SHELTER

SHELTER

a novel by
monte merrick

NEW YORK

Excerpts from "The Ballad of the Harp-Weaver"
by Edna St. Vincent Millay
from *Collected Poems*, Harper & Row. Copyright 1923, 1951 by
Edna St. Vincent Millay and Norma Millay Ellis.
Reprinted by permission of Elizabeth Barnett,
literary executor.

Printed in the United States of America.
For information address Hyperion, 114 Fifth Avenue,
New York, New York 10011.

Library of Congress Cataloging-in-Publication Data
Merrick, Monte.
Shelter / by Monte Merrick.
p. cm.
ISBN 1-56282-862-2
I. Title.
PS3563.E744P75   1993
813'.54—dc20   92-28087   CIP

FIRST EDITION
10 9 8 7 6 5 4 3 2 1

SHELTER

THIS IS THE PRIVATE PROPERTY
OF NELSON JAQUA.

KEEP OUT!

ARE YOU NELSON JAQUA?
THEN HOW COME YOU'RE STILL READING?
THIS IS PERSONAL PRIVATE PROPERTY.
GO READ SOMETHING ELSE AND LEAVE THIS
ALONE.

I DON'T BELIEVE THIS! DON'T YOU HAVE
ANY RESPECT FOR OTHER PEOPLE'S STUFF?
THIS IS NELSON JAQUA'S BOOK
AND NOT YOURS.

GO AWAY!

chapter one

I don't know what we would have done last summer if Mr. and Mrs. Shook hadn't killed their retarded son and walled him up in the basement. It would have been a really long summer with nothing to do.

The way summer works is that the first couple of weeks are so busy there isn't enough time to do everything. You get up early and cram it all in. When your dad tells you to mow the lawn, you mow it real fast so you won't miss out on anything. You've got a list a mile long of things to do and you wonder if you're going to get them all done before you run out of summer.

Then it starts to slow down after a couple of weeks. You've done all the good things on your list and the rest of them don't seem too good anymore. You think about getting a job. There's lots of time to mow the lawn, so you don't hurry with that. You kind of forget to mow the lawn at all and your dad yells at you. You start thinking that last summer was better than this one.

(Remember, Mr. Crisp said don't write like what you think is what everybody thinks. Don't use "you" all the time, use "I." Make it personal. Go over this whole thing again.)

Just when it looked like it was going to be a real long summer with nothing to do, Bobby Shook turned up missing.

Every night about sundown Mr. and Mrs. Shook walked Bobby around the neighborhood. He couldn't walk by himself. His arms flew every which way like they were attached to strings and the puppeteer had the strings all tangled. His feet went all over the place, too, and he couldn't walk in a straight line, like a drunk. His parents walked on both sides to help him out. He always had this big grin on his face like he was happy to be retarded and walking down the street with his parents. He'd drool and his mother would wipe his mouth with a blue washcloth. Kids said he peed his pants, too, but I honestly never saw that. He was older than us, either college age or older. Mr. and Mrs. Shook were older, too, more like grandparents.

Bobby and his parents lived in a really creepy house not far from my home. It stood on a little hill in the middle of the block, so it was taller than the other houses on the street, and it wasn't fixed up the way everyone else's house was. Most of the gray paint was peeling and the roof was missing some shingles. The gutters were filled with leaves and when it rained the water spilled over in big waterfalls. The windows were covered with white lace curtains that had turned yellow. A big maple tree stood in the side yard and towered over the house, making it even darker in the summer and more haunted-looking in the winter.

But there was something else I have to tell you about the house and then you'll really know why it was creepy. They had ivy for a lawn. Everyone else in our neighborhood had very nice lawns that they took care of. Ours was the worst because I was in charge of it and I never had time. At least it was grass. The Shooks had ivy and everyone knows that snakes hide in ivy.

Kids would never go up to their house on Halloween because it was so scary. They had this slanted porch with lots of loose boards. It would be real easy to fall off that porch into the ivy and have the snakes slither all over you, and that's just the kind of thing that would spoil any kid's Halloween. Even Maude, my little sister, wouldn't go to the Shooks' house. On Halloween Maude starts out early so she can go to every house within a ten-block radius and makes two different costumes so she can go around twice. Maude even likes snakes, but she wouldn't go to the Shooks'.

Nobody I knew knew either Mr. or Mrs. Shook personally. They kept to themselves and the only time you saw them was when they walked Bobby.

Cat noticed he was missing first. Cat noticed everything in our neighborhood because she was always roaming the streets, looking for action. At night she would dress in dark clothes, run through people's backyards and look in their windows. Once she said she saw Tim's parents doing it and I said, for God's sake don't tell Tim.

Cat's real name was Catherine, but that's not a good name for a boy. Cat was a girl, of course, but she wanted to be a boy and wanted a boy's name. She tried to make everyone call her Charlie for a while, but that never caught on and she settled for Cat. She wanted to be a boy so badly she once followed me into the boys' bathroom and I had to throw her out. That was Cat, thinking she could pee standing up.

Cat didn't wear dresses and shorts like other girls. She wore her father's sports coats and old men's pants from Goodwill that old men wouldn't even wear anymore. They looked good on her. Tim and I had a bet about what kind of underwear she wore, Jockey or boxer. We thought we'd never find out, but we were wrong.

She cut her own hair, too, just chopped it off with some scissors. It was all uneven and some parts she cut so close to her head, her skull shone through. That looked good on her, too.

She lived alone with her father on the other side of Thirty-ninth. He sold outboard motors and watched the fights when he came home from work. Her mother, the "Whore," came to town once in a while to take Cat shopping. She bought Cat dresses and purses and shoes and Cat acted real glad to have all that nice stuff, then when the Whore went away, Cat cut everything up into little bits and put on her old men's pants again.

Cat also had a pierced ear. She put a needle on the stove until it was hot, then shoved it through her earlobe. Even my mom doesn't have pierced ears and neither do any of my mom's friends. They wear these big earrings that clip on. Once I tried one on to see how it felt and it was like having a ball bearing hanging on your ear. I don't know why my mom doesn't have earlobes that hang down to her shoulders like women in African tribes. I don't see the point of putting anything on your earlobes at all. Why do they have to be decorated? Also, why do parents tell their kids to wash behind their ears? I was puzzled by that even as a tot.

(Remember, stick to your topic like Mr. Crisp said. Keep going back to your topic sentence to see if everything relates to it. You started out writing about a murder and now you're doing an essay on earlobes! Go over this whole thing again.)

I got to be friends with Cat one day when I was walking home from school. I read books when I walk and that day I was halfway through *The Agony and the Ecstasy*. It was a really giant book that weighed a ton and blocked my whole view, but it was so interesting that I couldn't put it down. I was a few blocks from my house when I heard a voice behind me say, "Freeze!"

I tried to remember what was in my wallet. I had a dollar in the dollar part, thirty cents in the change part, my blood-type card, a coupon for a free Popsicle, a picture of Carolyn Messinger who I had a crush on but might as well have been a one-eyed hunchback with a peg leg for all she cared, a rubber Tim gave me for a birthday present that I kept meaning to open up and try on, and a Don Drysdale baseball card because I knew a guy who collected those things and maybe I could trade him for something. There wasn't anything worth fighting for except the dollar and the rubber, so I froze and waited to be robbed.

"You almost stepped on this, Helen." Cat leaned down and picked a roller skate off the sidewalk right in front of me.

"Thanks," I said, not knowing what to say. Cat scared me, so I'd hardly said anything to her before except hi and I hadn't said much of that, because Cat didn't start conversations with things like hi. She started conversations with things like, "You almost stepped on this, Helen." She called people Helen who did anything dumb or klutzy because it reminded her of Helen Keller.

Cat pulled out a pack of cigarettes and offered me one, but I said no. I can't smoke because I had asthma as a kid. It's mostly gone now, except when I'm upset or doing something strenuous. But even if I didn't have asthma, I wouldn't smoke in full view of the neighborhood in case somebody reported it to my parents. Cat didn't care who saw her. She just lit right up. I felt pretty good walking with her, i.e., very brave.

"Hey, Nelson, have you seen the Helen Keller doll? Wind it up and it walks into the wall!" Cat laughed loudly. She didn't laugh much, but when she did it was usually at her own jokes. "You know how Helen Keller burned her hand? Reading the waffle iron!"

Cat didn't have a lot of friends. When she did have a friend, pretty soon the friend got mad at her and wasn't her friend anymore. This was because Cat always said what she thought and she didn't think too many nice things. Cat was somebody somebody made up the phrase "mad at the world" about.

We walked the three blocks to my house, not talking about anything in particular. I couldn't invite her in because my mom didn't like me bringing my school friends home without warning her. I was also afraid Cat would light up an L&M in our kitchen and start knocking off the Helen Keller jokes, so I said good-bye and thanks for noticing the roller skate. I didn't think that especially made us friends for life, but the next day at school she came straight up to me, started talking like it was perfectly normal and it was that way from then on. I didn't mind. There was something about Cat I liked. I couldn't get over those baggy men's pants and that haircut cut down to her scalp.

I'm talking about Cat like she's dead, but I saw her at school today. She was wearing a pretty dress and said hi like we were complete strangers. It's as if she doesn't remember last summer at all, how we investigated a murder and played strip poker and everything. Her hair is long now, almost to her shoulders, and I heard a girl call her "Cathy." I even think her pierced ear healed up. The past tense makes everyone sound like they're dead even when they're not. The only person who's dead is Bobby Shook.

"When was the last time you saw him?" she asked one Friday afternoon as we walked to the library to return some books and take Maude to Story Hour.

"I don't know. I guess it's been a while."

"Because he's dead. They killed him and buried him. Maybe they even buried him alive! He had to claw and scratch at the wall until his fingernails were broken and bleeding, then finally he suffocated to death!" Cat put her hands around her neck and squeezed, sticking out her tongue, popping her eyes and making a strangulated sound.

"I bet he's just away at a special retarded school. Maude, no!" I shouted. Maude had run on ahead and was crouched on the sidewalk, playing with a snail. I pulled her up and kicked it away.

"Can I take him home with me, Nelson, please?"

"You know Mom won't let us have pets and a snail isn't a pet anyway." This was a common occurrence. Maude liked insects and reptiles of all kinds, the more revolting the better. She had no fear of them at all. She put spiders down her *own* dress.

Taking care of Maude was my summer job. I was paid fifty cents a day, plus expenses. I had planned to work as a box boy at Safeway. The manager interviewed me twice and asked me to come back once more. I think I would have gotten the job, even though the first words out of his mouth were, "How tall are you?" Then my mom told me I had to start minding Maude Mondays through Fridays, from twelve-thirty to five.

Don't ask me why her name is Maude. Maude is a name for a little old lady who lives in a house with ten cats and tries to get you to cut her lawn for a quarter. It's not a name for a four-year-old blond girl with pale blue eyes. Maude's eyes look like whoever painted them in was running out of paint and had to water it down. I feel sorry for her that her name is Maude. But then look at my name: Nelson. Thanks a lot, Mom and Dad. Their names are Larry and Dolly.

"I'm telling you, Bobby Shook is dead," Cat insisted, handing Maude a cherry Life Saver to replace the forbidden snail. "They butchered him, cut him into little pieces, and buried him in the basement. I saw Mr. Shook unload this big truckful of cement bags and concrete blocks into his garage. Then they locked themselves in the house and haven't come out for weeks."

"How do you know they don't come out?"

"I've been watching them. There's an old treehouse down the block where those Wilson kids used to live. I watch from there."

"Maybe they have the flu," I suggested. Murder just didn't happen in our neighborhood. "There's got to be a reasonable explanation."

"Okay, what's the explanation for this? One night about a month ago I was walking by their house and I heard this terrible screaming. I crept up real carefully to the side of the house. It was coming from a window on the top floor. The curtains were closed, but there were shadows on them. Two people. The Shooks!" Cat said dramatically as if she was the host of a television mystery show.

"Mr. Shook had something in his hand, like a baseball bat or a poker or something and that poor retard was screaming for his life. I never saw him again. Explain that."

While Maude happily listened to the story of Peter Rabbit and I glanced through the books on the new fiction shelf, Cat suggested in a conspiratorial whisper that we go to the police with our suspicions. She excitedly described the patrol cars racing up to the Shooks' house and the officers hauling the murderous parents away. We'd get our names in the paper and perhaps a picture. Cat was good at imagining things like that.

The whole thing sounded pretty incredible, but the summer was starting to slow down and needed a little excitement, so I didn't tell Cat to forget it. I said we needed some hard evidence before going to the authorities, in order to avoid the humiliating spectacle of us being dismissed from the station house as "just kids." I suggested we start watching the Shooks' house on a regular basis to establish a pattern to their activities, if any. We could also make plans to gather more evidence. I'd enlist my best friend, Tim Wooley, into the investigation. Cat groaned. Tim was too stupid to be a part of anything this serious, she complained, but I suspected she simply didn't want to share the glory once we exposed the criminals.

It was true that Tim wasn't very smart. It hurt to watch him do his homework. He'd sit there and stare at it like it was in ancient Greek. I'd start out helping him a little and end up doing it all while he watched TV. He was older than Cat and me, but we were all in the same grade together. They held Tim back a year and would have held him back more, but it looked strange to have such a big, handsome boy in class with a lot of little kids, so they passed him.

Tim had dark hair and one big eyebrow that went straight across his forehead like somebody drew it on with a marker pen. He already had to shave a little bit around the chin. He was tall and strong, although he never did sports. He wasn't bad at sports, just not interested. I was interested, but bad at them. We began cutting recess together in sixth grade and had been best friends ever since.

So that's how we started watching the Shooks' house. I had the morning shift, Tim had the afternoon shift, and Cat took the night shift. Nothing much happened. The Shooks stayed inside. Occasionally I heard the sound of an electric saw ("chopping up Bobby into smaller pieces," Cat explained), but that was all. Since there was nothing to see, I got a lot of reading done.

The best book I read last summer was *Exodus* by Leon Uris, which was about the beginnings of Israel. It was exciting and informative. It was also depressing because I realized it would take me a long time, maybe even a year, to write anything that long or good. The problem is that my writing sounds really great while I'm writing it, but when I read it over it's disappointing. I'm very critical of my writing, which I shouldn't be because I'm just starting out. But I wouldn't be critical if it was good like Leon Uris. I'm critical because it's crap.

I've been thinking that maybe it's not such a good idea to write about what happened last summer. It doesn't have as much action, like war scenes and sex, as a couple of other ideas I have. I have an idea for a story about Israeli freedom fighters, which would have more of the above. It might be better to write a story that I'm not in, because I could be more objective. On the other hand, I seem to get about ten pages into everything I write and give up. Maybe I should write short stories. (Maybe you shouldn't write at all, Nelson, ever think of that?)

Dad just came in and asked me what I was writing and I said, "Nothing." I've filled up half a composition book, it's right on my bed where he can see it, and I say, "Nothing." And I wonder why parents hate their kids.

He asked me if he could sit down and I said sure. He asked me how things were going at school and I said fine. He asked me if there was anything I wanted to talk about and I said no. I figured I was in trouble for not mowing the lawn, but then I remembered that I mowed it two days ago. I used the edger and everything. Maybe I did a bad job.

He didn't say anything then for quite a while and didn't look at me either. I waited quietly until he got to the point.

"Nelson, do you know very much about sex?"

That was tough. If I said yes, I'd get in trouble for reading dirty books, but if I said no, I'd look like a complete moron. I couldn't think of a good response, so I didn't say anything. After a little bit, he spoke again.

"You're fourteen and that's not too young to know. I don't want you hearing the wrong thing from some kid in the playground. I'd rather tell you myself." Except he really didn't sound like he wanted to tell me himself. He seemed very nervous and kept picking at a scab on the second knuckle of his left hand. He skinned it putting up a new swing set for Maude a couple of weeks ago.

Then he said

THIS IS NELSON JAQUA'S BOOK AND IF
YOU'RE NOT NELSON JAQUA, YOU BETTER
STOP READING RIGHT NOW.

He said it was okay to masturbate! He said if I wanted to do it, just go ahead and not worry about it. He said everybody did it at some time in their lives and it never hurt anybody as far as he knew.

He has gotten really old. There are lines at the corners of his eyes and these big lines around his neck I never saw before. I hope my neck never gets like that. But it was interesting looking at him up so close.

I swear he told me everything there is to know about sex. I knew a lot of it already, but there were a couple of new parts. He kept picking at that scab even though you knew it wasn't ready to come off.

After a while he finished and I knew it was my turn to say something, perhaps ask a detailed question. I couldn't think of any, so I just said, "Thanks, Dad." He nodded, as if that's exactly what he expected me to say. Then he looked me right in the eyes for the first time since he came into my room.

I think he was trying to decide if he could kiss me. It would have been okay, but I guess he figured it wasn't right after he'd just told me all about ejaculating. So he patted me on the chest a little, said it was nice talking to me, and told me to turn out my light pretty soon. Which I did.

One really great thing about my dad is that he doesn't have hairs sticking out of his nose like Tim's dad. I really like that about him.

(Start this whole thing over! You're not telling your story. You're just putting in anything you want. You've got a whole paragraph about earlobes, not to mention nose hairs! How are you ever going to be a writer if you don't stick to your subject?

(This is the story of how you and your two best friends investigated a murder and what happened because of it. You've used up over one-half of a notebook and haven't even gotten to the action yet. How many books have you started to read and got disgusted with because they started so slow? Now you're doing the same thing yourself. Stick to your story or don't tell it at all.)

chapter one

Ben Levi dropped his machine gun, hunched himself down in the foxhole, and lit a cigarette. It was tough being an Israeli freedom fighter. He thought it would be an exciting, adventurous existence, but so far it was a lot of doing nothing. He wanted the fight to begin, even if he got himself killed. Anything was better than waiting.

The cigarette tasted good, although he wasn't supposed to smoke. He had asthma as a kid and smoking wasn't good for him. But what else was there to do in this dusty foxhole? There wasn't any light, so he couldn't read. It reminded him of the time when he, David, and Esther spent that summer in the treehouse watching the Steinbergs' house. They had killed their retarded son and walled him up in the basement. But this was much hotter.

He closed his eyes and thought of Sarah. Ben had never believed in love at first sight. He thought it was something that only happened in books, but then it happened to him. Beautiful Sarah, halfway around the world in Brooklyn. (Look up. Exactly half or more like a third?) He tried to put her out of his mind, but he couldn't. Sometimes he even masturbated thinking of her. He heard it was okay and that everybody did it.

(Does Leon Uris write about jerking off? What do you know about Israeli freedom fighters anyway? Write what you know!) (What if you don't know anything?)

*　*　*

I went up to Mr. Crisp after school today, told him I was trying to write a story and kept getting stuck. Did he have any advice?

He said I should just keep trying. Writing was hard work. When he was writing his books, he got blocked all the time. He just kept working at them and eventually it got a little easier. I didn't even know Mr. Crisp wrote books. He never mentioned them in class.

"Did any of your books come out? It would be great to read them," I said enthusiastically.

He suddenly looked very sorry he mentioned it. I assumed none of them came out, that's why he had to become an English teacher and here I was, bringing up the whole tragedy again. Good work, Nelson.

"Two of them were published, but we're talking about your writing, Nelson, not . . ."

"Two of them! That's neat! What are their titles?" I took my pencil out of my binder.

"They've been out of print for a long time. Let's get back to your work. Do you have a story to tell? A story that keeps you awake nights thinking about it?"

"Yes." This was not a lie.

"Have you outlined it? Do you know what happens? Who the main characters are?"

"Pretty much." I didn't want to tell him that it really happened and I don't have to make up anything. "It's really clear in my head, but when I start writing it down, it gets all confused. Pretty soon I'm writing about earlobes."

"Earlobes?" He seemed puzzled.

"That's just an example. I don't mean that I actually wrote about earlobes," I said quickly so he wouldn't think I was crazy. "Then I started writing this other story about an Israeli freedom fighter, but parts of my first story got mixed up with the war story, so I gave it up, too."

"Nelson, what do you know about freedom fighters?"

"Well, I could learn."

"Start with something you know. Choose a simple story and tell it as simply as you know how. You can get fancy later on."

He's very strict in class and nobody likes him much, but he was friendly to me and seemed glad to be asked for help. He doesn't have much hair, just a few blond strands that he combs over the top. When he gets excited, his head turns bright red and glows right through those thin hairs. His first name is George.

"When I wrote my first novel, I got frustrated just like you. I was actually pounding my head against the wall." Was this the reason for the hair loss? Remember not to get that frustrated. "I kept starting over and changing my mind. It took me two years to finish *Hothouse Flower* and it's only a hundred and forty-eight pages.

"Just tell the story, Nelson. No, let me rephrase that. Let the story tell itself. If it's a good story, let it loose and it'll unroll like a big carpet. Writing is difficult. It takes time and concentration. You need to work on your concentration. Your mind wanders a lot in class. But you can do it if you really want to. I think you should try."

I said thanks, that helps a lot and I started for the door. I liked what he said about letting the story unroll like a carpet, but I was a little worried about how he said it was a lot of work. He said that a couple of times.

"Nelson, would you like me to read what you've written so far and give you some specific help? It would just be between the two of us."

"No, that's okay, Mr. Crisp," I answered politely. "I don't want you to see it the way it is right now. Maybe later."

"I understand. Let me know."

How could I tell him that nobody can ever read this because of what it's about? Even if I finish it and by some miracle somebody wants to publish it, I'd have to say no. Because my parents would want to read it, right? Their only son publishes a book that gets rave reviews when he's only fourteen, of course they'd want to read it. They probably wouldn't even wait until it came out in paperback. They'd buy the hardcover. And they would be really hurt. They might never speak to me again or only speak to me to tell me they're moving away and changing their name. I don't want that to happen because things are going really good right now, like my dad comes in at night and talks to me about sex. I want to keep it that way.

So I don't know why I'm going to all the trouble of writing this down in the first place. I guess it's an exercise. I'll make all my mistakes with this story, then when I write about the freedom fighter, I'll write it perfect the first time. (Ha!)

I hope Mr. Crisp wasn't hurt that I didn't let him read my story. He said he understood, but that's the kind of thing people say and don't really mean. I don't think he was hurt. He's a writer, too, so he understands.

(Look for *Hothouse Flower*!)

chapter one

My friends and I, Tim and Cat, were watching Mr. and Mrs. Shook's house. They'd killed their retarded son, Bobby, and walled him up in the basement and we set out prove it. We watched from the old Wilson kids' treehouse, a little distance down the block. We watched for almost two weeks before anything happened. I had the morning shift, Tim had the afternoon shift, and Cat took the night shift.

Then, all of a sudden, one Sunday night

chapter one

---

*There was a knock on my window. It was my friend Cat. I was all
ready for bed and reading when she knocked. I was so surprised that*

chapter one

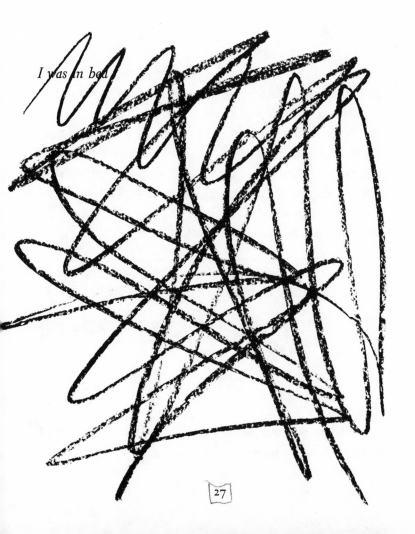

I was in bed

chapter two

The stillness of the night was shattered by three loud bangs. I jumped out of bed, flattened myself on the floor, and tried to figure out who was shooting at me.

I had been reading *Battle Cry* by Leon Uris and the war scenes were so real that the sharp, rapid raps on the window sounded like the rattle of a machine gun. I cautiously rose, pulled up the shade, and looked out. At first all I could see was my own pale, scared face. Then my eyes adjusted and I saw someone right outside the window, smiling and waving. It was Cat.

"They came out!"

I opened the window and told her to keep her voice down.

"They just got in their car and drove off," she continued loudly. "Let's go get Tim and wait for them to come back."

"My mom and dad are home." I could hear the rise and fall of their voices from the living room.

"So?"

"What if they come in and I'm not here?"

"Nelson . . ."

The problem with my name is that when somebody starts a sentence with it, it's usually bad news. Maybe it's because the accent is on the first syllable: NEL-son. It sounds like whoever is talking is just about to call you stupid. If you don't believe me, try it. (Is this significant? Avoid self-pity.)

"You're not a baby. They're not going to look in on you. Just come on."

"I'm in my pajamas." It was only eight-thirty, but I'd put them on early, brushed my teeth, and gotten into bed because I wanted to read my book without interruption. I was a little embarrassed to be in my pajamas in front of Cat. She had never seen me in them before and, anyway, they had choo-choo trains on them. I doubt that she expected me to be relaxing in a smoking jacket with a monocle in my eye, but I wished I was wearing something more adult.

"Well, put on some clothes."

"I'm supposed to tuck Maude in."

"Tuck her in and get your ass in gear, Nelson."

I did what she said, as always. I ran upstairs quickly, picked Maude's limp body off the floor where she had fallen asleep and deposited her in bed. I hurried back down to my room, changed into a dark sweater and jeans, climbed out the window, and we ran to get Tim.

Tim's family was watching Ed Sullivan, but Tim was in his room, smoking and looking at a dirty magazine. He had a whole collection and always offered me his old ones, but I was too nervous to take them. A paperback copy of *Lolita* was already hidden under my mattress and whenever my mother came in the room, it thumped like a tell-tale heart.

Tim didn't have to worry about his mom and dad checking up on him because there were too many kids in his family for Mr. and Mrs. Wooley to keep track of everyone. I never figured out how many brothers and sisters Tim had. Every time I went over there it was a different number. Tim was the second oldest. His older brother, Sam, was vice president of the junior class at Cleveland High, captain of the football team, a state champion debater, dated the cutest girl in school, and even had his own rock band. Tim would have had to grow wings and fly around the neighborhood to get any attention for himself.

Tim walked right through the living room, his parents didn't even look up from the television, and the three of us were settled in the treehouse by nine o'clock. It had high, fortresslike walls ten feet above the ground and once you were inside and had pulled up the rope ladder, you were safe. I watched the Shooks' house through a narrow chink in the wall while Tim and Cat shared a cigarette. It didn't bother them to be smoking the same cigarette, but if you told them to kiss each other, they'd be repelled.

Tim and Cat didn't get along. She thought he was stupid and he thought she was a bitch. It was true that Cat was sometimes a bitch, but I admired her for not caring what anyone thought of her. I spent much of my time worrying what other people thought, even total strangers. I worried what people in cars going forty miles an hour down the street thought of me. I worried what characters in books would think if they met me, like Michelangelo. The only two people whose opinion I didn't worry about were Tim and Cat. They had to like me. I was their only friend in the world.

"Pass it here." I reached for the cigarette.

"Nelson, you know you can't smoke. You want your asthma to come back?" Cat warned.

"It won't come back."

"I don't want you puking and passing out just when we need you. We're on watch."

"I'm not going to puke and pass out. Come on," I said, but she ignored me and I gave up the quest.

"Where do you think they went? The stores are all closed. Maybe a movie," Tim speculated.

"Why would people who stayed in their house for two weeks straight suddenly jump up and go to a movie?" Cat asked.

"It was just an idea."

"A dumb one."

Tim took the last drag off the cigarette and stubbed it out on the floor. A coffee can had been placed in the corner for cigarette butts, but it didn't cross his mind to use it. I was the only one who kept the treehouse clean.

"It was something important," Cat said. "They drove like a bat out of hell. I can keep up with any car for three or four blocks, but they lost me at Crystal Springs."

Cat could run; it was one of her talents. She ran everywhere. I drove her crazy by walking along, one slow step at a time, reading some giant book. She couldn't stand still for two seconds. In the middle of a conversation she'd suddenly dart up the street as if someone fired a starting pistol. Maude had a longer attention span. Compared to Cat, Maude looked like a Yogi in a month-long trance.

Cat hated school. The whole idea of school is to sit there and learn. They don't organize school around the idea of rushing from place to place. After about five minutes into a class Cat would ask if she could go to the rest room. Then she'd sharpen a pencil or get up and throw something in the wastebasket. She would open the window. A minute later she'd get up and close it halfway. Then she'd close it all the way and turn up the heat. Next she'd ask if she could get something from her locker. When she returned she would fish the thing she threw into the wastebasket out of the wastebasket. It never stopped. If somebody complained that she was being distracting, she'd tell them to "fuck off" and she'd get sent to the principal's office. She got terrible grades, but her father didn't care. He didn't have a high opinion of education anyway. He always said the only school worth going to was the School of Hard Knocks.

"Tim, you think nobody can see that, but I'm not blind," Cat said suddenly.

"See what?"

"You scratching your balls."

"I'm not scratching them. I'm adjusting them. They're caught."

"Don't talk about it!" Cat put her hands over her ears.

"These pants are too tight. My right ball keeps getting squashed and some hairs are all caught . . ." He shifted around and pulled at his crotch. "Oh, wow, that's better." He sighed with relief and winked at me.

"I'm going to throw up." Cat announced as she rolled on her back and tried to stand on her head. "Don't you think it's weird that men wear pants and women wear dresses? Shouldn't it be the other way around?"

The treehouse was rocking and threatening to fall out of the tree. "Cat, stop that!" I ordered, but she paid no attention.

"I mean, boys have things between their legs and girls don't. A dress would give you guys more room. Priests wear dresses, but they're all queer. Did any of them try anything with you, Tim?"

Tim was Catholic, but stopped going to church a couple of years before. I went with him once. I got an asthma attack from the incense, passed out, fell over and hit my head on the wooden bench. Tim laughed so hard he farted. We never went back.

"Wait! I've got an idea!" Cat rolled into a sitting position and dug in her pocket. "Here." She held something out to Tim in the dark.

"What's that?"

"A bobby pin."

"Gee, thanks."

"To pick the lock."

"What lock?"

"On their garage," Cat said casually, as if we broke into people's houses every day.

"Are you crazy? I'm not picking anything."

"Except your butt."

"What's that supposed to mean?"

"Going to the movies? Picking your seat out early?" Cat said and burst out laughing. This joke and a joke about Indian underwear were the only ones she knew that didn't involve Helen Keller. She expected you to laugh at her jokes, too, no matter how many times she used them. I bought her a joke book for her birthday in the hopes that she would widen her repertoire, but I doubt if she even opened it.

"When you aren't adjusting your balls, you're scratching your butt. What do you have, diaper rash? Try some baby powder. You think nobody's looking, but everybody sees. It's not making you any friends."

"Thanks for the advice, Miss Popularity."

"Cat, we can't break into their house," I interrupted. "We could get arrested."

"By who? The police don't care. If they did, the Shooks would be on death row right now. Look, it's easy. There's a little latch in there and all you have to do is stick it in, feel around until you find that latch and just flick it. Straighten out the bobby pin." She took it back and straightened it out.

"If you know how to do it so well, why don't you pick the lock?" Tim asked, still smarting from her ball-scratching and butt-picking criticisms.

"Do I have to do everything?" Cat complained loudly. "I'm the only one who watches the house. All Nelson does is sit up here and read." She whipped around toward me. "I bet you don't even look out at the house once. You just keep turning the pages. And all you do is sleep, Tim. I'm the only one working. If you two aren't interested, fine. But I'm not going to let them get away with this. That poor retard is missing. If they killed him, they have to pay. What if your parents killed you and buried you in the basement, wouldn't you want somebody to investigate? Would you just want to disappear off the face of the earth and nobody even bats an eye? We're Bobby Shook's only hope, but if you're both too selfish and lazy to do anything about it, I'll do it myself!"

Obviously, Cat didn't know how to pick the lock any better than we did. If she did, you can bet she would have taken the hair pin, broken into the garage and rubbed it in with a little salt.

She was right, I mostly read in the treehouse. I would occasionally glance out at the Shooks' house, but only between chapters. It was nice up there, quiet and green. The treehouse didn't have a roof, just a bunch of thick branches high above and the morning sun coming through them made leaf patterns all over my body and book. Sometimes a breeze would drift by and ruffle the leaves like people ruffle the hair of a small boy. Being in the treehouse was the way summer should be all the time.

It was also true that Tim slept in the treehouse. He slept a lot and I used to think that was why he was so tall. I was short because I never got a full night's sleep. Problems and stories spun in my head, keeping me awake long after I had turned off the light. Even after I had finally dozed off, I wouldn't sleep the full night through. I'd get up to drink a glass of water. I would hear a burglar. I envied Tim a lot of things—his height, his dark wavy hair always slightly rumpled and romantic, his soft, low voice— but mostly I envied him his sleep.

Tim took the bobby pin, heaved himself to his feet, and went down the rope ladder. He ran quietly up the street toward the Shooks' house. Cat and I watched him through the slits in the treehouse wall.

"Sucker," she said, and giggled.

Tim's tennis shoes made small padding noises on the concrete. He was lighter on his feet than I would have guessed. When he was directly opposite the house, he folded his five foot ten body into a commando tuck and dashed across the street. He crouched down in front of the garage and went to work. He looked pretty professional.

The Shooks' garage was at street level, dug into the little hill that the house was built upon. It was a narrow, one-car garage built when cars were smaller than they are now, perhaps in the time of the Model T.

Cat's shoulder touched mine as we watched Tim pick the lock. She smelled of Ivory soap. I hadn't noticed that Cat smelled like anything before. I don't go around smelling my friends. I wondered if she could smell me and what I smelled like.

"Come on, Timmy."

She said it under her breath as if she couldn't help herself. I'd never heard anyone call him Timmy before. I wish I had a name like Tim that could suddenly become "Timmy" in moments of high drama. You try that with my name and all you get is "Nellie."

I saw the car first. It was about four blocks away. From the position of the big double headlights I could tell that it was a 1958 De Soto Firesweep. I liked cars and studied them in my spare time. On September 27, 1964, I can get my driving permit.

A moment later Cat saw the car, too, and grabbed my arm. She looked at me and I nodded: It was the Shooks. There was no way to warn Tim; he was too far away and he wouldn't have heard us shouting to him anyway. Tim couldn't do two things at once, like pick a lock and listen for warning calls. He was still crouched in front of the garage door, working the bobby pin. I could imagine that eyebrow of his twisted with the effort. His shirt had come out of his pants and a white strip of his back, catching the light, glowed like a bike reflector. The car kept coming. It reached the end of the block. In another fifteen seconds it would turn into the driveway and the Shooks would see Tim trying to break into their house.

He disappeared. One moment Tim was crouched in front of the garage, fully absorbed in his work, and the next he vanished. Mr. Shook pulled into the driveway. He put the car in park, turned off the ignition, got out, and stooped to unlock the garage door. He was standing in the exact spot where Tim had been crouched just a second before. It was as if a trap door had opened in the sidewalk and Tim had dropped through. I started to ask Cat where he went, but she squeezed my arm harder. I looked again.

Tim was pressed against the left side of the garage, not three feet from Mr. Shook. He was hiding in the shadows and was doing a good job of it, except for his left leg. It was sticking out a little from the edge of the garage and one of those big headlights was shining right on it. All Mr. Shook had to do was turn his head to see it.

But he was too busy trying to figure out why his key wouldn't go into the lock. He tried another key. Then he tried the first key again. Then he went back to the car and talked to Mrs. Shook. She gave him her keys and he tried those, but they didn't work either. Tim must have jammed the lock with the bobby pin. Mr. Shook became frustrated and yanked on the garage handle a few times, trying to force the door open. This didn't work, so he began the long climb to the front porch. I could almost hear his labored breaths as he hoisted his heavy girth up those steep stairs. Mr.

Shook was a big man, easily weighing two hundred and fifty pounds, and wore baggy blue jeans with a tan windbreaker. He reached the porch and disappeared into the house. Mrs. Shook remained in the car.

I had been holding my breath so long my chest hurt. I let it out shakily. My breathing made a noise, though not a loud one, and Cat hushed me.

Tim was moving his leg. He must have noticed it was sticking out into the light and began pulling it very slowly into the shadow of the garage. Any sudden movement might catch Mrs. Shook's attention. She might get out of the car to investigate. Or call for Mr. Shook, who probably did the actual killing when it came time to slaughter their son. So Tim just inched that long leg into the dark and she never noticed.

Lights went on inside the house. Shortly afterwards the garage door opened and Mr. Shook came out. So they had a door from the basement into the garage. This information might come in handy later. Mr. Shook got back in the car and drove his wide, pink and black De Soto into the garage.

The taillights were extinguished, there was a slamming of doors, then Mr. Shook reappeared. He took hold of the rope to pull the garage door down, but didn't pull it. Instead, he let the rope go and walked out into the driveway. He looked first away from us, then turned and glared down the street toward the treehouse. Cat and I froze, even though we knew we were well-hidden. But Tim was directly behind Mr. Shook's shoulder, close enough to touch him. How could Mr. Shook not sense him there, I wondered, not feel him so near? Mr. Shook kept looking our way, not moving, just listening. It was so quiet he could have heard the hair growing on Tim's head.

Finally, Mr. Shook spun around, strode into the garage, and pulled the door down with a slam that echoed down the block.

It was a "do that again and you'll be sorry" slam that made my spine hurt. I expected Tim to come running right away, but he stayed until more lights went on inside the house: two on the first floor, then one on the second.

My chest was hurting again and I told myself it was okay to breathe. Tim was halfway up the block before I even realized he had moved. He sprinted silently under the cover of the big maples growing in the parking strips and I marveled at him. This was the kind of thing that made it worthwhile being Tim's friend: Out of the blue, he'd do something so surprising, so unexpected, I'd get a little rush. It was as if Tim was my son and he brought home a better report card than last time. Or he was retarded like Bobby Shook and suddenly made a little progress.

I let down the rope ladder and the treehouse tipped as Tim climbed up. He threw himself into a corner, panting and grinning. His big white teeth shone in the dark like they were plugged in. He held out the bobby pin.

"It broke off. I almost had it, too." Cat lit a cigarette and gave it to Tim right away. He sucked at it happily. Cat took the bobby pin and examined it.

"Cheap goddamn shit," she said and tossed it out of the top of the treehouse. I looked up to follow its path and saw stars dotting the angular spaces between the dark leaves above us. That night the universe seemed no more intriguing and mysterious than my own small, tree-lined neighborhood.

We stayed late in the treehouse that night making plans, most of them so crazy I knew we would never carry them out or even remember them later. We agreed to have conferences each morning at eight o'clock sharp at Cat's house to report our observations of the Shooks and to formulate plans to further the investigation.

When I crawled back through my window it was almost midnight, but I didn't get to sleep for another two hours. Every time

I started to drift off, a giggle would fizz up from inside me and spurt out like a shaken Coke. I was an accessory to a criminal act and it was the most exciting thing I'd ever done. I couldn't wait until morning when the three of us could get together and plan more criminal activities. It was going to be a good summer after all.

"Nelson, I'd like to speak to you before dinner," my mother said two days after our attempted break-in. The use of my first name first was an ominous sign, so I delayed going into the living room to see her until all other options had been explored. She was sitting in one of the big orange flowered armchairs, a drink resting on the marble table beside her. I could smell it from where I stood. A green olive was speared on a buccaneer's sword. My dad was away on business.

"Nelson, I want you to start minding Maude in the mornings now. I don't want her underfoot. I can't get anything done. I'll pay you seventy-five cents a day instead of fifty, and I'll put an extra dollar a week into your savings account for your future. That's three dollars and seventy-five cents a week, plus the additional dollar in your account. I think that's fair." She ate half of her olive.

"You mean, you want me to take care of her in the mornings instead of the afternoons, right?" I asked, just to clarify matters.

"The mornings *and* the afternoons."

"Mom!"

"The whole day. From eight to five. I'll pack lunches for you or, if I'm too busy, I'll give you money to buy lunch somewhere. Something nutritious. I don't want Maude eating a lot of junk." She looked at the other half of her olive, but didn't eat it. Perhaps she was wondering if it was nutritious.

"Mom, I can't! What am I going to do with Maude all day long? I can't think up enough stuff."

"Don't they have Story Hour at the library?"

"Just on Friday afternoon and I'm already taking her there."

"Take her to the park. She loves the park."

"We already go to the park. We go to two parks! She gets bored after an hour and she always wants me to push the merry-go-round really fast and you know I can't do that because of my asthma." Asthma was always a good excuse.

"Then just tell her you can't."

"Maude doesn't know what asthma is."

"Just tell her no. She'll mind. She's a good girl."

"Mom, I already do everything I can think of with her. I could maybe take her for a half-hour more, like noon to five . . ."

"Nelson, I want her out of the house. I can't get anything done."

I could never figure out what my mother actually did. She didn't read. She had a cleaning woman who came Thursdays, so she didn't have to clean. She clipped a lot of coupons and, when the cleaning lady arrived, went shopping. She also painted pictures and took painting classes, although she hadn't gone to class for some time. Half of the Grand Canyon was sitting on her easel at that very moment. She painted about one rock a week.

"Mom, I can't be with Maude nine hours a day. I'll go crazy!"

"You won't go crazy. Don't exaggerate." She ate a single peanut from a small silver bowl. "Take her to the zoo."

"We can't go to the zoo every day. They'll think we're strange."

"Who will?"

"The zoo people."

"Why on earth would they think you were strange? The zoo

is there for people to enjoy. There aren't rules about how many times you can go."

"I know, but . . ."

"Maude loves animals. I want to encourage that," said the woman who refused to allow even a goldfish in the house.

"What if I took her for the whole day once a week, say Mondays, and . . ."

"Nelson, I'm not going to argue. It's settled."

"I've got stuff to do in the mornings," I pleaded, determined not to give up without a protest.

"Like what?"

"Write."

"Write what?"

"A story."

"What story?"

"Just a story."

"About what?"

"Gladiators."

That stopped her. It wasn't a lie exactly. I had started a gladiator novel several months before, but quit halfway through the first chapter. Gladiators are hard people to write about. They don't do that much. They fight, they love, they fight some more, and then they die. It's not much of a life. On the other hand, it sounded a lot better than taking care of Maude nine hours a day.

"What do you know about gladiators?"

"Nothing. So I have to go to the library and look them up."

"Fine. Take Maude with you."

"What's Maude going to do at the library? She can't even read."

"Teach her." She bit the other half of the olive off the blue plastic sword, sucked the martini juice out of it, and swallowed it. I watched her, sickened.

"When do you want me to start?" I asked, hoping for at least a few days to adjust to my new schedule.

"Tomorrow."

"When am I going to mow the lawn?"

"Saturdays."

So that was it. That was the summer. No free time. No time alone in the treehouse, reading underneath the leaves. I had plans to write a novel about street gangs in New York. That would have to wait. For more than two months I would be keeping a four-year-old girl entertained from morning till night. Maude didn't even take naps. She had more energy than the sun.

I dreaded the reaction when I announced to Tim and Cat that I could no longer hold down the morning shift. There was bound to be a fight and I hated any kind of argument at all. I never raised my voice and never understood why anyone else did. I would rather just give in than get into a battle. I realize that writers should probably have arguments once in a while, because arguments often crop up in a story. One of the troubles with my New York street gangs story was that I hated to see the gangs get into a fight. The gladiators also got along really great.

So the following day I skipped our morning conference and took Maude to the park instead. This was a park with a large duck pond and was farther away than our local park. Perhaps Cat wouldn't think to look for me there. That she would find me eventually and give me hell was a given, but the longer I could postpone it, the better.

Maude and I fed the ducks stale bread and ate some ourselves. Then we got full and the ducks got full and I pushed Maude on the merry-go-round. She liked to go as fast as possible, then jump off, reel around dizzily, and fall down. This got tiresome, so I persuaded her to try the slide. It wasn't fast enough for the little hot rodder, so I fished a piece of wax paper out of the trash can and rubbed it on the scratched aluminum.

Maude soon tired of the park and we were out on the street again. We walked to the five and dime. I tried to interest her in a yo-yo, but Maude wanted a squirt gun. I was in a murderous mood, so I bought squirt guns for both of us. She got a dainty pink one and I chose a big black German Luger. Then we went to the dry cleaners because Maude liked how it smelled inside. The Oriental people came out from the back to look at the child who visited the cleaners just to smell it. Maude never asked to go into the Ann Palmer Bakery, which smelled great as far as I was concerned. She preferred the cleaners. She was a strange child.

Our next stop was the Rexall Drug Store soda counter where we ordered grilled cheese sandwiches and potato chips. My mother had not gotten around to fixing us lunches to take on our travels, so she gave me money instead. "Something nutritious," she repeated, as if I were an expert on nutrition. I guessed that grilled cheese sandwiches were healthy. I never died from one.

Cat caught up with us after lunch. I saw her running toward us and tried to duck into the barber shop for a quick trim, but Maude spotted Cat and started shouting and waving.

"Have you had a lobotomy?" Cat screamed as soon as she was within screaming distance. "Does eight o'clock at my house mean anything to you? Me and Tim waited an hour! You think I have nothing better to do all morning than sit around and stare at his ugly face?"

"Cat, I can explain." She ignored me, turned to Maude, and patted her head.

"Hi, Maude. What do you have there?"

"A squirt gun."

"Can I see it?"

Maude handed her the gun and Cat squirted me in the face. "It works good," she said, handing the gun back to Maude. I pulled my shirttail out of my pants and wiped my face. When I did, Maude squirted me in the stomach.

"Goddammit, Maude, that's enough!" I grabbed the gun away and put it in my shirt pocket, where it immediately began to leak. Maude whimpered pathetically.

"Don't swear at her. She's just a little girl." Cat dropped to one knee and tied the bow on the back of Maude's dress that had come undone. "Your big, bad brother is so mean to you, isn't he, Maude? And he's so untrustworthy. He doesn't do anything he promises, does he? I bet he promised you an ice cream cone today and he never bought you one, did he?"

"No," Maude said, suddenly perking up. "Nelson, you promised."

"Okay, we'll go to the Arctic Circle." There were at least half a dozen closer ice cream cones, but it was only one-fifteen and now my whole mission in life was to kill time. The Arctic Circle was a forty-five-minute walk away.

"My mom is making me take care of Maude all day now. What am I supposed to do? How can I watch the house?"

"Watch it with Maude," Cat suggested.

"I can't take Maude up in the treehouse. She'd fall out and break her neck, then *I'd* be on trial for murder!"

"Okay, you take the night shift," was Cat's next solution.

"I can't do that either, because I have stuff to do at night. I have the dishes and I usually tuck Maude in."

"Jesus, doesn't your mom do anything?"

"She's busy," I answered vaguely. I didn't want the night shift anyway. Reading would be possible only with a flashlight and that wasn't nearly as nice as reading in the leafy morning light.

"So you're telling me the investigation is over?" Cat said in her familiar "the world is against me" voice.

"I can help on weekends. But I guess during the week it's you and Tim."

"I can't trust him. All he does up there is sleep. And jerk off."

"Don't say that around Maude!" I was holding my sister's hand because Seventeenth Avenue was a busy street. I didn't want her to dart into traffic and be leveled by a truck, much as I would have delighted at such an event.

"She doesn't know what it means. You probably don't know, either," Cat added bitingly.

Maude was whining for her squirt gun, so after a brief lecture about the responsibility of owning a firearm, I returned it to her. It was out of water, so I filled it from a hose coiled in a nearby garden. An old lady came out on her porch and yelled at me for using the hose without permission. I pointed to Maude and said it was for my little sister whose squirt gun needed refilling and could we have just a little, ma'am, please? I found myself slipping into a southern accent to make the poor white trash act more convincing. Seeing Maude, the mean old lady magically turned into a sweet old lady and ran inside to get Maude a cookie and a glass of lemonade.

"Maude, that's instead of the ice cream cone," I told her, remembering my mom's instruction not to feed her too much junk.

"But you said I could have an ice cream cone, you promised!"

"I don't want you spoiling your dinner," I replied, trying to picture dinnertime. It seemed as far off as college midterms or a fraternity beer bash.

"What do you think the Shooks do for food?" Cat asked, suddenly trying to balance on one toe atop a fire hydrant.

"They've been in there two weeks. Who has that much food without going to the store? Unless they eat *him!*" Her eyes glistened.

"Come off it, Cat."

She jumped down from the fire hydrant and did a cartwheel. "Well, how do they get food, Nelson? You're the smart one. You explain it."

"They have it delivered," I answered. Cat whirled around to look at me and, I'm not kidding, my hand went to my gun.

"How do you know that?"

The sweet old lady came out of her house and gave Maude the lemonade and cookie, but didn't bring anything for me and Cat. I guess we were either too old for treats or not cute enough.

"How do you know that, Nelson?" Cat demanded.

"Shhh."

"How?"

"I'm guessing. But it makes sense." I ran up on the porch to collect Maude. The sweet old lady turned back into a mean old lady, told me that using someone's hose without permission was stealing and if it ever happened again she would call the police, then turned back into a sweet old lady, tickled Maude's chin, told her to come back any time, and gave her a penny. Maude immediately wanted to go to the railroad tracks so she could put the penny on the rail and wait for a train to come along and squish it.

"If they get their groceries delivered, how come we've never seen it?" Cat asked as we walked in the direction of the train tracks. "We watch the house all day. I've never seen a delivery truck, have you?"

"Maybe they do it early. The earliest I've ever gotten to the treehouse is a little after eight. Maybe they come before that."

"Safeway doesn't deliver."

"No, but the Little Store does."

"What time does it open?"

"Seven." The actual name of the Little Store was the Thirty-eighth Avenue Market. Although my mother did her major shopping at Safeway, the Little Store was good for last minute things: a carton of milk or a box of Minute Rice. It was owned by Mr. Walsh, a friendly bald man who lived behind the store with his invalid wife. He didn't have children of his own, so he didn't mind kids hanging around the store. Mr. Walsh allowed you to look around even if you didn't need to buy anything and, unlike other storekeepers, never watched to make sure you weren't shoplifting.

The Little Store was small and crowded, with merchandise stacked all the way up to the ceiling. It was always warm inside when the day was cold and cool inside when the day was hot. It smelled good, of soap and fresh fish and coffee. The penny candy machines by the door had just enough prizes in them that you would occasionally get one with your gum or jawbreakers. You didn't even need money at the Little Store. You could charge anything you wanted to your parents' account. Mr. Walsh would write the amount on a small receipt pad and never ask if your mom and dad authorized the purchase. If you had a dream in which you came home and your house had suddenly turned into a store, it would be just like the Little Store.

As soon as we were in sight of the railroad tracks Maude ran ahead and put her ear to the track to listen for a train. I hoped one wouldn't suddenly appear and slice her head off, as this would be hard to explain to my parents.

"Okay, say you're right," Cat grudgingly allowed, "say they have their groceries delivered. It still doesn't get us anywhere."

"I didn't say it did, Cat."

"It doesn't get us inside that house."

"I know."

"That's what we've got to do if we're ever going to solve this thing."

"One's coming!" Maude piped up. I listened to the track; it hummed and the steel vibrated a little against my cheek. We positioned the penny on the silver rail. We did this at least once a week.

"Come on, Maude, let's get back."

I led her away from the tracks and held her hand tight. Cat stood beside me. We waited anxiously for the train's appearance, which suddenly took on an almost mythic importance in our young lives. The signal turned from red to green and I felt Maude's little body move closer to mine.

When the train zoomed by, Maude hid her face in my side so she wouldn't have to watch the penny get squished. It was a Union Pacific passenger train with a Roof Garden restaurant car, and I saw people sitting in the bubble top having snacks and cocktails. A number of them looked down at us. I wondered what they thought of me.

Maude wanted the penny as soon as the train passed, but I held her back as I knew it would still be hot. We looked at the coin. It was flattened to the size of a quarter and was a pale coppery silver, a special color reserved for a squished penny. I squirted some water on it and it sizzled.

"I've got it!" Cat suddenly exclaimed.

"Got what? Not yet, Maude!"

"How we're going to break into the Shooks' house."

I tested the penny. It was still a little warm, but no longer scalding. I gave it to Maude, who examined it with a specialist's eye. She had about seven of these already. Predictably, she announced that this was the best one yet.

"Nelson, pay attention."

"I am. How are we going to break into the house, Cat? I'm listening."

"I'm going to get a job as a delivery boy at the Little Store!" she said brightly. She would have added, "Elementary, my dear Nelson," but Cat didn't read much.

Of course I said, what a good idea, why didn't I think of that, you're a genius and so forth, because I knew she wouldn't get the job and it would be one more example of how the world was against her. Cat had a grudge against the world. I didn't exactly have a grudge against it, but I felt it hadn't really lived up to my expectations, either.

A day later Cat caught up with us at the golf course where we were looking for lost balls. This, as you can imagine, was something Maude enjoyed more than I. Maude had once found a green golf ball that glowed in the dark, and she was hoping for other colors, too. I read, one eye on my book, one eye on Maude, in case she fell in a sand trap.

"Nelson, tell me why you can just walk into Safeway and get a job as a box boy when you're a ninety-pound weakling dwarf with asthma and I can't even get a job at the fucking Little Store?" Cat demanded furiously.

"Don't use words like that around Maude."

"She's got to learn them sooner or later."

"No, she doesn't. Anyway, I didn't get the job at Safeway. I was going to have my third interview."

"Yeah, but you would have got it and you know why? Because you have a lousy dick between your legs and I don't!"

"Don't use that word in front of her, either."

"Nelson, I found a balloon. Blow it up for me, please," Maude asked, holding a used rubber to her mouth. She was trying to inflate it and, possibly, twist it into a bunny rabbit.

"Goddammit, Maude, that's not a balloon!" I grabbed the rubber, threw it away, and rushed her to the clubhouse. She cried and thought I was being mean. I made Cat take Maude into the ladies' room to scrub her hands thoroughly and rinse her mouth, while I went into the men's room, washed my own hands, and then sat in a toilet stall until I stopped feeling sick to my stomach. It was Thursday. I still had a day and a half of trying to keep my little sister from getting run over, being decapitated, or contracting syphilis. The following week I would have five more days of this nightmarish existence, and the week after, five more. The back of my neck ached and a vein throbbed over my right eyebrow, the beginnings of a headache. I picked up some aspirin in the clubhouse shop and went to find the girls.

"Where have you been, Nelson? We've been waiting forever!" Cat said with typical impatience. After I made sure that Cat had carefully cleansed Maude's hands and mouth, I bought us all lunch. My mom had again been too busy to fix sack lunches and gave me money for the meal. "Something nutritious," she said as she drew two crisp bills from her purse, "not junk."

We sat at the counter in the clubhouse restaurant. Maude ordered a Green River, I had a chocolate shake, and Cat a cherry Coke. I ordered hamburgers and French fries all around.

"He didn't even interview me," Cat said, recounting her humiliation at the Little Store. "He didn't even have me fill out a form or say he'd think about it. He said it was his policy to just hire boy delivery boys because some of the loads were heavy, canned goods and stuff, and he didn't want me to hurt myself. How could I hurt myself? Drop it on my toe?" Cat pulled out a pack of cigarettes, but I made her put it away. "I told him I was never coming back to his lousy store again, only I didn't say 'lousy,' if you know what I mean. I said he was a lousy discriminator. Was that the right word?"

"From discriminate. Yes."

Our hamburgers came. The soda jerk was a bony blond fellow I recognized as the drummer in Tim's brother's band. He was trying to grow a mustache and a few pale strands like insect legs were stuck to his upper lip. Cat tried to make small talk with him, but he pretended to be busy. Later he offered Maude a free ice cream sundae, which I said she couldn't have, then presented her with a yellow and red striped pinwheel.

"Okay, there's a simple solution to this whole thing." Cat was having her cigarette as we walked toward Crystal Springs Park, a small park with swings that attracted Maude because they swung particularly high and there was always the chance of flying out and shattering every bone in her small frame. "It's very simple. Tim's got to be the delivery boy."

This made sense. Tim was the delivery-boy type. There was no chance he'd hurt himself lifting bags of canned goods. He had built-in muscles, muscles from doing nothing but sitting in his room, smoking and listening to forty-fives. He made noises in early summer about getting a job, but typically had done nothing about it. He regularly borrowed money from me because his parents had too many kids to give him much of an allowance. Getting a job at the Little Store was the perfect solution. Cat thought so and I thought so. Unfortunately, Tim didn't think so.

"All work and no play makes Tim a dull boy," he said when we suggested the idea, but this was the wrong thing to say to Cat and me. I was angry that his parents didn't make him work like mine did and Cat already thought him a dull boy. He put up a half-hearted fight, but caved in before long.

Tim asked me to go along with him the next day to apply for the job. Sometimes I wondered if Tim could do anything by himself except go to the bathroom and sometimes he wanted me to accompany him in there, too. When we arrived at the Thirty-eighth Avenue Market, Tim immediately headed to the back to talk to Hugo, the stock boy. Meanwhile, Maude marched up to Mr. Walsh to ask for the free Pixie Stick that he gave her each time she came to the store. He let her behind the counter to make her selection, and since Maude found it necessary to consider the pros and cons of each of the twelve flavors before deciding, I knew she would be occupied for some time. I joined Tim and Hugo.

Hugo was a part-time engineering student at Multnomah Community College, but I don't think he went to class much. He didn't need to learn engineering, anyway, because he already had quite a little business going. He sold black market items to neighborhood kids, products they couldn't get by themselves: hard liquor and beer, muscle relaxants, cherry bombs, and firecrackers. He also offered plastic dog shit and throw-up. He could find back issues of *Mad* and *Cracked* and get any dirty magazine you wanted. He charged ten percent above the price of each item and had a regular clientele. When I approached them, Hugo was telling Tim that he could get his hands on a magazine "that'll make your pecker stand up and salute." Tim thought this was a good investment and asked me for some money. I said it was about time he applied for that job. Tim got the beaten-down look of a lifetime member of a chain gang and wearily shuffled up to the front counter, his broad shoulders already slumped from the idea of the back-breaking work.

This is how it was with Tim: He walked up to the counter, took a strip of beef jerky from a jar on the counter, and dug in his jeans for change. He said, in a virtual whisper, that if Mr. Walsh needed another delivery boy he'd like to apply for the job, but if he didn't, don't worry about it. Tim put a dime and five pennies for the beef jerky on the counter. Mr. Walsh shoved them back at him, said that Tim didn't need to apply for the job because the job was already his and the beef jerky was on the house. Mr.

Walsh told Tim he could start tomorrow and added, "It's not much of a job, but it could work into something better down the road." He was practically telling Tim he could have the store when he retired. I would have been excited to get a job so easily, but as we walked away from the Little Store Tim had the same dazed look he always did, as if someone had just hit him on the head with a frying pan.

Tim's schedule was Mondays, Wednesdays, and Fridays, eight to six with an hour off for lunch. Another delivery boy covered Tuesdays, Thursdays, and Saturdays. The Little Store was closed on Sundays. When Tim wasn't delivering groceries, he swept up and helped Hugo stock the shelves. He wore an apron with his name stitched on it in big looping writing, as looping as you can get with the name Tim. He complained about the job for the first few days, then began to complain less and less. After a week he didn't complain at all. He delivered groceries all over the neighborhood, but never to Mr. and Mrs. Shook.

Every day I found something to do with Maude. We went to the pet store to look at pets we weren't allowed to have. We started Christmas shopping. We were regulars at the zoo and the parks. We went to movies and visited department stores to watch game shows on TV. I found a library with Story Hour on Friday mornings, so we added that to our weekly schedule. I enrolled Maude in swimming lessons at Reed College. Maude swam, I read.

Around the first of July I got a new job.

"Nelson, I want you to start fixing Maude's dinner. She needs to eat at six o'clock every night, and that's exactly when your father gets home from work. I'm too busy to feed her then."

At six o'clock the living room became off-limits. My mother and father had drinks and talked, and we were forbidden to enter the room. If we had something important to tell them, like the house was on fire or an atom bomb was about to explode directly over 7208 S.E. Thirty-second Avenue, Portland, Oregon, we had to stand in the doorway and say it from there. Maude had trouble with this rule and was always running in to tell our parents what we did that day. They would be sweet and patient with Maude, then yell at me for not keeping her out of the living room during cocktail hour.

My father is tall, which doesn't explain why I'm short, and he looks like he'd be the vice president of an important department store chain, which he is. When he isn't working he likes to fish, and every summer except the one I'm writing about we went camping. He thought there was nothing better than to sit perfectly still for hours on end in a small boat with his line stretched into the lake. He didn't even seem to care if he caught anything. He liked me to fish with him, and this was torture for me.

My dad's other interest is collecting stamps. He has a huge stamp collection that is so boring it makes fishing seem exciting. He doesn't even collect American stamps with presidents and the English language on them. His specialty is French stamps, which pretty much all look alike, only in different colors. When I was younger my dad bought me a stamp-collecting kit for my birthday. I worked on it in the backyard one afternoon. I put about half the stamps in the album, then a big wind came up and blew away the rest of them, which saved me a lot of trouble.

My father and I didn't have a lot in common. He was thirty-eight, I was thirteen. He was married, I wasn't. He had two kids, I didn't have any. He liked to fish, I liked to read. He collected stamps, I didn't collect anything. I liked my dad all right, but wouldn't say I was passionately in love with him. If he was going to be executed in the electric chair, I'd try to pull the plug out of the socket. But if he was being executed by a firing squad, I wouldn't throw myself in front of his body.

"I'll cook everything," my mother said, continuing to outline my new responsibility. "I don't mean you have to cook for Maude. I'll cook and leave her dinner and yours in the oven or on the stove. But I want you to sit with her and make sure she eats everything on her plate and drinks her milk. I'll add another quarter to your pay, so you'll be earning a dollar a day. I'll still put a dollar a week in your savings account, and I'll add another dollar every two weeks, making a total of six dollars a month in your account for your future.

"Okay." I didn't want to get into an argument. Anyway, I could always read at the table, which wasn't allowed when I ate with my parents.

"And no reading at the dinner table," she added. "I want you to talk to Maude."

"Mom, I talk to her nine hours a day!" I knew I was whining. It was the same whine that Maude got in her voice when I told her she couldn't do something. The Jaqua whine. "I don't have anything else to say to her."

"Talk about what you did that day."

"We talk about that on the way home from whatever we did that day. Mom, she's four years old . . ."

"I know how old she is. I don't want a fight about this. We have a rule about reading at the dinner table."

"Why can't you do something for Maude? Why do I have to do everything?" I asked, knowing full well that there would be no satisfactory answer to this question. She was the parent, I was the child. A headache that began that afternoon at the zoo banged at my head like a prisoner kicking his cell door.

"You don't do everything, Nelson. You have a bad habit of exaggerating all the time," she criticized, a wild exaggeration in itself.

"I get her dressed, I fix her breakfast, I have her all day. Now I have to make her dinner . . ."

"I didn't say you had to make her dinner. I just want you to be sure she eats it. Nelson, I won't stand for you talking back this way."

"It isn't fair."

"You have a lot to learn about life, Nelson." This was undeniable, but hardly apropos. Still, she acted as though the matter was settled and turned to leave the kitchen. I couldn't let her get away with it; I had to make one last desperate, self-pitying plea.

"My friends don't have to take care of their brothers and sisters! Tim doesn't. He has a real job." I didn't mention that I practically had to light his shoes on fire to get him to walk ten feet to ask Mr. Walsh for the position.

"I don't care what your friends do. Anyway, I've seen your friends. Who is that strange girl? I don't want you spending time with her."

"Cat?" I couldn't believe this. Now she was forbidding me to have friends.

"She smokes. If I ever catch you smoking, you'll be sorry," she warned. I'm sure I don't need to tell you that my mom smokes a pack of Chesterfields a day and collects the trading stamps that come in each package. Last time she traded them in she got an iron.

"I don't smoke!" I yelled. "Why can't I even have a friend? Why do you treat me like a little kid all the time? I'm thirteen! I'm a teenager!"

"Don't remind me."

"In five years I'll be eighteen and I'll be gone! What are you going to do then? Who's going to take care of Maude then?" Why was I pursuing this when I knew it was hopeless? The last thing I wanted was a fight with my mother; I knew her power to make me miserable. Still, the question burst out of me. Perhaps I really wanted to know, for Maude's sake.

"By then things will be different," she said. "They'll have to be." She didn't explain further and walked to the kitchen door. "You're too young to understand," she added wearily, as if she realized this was something every mother since caveman days had said to her child and wished she could come up with something slightly original.

"I'm not too young!" I shot back at her, but she was already gone.

"Be sure to do the dishes. You still have your regular chores," was the reply from the other room.

I threw the dishes into the sink and turned on the hot water full blast. My mom always made me wash the dishes thoroughly before putting them in the dishwasher, another version of cleaning up before the cleaning lady comes. I dumped half a bottle of detergent in the sink, then put the sudsy dishes in our new Hotpoint without rinsing them, hoping the pressure from the bubbles would blow the dishwasher out of its built-in place under the counter. I switched on the disposal and deliberately let a fork slip down the drain. The teeth-aching sounds of metal chewing on metal were good for my soul, but hard on my headache. I fished the mangled fork from the disposal and threw it away. I took the lid off the roasting pan in which my mother had made a pork roast and slammed it down on the counter.

"I heard that, young man."

I speared the remains of the roast, tossed it on a plate, wrapped it in aluminum foil, and heaved it into the refrigerator. Then I washed the roast pan and hurled it in the direction of the dish drainer. I miscalculated the power of my pitch (why couldn't I throw so well on the baseball diamond?), the pan bypassed the dish drainer altogether, and scored a bulls-eye on a ceramic vase in the shape of a maid holding a basket of flowers. The vase catapulted to the floor and shattered. I felt much the same as I did after I finished playing with myself: satisfied, but hopeful nobody would find out.

"What is that?" my mother said, looking down at the pool of water, the bright blue irises with green stalks and the scattered shards of a Bavarian flower girl.

"I didn't do it," I said automatically.

"That pan just flew across the counter by itself?" my mom asked with withering sarcasm. I had no rebuttal. "I bought that vase on my honeymoon, do you realize that?"

"I'll buy you another one."

"How will you do that, Nelson? It was nineteen years ago. Do you think a store stocks the same merchandise nineteen years in a row? Your father is in retail. You should know better. Anyway, that vase was handmade, one of a kind."

"I'll get you something nicer."

"That is not the point," she said, her voice rising and sharpening. "It was priceless to me. It's a memory of a very special time. Nothing can replace it."

"I didn't know you went to Germany on your honeymoon." I switched to a conversational tone. "I'd like to ask you about that sometime. I'm interested in European culture . . ."

"We went to San Francisco," she interrupted, "then drove down to a little town that is fixed up like a German village. Don't try to talk your way out of this, Nelson."

"It was an accident."

"Well, I'm going to have to take this out of your salary," my mother said, moments after she had proclaimed the little fräulein priceless. "You'd better start learning to have respect for other people's property. Your father is not going to be happy with you."

With the threat of more than monetary punishment hanging in the air, she left the kitchen.

As I was sweeping up the fragments of the demolished flower girl—a sliver of basket here, a chunk of bosom there—I noticed a faint label on the white, unpainted base: "Made in Korea." But perhaps the vase was handmade anyway, a Korean one of a kind.

chapter three

Last summer the Fourth of July fell on a Wednesday. Since the Little Store would be closed on the Fourth and Wednesday was one of Tim's scheduled work days, Mr. Walsh asked him to work on Tuesday the third, instead. Tim arrived at the store as close to on time as he ever did, four minutes after seven o'clock. Mr. Walsh was on the phone with Mrs. Shook. She wanted some groceries delivered.

We had an emergency meeting that night in my backyard to hear all about it. I had fed Maude and she was happily playing "Accident" in her room. This, her new favorite game, involved running her dolls over with my old toy trucks, taking the victims to the hospital in an ambulance, then, as soon as they were mended and on their feet, running them over again. While Cat and I waited for Tim in the backyard, I heard Maude's high-pitched voice imitating a siren and I knew there had been another accident with one of her dollies, possibly a fatality. Otherwise, the night was quiet. The low murmur of voices came from the living room where my mother and father were talking. Once in a while I heard the sharp crack of an ice tray.

"Where is he?" Cat asked impatiently. She had already smoked two cigarettes, one of which she ground out on our new redwood picnic table. I complained, but she ignored me. Then she caught me leaning toward her and sniffing to see if she still smelled like Ivory soap.

"What the hell are you doing?"

"Trying to get some air. I'm all stuffed up."

"You think there's more air over where I am? We're outdoors, Nelson. There's air over by you. Use your own air and leave mine alone."

"I lost my balance for a second. Sorry."

The sirens finally stopped and I went inside to put Maude to bed. She was lying on her yellow and red braided rug, clutching a dump truck like a teddy bear. Sleep came upon Maude all of a sudden, creeping up behind her and pouncing. She would keel over and drop to the floor like a gunslinger felled by a single bullet. I picked her up and slid her gently under the covers, although she wouldn't wake even if I lifted her, threw her toward the bed, and missed. When Maude was asleep, she was asleep. When she was awake, look out.

By the time I returned to the yard, Tim had arrived and Cat was bombarding him with questions. He ignored her, pulled a beer from a small paper bag, and asked me for a church key. I ran back in the house, making him promise not to start his story until I got back. My mother had been too busy to make dinner that evening and the kitchen smelled of burnt baked beans and cut-up hot dogs, the culinary feast I had prepared for myself and Maude. The charred saucepan was still in the sink where I abandoned it. (I read when I cook, too.)

"Nelson?" my mother's voice projected from the living room.

"Yes, Mom?" I rummaged in the kitchen utensil drawer for a

can opener. I recognized a melon-ball-maker I had given my mother a few Christmases back, a last minute stocking stuffer. I remembered her forced joy when she unwrapped it.

"Nothing, I just wondered if that was you."

"Yeah, it's me." I untangled the can opener from a wire whisk and hurried outside. The beer made a nice spurt when Tim pierced the can. He took the first sip, then passed it around. I don't like beer, but that night it was just the thing to cut through the greasy taste of hot dogs and burnt baked beans that still lingered in my mouth, as well as in the kitchen sink.

"Okay, tell us." Cat was literally sitting on the edge of her seat, the top of the new picnic table. I sat at her feet and Tim stood with one foot on the bench, his too-short pants leg riding halfway up his calf.

"They have their groceries delivered on Tuesdays as soon as the store opens. Mrs. Shook used to come in to do her shopping, but she started calling up and ordering over the phone about a month and a half ago. I asked Mr. Walsh why, but he didn't know."

"We know why," Cat said knowingly.

"What did they order?" I asked. Tim reached into his back pocket and drew out a crumpled piece of paper: the grocery list. Cat was awestruck. When she took the list her hands were actually shaking.

"Bon Ami! That's for heavy-duty cleaning, like bloodstains!" She squinted at the list; in the near darkness the penciled items were almost illegible. "Stain remover, too. There's lots of cleaning stuff on this list. I'm going to have this handwriting analyzed. The same Gypsy woman who pierced my ear does palm reading and handwriting analysis."

Tim looked at me. Neither of us said anything, but each knew what the other was thinking: So Cat hadn't pierced her own ear after all. We never doubted it or questioned her when she said it didn't hurt; it was the crazy kind of thing Cat would do. In fact, a Gypsy had done it and, if the truth were known, Cat probably yelled like a stuck pig.

"She read my palm for a quarter," Cat continued, still peering at the list. "She didn't know a thing about me and the things she said were incredible."

"Like what?"

"She said I was destined for greatness."

"How?" I asked, a little alarmed. I secretly hoped that I was destined for greatness, but if Cat was destined for greatness, this would probably decrease my odds. It was unlikely there could be two greats from the same small neighborhood. It wasn't the Left Bank of Paris.

"She can't tell you everything. Anyway, she's got all sorts of powers and I bet she can look at this and tell if it's the handwriting of a murderer or not. I already know they're cracked. Look at the way they make their Rs."

"They called the order in, remember?" Tim said. "That's Mr. Walsh's handwriting." Cat's face fell in disappointment. Perhaps she was looking for an excuse to go back to the Gypsy fortune teller. I made a mental note to go there myself, with Maude. It was somewhere we hadn't been.

"I'll keep this." She folded the grocery list carefully and slipped it into the inside pocket of her sports jacket. Underneath she wore a blue Cub Scout shirt and a string tie with a small jeweled American flag on it. I was surprised and touched by this; I never would have categorized Cat as patriotic. "Now tell us everything," she said to Tim. "Don't leave out a thing."

Tim started. His soft, breathy voice made the story even more suspenseful. Night had fallen and there was a sweet smell in the air. I thought the aroma came from a lilac bush in the corner, but the smell grew stronger when Tim leaned toward us and I realized he had put on some cologne. That and Cat's little jeweled flag made the evening really special.

"There were three sacks, packed pretty tight," Tim began. "I loaded them on my bike and rode over there. It was about quarter to eight when I got to the house." Mr. Walsh had a special heavy bicycle for deliveries. Groceries could be stacked in the wire basket on the handlebars and in a wooden box on the back fender. You had to be strong to control the bike when it was loaded down and that was probably one of the reasons Mr. Walsh wouldn't give Cat the job. She frowned a little at the mention of the bike, but didn't say anything.

"I parked down by the garage so I could get a good look at the new lock." The morning following our attempted break-in, Mr. Shook had left his house at nine thirty-two, was gone forty-six minutes and, when he returned, spent twenty-three minutes replacing the broken lock on the garage door. I reported this at our first morning conference of Tuesday, June nineteenth. Two days later my mom put an end to my Shook-watching career.

"It's a Yale lock," Tim went on. "Heavy-duty. I wouldn't even try picking that kind," he added, the hardened professional. "So then I carried the groceries up the steps . . ."

"All three at the same time?" Cat was thinking of those sacks "packed pretty tight."

"Yeah, I didn't want to go down those steps again. They're killers." At the word "killers" an involuntary shudder passed through me; I suddenly realized what a dangerous game we were playing.

"I rang the bell. It's black and it has a little quarter moon on it, right on the button. Whoever heard of a black doorbell with a quarter moon on it?" Tim paused for us to ponder this curious feature. It was just the kind of doorbell a kid would be afraid to push on Halloween night. It seemed like a detail with hidden significance. Everything could be a clue.

"Nobody came at first. I wanted to look through the window but Mr. Walsh said that's the one thing a delivery boy never does. You're supposed to wait, count to twenty, then try again. You're never supposed to ring a third time. If they don't come, you leave the groceries on the front porch and make sure they're protected in case it starts to rain." Tim gulped some of the beer. His prominent Adam's apple, sharp and pointed, bobbed up and down as he swallowed.

"I was just about to do my second ring when I heard footsteps. High-heeled footsteps, so I knew it was Mrs. Shook. Tap, tap, tap. She opened the door just a little. It was on one of those chain locks. She looked out, kind of surprised-like, like she wasn't expecting anyone. I told her who I was . . ."

Cat gasped. "You said your name?"

"No, just that I was from the Thirty-eighth Avenue market with their groceries. She closed the door, took off the chain lock, opened the door again, and unlocked the lock on the screen door."

"What kind of lock?"

"Just the hook and eye kind."

"Was the front door locked when she opened it?"

"Right. I heard the bolt go back. I forgot."

"Don't forget anything," Cat reprimanded.

"She opened the screen door. I had one sack in each hand and the other in between. She asked if she could help, but I said I could do it. She held the screen door open and I went inside."

"What did it smell like?" This was my question, a writer's question.

"Well, it didn't smell like there was a rotting body in there, if that's what you mean. But it didn't smell good, either. It smelled like there wasn't a lot of fresh air inside. You know, real stale. But it didn't smell as bad as your house, Nelson."

"Yeah, Nelson, your house smells like a French whorehouse," added Cat.

"When were you ever in a French whorehouse?"

"In a former life. The Gypsy fortune teller said I've had many lives," she said, glancing at her palm.

"What your house really smells like is somebody pissed in a rose garden," Tim complained.

"It's hyacinth spray my mom uses," I explained, trying not to be defensive. She would burst into a room and spray that can around like a Marine taking on a Jap machine-gun nest. I finally made her promise to stay out of my bedroom, but the smell drifted in anyway, under the door or through the furnace register.

"It was pretty dark in the Shooks' place," Tim went on. "The curtains were all closed and they have dark carpets on the floor, Oriental-style carpets or something. You walk in the front door and there's a staircase that goes straight up to the second floor. On the right there's like an open doorway, no door or anything, and that's where the living room is, with couches and a TV. On the right there's this arch . . ."

"You mean on the left," I corrected, helpfully. Tim couldn't tell left from right unless he made a writing motion with his hand. He was right-handed, like me. Cat claimed to be ambidextrous, but had yet to prove it.

"I mean the left. An archway into a dining room with a big table and chairs. That's where we went. She seemed sort of nervous, 'cause at first she had me put the groceries on the dining room table, then she made me pick them up again and take them in the kitchen. She's pretty small—about as tall as your mom,

Nelson, but a lot older. And fatter than both our moms." No mention of the Whore and Cat let it pass.

"Was any of Bobby's stuff lying around? Toys or retarded-type things?" Cat asked.

"There was a picture in a gold frame on the thing in the dining room. You know, the thing with drawers and cupboards where you keep the good silver and china and shit. You know what I'm talking about." We all thought for a moment, but none of us could remember what it was called. "But it was an old picture when he was about our age. That was the only sign I saw of him. So I went in the kitchen and put the groceries on the table in there. That was the only part of the house that was bright. The curtains were open and the sun was coming in." I was impressed with Tim's grasp of detail. I could see the bright kitchen, could imagine its abrupt contrast with the musty, gloomy house. "Then she didn't have her purse, so she went to get it."

"And left you alone?" Cat's eyes widened.

Tim nodded. "For about three minutes or so. I looked around. There was something cooking on the stove, I couldn't tell what. Big lumps of something in a sauce."

"Boiled retard balls," Cat suggested.

"There were some sharp knives in the drainer thing on the sink. Other than that there wasn't anything suspicious. I couldn't go looking in the drawers, because I knew she'd be back any second. It was real quiet, just that pot bubbling on the stove. Then I realized that right there, right in front of me, was the door to the basement. It was partway open already. I listened for Mrs. Shook's footsteps, but I didn't hear her. She's kind of tubby, so I figured I'd hear her when she came back. I snuck over to the door and opened it a little more. It creaked."

I wondered if the door really creaked or if Tim just added that for dramatic effect. In any case, it was a nice touch.

"There's a wood staircase, unfinished wood, going down to the basement. There's a landing about halfway down, then the stairs turn and go out of sight. All I could see was the washer and dryer and some stuff hanging on a clothesline. And a concrete wall."

"The wall!" Cat clutched my arm.

"I don't know if it was *the* wall," Tim continued. "It was made of gray bricks held together with motor. Motor? Is that right?" he asked me, the word expert.

"Mortar."

"Of course it's *the* wall. He's behind there, rotting. The ants and maggots are crawling in through his eyes and feasting on his brain!" Cat made feasting sounds with her mouth, then jabbed me in the side.

"Ow!"

"Anyway, I knew Mr. Shook was down there, because I heard sounds. It sounded like he was using a planer." Tim, whose father was always down in his own basement building something from plans in *Better Homes and Gardens,* knew the sounds of carpentry. "Then I heard her coming back, so I put the door back to where it was before and stood exactly where I was when she left.

"She came in and said, 'Sorry this is taking so long,' then she went to the basement door, opened it, and yelled down, 'Chuck!' "

"His name is Chuck?" Cat asked, incredulously. True, it didn't sound like the name of a mass murderer.

" 'Do you have some change for the delivery boy?' The planing stopped. Then Mrs. Shook took this plate off the kitchen table and held it out to me. 'Have a cookie,' she said. There were a couple of different kinds, ones with chocolate swirls and some red ones."

"Red cookies?" Cat's eyes glistened.

"Cherry," I said, trying to avoid a reference to blood-flavored treats.

"Did you take any?"

"One of each."

"You didn't eat them!" Cat exclaimed. Tim didn't answer. He drained the beer, belched, crumpled the can with one hand, and threw it into the yard where I would be sure to run over it with the lawn mower, then reached into his shirt pocket and took out two cookies wrapped in Kleenex. One was a shortbread cookie with a chocolate spiral and the other was tinted a pale red and decorated with silver balls.

"I'm not going to touch them. I just want to look," Cat said, scrutinizing the sweets. "We have to be careful of fingerprints." I said I doubted if fingerprints showed up on cookies, so Cat took them and studied them closely. I almost expected her to pull out a magnifying glass.

Tim went on with his story. It was completely dark now and the sky looked as if someone had tipped over a bucket of stars.

"I heard some heavy boots on the stairs. Clump, clump, clump."

"Chuck."

"I wasn't scared up till then, but I suddenly remembered I was the one who broke their lock and maybe this whole thing about the change was a way to get him upstairs so he could catch me. I said, 'That's all right, I don't need anything,' and started to back out of the kitchen, but Mrs. Shook grabbed my arm and said, 'We always give the delivery boy a tip.' "

"The better to eat you with, my boy!" Cat said and cackled.

"Before I could break away he came through the door. He's really big, six foot two at least. He was wearing overalls and a Western shirt, one of those Pendleton shirts, I think. He didn't say anything at first. He just took out his wallet and handed some money to Mrs. Shook. Then he looked at me. Stepped up close, looked me right in the eye and said, 'What's your name?' "

Cat and I held our breaths. Tim's voice was a good story-telling voice, low and whispery, and we strained our ears to hear every word. I wish I could write in a whisper like that.

"What did you say? You didn't tell him!" Cat was digging her fingernails into my arm.

"I tried to think of a fake name. I had to think real fast and you know me and thinking fast." Tim laughed a little. His perfect teeth glinted. "Finally, I just said the first name that came into my head."

"What?"

"Nelson."

I felt sick. The two sips of beer I had taken churned in my stomach like suds in a washing machine.

"What did he say then?" Cat asked, breathlessly.

"He said, 'We had a cat named Nelson once. *But I ran over it!*' "

There was a deadly silence, then Cat burst into loud peels of laughter. Tim looked at her, grinned, and started laughing, too. Cut-up hot dogs and baked beans shot up from my stomach into my throat. I gulped them back down and acid fumes burned my nostrils. I once saw a dog vomit on the street and lick the hot stuff up off the pavement. That was the only time in my life I was glad I didn't have a dog.

Without warning the back door opened and my father appeared. He didn't come outside, but stood framed in the light from the house: a tall, slim figure swaying in the doorway. The ice in his glass made a gay, tinkling sound, like wind chimes.

"What's going on out there?"

"Nothing, Dad. It's just us," I said quickly, poking Cat to make her shut up.

"Who's us?" He didn't sound mad, only curious.

"Me and Tim and Catherine."

"Good evening, Mr. Jaqua." Cat always put on an accent when she spoke to other people's parents, a slight English accent.

"What were you laughing about? What's the joke? I need a good laugh."

"Nothing, Dad."

"I laugh about that a lot myself," he said ironically. I hoped he wouldn't come out and he didn't. But he didn't go back inside, either. He lingered in the doorway, letting in the moths.

"Mr. Jaqua, is it all right if Nelson comes over to my house this evening? My father is expecting us," Cat asked in her cultured tone. I almost expected her to add, "for tea."

My father threw out his arm with an abandon that made his drink slosh over and said loudly, "Why not? It's the Fourth of July!" as if it was his responsibility to open the festivities. Then he turned and weaved back inside, closing the door behind him. A minute later I heard the crack of an ice cube tray.

As we walked to Cat's house, Tim finished his story. "Mr. Shook went back downstairs, Mrs. Shook gave me a dollar tip and another cookie, and showed me to the door. She said, 'Take care, Nelson.' I went down the steps, got on my bike, and rode back to the store."

"What happened to the third cookie?" Cat was cradling the other two in her hand.

"I ate it."

We heard the first gentle pops of firecrackers far away. There was a little bit of a moon, about as much as Tim said was on the Shooks' doorbell.

"We've got to get down in that basement. We've got to tear down that wall and find the body," Cat said eagerly. "Can't you see it? The police cars swarming all over. 'Come out with your hands up!' We'll be famous at Cleveland before we even get there," she added, perhaps picturing an assembly in our honor. Frankly, I wouldn't have minded a little bit of fame before entering the huge high school. Our class had gone there on a field trip in May and the teeming halls and swarming crowds reminded me of descriptions I had read of Manhattan.

We walked in silence the rest of the way to Cat's house. The houses were smaller in her neighborhood and the yards weedier. One lawn featured a car propped up on wood blocks. Another house was just a burnt-out shell boarded up with thin sheets of plywood. "Fuck yourself!" was written across them in orange spray paint.

"You guys like vodka?" Cat asked, opening her front door. The door wasn't locked; Cat and her father said they had nothing worth stealing. "I've got a whole bottle. My dad's not really here. He's in Reno gambling. Let's make popcorn, drink vodka, and play strip poker."

Tim didn't know how to play poker and neither did I. Cat tried to teach us and although I picked it up pretty fast, Tim couldn't make any sense out of it. He had trouble remembering which was better, a flush or a straight. He knew three of a kind when he saw it, but a full house baffled him. Cat wrote up a little chart for him to follow, but he couldn't follow it. That big eyebrow was all wrinkled and he lost every round. We told him to put his shoes and socks back on and we played Strip 21 instead.

First, we agreed on the rules. Whoever went over twenty-one took something off. If nobody went over, the person with the lowest score took something off. Anything you were wearing counted.

Tim still lost the first couple rounds. I asked him if he understood the rules, and he said he did—he just kept getting bad hands. He took his left shoe off and Cat and I pretended to be sick at the smell. Those first few rounds were fun.

I had my vodka in orange juice because I could barely taste the vodka that way. Tim mixed his with tonic water. Cat had hers straight, with a little ice. She must have been showing off; she couldn't possibly have liked it. It tasted like chilled gasoline. A big salad bowl full of popcorn was placed in the center of the floor. We had used a whole stick of butter on it and the cards were greasy after a couple of rounds. A picture of two poodles, black and white, decorated the backs of the cards. They must have been the Whore's.

On the third hand, I got a Jack and a five, then a nine, and my right shoe came off. Cat had twenty-one almost every hand, but I didn't believe she was cheating. She was the kind of person who would naturally have good luck with cards. Her father went to Reno with his friends from the outboard motor business every Memorial Day, Fourth of July, and Labor Day, so she had gambling in the family. It wasn't until the fifth round that she lost a shoe. She wore men's brogues, which were too big for her feet, and thick oatmeal-colored socks to make the shoes fit.

It was exciting. Somebody was going to be naked in that room and it could be any one of us. When Cat went to the kitchen to get more ice for our drinks, Tim and I looked at each other and laughed. We didn't say anything, just laughed and shook our heads, amazed to be doing this. Tim had green eyes. Usually when people have green eyes, they're not very green. Tim had very green eyes and when he laughed they turned greener.

Then Tim had to take off his shirt. He had an undershirt on, but that's when the game started to get serious. We didn't laugh or chatter anymore. It was so quiet we could almost hear the ice melting in our drinks. The snap of a card sounded like a fire-cracker.

My shirt came off next, then Cat had a couple of bad rounds and took off her other shoe and both socks. Tim lost the following round with nineteen. It was a tough break, but I had twenty and Cat had twenty-one, as usual. Tim took off his undershirt. Tim had good shoulders, broad and big-boned. In science class Dr. Unger told us that shoulders were hereditary: Some people get nice square ones like Tim's and other people get strange sloped ones like mine. Mine are so sloped they barely count as shoulders. Maude always complained when I put her on my shoulders be-cause she slid right off. Tim could have put two or three kids on his shoulders without any problem.

I dealt the next hand, dealing myself a beautiful twenty-one. Tim got nineteen again and Cat went over. She took out her pierced earring and all hell broke loose.

"An earring isn't clothing," Tim said in a loud no-you-don't tone of voice. He was soft-spoken and shy and only raised his voice around Cat. "We said any piece of *clothing.*"

"We said anything we're *wearing,* bird brain! I'm *wearing* this earring!"

"That isn't fair! Boys don't wear jewelry, so of course you're going to win!"

"You're wearing a ring!" Cat shouted back. "That's jewelry!"

Tim looked down at his ring in surprise. He'd forgotten all about it. Before we started I had carefully counted every item I was wearing, a grand total of nine.

"A ring isn't jewelry, it's a ring," Tim said defensively.

"So is an ear-*ring,* bozo!"

"Cat's right, Tim, the earring counts," the voice of reason interrupted. "We said anything we wore and Cat is wearing the earring. We can't change the rules in the middle of the game," I added. Tim sulked and poured his drink down his throat.

Cat shuffled in silence and the gold bracelets on her wrists jingled. She hadn't been wearing them earlier in the evening. They consisted of ten thin bands held together by a single clasp, but I suspected that each band could be taken off separately. She sported other jewelry, too—a couple of rings and a necklace—that I'd never seen before. She must have put them on when she went to get ice for our drinks.

"Cat, you didn't have those on when we started," I cautiously began. I would have let her get away with slipping the jewelry on mid-game just to avoid a fight, but I was dreading losing and baring my white, thin-chested body.

"What?" she answered innocently.

"Those bracelets and those rings."

"Sure I did." She quickly dealt the cards.

"No, you didn't," Tim interjected. "I remember because when we were in Nelson's backyard, I was looking at your wrists and you didn't have anything on them, not even a watch."

"Who said you could look at my wrists?" she screamed.

"Everything you didn't have on before comes off, Cat. The necklace, too," I said.

"Well, I had the fucking earring on before!" She tore the bracelets off her wrist and threw them across the room. The clasp broke and the thin bands went rolling in ten different directions.

"No one's disputing that," I said, impressed by my handling of the affair.

"Tim's disputing it! I don't know why you guys never trust me," she mumbled, pulling off the rings and necklace she had put on illegally. "Christ, you'd think I was public enemy number one. I don't even know why you play with me if you think I'm such a big criminal."

"Come on, let's look at our cards," I said as I studied my nine of hearts and seven of clubs. Cat took a sip of her gasoline on ice and glanced at her down card. I was pretty sure Cat wasn't really angry with us. She knew we wouldn't let her get away with ten gold bracelets miraculously appearing on her wrists. She was just afraid she was going to lose. In no time at all she could be nude in a bedroom with two boys who were partially nude themselves. This terrified her. I got scared just knowing that Cat, who never got scared, was scared.

When I get scared I do things without thinking, like take a card when I should hold. I had sixteen, but when Cat asked if I wanted to be hit I said yes and, of course, got a face card. My undershirt came off. My sloped shoulders never seemed so sloped. My skin was too pale for words.

Next hand I got fourteen and held, determined not to make the same mistake again, but this time I was too low and had to take off something else. I removed my dog tag. In our stockings the previous Christmas both Maude and I received dog tags with our names and addresses printed on them, a gift probably inspired by my dad's long-ago days in the army. I could see Maude needing identification—she was a little girl who might forget where she lived—but I was insulted and had no intention of ever wearing the thing. I put it on to please my father and somehow never took it off. Now, suddenly, I was grateful for it. I expected a storm of criticism for claiming a dog tag as clothing, but Cat said nothing and Tim was too busy counting how many things he still had on.

Cat lost twice in a row. First she took off her string tie with the jeweled American flag. When she lost the second time she stood right up, unbuttoned her old men's pants and let them drop to the floor. She wasn't wearing Jockey shorts like I once guessed or boxer shorts like Tim had supposed. She wore delicate cream-colored panties with strips of lace around the legs. They were shiny, either satin or silk, and the most feminine piece of clothing I'd ever seen Cat wear. She said she always destroyed the clothes the Whore bought her as soon as the Whore left town, but, seeing those panties, I began to wonder.

I had been friends with Cat almost a whole year without ever seeing her legs. She never wore a dress to school even though the rule was that girls had to wear dresses Monday through Thursday; Friday they could wear pants or culottes. Cat's legs were smooth and slim as two baseball bats and her kneecap sat on top of her knee like a little hat.

The three of us were tense and competitive now. Cat freshened our drinks without asking if we wanted more and the only words spoken were "Your deal" and "Hit me again." I had three items of clothing left: my belt, my pants, and my underpants. Tim had his pants, underpants, and, instead of a belt, his ring. It was hard to tell what else Cat was wearing, but she was definitely ahead.

Tim dealt me a twenty. Cat had a seven of diamonds up. She looked at her turned-down card and asked for another. She held. Tim took a sip of his drink. He had a nine of spades up. He looked at his hidden card. I knew he was counting because that eyebrow was doing funny things. He held. We showed our cards. Cat had twenty-one, as usual. Tim and I both had twenty.

"You guys both have to take something off."

"Cat, it's a tie. It doesn't count," I reasoned.

"Those are the rules."

"We didn't decide what we'd do in the case of a tie."

"We said the person with the lowest hand has to take something off. You're both the lowest."

"We can't *both* be the lowest," Tim protested.

"If we're both the lowest, that means nobody's the lowest and nobody has to take anything off," I argued, trying to fight down a note of hysteria in my voice.

"Nelson, it's just a game," Cat said, forgetting that five minutes before she had flung her gold bracelets across the room in a juvenile rage.

"How come you always make up the rules?" Tim spat at her.

"Who should? You? You can't even add!"

"Fuck you, cunt!"

"Look," I said quickly before Cat could take a swing at him. "Let's do this. In case of a tie, we'll cut the deck. Tim and I will cut and the guy with the lowest card takes something off."

Cat shrugged. "Do what you want. I'm not interested in seeing your naked butts, anyway," as if the game totally bored her.

"Okay, Tim? Here's the way the suits go. Spades are highest . . ."

"Hearts are highest." This was Cat, the expert.

"Spades are highest, but just so we don't get into a fight, for this game hearts are highest, spades are second, then diamonds, and clubs are lowest. Okay?"

Tim nodded. I cut the deck and got a seven of diamonds. I felt the vodka burning a hole in my stomach.

"Hearts are highest and then what?" Tim asked as his hand hovered above the deck.

"We just told you, dimwit!" Cat yelled. "Hearts, spades, diamonds, clubs! Nelson has the seven of diamonds! Cut!" After just saying she wasn't interested in seeing our naked butts, she seemed pretty anxious to see how this would turn out.

Tim cut the deck and got a six of clubs. He furiously threw the cards down and started pulling on his ring, a silver band imprinted with Indian designs that he got when he was twelve on a trip to Carson City, Nevada. It was a ring for a twelve-year-old and it wouldn't come off his fifteen-year-old finger. He pulled and yanked and twisted it. His knuckle cracked, turned red, and the skin around the base of the knuckle began to wear away. I expected him to draw blood any minute.

"It won't come off," he said.

"Then take something else off, dumbhead."

"I want to take my ring off."

"Then do it and stop holding up the game!" Cat yelled.

"It won't come off!"

"Then take something else off!" My own knuckle hurt just watching him work that ring. His face was flushed and his eyes were watering, whether from frustration or pain I couldn't tell. I hated this. Why didn't Cat let up on him? Tim had enough problems without her making him burst into tears in public. He was dumb, his family ignored him, he had practically no friends but me, all he did was sit in his room and look at dirty magazines, and even being good-looking didn't help because he was so bashful around girls he could hardly speak. True, he had a job, but it was probably the only job he would ever have. He would work at the Little Store his entire life, Mr. Walsh would leave it to him in his will, and Tim might end up taking care of crippled Mrs. Walsh in the back room as well.

"Cat, shut up! Can't you see he's trying?" I said angrily.

"For crying out loud." Cat wearily set her glass down on the floor. "Come here, Tim." She took his hand. It was a wide, thick hand with fine dark hairs sprinkled across the back. Cat dipped her fingers into the pool of butter at the bottom of the popcorn bowl, rubbed the butter around Tim's ring, and simply slid it off. Tim was awestruck, as if she had just cured a leper. Cat rubbed her buttery fingers on a rolled-up napkin, Tim rubbed his on his pants, and I shuffled.

When Tim flipped over his next hand and announced proudly

that he had twenty-one, I expected another fight. But Cat didn't say a word. She sat silently behind her ace of diamonds and Jack of hearts and simply smiled. She knew I was going to have to be the bad guy this time. I had nineteen.

"Tim, I hate to tell you, but that's twenty-two."

"Eleven and five is sixteen, right? An ace makes seventeen and five is twenty-one," he said with complete confidence.

"Seventeen and five is twenty-two, Tim. Cat, tell him." She said nothing. I reached for the pad of paper and pencil Cat had used for Tim's cheat sheet, made Tim put one mark for each point in his hand and count them up individually. Even after it was clear that seventeen and five made twenty-two, not twenty-one, he stared at the score, trying to find a loophole. He gulped his drink. His Adam's apple bobbed up and down. If this was a horror movie, it would have shot out of his throat and attacked me.

He nodded, finally convinced. He reached in his back pocket, took out his wallet, and tossed it on the rug.

"No, no, no!" This was Cat, of course. "You don't wear a wallet. You carry it. Only things you're wearing count."

"Get fucked, Cat!" Cat shrugged. He took some change out of his pocket and threw it at her. She ducked the coins and they scattered across the room. "I suppose that doesn't count, either!"

"Bingo."

When he jumped to his feet I fully expected him to march out of the room and not even come back for his shirt. But he didn't. He unzipped his jeans, pulled them off, and flung them at Cat. She ducked again. More change rattled and rolled on the wood floor. Tim sat down and poured another drink. The front of his underpants looked white and freshly laundered. I had been thinking about mine ever since the game began and was pretty sure that the last time I did my wash was a week and a half before, and I only had a week's worth of underpants.

I must have been concentrating on that and not the game, because I took a third card when I already had a six and an ace. Tim and Cat both showed face cards and were holding, so I assumed they had twenty-one or close to it. Cat hit me: a five of diamonds. I took another card. A three of spades. I had four cards which still only added up to fifteen. I took another. A two of clubs. Five cards and I was back where I started with seventeen. I took one more. Dolt. If you've had five low cards in a row, it's a safe bet the next one will be high. The queen of hearts smirked at me. My belt came off.

I only had my jeans and underpants left, but Tim only had his underpants. What did Cat have on, I wondered? Her panties, of course. I assumed she wore a bra under her shirt, but did she have any other jewelry she would try to pass off as a wearable item, like a diamond in her navel? I wondered if a tampon counted. If she had one in, would she take it out? If so, what would Tim and I do—faint dead away or try to argue?

Cat lost the next couple rounds. The Cub Scout shirt came off, but under it was a man's undershirt, the athletic kind with no arms. Then the undershirt was removed to expose a frilly white bra. She was like one of those Chinese boxes with another box inside it and another box inside that and still another box inside that. Could she possibly be wearing anything under her bra, like pasties?

The bones in her chest lay in narrow, even strips under her translucent skin. I wanted to reach out and touch them. If I had a little mallet, I could play them like a xylophone. I started to worry about getting an erection.

Cat dealt, then sat back confidently and used a finger to stir the ice in her drink. I knew she had twenty-one from her satisfied expression. Tim's fingers moved as he anxiously counted. He counted again, then proclaimed, "Twenty-one!" and flipped over his down card. This time he really did have twenty-one. I had another lousy nineteen.

They watched me take off my pants, not even politely pretending to look elsewhere. I unbuttoned the single button and lowered the zipper with the slowness of a striptease artist. I started to remove my pants while I was seated, but my underpants started coming off with them. Cat saw part of my ass, a preview of coming attractions. Finally, I stood up and, as if making a presentation, pulled my jeans down to my ankles. Cat studied my crotch with connoisseurlike interest. I quickly stole a glance at it myself. The front of my Jockey shorts was unstained. I hoped the bulge looked big enough, but not too big.

It was Tim's turn to deal. Nervously I gulped the rest of my drink. We had run out of orange juice, so I drank the vodka on the rocks. It no longer tasted like gasoline, but like the coldest, clearest water in the world—like a piece of a melted glacier.

Tim dealt me a two of diamonds up, a ten of diamonds down. Cat had her usual face card showing and Tim showed an eight. They were holding. I had to take a card.

"Hit me," I said. Tim tossed a card toward me, it caught on the rug, and flipped over: a six of clubs.

"I'll keep it," I said quickly and pulled it close to me.

"He has to take another card, doesn't he?" Tim asked anxiously. If Tim had a face card down, which was likely, we were tied. We both just had our underpants left.

Cat realized the gravity of the situation. She considered the dilemma with un-Cat-like patience, all the while stirring her drink with her finger. Bright red polish adorned her nails. Did she usually wear nail polish? I couldn't remember. There was always something new to notice about Cat, an unexpected benefit of her friendship. "As I recall, the rules are that Nelson has a choice," she said after a period of deliberation. "If he wants to keep the card, he can. If he wants to turn it back in and take another, he can do that. It's up to him."

Were those really the rules or was Cat just making them up because she could see how deathly afraid I was of losing? Goose-bumps covered my body. My glass shook in my hand. There was no question of an erection. I realized how much I liked Cat. She tried to be tough, but inside she was really sweet and considerate. Standing up for me in this way gave me renewed respect and admiration for her. Then I had a sudden thought: Cat made up the rule because she wanted to see Tim's naked body more than mine.

"I'm keeping it," I repeated.

So I had eighteen. If Tim had a face card down, he also had eighteen. Cat probably had twenty-one. We each took a breath and flipped over our cards. Cat didn't have twenty-one. She had eighteen, too. So did Tim.

"Three-way tie. Cut the deck." Cat reached for it first and cut. She drew the ace of hearts.

Tim and I looked at each other. "Go ahead," he said, gravely. I cut the deck. A jack of spades. I wasn't in the clear yet, but the odds were good that Tim would draw a lower card. His brow furrowed. I had shakily cut the deck almost to the bottom and he didn't have a lot of cards to choose from. I guessed that he was already preparing his defense, arguments for a redraw forming in his mind. His big hand fumbled with the few cards that were left. He made his cut. He turned over the card: the king of spades.

So I lost. And all of a sudden it didn't seem like such a big deal. What did it matter if I took off my underpants and everybody got a good look? A person's body doesn't count. The important thing is who you are inside. I'm a pretty nice person, I reminded myself. I've never murdered anyone. I take care of my little sister and she hasn't been run over by a truck yet. I'm a good student. I do everything my parents tell me except mow the lawn, which I do on occasion. I don't steal things, don't smoke, and this was practically the only time in my whole life I drank. I help Tim with his homework and don't ask for anything in return. I don't tell Cat to drop dead although she sometimes deserves it. If they don't like my body, I thought, then we have something in common. *I* don't like my body. If they laugh at it, I'll laugh right along with them. Anyway, I reasoned, it doesn't matter to Tim and Cat what you look like naked; they love you for who you are. Have a sense of perspective. When all is said and done, there are more important things in the world than losing a stupid, infantile game of strip poker.

I took out my retainer. I didn't even remember I had it in until I was reaching for the elastic band of my Fruit of the Looms. A popcorn husk had lodged under my retainer wire and I was trying to free it with my tongue when it occurred to me that you *wear* a retainer. Nobody could dispute that. I let go of my waistband, reached into my mouth, took out the little plastic palate and set it carefully on top of my undershirt. Cat and Tim stared, too dumbfounded to speak.

I had won. I wasn't going to have to show my bare body to the world after all and the realization made me want to giggle with pleasure. I knew that I'd get twenty-one or close to it on every hand from then on until somebody else lost. I was so relieved, I poured myself a drink. I had to stop myself from lifting the glass in a little toast.

It was over real fast after that. I got twenty-one on the next round as I knew I would. Cat drew seventeen, but Tim went over by a mile, as if he didn't want to postpone the inevitable. He wasted no time. He stood up, turned his back to us, pulled down his shorts and tossed them away. He leaned down, grabbed the vodka and took a swig right from the bottle. Then he turned to face us.

"Ta-da!"

Last summer Tim could easily pass for eighteen. He could sometimes buy beer, which meant he could pass for twenty-one. Naked, he was somewhere between the two. He certainly didn't look fifteen, clothed or unclothed. Cat looked exactly her age, thirteen years and ten months. I can still pass for twelve when I'm going to the movies, meaning I can get in for thirty-five cents instead of fifty.

Tim was a little red in the face, but that could have been the vodka. He sat down, crossed his legs Indian-style and smiled sheepishly. Now that the game was over he seemed almost proud to have lost. He certainly had nothing to be ashamed of and he knew it. There was a respectful silence. Someone was finally naked.

"Okay, Nelson," Cat said, "let's go." I looked at her quizzically, not catching her meaning. I didn't even understand when she reached behind her back, unhooked her bra and started to take it off. What was she doing, I wondered? She won. Why was she removing her bra? Then it slowly dawned on me that Cat and I were going to take our clothes off, too. I was immediately panic-stricken. What was the point of winning if we were all going to lose eventually?

Cat's breasts were pointier than I expected. They were curved at the bottom, but rose to a sharp point with a wide pink nipple spread over the tip. They clung to those strips of bone in her chest like giant raindrops, white and soft. It was strange to see Cat as a girl.

Then she stood up, pulled down her cream-colored panties with lace trim and there was that part of her, too. She sat down cross-legged just like Tim with a big, proud grin on her face just like his. The game had been nerve-racking and had us all on edge, but now that it was turning into a Roman orgy, Cat and Tim were totally relaxed. They seemed as comfortable as nudists in a nudist colony.

They turned toward me. I suddenly regretted the brilliant stroke of taking out my retainer. If I had lost the game when I was supposed to, I'd already be nude and wouldn't have to worry about it now.

I've studied the works of Michelangelo. After I read *The Agony and the Ecstasy* I checked out art books from the library and made a survey of his statues. The guys he carved, like David and the other guys, were about my size in the genital area. Of course, they had muscles and were tall and handsome, things I can't fall back on. But as far as genitalia goes, according to Michelangelo, I'm in proportion. I was never especially embarrassed in the locker room at school. I guess some guys were a little bigger and others smaller, but it never worried me particularly.

So I don't know why I didn't take off my shorts right away. The longer I waited the more I was inviting some insulting comment. "What are you, Nelson, deformed?" I could imagine Cat saying. I took another drink for courage and, as it dribbled down my throat, tears stung the corners of my eyes. It was straight vodka and not even cold anymore, as we had used up all the ice. I felt excited by Cat's naked body so close to mine and Tim's cologne was stronger now that he had taken off his clothes.

It was now or never. I lifted my butt off the floor and wiggled out of my underpants. I didn't fling them away with the careless abandon of Tim and Cat. I kept them close by. My friends looked me over without shame. I shrugged a little, excusing myself for any deficiencies. Then Tim looked back at Cat's physique to see if there was anything he missed. Cat looked from me to Tim for comparisons, but made no verbal judgment. I took another drink. I wished somebody would break the silence.

Cat started to laugh. At first I thought she was laughing at me, then saw that she was merely happy and couldn't contain herself. Cat rarely laughed and this was too bad, because she had a big laugh, the kind of laugh that makes you laugh, too, even if you don't care for what she's laughing about. Tim laughed his breathy, more staccato laugh and pretty soon I relaxed a little and joined in. Then I got the hiccups, which made everyone laugh even more.

Tim said he had to take a piss and stood up to go to the bathroom. Cat said she'd always wanted to see a boy take a piss. Pretty soon we were all in the bathroom, Tim and me peeing from opposite sides of the bowl while Cat studied our different styles. Tim didn't hold on to his penis when he urinated. He put his hands on his hips and just stood there while it happened all by itself. I wondered where he learned to do that, if his dad taught him or if he had copied some boy at school. Once I tried it and spent the next half hour cleaning the bathroom.

Then Cat peed for us, but you really couldn't see anything. There was just a sweet, ladylike tinkle. I found it kind of sexy.

After that I can't remember much. We went back to Cat's room and drank some more and talked and the next thing I knew I was back in Cat's bathroom, my head in the toilet bowl, vomiting. It seemed as if everything I'd ever eaten in my whole life from pabulum to the cut-up hot dogs and baked beans from that night's dinner was coming up. Cat's and Tim's hands were soft on my back and shoulders as they patted me and told me to relax, it's okay, you're going to be fine. They spoke in gentle, comforting voices that took my mind off the acrid fumes burning my throat and sinuses. At one point Cat flushed the toilet because it was getting full. Then I started puking again into the fresh bowl.

They helped me to the bed, Tim walking on one side, Cat on the other. One of Cat's breasts brushed against the side of my chest, my first female breast. Someone covered my still-naked body with a blanket and, as it settled down on me, so did sleep. For the first time in months I didn't toss and turn and wait for sleep to come. I closed my eyes and was gone.

A minute later Tim shook me awake and told me it was time to go home.

"What time is it?"

"Twelve-fifteen." Tim was dressed. Cat had also dressed and was quietly cleaning the room. It had been a little before nine-thirty when I took off my watch in the strip poker game. I got sick about an hour later.

"How do you feel?"

"Okay." And I did, except for a tight metal band around my head.

"Do you want me to help you get dressed?" My clothes were folded and piled neatly at the foot of the bed. My retainer sat on top of them like a small crown.

I said I could dress myself, so Tim searched for his change under Cat's dresser while I slipped on my clothes. They had been drinking as much as I, but didn't seem drunk or even tired. They appeared refreshed and adult. I felt like their child.

We said good-bye to Cat at the front door. She put her face next to mine and kissed my cheek. She smelled clean, as if she'd just taken a bath, even though I knew she couldn't have. She didn't kiss Tim.

Tim and I walked as far as Thirty-fifth Avenue together. There was a slight mist and the streets were deserted. Tim said nothing and neither did I. I worried that Tim was mad because Cat kissed me and not him, but he didn't seem mad, only quiet. When we got to the cut-off to his house, we said goodnight, and Tim walked away up the street. I watched him until he disappeared under the fat summer trees. What would become of Tim, I wondered? I imagined I would always feel a little bit responsible for him.

It wasn't until Tim was out of sight and I no longer heard the light tapping of his shoes on the sidewalk that I realized I never asked him what happened during the nearly two hours that I was asleep.

*   *   *

I found *Hothouse Flower!* I was browsing in one of the used bookstores downtown and there it was, right beside *Hawaii.* I was excited to find my English teacher's out-of-print novel and immediately grabbed it, but then I noticed that the author's name was George Mitchell, not George Crisp. I figured there must be two books with the same title and started to return the paperback to the shelf when I caught a glimpse of the author's picture on the back cover. It was Mr. Crisp, all right, a lot younger and with a lot more hair. George Mitchell must be his *nom de plume* (pen name). If I was going to choose a *nom de plume,* I'd make it a little more exciting. The book was marked down from fifty cents to twenty-five. On the front cover a review stated that the novel was "Lusty, earthy . . . characters you will never forget!" and there was a painting of a woman wearing a red dress torn half off her body. A man was grabbing her and kissing her throat with most of his clothes torn off, too. I bought a copy of *The Prince and the Pauper* along with it, so the bookstore owner wouldn't think I was only interested in lusty, earthy books.

The story was about a girl named LuAnne whose mother died when she was little and whose father drank all the time, beat her with a switch, and tried to crawl into bed with her at night. She ran away from home when she was sixteen and became a prostitute because she couldn't find a decent job. Then this man named Paul, who didn't look anything like the guy on the cover, visited her once and fell in love with her. He asked her to marry him, but LuAnne was making good money in the whorehouse and didn't want to give that up, although she liked Paul very much. Paul was jealous of the other men who came to see LuAnne, so he paid her a lot of money to sleep only with him. This was expensive and pretty soon Paul was broke. LuAnne didn't get rich, though, because the madam of the whorehouse took most of LuAnne's money and just gave her a small percentage. Finally, LuAnne decided to quit the whorehouse life and accept Paul's proposal. Paul had to admit that he'd lied; he had a wife and two children at home. But he said he truly loved her, wanted her to be his mistress, and still sleep only with him. LuAnne refused and, at the end of the story, she was walking down the road, disillusioned and heartbroken, trying to hitch a ride out of town. I got the feeling that there were going to be more books with the continuing adventures of LuAnne, but the store didn't have Mr. Crisp's other published work.

It was really sexy. Paul and LuAnne went to bed all the time and it was described very accurately as far as I could tell. There was one part where he "entered her from behind" that I wasn't sure about, but otherwise it was very convincing. It's hard to believe Mr. Crisp wrote it, as he doesn't seem to be the kind of man who would have thoughts like that. Maybe he was different when he was younger and had more hair. I wanted to tell him I read his novel and enjoyed it, but thought it was best to do this in private. Yesterday he asked me to stay after class and waited until the other kids left the room before he spoke.

"Nelson, how is your writing coming along?" he asked, packing up his briefcase.

"Okay."

"Are you still having trouble sticking to your story?"

"No. What you said was really a big help, Mr. Crisp, especially the part about not getting in the way of the story and letting it unroll like a big carpet. It's going really good now." This was a lie because I haven't written anything for three weeks. But when I do write, it goes a little smoother.

"Well, if you ever want me to read any of it, Nelson, I'd be happy to. I wouldn't show it to anybody else or talk to anybody about it. It would be just between the two of us. Two writers."

He smiled. He has a nice smile, with small evenly spaced teeth. I wondered if LuAnne kissed that mouth. I wondered if he "went down" on her with it, if that's what I think it is.

"Thanks, Mr. Crisp. I really appreciate that. I'll let you know if I ever want you to read any of it. Oh, by the way, I read your book!"

If I'd pulled out a gun and shot him in the foot, he wouldn't have been more surprised. He flushed a bright red and the top of his head glowed as brightly as the light on a police car.

"What . . . what book?" he stammered.

"Hothouse Flower. It was great!" I said enthusiastically.

He hurried to the door and pulled it shut. Then he returned to me and spoke in a hushed, threatening tone. "What makes you think I had anything to do with that?" The friendly Mr. Crisp was gone. I was afraid he was going to turn me in to the principal for reading dirty books, even if he had written them.

"Don't you remember you told me you wrote two books and

one of them was *Hothouse Flower,* but it was out of print? Well, I found it and read it and I really liked it a lot!"

The color drained from his face until he was a grayish green. He put a hand on his desk for support and looked like he might be sick. I glanced around for a wastebasket.

"What did you do with the book?" he asked in the resigned voice of a murderer who has just been exposed by Perry Mason on the witness stand.

"I have it."

"Here?" His eyes widened in alarm.

"No, no, at home." I resisted the impulse to reach out and comfortingly pat his shoulder. He isn't very tall. Every teacher looks tall when he stands in front of the classroom, but now that I was talking to Mr. Crisp, writer to writer, I realized how slight he is. His shoes aren't much bigger than mine.

"Who else have you told about this?"

"Nobody."

"You haven't told any of your classmates? Or shown it to them?"

"No, Mr. Crisp."

"What about your parents?"

"Of course not."

This seemed to reassure him a little and he was able to stand without holding on to the desk. He walked over to me. He smelled of smoke. He must smoke in the teacher's lounge. (Paul smoked, too.)

"Nelson, I want you to promise that you'll never bring that book to school or show it to any of your friends or talk about it to anyone. Will you promise me that?" It occurred to me to say, "Sure, Georgie, as long as you give me an A this term," but having no previous blackmailing experience, I just said yes.

"I'm going to hold you to that," he said, turning back to his desk and continuing to put papers and textbooks into his briefcase.

"Mr. Crisp, you know when you said I should write about what I know about instead of working on my freedom fighter story? Well, I was wondering if everything in *Hothouse Flower* happened to you or somebody you knew? It seemed so real."

"No, Nelson. It was just a story I thought up. That was the first thing I wrote and it was very imitative. There wasn't any of me in it at all, which is one of its problems. It was kind of *my* freedom fighter novel."

"Yeah, except you finished it and it came out."

"Only in paperback," he added with a note of bitterness. "Anyway, to answer your question: No, it wasn't based on personal experience. I guess there were a couple of things in there that happened to me, but just one or two." (Entering from behind? I didn't ask.)

"Well, I really thought it was great and I'd like to read your other book, too. I'm going to look for it."

"All right, Nelson. You can go." He seemed kind of eager to wrap this up. He snapped his briefcase shut. On his desk was a framed picture of his pretty wife. I suddenly realized that if her name was Sugar, she'd be Sugar Crisp. I laughed out loud and he looked at me, expecting me to tell him what was so funny. I felt bad for thinking such a dumb thing after he had taken the time to ask about my writing. I turned quickly and walked to the door.

"Remember your promise," he reminded me.

"Oh, sure, Mr. Crisp," I answered. I turned the knob and pulled the door open, then remembered a favor I meant to ask.

"Mr. Crisp, I wondered if . . ." I closed the door again and stepped back into the room. "I won't bring your book to school or anything, but maybe sometime, some weekend, could I bring it to your house so you could autograph it for me? If that isn't too much trouble."

"Nelson, I didn't really write that book for young people."

"I know. That's what I liked about it," I said honestly. "I don't want to read things about young people. I know what it's like to be young. I want to read about people I don't know about. I didn't care that LuAnne was a prostitute. It wasn't her fault. Her father was mean to her, so she had to run away. She was a nice person at heart and at the end I hoped she'd meet a man who wouldn't lie to her and treat her bad, and she could be happy. I don't see why I should read *Tom Swift* or something that could never happen in a million years when there's all sorts of books about real people and real things that are much more important. They should put *Hothouse Flower* in the school library. They should be really proud that you wrote it and your other book, too. I think it's inspiring."

Mr. Crisp looked at me with a surprised expression. "You really liked it, didn't you, Nelson?"

"Oh, yeah! It was better than *Lolita*!"

He laughed. The nice Mr. Crisp was back. I could see why LuAnne fell in love with him. He said he'd be glad to autograph the book for me. Then I said I'd see him tomorrow and he said he'd see me tomorrow and we both forgot that tomorrow was Saturday and we wouldn't see each other till Monday.

Maybe I'll let Mr. Crisp read this sometime, even though I swore I'd never let anybody see it until everyone in it has been dead for fifty years. But I promised to keep his book a secret, so maybe he'll keep mine a secret. I liked it when he said, "It would be just between the two of us. Two writers." I don't know if I have the nerve to show it to him or not, but if I ever do, I think I can trust him.

chapter four

It was a week before I saw Cat again. This was the longest I had spent away from her since we became friends and I missed her. I knew why I didn't go looking for her—I was embarrassed about throwing up and having to be taken care of like a child—but I couldn't understand why Cat didn't come looking for me.

Tim also kept a low profile during the days following the strip poker game, so early Monday morning I walked to the Little Store to see him. I had Maude in tow, of course. Mr. Walsh was in the back with his invalid wife, so I put five cents on the cash register and took two Pixie Sticks, grape and lime, for Maude.

"I got another day," Tim told me as he diligently polished the meat display case. He was really putting some elbow grease into it.

"Another day?"

"Saturdays." A fat gray salmon stared up at me from inside the case. It had a cherry in its mouth. I was reminded of the stuffed olives my mom and dad put in their drinks and my stomach did a flip-flop. "Now I work every day except Tuesdays and Thursdays."

"That's a lot of work," I cautioned. Tim shrugged, unperturbed by the grueling schedule. "Too bad you don't work Tuesdays, then you could deliver to the Shooks' house every week and really keep an eye on them." The bell on the front door jingled and a customer came in, a woman wearing a yellow print dress and a hat with a big bow. She looked like she'd just been to the Easter Parade.

"I was thinking about the card game the other night," I said with a nervous laugh. "Do you believe we peed in front of Cat?"

"Come on, Nelson, this is a store. The customer could hear you." Tim wiped his hands carefully on his polishing rag and went to stand behind the front counter. I checked on Maude. She was chewing on one of her Pixie Sticks and looking at packages of plastic hair clips and barrettes. I followed Tim to the counter.

"Since when do you work the cash register?"

"I'm supposed to wait on the customers when Mr. Walsh is in the back."

"And work the cash register?" I asked in shock. This was the boy who couldn't count without looking at his fingers.

The woman in the flowered dress put her purchases on the counter: an economy-size box of detergent, a package of bologna, a jar of Vaseline, and a can of cat food. The detergent didn't have a price and Tim sent me to aisle four to check it. Maude trailed after me, bugging me to buy her some multicolored barrettes with farm animals on them. I ignored her.

Tim rang up the woman's purchases. He was clean-shaven and his hair was combed for probably the first time in his whole life. He squinted a little at the cash register keys as he entered the figures. Tim had glasses, black horn-rims, but didn't wear them much. When he did wear them, he looked even better than without them.

He took the customer's money, made change, bagged her groceries, and even chatted a little about the weather. She asked if they were going to stock more of her regular cat food, because her cat was particular. He assured her they would and wrote down the brand on a little pad. "Bye, Tim," she said as she left, flashing him a smile. She wasn't young, but she had large breasts that pushed and strained at her bright dress like baby dinosaurs being hatched.

"How does she know your name?"

"She can read," he answered, glancing down at his apron where his name was embroidered in blue thread. I remembered that he had one in red, too. I wondered how many different colors he had.

"What do you think the Vaseline was for?" I asked, raising my eyebrows suggestively. Tim gave me a look warning that if I kept up the dirty talk, he would throw me out of the store. He certainly was taking his responsibilities seriously. He acted like he was in command of an Allied submarine. I followed him back to the meat case, which he continued to polish even though it looked about as polished as it would ever be. Maude hounded me about the barrettes until I gave in, then Mr. Walsh came out of the back and told Tim to take a break. We went outside and he had a cigarette.

"What did you do on the Fourth?" I asked, watching Maude feed her grape Pixie Stick to some ants.

"We went to the amusement park at Jantzen Beach," Tim answered, groaning. "The whole family. Jesus. You can imagine what that was like." I could. I pictured the Wooleys' station wagon crawling with kids, like an ant farm on wheels. "I spent most of the time trying to find somebody. Jimmy would get lost and I'd find him at the little motor boats, then Pam would get lost and I'd find her at the cotton candy machine, then Terry would get lost and I'd find him at the bumper cars. I hardly got to go on any rides." Still, it sounded better than my Fourth. I finished a 600-page novel about life among the Puritans and started another massive tome, the story of Andrew Jackson's wife.

My mom and dad ordered in Chinese food while Maude and I ate peanut butter and jelly sandwiches. I went by myself to watch the fireworks, then came home and tried to find the good parts of *Lolita*.

"Did you go on the roller coaster?" It was a big, dirty white roller coaster that looked like it could collapse any minute. A high school boy had been killed on it a couple of years before, making it even more menacing. I had taken Maude to Jantzen Beach a couple of times already that summer, but I couldn't go on any scary rides because she was too little.

"Yeah, a couple of times. You should have seen the line. It was about a half-hour wait. But we got to ride in the front car once."

"That's where that kid got killed."

"Yeah, but he was standing up and showing off, the jerk. It's safe if you follow the rules. Cat wanted to ride with no hands but I wouldn't let her."

I didn't say anything for a while because I was having trouble breathing. My lungs wouldn't suck air in or blow it out. I tried to remember how long a human brain can survive without oxygen before permanent damage sets in; the ballpark figure of six minutes came to mind. My ears had plugged up, too, so that sounds sounded very far away. A car driving by could have been driving on the other side of the moon. In addition, a high-pitched whine had begun in the center of my head, as if an insect was trapped in there. I hoped it wasn't an earwig because I'd just seen a television show in which a man was killed when someone planted an earwig in his ear. It ate through his brain and wiggled out the other side.

"Is Maude supposed to be eating the ants?" Tim asked quietly, as if the question could have two answers.

"Maude, come here!" She trotted over, her face smeared with

purple from the Pixie Stick. I opened her mouth and checked inside. It looked antless. I took out a handkerchief I carried for little emergencies like this, licked the corner, and started cleaning her face. Every Christmas I received a set of three monogrammed linen handkerchiefs from my grandmother, my mother's mother. Apparently she thought I walked around the neighborhood in a three-piece suit with an initialed handkerchief jutting out of my pocket. As far as I was concerned, they were only good for cleaning Pixie Stick stains off my little sister's face.

"Don't eat the ants."

"There's chocolate covered ants in the store." I once made the mistake of pointing these out.

"Those are special ants, raised in antiseptic conditions," I said, improvising. In fact, it was possible that the ants (protein) were better for her than the Pixie Sticks (sugar), but I wasn't sure. Then Maude wanted to put all six farmyard animal barrettes in her hair at once. I discouraged her from this ostentatious display and attached a pale pink pig to her head.

"I've got to get back to work," Tim said, tossing his cigarette into the gravel and crushing it with his loafer.

"So Cat went with you and your family to Jantzen Beach." I tried for a casual tone, but my voice shook like an old person's.

"Yeah. Her dad was out of town. She was going to be all alone, so I just asked her."

"That was nice of you. I don't know how her dad can just leave like that," I said, although I would have been delighted if my parents took a weekend off, freeing me to do whatever I liked.

"Cat isn't so bad when she isn't being a bitch." Tim took out a crumpled package of butter mints, put one in his mouth, and offered me one.

"That's what I kept telling you but you never believed me."

"Yeah, well . . . ," Tim said, not completing the sentence or admitting he was wrong. He switched the subject. "Mr. Walsh gave me a raise."

"That's great," I said, wondering if he paid for Cat's rides on the roller coaster.

"Well, see you, Nelson."

"See you." I watched him walk back into the store. He wore his apron well. I think it was his height.

Maude and I were on our way to Berkeley Park for the first time in a week that would be filled with visits to one park or another. I walked fast, too fast for Maude. But I had to think and it was hard to think and walk at a four-year-old's pace, especially a four-year-old who found every blade of grass interesting. "Nelson, stop going so fast!" she complained. I let go of her hand and kept walking.

Why did Tim invite Cat to the amusement park and not me? I couldn't get the question off my mind. True, her father was out of town, but I'd never known Tim to be a humanitarian, especially when it came to Cat. He thought she was a bossy bitch. She thought he was stupid and disgusting. Remember when he scratched his balls. Remember the strip poker game where he called her a "cunt" and she called him "dumbhead" and "dimwit." It was hard to believe they survived a ride on a roller coaster together. And he said they rode it more than once.

Maybe Tim just wanted company and knew that if he asked me along, I'd have to bring Maude. The last thing he needed, with all his brothers and sisters, was another kid. Cat might be a bitch, but she was a solitary bitch. Still, he could have invited me. I helped him with his homework and lent him money when he needed it. I think I deserved this courtesy.

"Nelson, stop!" Maude was crying and calling to me. I turned to look back. She stood on the far corner of Henderson clutching her Pixie Sticks. The pink pig had slid down a lock of hair and dangled beside her cheek. The inevitable sandal was unbuckled. She looked as plaintive as a poster child.

"Okay, Maude. I'm waiting for you."

"I have to hold your hand," she sniffled.

"Come on. It's okay. You can cross the street by yourself. You're a big girl. Go ahead." She didn't move. It seemed like Maude had been four years old for ten years. "Come on! Hurry!" She still didn't budge. "Now!" I shouted.

She stepped off the curb and ran into the street. Suddenly a car appeared out of nowhere, speeding up Henderson at forty miles an hour. Maude saw it coming and froze. Should she go back, should she go forward? She didn't know, so she did nothing. She was too far away for me to rescue her and, anyway, I couldn't move. My shoes were bolted to the sidewalk. There wasn't even time to scream. I just had to stand there and watch a turquoise Chevrolet Bel Air mow down my little sister.

The car screeched to a halt one half foot from Maude. There was a crash of glass breaking, then silence. A little breeze lifted the edge of Maude's skirt and it touched the front bumper of the car. That's how close she was from death.

Maude scampered up the curb and ran to me. The woman in the Bel Air was leaning forward, hugging the steering wheel. I wondered if she hit her head and if I'd have to clean her up with my grandmother's handkerchief. Then she turned and looked down the block at me. "If looks could kill" flashed through my literary mind. She knew me, all right: the slime brother who was so wrapped up in his own problems he couldn't walk ten yards to help his baby sister cross the street. The woman glared at me, willing me to come back and stand in front of her Bel Air so she could floor it, run me over, back up, and run me over a couple more times to make sure the job was done.

I grabbed Maude's hand and ran. I longed for Cat's fleetness as we sprinted down the block. My lungs began to ache and clutch almost immediately. We cut across a lawn on the corner and ducked behind the nearest tree. I expected the Bel Air to appear any second in hot pursuit and, while I tried to catch my breath, looked around for a better hiding place. I thought about the crash I heard when the woman slammed on her brakes. Once I'd dropped a whole cardboard box full of Mason jars and it sounded just like that. I bet she had them on the back seat. Yeah, she looked like a canner.

When the Bel Air didn't appear and I realized the woman wasn't going to chase us, I felt my lungs begin to clear. The congestion reminded me of the days I spent on our living room couch, gasping for air like a fish on the bottom of a rowboat, convinced I was going to die. My mother would sit beside me, her fingers raking through my damp hair, and say, "Relax, honey, just relax. You'll be better any minute." I hadn't had an attack for several years and thought I was over them for good.

"Isn't he sweet and furry?" Maude cooed. She was playing with a caterpillar she found on the tree. "Can I take him home, Nelson, please, please? It's not a pet."

She had almost gotten killed and thirty seconds later she had forgotten all about it! This drove me crazy about her. Maude wasn't worried about the woman in the Bel Air chasing us. She was worried if our mother would let her adopt a stupid caterpillar. When was she going to learn there were more important things in life, that a pet wouldn't solve anything? She had to grow up sometime. She might as well start right now. I snatched the caterpillar from her, threw it down, and ground it into the side-walk with my foot. Maude stared in horror.

"How many times have I told you to look both ways before you cross the street? How many? Is that so hard to remember? Get your pea-size brain off caterpillars for a second so you can remember something important for a change! You just ran out in front of that car and almost got yourself killed! How do you think I would have felt if that woman hit you? You think I would have liked going home and telling Mom and Dad that you're dead? Smeared all over the street like that fucking caterpillar? Don't you ever, ever do that to me again! You get no more Pixie Sticks for a week!" I grabbed them away from her. "And you can't have your barrettes any more today." The pink pig still miraculously clung to a blond strand of hair. I yanked it off. "Now, tell me, what are you going to do before you cross the street every single time from now on?"

Now, of course, she was crying so hard that she couldn't answer. I didn't care.

"Answer me! *What are you going to do?*"

"Look . . ." (sob, gasp) ". . . both . . ." (gasp, sob).

"What?"

". . . ways."

"Say it again!"

"Look . . ." (sniffle, snort) ". . . both ways."

"Again!"

"Look both ways."

"Again!"

My mother ate with us that evening; my father was in Salem on business. She asked what we did during the day. Maude was too busy dissecting her tuna casserole to mention that she had almost been run over by a two-ton automobile. She dug out the peas and put them in one pile. She pulled out the potato chips and put them in another pile. She moved the tuna fish into a third pile. Then she ate each element separately. This, of course, negated the whole point of a casserole, but my mother didn't say anything. You can imagine what she would have said if I took my casserole apart.

"Nelson, after you put Maude to bed, I want to talk to you in the den." The casualness with which my mother said this as she rose from the kitchen table could only mean one thing: She knew. The woman in the Bel Air must have tracked me down, reported the near accident, and now I had to face the consequences.

Despite my efforts that night to interest Maude in a game of Chutes and Ladders, she insisted on playing Accident with her dolls. It made me queasy to see them run down time and time again by dump trucks and fire engines. I tried to use the game as a way to enforce the rule of looking both ways before crossing the street. I'd position a doll at the street corner, turn its head carefully left and right, then cautiously move it out into the street. It didn't matter. Maude would grab a moving van and mow the doll down.

It was almost eight-thirty before Maude fell asleep. I knew my mother was waiting for me, but I delayed the confrontation as long as I could. I went to my room and took two aspirin with the remainder of a flat Coke. I'd had a headache ever since Tim told me about his Jantzen Beach outing and couldn't shake it. In fact, I'd been getting headaches more and more frequently. Well, I was under a lot of pressure, I reassured myself as I waited for the acidic little tablets to unfurl in my stomach. I needed a vacation from summer vacation.

As I walked into the den for the talk with my mom, I reviewed my strategy. I would be contrite. I would admit that I had been careless and untrustworthy. My mind occupied by matters other than the welfare of my baby sister, I had almost caused her violent death. This, I knew, was unpardonable. Quite clearly I could not be trusted. Therefore, I should get a job—something like Tim's position at the Little Store—and, with time, hard manual labor would teach me responsibility. I hoped to produce tears during my confession.

She was sitting in the big brown swiveling armchair behind my father's desk, her left leg tucked underneath her. A swiveling chair is fun for the person who's swiveling, but it's terrible for anyone else. The person who sits in the swiveling chair can't help but swivel. It's human nature. The other person just has to sit there and watch.

She asked if Maude got to bed all right. This was obviously the prelude to, "She could be in her coffin right now, young man!" I considered confessing up front before she made the accusation. This could show sincerity. It could also show stupidity. I told her Maude was all tucked in and fast asleep and left it at that.

"I'll go in and kiss her good night in a minute," my mother said, swiveling. She took a sip of her drink. There were interlocking water rings on the desk top, like the Olympic symbol. I wondered if that's how they came up with the Olympic symbol. I realized my mind was wandering.

"How much do you love your father?"

I blinked. Blinking was my only reaction. I couldn't think what else to do. I hoped the question was a rhetorical one and my mother didn't really expect an answer. But she kept looking at me, swiveling and waiting. I blinked some more.

"I don't know." My sloped shoulders rose and fell in what I hoped was an ironic gesture.

"You must know, Nelson. How much?" my mom asked, pressing the issue. Did she want a percentage, I wondered? A number on a scale from one to ten? All that came to mind were the amounts you mortgaged properties for in Monopoly. Should he be Marvin Gardens or Pennsylvania Avenue? Would I show filial pride by declaring him Boardwalk?

"A lot, I guess."

"You guess?"

"I mean, a lot."

"What do you love about him?" She sounded curious. She even stopped swiveling to hear my answer.

"Well, I liked it a lot when we went to British Columbia that summer and I caught that gigantic fish." If I had been hooked up to a lie detector, I would have blown a fuse.

"When was that?" She went back to swiveling. I wished she would go all the way around just once. It would relieve the tension.

"Two summers ago." Just as I was nodding off, rocked to sleep by the gentle motion of the boat, I hooked a huge trout. My Dad helped me reel in, but I was given full credit for the catch. He made me hold the fish by its gills while he took a picture with his new Polaroid camera. I could have waited practically my whole life to see this shot, but with the Polaroid it came right out. There I was, trying to smile with fish blood running down my arm. "You remember," I prompted. "Lake What-cha-ma-call-it."

"Oh, yes," she said, as if this was the exact name of the lake and it suddenly brought back a flood of fond memories. I was lying about enjoying the trip and she was lying about remembering it at all. This conversation was not going well.

"Nelson, what I'm really asking is how you'd feel if your father and I got a divorce. Would it upset you?"

I wanted to lie down. My favorite place to lie down was the living room couch. Whenever I was sick as a child, that's where I would station myself, rather than in my room. If I went to my room there was always the chance that my mom or dad would say, "Call us if you need us," close the door, and promptly forget I even existed. It was better to lie on the living room couch, my poor feverish body in full view, impossible to ignore. I got the most out of my fever that way. The only problem was that the living room couch was covered in lime green material with little gold threads. If you stare at lime green material with little gold threads for too long when you're sick, you get even sicker. But it sounded good right now.

"Divorced?"

"I'm sure you realize your father and I have been having problems," she said, mixing her watery amber drink with a swizzle stick. How could I have realized they were having problems? They never yelled at each other. They never threw plates or spent the night at a friend's house. No, I thought they were getting along fine. I thought it was me who was having the problems.

"Not really."

"Well, you don't need to know about all that. I just want you to know that it's something we're discussing. I don't want it to come as a surprise." I hoped my mother was making a joke, but I suspected not. "I'd like you to think about who you want to live with, your father or me."

"Okay."

"Who do you think you'd like to live with?" she asked, swiveling.

"Oh, you want me to decide right now?"

"I want you to think about it, Nelson. But without thinking, just right off the top of your head, what would your answer be?"

Obviously, there was only one right answer. "You," I said, reassuringly. If and when my dad asked the same question, there would be only one right answer for him, too.

"Your father has been seeing another woman," she went on. Now I *really* wanted to lie down, it didn't matter where. "It's been going on for years. Seven years, to be precise. I, of course, just found out. The last one to know, I guess." She was forgetting me, but I didn't correct her. "I know this woman, too. Socially.

We've been out to dinner with her and her husband. She's married, too, of course." She sipped her drink. "He doesn't love her, he says. It's just a physical attraction. That's supposed to make me feel better, I suppose." Another sip. "He says it's over and it'll never happen again. He expects me to believe that, as if I could believe anything he says after this." Swivel, sip. "He's seen her for almost half of our married life. He's been having fun while I've raised two kids, kept the house running, put dinner on the table. I haven't been having any fun. And don't think I haven't had offers, either. I've had lots of offers. Offers from friends of his. But I had this crazy notion about till death do us part. I had this idea you were supposed to keep the promises you made on your wedding day. I guess I'm old-fashioned that way."

She rattled the ice cubes in her drink. It reminded me of the Mason jars, which reminded me that I got away with nearly killing my sister. I took no comfort in it. "So, what do you think I should do, Nelson?"

"What?"

"Do you think I should do it?"

"Do what?"

"Get a divorce."

She wasn't kidding, either. She was asking a thirteen-year-old boy if she should divorce my father. Like before, there was only one right answer.

"I don't think you should."

"No?"

"Uh-huh."

"Why not?"

"I don't think he meant it."

She got up from her chair and walked to the narrow built-in bar in the wall. She picked a couple of ice cubes out of the ice bucket with a pair of gold tongs, taking care to select the very best cubes, as if it made a difference. Then she raised a bottle of Scotch and poured some in her glass.

"Can I have one?"

I couldn't believe I said this. I was still shaky from the third of July vodka. I swore I'd never have another drop of alcohol the rest of my life and here I was, not even a week later, asking my mother for a belt of Scotch! I really wanted it, too.

She chuckled softly like it was a good joke, put the bottle down, and returned to the chair. She tucked her left leg under her again and began to swivel.

"So, you don't think he meant it."

"No. You know how sometimes you do something really stupid because you're just not thinking or you've got your mind on a million other things? I do that all the time. I'm not paying attention and I'm off in my own little world and before I know it something's happened that is really terrible that I never meant to happen in the first place." I knew I was confusing the Bel Air lady and Maude with my father and the Other Woman, but it was too late to turn back. "I think it's the same with Dad. He wasn't thinking right or had his mind on other stuff and it just happened. I'm sure he's telling the truth when he says he doesn't love her and it won't happen again. I believe him and I think you should, too."

My mother paid close attention during my summation and when I finished continued to look at me for a long time. She appeared to be seriously weighing my argument. The swiveling had stopped, but now she was spinning her sweaty glass on the desktop. Finally, she picked it up and took another sip.

"Men always stick together," she said. This was so bitter and so final I couldn't even take pleasure in the fact that she called me a man. "You can go, Nelson."

As I walked to the door, I cursed my inadequacy, my clumsiness. I'd had a chance to save my parents' marriage. If I'd just said the right thing they would have seen the folly of their ways, patched things up, and lived happily ever after. But the moment came and all I did was babble incoherently. I pictured us all on *Divorce Court,* Maude and I seated in the front row with my arm draped protectively around her little shoulders, while our parents flung accusations at each other. Perhaps the Other Woman would make a surprise appearance.

"Nelson, one more thing," my mother said as I reached the door. I stopped reluctantly. What new horror awaited? I had to restrain myself from bolting from the room. I looked at her, braced for fresh disaster.

"Nelson, you're doing a very good job taking care of your little sister. Thank you."

I could think of nothing to say.

"Did I pay you for last week?"

"No, but that's okay," I said quickly.

"No, it's not okay. I promised to pay you and you should have at least one parent who knows how to keep a promise." She looked tired and thinner than I remembered. She took her purse from the desktop, opened it in her lap, and looked inside. This little task seemed to consume all her energy. "How much were your expenses?"

"I'd have to look. I have it written down." I wanted out of that room so badly.

"Just give me a rough estimate."

"One seventy-five, maybe." Her wallet bulged with unused coupons. She thumbed through the coupons, but found no currency.

"Will you take a check?" She laughed a little. "No, I have it," she said, abandoning her wallet and scraping the bottom of her purse for change. It seemed to take forever for her to collect enough to pay the outstanding bill. She counted the coins carefully, then held them out to me. I walked over to the desk.

"Here's six dollars and twenty-five cents," she said, dropping the heavy assortment of change in my hand. "That's your expense money, plus last week's salary, minus fifty cents for the vase you broke. We'll take fifty cents out of your salary each week for the rest of the summer, but I'll still deposit one dollar in the bank for your future as well as your bonus dollar for the past two weeks. Plus one more dollar from last week that I didn't get around to, so that's three dollars I owe your account." My finances were so complex my head reeled. "Remind me," she said, swiveling again.

I couldn't sleep. I read until my eyes were tired, then turned out the light and lay down, but I was still wide awake. Too much had happened that day—Tim, Cat, Maude, the driver of the Bel Air, my mother, my father, and the Other Woman all jockeyed for the honor of my attention. I tried to clear my head and think of nothing. This was impossible, so I pretended my body was going to sleep, starting with my feet. My feet were asleep, my calves were asleep, my thighs were asleep. But by the time my thighs were asleep, my feet had woken up. I took some aspirin. I masturbated. Nothing was working, so I got up, dressed, opened the window, and jumped out.

I started running. Maybe if I ran long and hard enough, I thought, I'd be tired enough to go to sleep. After a block my lungs started to throb, but I kept going. My sinuses felt like someone had stuffed them full of steel wool. By the time I got to Tim's, I could barely draw a breath. Lights were on at the front of the house and the television was blaring. Rock 'n' roll music poured out of the garage, Sam's band practicing. I didn't want to see anyone but Tim, so I went around to the back of the house and looked up at his window on the second floor. It was dark. I selected some dirt clods from the garden and threw them. A few hit, but there was no answer.

I ran to Cat's. I felt dizzy and even a little drunk. I wondered if leftover vodka was being activated by all this movement. My wheezing, gasping breaths sounded deafening in my ears, and I wondered if they might wake sleeping children and alarm attack dogs. I knew I should slow down and try to relax. There was no hurry; my parents weren't divorcing tonight. But I had to talk to someone, and not even about that. I needed some company that wasn't a four-year-old girl with a love of caterpillars and Pixie Sticks. I wanted to hear someone swear and tell a bad joke and call me "Helen."

I peeked through the front window of Cat's house. Her father was watching a Gillette commercial. I could have walked right in and he probably wouldn't have even looked up from the TV, but still I went around to the back. Cat's light was on. I heard her big, loud laugh and immediately felt my lungs let in a quart of cool night air.

Her room was on the ground floor, but the window was too high to reach. I jumped up to knock on the pane, but missed and rapped my knuckles against the aluminum siding of the house. I decided to simply shout her name and had opened my mouth to do this when I heard Tim say, "I felt so stupid!" and laugh. Then I heard Cat laugh. The two of them laughing.

Now I wonder what would have happened if I had called out her name anyway. Cat would have come to the window, seen me, invited me in. She and Tim would have asked why I was upset. I might have told the truth and I might not have, but that's not the point. The point is this: What happened afterwards would not have happened and the rest of the summer, the way it happened, would not have happened, either. It would have been an entirely different summer if I'd just opened my mouth right then and yelled, "Cat!"

I ran instead. Now I didn't know where I was going. There wasn't anywhere else to go. I crossed people's lawns, ran through their backyards, and down the alleys behind their garages. I knew all the shortcuts through the neighborhood and I took them, even though I wasn't going anywhere I needed a shortcut to. I could only breathe a little now through my mouth, breaths that felt on fire. My eyes teared from the pain and the neighborhood was blurred. I stumbled over a red scooter on the sidewalk and hit the pavement hands first. I skinned my palms raw, but was almost grateful for this new wound. It took my mind off my seared lungs. I jumped up and kept running. That night I was one swift ninety-eight-pound bullet of pain.

I ended up at the Shooks. The house was dark. The sky was dark, too. Stars were visible, but none of them looked organized into constellations.

I never believed the Shooks killed their retarded son and walled him up in the basement. That kind of thing just didn't happen in our neighborhood. It was the kind of thing Cat made up when she ran out of Helen Keller jokes and the Indian underwear routine wore thin. Did she believe it herself? Maybe, maybe not. You get Hardy Boys and Nancy Drew books for your birthday and Christmas and begin to think all sorts of mysteries and adventures will happen to you as they do to the characters in the books. But your biggest adventure turns out to be when your parents split up and ask you to choose between them, and your biggest mystery is why your mother ran off with the bank loan officer who refinanced the mortgage on your house, which is what the Whore did.

Yes, the Shooks were acting strangely and their son was missing. That didn't mean, however, that he had been murdered. The

Shooks looked like nice people, at least as nice as anybody. They walked Bobby in public and weren't embarrassed when he drooled and his arms flapped this way and that. Mrs. Shook offered Tim three cookies when he delivered the groceries and gave him a dollar tip. The Shooks didn't seem to be the kind of people who would kill their son because he wasn't like normal boys or because they were tired of taking care of him. Nobody could be that cruel.

But parents do kill their children. Read the paper. They stuff their newborn babies in trash cans, walk away, and forget they ever gave birth. Others starve their children to death. They beat them with belts and burn them with cigarettes. Fathers rape their daughters. They hit their sons with hammers, pieces of firewood, and the handles of guns. They set fire to the house with the family asleep inside. Women stick coat hangers up themselves, murdering their children before they are born. People sign their kids away, give them away to total strangers, and never think of them again.

Cat said she heard Bobby Shook screaming one night and saw his parents' shadows on the bedroom curtains. Maybe Bobby was having a nightmare that he couldn't wake up from and maybe his parents were fussing over him and stroking his forehead. But perhaps he was tied to the bedpost and they were hitting him with a baseball bat. There was no way of telling. He could still be in that house, chained in his room or down in the basement, hungry and hurt and too retarded to know that his own parents wanted him dead. If this was so, somebody should try to help him. He had rights. He deserved someone to care about him, even if it was only me.

There was a large tree beside the house, as tall as the house and with long, thick branches full of leaves. The bark of the trunk felt good, cool and rough, as I climbed it. Several big knots served as footholds. I grabbed the lowest branch, pulled myself up, and straddled it. This wasn't as hard on my lungs as running and even relieved the pressure a little. I should have tried tree-climbing long ago.

Standing on that first, sturdy limb, I was even with the living room window. The faded, yellowed curtains were closed. I remembered Tim's description of the interior: in the foyer, a stairway to the second floor; to the left, an arch into the dining room; to the right, an open doorway to the living room. I pulled myself up to the next branch, then the next. They were conveniently spaced.

I was now between the first and second stories. There were two windows on the upper floor, both dark and both with lace curtains. The nearer window, the one Cat had seen shadows on and heard screams from, had a screen on it. It was a small screen with a sliding panel that filled only the bottom half of the window. I knew those screens. They are temporary screens, summer screens. They aren't nailed or fastened into place; they're held only by the weight of the window above. It's the easiest thing in the world to kick them in. The branch above my head led to the window like a path.

I dropped silently to the ground and sprinted the three-and-a-half blocks home with no problem. My chest had cleared and I could breathe again through my nose. I almost wished my house was farther away so I could run farther. I wondered if this was what they called a second wind. Whatever it was, it felt good to have my legs pumping up and down and my lungs behaving themselves. It felt good, too, to know that I could get into the Shooks' house any time I wanted. Tim couldn't. Cat couldn't. Only I could. I jumped six big squares in the sidewalk and cleared them, except for a fraction of my heel touching the far crack of the sixth square. It was a record for me and, I'm sure, for anyone on my street.

chapter five

We were at the crematorium. It was one of Maude's favorite places to go, but I didn't take her there much. The big, gloomy stone building surrounded by a black iron fence didn't seem like a healthy place for a little girl. Although the grounds were open to the public from nine to six, nobody but us seemed to visit. I liked it because it was peaceful. Maude liked it because of the swans.

Swans glided prettily in the pond under the weeping willow trees. You could feed the swans from the edge of the water or drop bread crumbs to them from a wooden bridge that crossed the pond. I didn't let Maude feed the swans up close because swans are rumored to be mean and might bite her little fingers. I often thought about ringing the bell and asking for a tour of the crematorium. But desperate as I was for things to do with Maude, I didn't think a trip through the burn house would be wise.

The crematorium sparked Maude's desire for more animals, so afterwards I took her to the zoo. I purchased a Zoo Key, a plastic key in the shape of an elephant that turned on a tape recorder in front of each cage. The tapes told interesting facts and figures about the animals, which Maude listened to breathlessly, her little mouth hanging slightly open in awe.

She cried when we left. I promised we would come back next week. She asked if the llama would still be there, as if it had an urgent business trip coming up or might be out to a ball game. I assured her that the llama would be there next week and so would we.

The following day we went shopping for my father's birthday. In Lipman's department store downtown I debated between a gold pen and pencil set and a wooden duck paperweight. Neither seemed like something he would like, but I didn't know how to get my hands on a rare French stamp. Finally I decided on an imitation-leather shaving bag, since he traveled so much. I took time and care in making my selection, but my approach was cavalier compared with Maude's.

She started at one end of the dime store where I took her to buy her gift and carefully considered each item on display from a five-cent ball and jacks set to a folding chair. Her final choice was a plastic key ring with a small fish imbedded inside. "Daddy likes to fish," she said in explanation. The key ring was her second choice; she really wanted to buy him some Jockey shorts, but didn't know his size. I suggested the large size. "Daddy isn't large, he's tall. Where are the tall sizes?" The manager of Coronets seemed relieved when we left.

We had hamburgers and French fries at the Arctic Circle. I bought a newspaper and paged through it, looking for an activity to fill the long afternoon. A supermarket was having a carnival. We took a bus the nearly fifty blocks to the fair and rode the Ferris wheel and rocket ships a dozen times each, then strolled home. We stopped at a park along the way.

Wednesday morning we went to the library to return some

books, even though they weren't due for a week. I browsed until Maude got cranky, then we walked to Beckwith's Bicycle Shop to see if the price had come down on an English Racer three-speed I desperately wanted. It hadn't. Maude test drove a tricycle. Then it was time for Maude's swimming lesson. I changed her in the men's locker room at Reed College and tried to keep her from looking at the naked boys. She looked.

After her lesson, I thought about dropping by the Little Store to see Tim. Maude hadn't had a Pixie Stick for several days and was squirming like a drug addict. But Tim had been so serious the last time we visited him at work that I thought he might not want us bothering him again right away.

Instead, Maude and I went downtown to the art museum. This was a strange place to take a four-year-old, but I was running out of ideas. Maude thought the idea of the museum was to award a prize to the very best picture and she judged each one fairly and impartially. She gave first place to a Renoir, a pale and fuzzy painting of a girl combing another girl's hair. The kid had taste.

We lunched at the museum coffee shop (tuna sandwiches and Korn Kurls), then walked down to Broadway to see a movie. I read the titles out loud, carefully avoiding *The Music Man,* which we had seen last week and I knew Maude would want to see again. She liked the sound of *The Days of Wine and Roses,* but I told her that wasn't for little girls. I tried to interest her in *Mutiny on the Bounty.* I had, of course, read the book.

"What's it mean?" Maude asked.

"Well, mutiny means fight. And the *Bounty* was a boat. So, it's sort of "The Fight on the Boat." That sounded exciting to her, so I purchased two tickets. The lady at the box office looked down at the little form of Maude.

"This isn't a movie for children."

"She's very sophisticated," I answered. Inside, we bought lots of candy because it was a long movie. We sat close to the screen so nobody would sit in front of us and block Maude's view. I leaned back, resting the nape of my neck on the cool metal edge of the seat, and relaxed for the first time in days. The next three hours were taken care of.

The plan was for Maude to eat a little bit of the candy, watch a little bit of the picture, then doze off. Instead she ate most of the candy, stayed awake until right before the mutiny, then threw up. I took her to the bathroom to clean her up and by the time we got back to our seats, they were on their way to Tahiti. Maude whined that it smelled like throw-up in the theatre and there wasn't enough fighting on the boat, so we left.

I dragged her up the street to the bus stop. The headache that had eased when we sat down in the movie theatre made a comeback, and each step sent a strong pang shooting up my spine to my throbbing skull. Maude began to drop hints about going to Newberry's soda fountain for a hot dog.

"So you can puke that up, too?"

"I won't, Nelson."

"Yes, you will. You'll barf it up on the bus and make another big mess that I'll have to clean up. You're not a big girl. I wanted to see that movie. We do everything you want and then the one time we do something I want, you ruin it. You don't deserve a hot dog. You can have a hot dog for dinner. If you puke it up at home, at least we have a mop!" Of course, she was crying by now.

On the bus, people smiled at Maude and made funny faces to cheer her up. One man offered her a Tootsie Roll Pop. "She can't have that!" I snapped and for a second I thought he was going to hit me.

It was still too early to go home. Suddenly I wished we'd stopped for that hot dog as it would have killed some time. We were now on the east side of the river and I couldn't think of any hot dog places nearby. Maude started talking about how much she liked the movie.

"How come we left before they got to Titty?" she asked. "Can we go back some time and see the rest of it, Nelson?" I had to get rid of this little girl. If I didn't, I might push her into traffic or return to the zoo and toss her into the leopard's cage. The rest of the summer stretched ahead as one Maude-filled day after another. Before it was over, one of us would be dead.

I suddenly remembered that the Dairy Queen offered hot dogs on the menu. On the way there, I bought *The Sellwood Bee,* a neighborhood paper. Waiting for our order to be filled, I read the classified ads. There were five ads for baby-sitters. I made some calls from a pay phone while Maude happily ate her wiener and most of mine, too. At three-thirty I dropped the little girl off at the house of Mrs. Grace DeWitt, a gray-haired lady I'd never seen before in my life.

"I'll be back at five, Maude." I kissed her with brotherly affection. I felt more like biting her.

"Where are you going, Nelson? Take me with you!" she wailed, as if the brief separation would be an unendurable agony.

"I have something very important to do. I'll be back soon." Without further ado, I ran down the stairs and up the street.

I went to the Little Store to talk to Tim, but he was making a delivery. Mr. Walsh was in the back with his invalid wife and Hugo was holding down the fort. He sold me a pack of cigarettes and I asked if he could get his hands on some sleeping pills. He thought he could, but it might take a day or two. He didn't ask what they were for.

I went out back, lit a cigarette, and smoked it. I smoked it all the way down to the filter, then lit another one and smoked that, too. Then I went back into the store and asked Hugo to sell me a beer, but Mr. Walsh suddenly appeared and I bought a Mounds bar instead. I walked to the park and made plans for the rest of the summer.

Mrs. DeWitt charged fifty cents an hour. If I left Maude there four hours every day, it would cost me two dollars a day. This was twice what I was getting to take care of her, but I could take money out of my small savings account. My savings were supposed to be for my future, but I wouldn't have a future if I couldn't get away from the blond-haired, blue-eyed albatross a little each day. I could also cheat on my expenses. Bus fare, Zoo Keys, movie tickets, and lunches were all paid back to me. I had been scrupulously honest until now, but I could start padding my expenses and my mother, preoccupied with her messy divorce, would never know the difference. Maybe I could find a cheaper baby-sitter. Or I could get a part-time job in the afternoon.

The park was deserted except for a thin, waiflike girl who wore her dark bangs so long her eyes were completely covered. I had seen her there before. She always sat with her back against the trunk of a tree, drawing on a sketch pad. She looked up at me a couple of times and scowled as if I was spoiling her picture by being in the park. Well, it was a public park and who was she anyway, Grandma Moses? She left a minute or two later.

I smoked another cigarette and ate my Mounds bar. Then I put my head between my legs so I wouldn't pass out. Somewhat recovered, I went to the upper level of the park and watched some kids throw a Frisbee around. I hoped they would throw it to me, but they didn't. After that I walked to Safeway to talk to the manager about an afternoon job. He had been transferred to another store and the new manager wasn't around. All too soon it was time to pick up Maude. I paid Mrs. DeWitt and asked if I could bring Maude back tomorrow afternoon. She said sure.

· · ·

"Nelson, come in here a moment, please," my father said after I had fed Maude canned spaghetti and frozen corn and put her into her pajamas. My mother and father were in the living room, sitting in the matching floral armchairs. Since it was cocktail hour and the living room was off-limits, I knew they had something serious to discuss. This would be the official announcement of the divorce and they would ask who I wanted to live with, mother or father. Quite honestly, I didn't want to live with either of them. I wasn't sure where I wanted to live, unless it was in one of the novels I had read that took place in a different time, a different country. Every time and place seemed better than the one to which I was attached.

"Nelson, come here," my father said. He was wearing a tie I had given him two Father's Days before. I wondered if he really liked it or if he just put it on because he felt he had to wear it once or twice. I imagined him saying to his co-workers, "My son bought this for me," then laughing and adding, "Well, what can you do?"

"I understand that you dropped Maude off at a stranger's house this afternoon and left her there. Would you like to explain this to us?"

My father didn't sound angry. He sounded like there must be a perfectly good reason for my behavior and if I simply explained, he would accept it. My mother didn't say a word. She sat with her legs crossed as if she'd already decided that I was to die.

"I had something important to do," I said, trying to keep the old man's quaver out of my voice.

"What was that, Nelson?"

"It was something that she couldn't come with me for and it was only an hour and a half."

"What was this important thing you had to do, Nelson?" he asked again.

My mind spun as I tried to think. I could hear it turning. It made the sound a car makes when it is stuck in the snow.

"It wasn't that important," I said, weakly. Usually I was good in situations like this, but my head was cloudy from the afternoon cigarettes.

"Did you know this woman?"

"No, sir."

"How did you find her?"

"In the paper."

"You just picked someone out of the paper. Do you realize that woman could have been . . ." He didn't say what she could have been. "That she might not have been a nice lady? That she might have hurt your little sister?"

"She didn't, did she?"

"That's not the point!" He sounded angrier now. "In case you don't know, Nelson, I'll tell you. There are people who do mean things to little children. They hurt them. They do things that I hope you never have to know about in your life. Do you think your mother and I just pick someone out of the paper to baby-sit you and your sister? We check these people very carefully because we don't want anything to happen to you. If anything ever happened to either of you, I don't know what we'd do. If anything had happened to Maude this afternoon . . ."

"Nothing happened!" I interrupted.

"I know nothing happened, because this woman called your mother to make sure that she knew about this." All summer I had drilled Maude on her phone number and address. My good intentions, as usual, turned against me. "Your mother asked for some references, checked up on her, and she's fine. But it could very easily have been the other way around." I lowered my eyes as a humbling gesture and focused on his tie clip. It had a stagecoach on it. I gave him that, too.

"Nelson, your job is to take care of Maude," he lectured sternly. "*Your* job! No one else's. If you ever, ever do anything like this again . . ."

"He won't do it again," my mother interrupted and I expected her next words would be, "because he's going to fry in the electric chair tomorrow morning." But she didn't have to say it. It was understood.

"No, I won't, I promise." The living room floor was tipping like an amusement park ride. If I fainted and fell down, would I gain sympathy or would they just kick me?

"I want to know what you did for the hour and a half that Maude was with Mrs. DeWitt," my father said a little more calmly.

"Nothing."

"That's not an answer, young man."

"It's true." It was true, but it's the kind of thing a parent will never believe.

"I want an answer, Nelson, and I want an answer right now."

"I went to a dirty movie."

This was a calculated risk. I was hoping he would now be mad at me for going to a dirty movie and totally forget that I dropped Maude off for an afternoon with the child molester.

"How did you get into a dirty movie? Don't you have to be twenty-one to go to those things?" my father asked, curiously.

"They don't care."

There was a long pause. I worried that my dad would ask for the name of the movie, but I had one in mind just in case.

"Nelson," he said quietly, "I don't want you going to those things. If you have a curiosity about sex, you come to me and ask. I'll tell you anything you want to know." I thought about asking a few questions about the Other Woman, but I didn't want to turn this into a family brawl just when it looked like it was winding down. "Those places aren't for you. There are people who go to those things, men who go to them who have all sorts of ideas about young boys like you and I don't want you anywhere near them. Your mother and I would feel terrible if something happened to you. Terrible." He really sounded like he meant it, too. I felt tears welling up.

"Nelson, come here," he said gently. He sat forward in his chair and I took a couple steps toward him. "Come closer." I did, stopping at the end of his knees. If he put his arms around me and hugged me, I knew I was going to cry. I didn't want to cry in front of my father because I wanted him to think of me as my mother did, as a man.

He hit me. Maybe he was aiming for my cheek, but he got me right across the ear and the side of the head. In seventh grade our music teacher brought a tuning fork into class. She rapped it on her desk and the sound made me want to crawl out of my skin and leave it lying on the floor like snakes do. When my father hit me that evening my head rang with the same rapid, tormenting vibration.

"Don't you ever, ever do that again!" he shouted. Spit flew out of his mouth and a drop landed on my cheek. I turned and ran out of the room. My mother never even blinked.

Sleep didn't come easily that night. My brain throbbed with all the arguments I could have used with my dad. I should have asked if he had to take care of his sister all day long when he was thirteen. I should have thrown the Other Woman in his face. I fell asleep around five in the morning and two hours later Maude was tugging on me to get out of bed. At eight we set off to find Cat.

"Nelson, can we go see that nice lady again?"

"What nice lady?"

"That nice old lady baby-sitter. Can we go see her again today?

She was nice." It would be another nine hours of trying not to strangle a four-year-old child.

It had been over a week since I'd seen Cat and I was tired of waiting for her to come find me. If she kidded me for pissing and throwing up in front of her, so be it. Those were the facts and, anyway, our friendship was bigger than such trivialities. I needed her company, needed a dose of her "don't give a damn" attitude.

Halfway to her house I chickened out for the usual reasons and we veered off to Berkeley Park once more. I carried two fat books, a steamy one by John O'Hara and *By Love Possessed.* Maude begged me to play on the teeter-totters with her, which she knew I hated. She loved them, especially when I came down hard on my end and she bounced violently up in the air. I found myself bouncing her harder and harder, hoping she would lose her grip, fly off, and get caught in a tree. When I realized this wasn't going to work, I went over to the swings. Maude tried to entice me with the joys of the tether ball and when I said no, she pretended to cry. I told her to go play by herself. I opened one of my books and started to read, swinging compulsively back and forth.

The last time I saw her, she was on the merry-go-round. Some older kids were pushing it as hard as they could and Maude was squealing with delight. The faster the better as far as Maude was concerned. I imagined her in twelve or thirteen years speeding down the highway in a red convertible, an open bottle of whiskey beside her and her white scarf blowing in the breeze like the heroine of the John O'Hara novel I was reading.

Twenty pages and fifteen minutes had gone by before I realized I hadn't heard Maude laugh or squeal for a while. I looked up. The park was nearly deserted. The older kids had gone. A couple of young mothers with babies in carriages were sitting at a picnic table, having sandwiches and talking. A teenage girl was practicing her baton. Three pimply boys lay on the grass, smoking and watching the baton twirler. Maude had vanished.

I ran to the young mothers and asked them if they'd seen a four-year-old blond, blue-eyed girl in a pink shift with a big red apple on it. They hadn't. I tried to be calm and not let them see my panic.

The park had two levels. The slides, merry-go-round, teeter-totters, and swings were on the lower level, then the grass gently sloped up to a large, flat area containing two baseball diamonds. In the center of the park was a small brick building housing the maintenance office and rest rooms.

I ran into the women's bathroom, yelling, "I'm looking for someone!" but the three stalls were deserted. In the men's room a boy on roller skates was writing something obscene on the wall above the urinal. He was no help.

A Little League team was practicing on one of the baseball diamonds and some college-age boys were playing tag football on the other. There was no sign of Maude.

The only thing to do was to return to the lower level and search it foot by foot. I ran back and forth, zigzagging madly across the park, calling out her name. My heart thumped and my lungs tightened and squeezed, aggravated by both the running and my terrible anxiety. How could I report to my parents that I lost my little sister? If my father had hit me for dropping her off with a baby-sitter, what on earth would he do to me for permanently misplacing her? I thought about enlisting the three pimply boys in my search, but they were intent on trying to catch sight of the baton twirler's crotch and didn't look like they wanted to be disturbed.

I found Maude behind a bush, her underpants down around her ankles, squatting and contentedly peeing. She held a blade of grass between her fingers and was blowing through it, trying to get it to whistle. I grabbed her by the strap of her shift and yanked her up.

"How many times have I told you never, never, *never* to go out of my sight? How many times? What do I have to do, beat it into you to make you understand?" I was screaming and knew my voice carried across the park, but I didn't care. "Are you some kind of mental retard or something?"

"I had to wee-wee."

"I don't care! You come and ask me! I'll take you to wee-wee! You don't go off by yourself! I'm not going to take this anymore, you little shit!" I swatted her behind, not hard, but hard enough so she started wailing and peeing again. The urine ran down her legs and into the panties that were stretched between her sharp little ankles. "If something happened to you, who'd get the blame? Me! I'm always the one! You can just do whatever you want and I have to pay for it! Well, from now on you do exactly what I say or I'm telling Mom and Dad you're a bad girl! A bad, bad girl and you get no Pixie Sticks today or for the rest of the week, you hear me?" It was already Thursday, so this wasn't as cruel as it sounds. "No more treats at all and no more zoo until you learn to behave. And now you've peed all over yourself. I can't believe you're four years old. You act like a little baby." I yanked off her panties and sandals. She was weeping uncontrollably.

"Hey, take it easy on her, kid!" Incredibly, this was one of the pimply crotch-watchers.

"Mind your own business!" I yelled.

"You wanna try and make me?"

Until that moment I had lived my life in a manner to ensure that nobody, especially someone older and larger than I, would say to me, "You wanna try and make me?" But something had gone wrong and here it was, high noon. The gangly teenage boy with

Camel-stained teeth ambled to his feet and walked over to me. I pulled out my grandmother's handkerchief and quickly wiped Maude's legs. Her urine smelled sweet and tart, like a liqueur.

"Hey, runt. Who's that? Your little sister?" He had flamingo legs, two tubelike projections wrapped in worn blue jeans. Angry red dots crossed his cheeks, as if somebody sprinkled on his acne. He didn't look like he ate a green vegetable with every meal.

"Yeah, what's it to you?" I shot back at him. I never thought of myself as somebody who would ever say, "what's it to you?" I thought I was above that kind of talk.

"How come you're so fucking mean to her? She's just a little kid. Weren't you ever a little kid?" I tried to picture *him* as a little kid and couldn't. "Hey, little girl, what's your name? Want some gum?" He crouched down. His knees made a loud crack, as if this was the first time he had ever bent them. He pulled out a pack of Black Jack and offered her a stick.

"She can't have it!" I shouted.

"I want it!" Maude bawled, although she didn't like stick gum.

"Sure you can have it," he said with a yellow-toothed smile. Maude reached for the gum, but I jerked her arm back.

"I said no more treats today! Come on, Maude." I grabbed the soaking panties and sandals with one hand and Maude's trembling hand with the other. The Camel Kid reached in his pocket.

"She can have the gum, punk," he said, and the switchblade made a small, precise click as it slid out. It gleamed in the sunlight. I stared at it. The only switchblade I'd ever seen was in *West Side Story.*

"Pretty knife!" Maude said, enthusiastically. The Camel Kid held out the stick of Black Jack to her again and this time I didn't try to stop him. Maude took the gum, although now she preferred the knife. The kid and I stared at each other. I wondered what I'd do if he came at me with the switchblade. Dance?

But he just laughed, turned away, and started walking back to his buddies. As I dragged Maude toward the exit, he yelled at my back.

"Asshole!"

I ignored him. I wanted out of that park so bad. We hurried toward the narrow concrete path leading to the street.

"Stop, Nelson, I want my gum," Maude demanded.

"I said you can't have it! Are you going to obey me or not?" She started bawling again. The park had been strangely deserted when I was frantically searching for Maude and could have used help, but, now that I was as vicious with her as a SS storm trooper, it was crowded with the curious. They glared at me, hating me for mistreating the innocent ragamuffin, this angel with an apple on her dress. I hated them back. They didn't understand. It's easy to love a four-year-old girl you don't have to watch over day after day, stopping her from picking up slugs, and feeding her something nutritious. I couldn't wait to be out of the park, away from their angry, judgmental glares. The exit seemed to move away as we went toward it.

Then I saw them. They had just come into the park. Tim and Cat didn't see me, because they were looking at each other, talking quietly, and holding hands. Walking in the park, hand in hand.

"Look, there's Tim and Cat!" Maude stopped crying on a dime, proof that her hysterics were fake. Kids are such fakes. She raised her hand to wave and opened her mouth to shout to them, but I jerked her up in my arms, turned and ran the other way. Maude felt as heavy as a sack of concrete. It seemed a mile to the other side of the park where there was a second exit, but I ran as fast as I could and prayed Tim and Cat wouldn't spot us. I dropped one of the library books in our flight, but I didn't stop. I would come back at night to retrieve it.

"Nelson, stop! It's Tim and Cat!"

"Shut up!" I ordered. A moment later we reached the exit and were out of sight. I set Maude down and she started to cry again. "I wanted to see Tim and Cat," she whimpered, longing for company other than mine. I didn't entirely blame her. Her sandals were dry, so I put them back on, reminding myself to give her a long bath before dinner.

"Come on, let's go get an ice cream bar." A minute before I had said no treats for the rest of the week, but you have to be flexible with a kid. "What do you want, a Fudgsicle or a Creamsicle? Or maybe a Nutty Buddy?" Maude stopped crying to think and we set out for the Little Store.

Maude said it felt good to walk around without underwear and made plans to do this the rest of her life. She had completely forgotten that I called her "a little shit" in public, forgotten that I had almost been stabbed to death by a juvenile delinquent, forgotten that I practically yanked her little arm out of its socket. I wished I could forget things so easily.

But how could I forget that I had just seen my two best friends walking hand in hand in the park like the lovers in a teen romance movie? Only the soft strings of the sound track were missing. Perhaps it had been a hallucination. This was the fourth day in a row that a headache stabbed at my head; perhaps I was losing my mind. But Maude had exclaimed in her pip-squeak voice, "Look, there's Tim and Cat!" So it was really them, really walking hand in hand.

The only time I'd ever seen them touch was the day Cat slugged Tim. We had just started watching the Shooks' house. It was a Sunday and all three of us were jammed into the treehouse, talking and kidding around. Tim and I were ganging up on Cat, making fun of her clothes, her old men's pants and string ties. Tim's breath smelt of beer and he was talking more loudly than usual. He said something about Cat probably not having any tits and she slugged him. Her fist landed hard on the bridge of his nose, there was a loud crack, and blood spurted down Tim's face. He put his hand to his nostrils, then looked at his fingers dispassionately as if he'd never seen his own blood before and the sight interested him. For a second, I thought that was the end of it.

Then he went for Cat's throat. He got his big hands around her neck and started squeezing. It was not pretend; he was really trying to kill her. Cat screamed, a good scream, a horror-movie scream. I tried to pry Tim away from her. It wasn't easy—he was strong—but he finally let go.

"Cunt!" he shouted, spraying blood all over us. I took out my trusty grandmother's handkerchief and tried to clean him up.

"Look what you did to my hand! It's broken!" Cat screamed back.

"Me? You hit me! If you broke my fucking nose, I'm going to kill you, you filthy cunt!"

"Tim, stay still!" I said, trying to administer to him.

"Nice language, Timothy." Cat examined her hand. "It's broken all right. These two fingers."

I was resident doctor. Maude frequently needed patching, so I carried a few loose Band-Aids in my pocket and a small bottle of Bactine for minor cuts and scrapes. I got Tim to hold the handkerchief to his nose and lean his head back while I examined Cat's fingers. They were long and slender. They didn't look swollen, only a little bruised.

"I think they're just sprained," I said with my best bedside manner.

"How come you're always on his side?"

"I'm not. I just don't think they're broken."

"I can't *move* them! They're *broken!*" she insisted.

"They look fine to me, Cat."

"Fuck you, Nelson."

"Okay." I shrugged and she flipped me the bird. It wasn't until her finger was raised straight and tall in front of my nose that she realized this was one of her supposedly broken fingers. She quickly hid her hand in her lap, cradling it like a wounded bird. I started laughing, then Tim laughed, too, and even Cat had to laugh at herself. Then Tim blew his nose in the handkerchief and tried to shove the bloody snot in Cat's face. We pushed each other around and laughed until our stomachs hurt, and that was the only time I ever knew them to touch. Now they were walking hand in hand in the park.

To my knowledge, Tim had never held a girl's hand before. Girls liked him because he was tall and dark-haired and soft-spoken. But if they tried to start a conversation with him, he'd look down at the floor, dig a finger in his ear, examine the earwax, take out his glasses, polish them, put them on, brush some dandruff off his shoulder—anything so he wouldn't have to answer. He had never walked a girl home, as far as I knew, much less strolled romantically in the park.

Cat wasn't even a girl, really. She dressed in men's clothes, her hair was cut shorter than any crew cut, and she talked dirtier than any boy I knew. She didn't even like Tim. She thought he was a dunce, that all he ever did in the treehouse was jerk off. But there she was, holding the hand that she accused him of jerking off with. This wasn't consistent. Instead it was like a recurring dream in which a dear friend claims not to know you, or the one where you come home and your parents have given your room away to someone else.

The park was quiet that evening when I returned to get my library book. There it was, right where I'd dropped it: *By Love*

Possessed. In a corner of the park, a boy and girl were lying on the grass, his hand inside her sweater. I wondered if I'd ever be by love possessed. I played on the swings for a while, swinging as high as I could. I went home around nine.

Friday passed and on Saturday I went back to *Mutiny on the Bounty.* I bought the souvenir booklet in case my father wanted proof that I hadn't gone to a dirty movie. Ever since he hit me, I had been sneaking around the house like a burglar. I stayed mostly in my room, but if I had to go to the bathroom, I waited until I was sure I wouldn't run into him in the hall. I crept to the kitchen only when I knew my parents were in the living room. I'd grab something portable, a piece of bread or a handful of grapes, and take it back to my room to eat. Sunday morning I didn't feel well, so I stayed in bed. Sunday afternoon I went over to Tim's.

His house was noisy and chaotic as usual and, like always, I saw a child I'd never seen before. Maybe it was a neighbor kid, but I pictured Tim's brothers and sisters multiplying and dividing like amoebas.

Tim was sitting on his bed and staring at the wall like a mental patient. He seemed pretty glad to see me.

He had the messiest room I'd ever seen. Clothes were scattered everywhere, along with dishes, glasses, and empty pop bottles. All of them had a little something in or on them: the crust of a sandwich, a last swallow of milk, a ground-out cigarette butt floating in moldy RC. Ashtrays looked like they hadn't been emptied since smoking was invented. A hi-fi was on a table beside his bed, but not a single record was in its sleeve. A typewriter stood on his desk and, beside it, a *Learn to Type* book was open to Lesson Two. A chicken bone lay on top of it, perhaps marking his place.

He did have one great thing, an electric train with a track

running all around his room: under his bed, over the dresser, across his desk, and along the floor in front of the door. He built trestles to support the long track, an engineering feat as impressive to me as the bridge on the River Kwai. Parts of the track were unhooked and the little people, traffic signals, and trees were mostly knocked over, but it was a nice train set. It made his room.

"Come on in." He got up and kicked some things out of the way, making a path. "I've got to clean this place up," he said in a voice that made it sound as though it wouldn't happen in our lifetime. "What's new?" He took a bath towel off the back of his desk chair and turned the chair around for me. On the seat was a plate holding a shriveled watermelon rind. "Plant it," he invited, tossing the watermelon plate elsewhere.

If he had seen me running from him in the park on Thursday afternoon, I was sure he would mention it. I planned to say that Maude had suddenly become sick and I had to rush her to the doctor. Kids are always mortally ill one day and perfectly fine the next. If he didn't bring up the episode, I was going to try to get him to talk about Cat.

"What've you been doing?" I asked casually, lifting the carcass of a Mercury rocket and brushing off some of the dust. It looked like all it needed was one side panel and a fin.

"Not much. I've got to finish that one of these days," he said in the same sad voice he used when talking about cleaning his room. "The store takes up a lot of time."

"Yeah. I've been baby-sitting Maude."

"She's a good kid." Tim liked little kids. I could take them or leave them.

Tim picked a pair of jeans off the floor and went through the pockets for change. There wasn't much. He tossed the jeans on his dresser, but they slipped off and fell to the floor. He didn't notice.

"How's Mr. Walsh?" I asked, trying to keep the conversation lively.

"Fine."

"You ever see that wife of his?"

"Not yet."

"You think she really exists?"

"Oh, sure." Tim started putting together a section of the railroad track. Our conversations always started like this, a few words back and forth, incomplete sentences, not much flow. We both pretended we couldn't care less about the other guy. Then, after a while, we'd warm up, the talk would develop a rhythm and you couldn't shut us up. But it always took a while to get rolling.

"I was thinking about the other night. The Fourth. The third, really," I said, as if it had been the most tedious night of my life and only came to mind after I'd thought about every other night of my life. Tim grunted. "I haven't seen Cat since. Have you?" I linked a box car with a flat car. I'd always wanted an electric train and asked for one every Christmas, but never got it.

"Not really. Does it smell in here?" He glanced around and sniffed. "It stinks in here, doesn't it?" I shrugged and he grunted again. He started clearing underwear and crusty socks off the track all around the room.

"Nobody won our bet," I said, after a decent interval.

"What bet was that?"

"Remember we bet whether Cat wore boxer shorts or Jockey shorts? I said Jockey, you said boxer. Did you see what she was wearing? Those cream-colored panties with lace around the leg holes? I bet the Whore bought them for her, even though Cat says she cuts up everything the Whore buys."

"That's bull. She doesn't cut up anything. Her closet is full of stuff like that. All this fancy shit her mom got her."

"Really?" He crawled under the bed to clear off the track under there. I added a coal car to my section of train, then a caboose. "How do you know?"

"She showed me." Tim emerged from underneath the bed with a dirty magazine and a spiral notebook. He shoved the dirty magazine under his mattress and sailed the spiral notebook toward his desk. It hit the edge and fell into a wastebasket. He didn't bother to retrieve it. "She showed me her whole closet."

"No kidding? When?"

"After you passed out." He took the four cars I had strung together and set them on the track, then went in search of the engine.

"Yeah, I meant to ask you what you did all that time. It was like two hours or something. What did you do?"

"Nothing much. We drank some more."

"You drank *more*?" My stomach rotated.

"I wasn't that drunk. Neither was Cat. You were the one who got plastered." He found the engine under a dirty sweatshirt with black stains on the back and under the arms, as if Tim sweated ink.

"How come she showed you her closet? That's kind of a weird thing to do, isn't it?" I kept it casual. If I showed too much curiosity, he might clam up.

"We were just talking about our parents, you know, the usual complaining bullshit, and she opened up her closet and showed me all that stuff her mom bought her. Tons of stuff. She put on a couple of things."

"She *modeled* for you?" This was hard to imagine.

"They looked good. I told her she should wear them to school instead of that crap she wears, but she said she never would." Something was wrong with the track. Sparks shot out from the wheels of the engine, but it didn't move. Tim looked for a short along the line.

"What else did you do? Don't tell me she modeled for two hours."

"Nah. She just put on a couple things. I don't know," he said vaguely as he examined a piece of twisted track. He started bending it back into shape. "Just talked. Played this game."

"What game?"

"We made it up. She could ask me a question, anything she wanted, and I had to tell the truth. Then I could ask her something. We played that for a while."

"What did she ask you?" I realized it really did stink in his room. Maybe it was lack of air. I looked at the window and wondered if it had ever been opened.

"Oh, you know, what girls I liked at school. If I had a crush on that—what's that bitch's name?—Connie. Can you believe she thought that? I can't stand that pig." Connie was one of many girls who came up to me during the school year and asked when Tim's birthday was so she could get him something. On Valentine's Day he received a massive stack of valentines from various girls. I got four, three from my teachers.

"What kinds of questions did you ask Cat?" I stifled a phony yawn to show my complete disinterest.

"I asked what girl had the best tits in school. I figured she'd know, since she saw them naked in gym all the time."

"Who did she say?"

"Laurie Cooney. Another stinking cow." Tim's general opinion of girls, in fact of mankind, was pretty low.

"What other questions did you guys ask?" He had reshaped the mangled piece of rail, reattached it, and now was straightening sections of track all around the room.

"Shit, I can't remember. It was over a week ago."

"It must have been really interesting," I encouraged him. "I've never talked with a girl that way. There's all sorts of things I'd like to know."

"I remember. She asked me what it's like to have a dick."

My jaw dropped. "How did you answer that?"

"I said, 'How should I know? I don't know what it's like *not* having one.' She said that wasn't an answer, so she got a free question. Typical, she just made up the rules as she went. I said, 'Get fucked' and she said, 'Don't be as dumb as you look'—the basic routine. Finally, I said, 'I don't give a damn. Ask away.' And she says, 'What's it feel like when it gets hard?' "

I couldn't believe this conversation happened when I was lying not three feet away. How could they discuss these things and not include me? Not that I was eager to describe to Cat such an intimate feeling, but I would have liked to have been conscious to hear Tim try to describe it.

"Jesus," I gasped, "what'd you say?"

"I told her, I guess. I don't know how to put it in words exactly, but I tried. Then I asked her if she got the same feelings even though she didn't have one. She said, 'Yeah. It's a little different, but yeah.' "

"Cat?" I asked, trying to picture her with a hard-on.

Tim shrugged. "She's human." He cleared a dustball, like a small tumbleweed, off the train track. "Then it was her turn. I'm trying to think what she asked then." My mind reeled at the possibilities. "Oh, I know. She asked how often you get an erection. 'Once a month? Twice?' she says. I told her. Man, you should have seen her face at that one," he said with a proud chuckle. "Then I asked what it felt like when she had her period. You know, it was one of those real philosophical discussions. World issues. Real adult." Tim flipped a switch and the train started running. It chugged under the bed.

"How long did you play this?"

"Till we ran out of questions. Then we just talked about stuff. What it was going to be like at Cleveland. What we thought maybe we wanted to do when we were out of school. More crap about our families."

"And after that you woke me up?"

"No, it was only about eleven-thirty by then."

Tim had set up trees and stations all along the track, little people waving at the train and cars stopped at striped barricades. He must have gotten a couple of pieces every birthday and Christmas. If I started getting a piece or two for every birthday and Christmas from now on, I wouldn't have a train set as big as Tim's until I was at least twenty-five.

"Then what did you do?" I hoped Tim couldn't hear the nervousness in my voice. I felt like a terminally ill patient who can't resist asking how long he has left to live.

"We took a bath."

"A bath?"

"In the bathtub."

"Together?" I recalled when Cat kissed me goodnight she smelled like she had just bathed. I also remembered she didn't kiss Tim; perhaps she thought it improper after a detailed discussion on menstruation and boners.

"What did you do in there? Wash each other?" An edge was creeping into my voice and I tried to control it.

"Just our backs a little. We played this other game. Sam and me played it when we were kids. You write something, a word or a title of a movie or something, on the other person's back and they have to guess what it is just from the feel of the letters. You ever played that?

"Who would I play it with, Maude? She can't even read!" The edge again.

"Well, we played that for a while and then we were getting pretty wrinkled, so we got out and dried off and dressed and then I woke you up."

The train was running smoothly now, making a pleasant whirring sound. There's nothing like the sound of an electric train going around a track. It's soothing.

"How could you do all that with me lying right there?" I asked, fighting a rising hysteria.

"What do you mean?"

"I mean, I was right there."

"Nelson, you were dead to the world."

"You guys are my best friends."

"We took care of you, didn't we? You were a mess. Slurring your words and saying, 'I'm thorry I'm thick. I'm tho thorry.' If you could have seen yourself, Nelson, like some wino."

"For all I know you two fucked and I was in the same room!" I shouted. My face flushed crimson and tears poked at the corners of my eyes. I didn't know what I'd do if I started to cry. Throw myself in front of the train, I guess.

"Come on, Nelson, you know we didn't do that."

"How do I know?"

"Cause I'm telling you."

"Oh, I guess I'm supposed to believe you after you lied to me."

"When did I lie?"

"You said you haven't seen Cat since that night and I know you have, because I saw you walking in the park holding hands!"

"What are you doing, spying on us?"

"And you were at her house, too, Monday night, because I heard you laughing. You were probably laughing at how stupid I looked when I got sick! That's two lies and I'm supposed to believe you now?"

He didn't say anything right away. He slipped some forty-fives back in their brown paper sleeves.

"I thought you wanted me and Cat to be friends."

"I do. Of course I do."

"You're always telling me she's really nice, not really a bitch. It's just because of the Whore running off and how her dad never talks to her. And she doesn't feel she's pretty, so that's why she dresses the way she does and cuts her own hair."

"I never told you that," I angrily denied. This must have come up during the modeling session.

"Anyway, you're always telling me to be patient with her and nice, but the minute I am, you get all bent out of shape."

"Are you guys going together?" I asked with abrupt, district-attorney-like directness.

"Nelson . . ." My first name first. It always meant bad news. He didn't have to say they were going together; of course they were going together. They were probably getting married. I wondered if I would be best man or even be invited to the ceremony. I pictured Sam's band, the Bandits, playing at the reception. What would Cat wear, a tuxedo? "You're really out of control, buddy," Tim went on. "Cool down. What's the matter with you?"

"Nothing," I said and focused on the train climbing the track to the windowsill. He was right, I was overreacting. It was my fault I had gotten sick and missed out on the fashion show and the truth game. There was no law against Tim visiting Cat at her house or them strolling together in the park. I wanted them to like each other; God knows we all needed friends. "I'm just sick of taking care of Maude every day," I said in weary explanation.

"Don't worry. Summer's half over already. Next year we'll be in high school."

It was the moment to talk to him, to tell him what was really wrong. That my parents were getting divorced. That I was being asked to choose between them and didn't want either one. That my father hit me. That I almost killed my little sister. That I felt bad about it, but almost wished I had succeeded. If it meant jail, at least I would know where I'd be living and with who. It was time to tell somebody that I had a headache that wouldn't go away no matter how much aspirin I took. That I knew I was sick, but was too scared to go to the doctor and find out what was wrong.

I didn't tell him any of it. Our friendship had its boundaries. I just kept watching that train go round and round, under the bed, over the desk, and past those people with their hands up to wave.

"Hey, Nelson, you want this train set?" Tim asked, breaking the silence. "I'm going to get rid of it anyway. If you want it, you can have it."

Consolation prize. He got the girl, I got the train. Thanks a lot, Tim. Couldn't he see that I had problems an electric train, no matter how many pieces it came with, wouldn't solve? Did he think I was so pathetic, so much of a charity case? I deserved more from him. I would have done anything for Tim. I loved him as much as I loved anyone and this was all I was offered in return. He was even too dumb to know how much he hurt me. The worst part of it was that I really wanted the train. I thought it was neat.

"Nah. Thanks."

As I walked away from Tim's house, I thought how lucky Bobby Shook had been. He didn't have any friends, so he never worried whether they were going together or not. He was too lame-brained to know he had any problems at all. When he walked down the street, he always had a big happy grin on his face. Maybe you had to be retarded to be happy.

Or a child. The smallest thing could move Maude into a state of bliss. She didn't know our parents were getting divorced. She wouldn't care if Tim and Cat took a bath together. She'd think it was fun and want to get in, too. She had someone to take care of her all the time and her biggest problem in life was whether she should have an orange Popsicle or a lime one. She cried sometimes, but much of it was faked and she was over it in a second. I couldn't even remember the last time I got over something.

I walked. I went to the same places I went with Maude every day: the park (crowded), the library (closed), the drugstore (closed), the crematorium (open). It was my routine and I couldn't vary it, even on my day off. The golf course, the park with the ducks, the railroad tracks. I didn't want to go home where I'd have to sneak around, avoiding my parents who disapproved of me. Anyway, I was tired of their endless talk, punctuated by the sharp crack of an ice tray.

I went to my old school. It already seemed small and distant from me. Tim said, "Next year we'll be in high school," as if that would solve everything. But the field trip to Cleveland High frightened me. The halls were thick with students running to class, slamming lockers, practicing pep-rally routines and scenes for drama class. Bells were sounding and announcements being shouted through loudspeakers. An assembly looked as massive as a political convention. The students all seemed self-assured and mature.

It was almost dark when I stole in through the back door of our house. "Is that you, Nelson?" my mother called out. I said yes and waited for my parents to call me into the living room to tell me they were sorry for being so angry and to cheer up, because they weren't getting divorced after all. But they said nothing.

I examined my face in the bathroom mirror. It was a round, undistinguished face without a trace of color. I searched for signs of character, but couldn't identify any. My blond clipped hair made my face even more pale and bland. I tried to determine if I resembled my mother or my father, but, to my eye, I didn't look like either of them—a mutant.

I took off all my clothes and looked at my body in the full-length mirror. My skin seemed unnaturally white and, on impulse, I turned off the light to see if I glowed in the dark. I wondered what Cat thought of my body when she saw it naked for the first time. I couldn't imagine.

I knelt on the floor and put my head over the toilet bowl, as I had when I threw up in front of Cat and Tim. I glanced over my shoulder at the mirror to see what I looked like in this position. It was not flattering.

I didn't resemble my parents, but my body did remind me of someone; who? Not Tim, certainly. Not Cat. I didn't know any other naked people.

Then it came to me: Maude. When she was three and a half, Maude went through a naked period. She loved to run around the house nude, especially when my parents had friends over. Maude would make a surprise appearance, darting in and among the guests. They would pat her on the head, tickle her in the ribs, and Mom and Dad would laugh. Nobody saw Maude's nudity as improper or provocative. My body was just as innocent, not sexy in any way. I'm not saying that if I went running through the house naked my parents would be delighted and their guests charmed. I'd be horsewhipped. What I'm saying is, if I ran through the house naked, nobody would say, "I want to take a bath with that guy."

I didn't even read that night. I turned off the light, crawled into bed, and fought off the desire to get a teddy bear from Maude's room. I tried not to think about Tim and Cat, but all I could think about was Tim and Cat.

I wondered if they were in love. I wondered if my father and the Other Woman were also in love, although he assured my mom it was just a physical attraction. If it was just sex, why was my mother so upset about it? She must have slept with my father plenty. They were married nineteen years. If they had sex with each other an average of once a week for nineteen years, that's nine hundred and eighty-eight times. That seems like a lot. I can't think of anything I've done nine hundred and eighty-eight times.

Maybe my mom is afraid the Other Woman is going to beat her record, I thought. But the Other Woman would have to have sex with my dad one hundred and forty-one times a year in order to tie with my mom. My father travels a lot, but not that much. (Unless the Other Woman and my dad have sex three or four times every time they see each other. She could catch up that way.)

It was more than numbers, I decided after thinking some more. It was a matter of trust. My mother trusted my father to only sleep with her, then she found out he'd been screwing this Other Woman three or four times a day. She was upset in the same way I was upset with Tim and Cat. I trusted them, but they took a bath together and went walking hand in hand in the park without me. They cheated on me just like my father cheated on my mother. I suddenly realized what a dumb thing I said to my mother when she asked if she should divorce him: "He didn't mean it." Of course he meant it. Tim and Cat meant it, too. Tim didn't apologize for sitting naked with Cat for hours at a time or for writing on her soapy back. He didn't apologize for lying, either. I suddenly changed my mind: My mother *should* divorce my dad. I would live with my mom and visit my father on Christmas and Father's Day, that's all.

My head hurt regardless of whether I lay on my stomach, my back, or my side. I put my head under the pillow, but then I couldn't breathe. I ran cold water on a washcloth and put it on my forehead. It was warm in three minutes. I took more aspirin.

Headaches were now a daily event. They always started in the same place, over my right eyebrow. After an hour or two they would crawl across my forehead, around my head, and down the back of my skull to the nape of my neck. The hairs there would sting. A sudden movement would make my head ring like a gong.

While Maude was listening to "The Shoemaker and the Elves" at the library one Friday afternoon, I looked up brain tumors in a medical encyclopedia. My symptoms were exactly those described in the book. The author said: "See your doctor immediately." I took aspirin instead.

At first I took two every four hours, as per the instructions on the bottle. When that had no effect, I started taking more. I experimented with different kinds, paying close attention to the medical experts who preferred this or that brand in television and magazine advertisements. I mixed brands together to see if that helped. I tried not to read the warnings on the labels: "If pain persists for more than 10 days . . ." It had been more than ten days. Sometimes I'd carry five different bottles in my pockets so I could try various brands at various times of day and I rattled when I walked. I'm sure one of the reasons I vomited so much at Cat's the night of the strip poker game was the aspirin. I'd had twenty-five that day.

There was a high hum in my head, constant and unnerving. My ears were so sensitive that a loud noise—a shout, a scream—would pierce my eardrums like a hypodermic needle. Maude was capable of producing shrill sounds without warning and this made me even more short-tempered than ever. My skin felt stretched across my face, as if someone had adjusted it too tightly. I was constantly tired, but still couldn't sleep at night. I stole pills from my parents' bathroom and took them, hoping they were sleeping pills. Then Hugo came through with the sleeping pills I had ordered. I gave him eight dollars for twelve pills concealed in a Pez dispenser. The pills were so strong that in the mornings Maude had to jump on me to wake me. I felt groggy all day and couldn't wait until night when I could take another pill.

Then it started to hurt to pee. My penis burned so badly that I became afraid to urinate. I would hold it in as long as possible, sometimes six or seven hours. My bladder was as swollen as a loaded water balloon. Each step brought a sharp pain and the danger of sudden embarrassment. When I finally relieved myself, it was like pissing hot coffee and once steam rose out of the bowl when my urine hit the toilet water. I was fascinated and terrified at the same time.

I didn't tell anyone I was sick; to say it aloud would make it too real. Anyway, who would I tell? How could I tell my parents when they wouldn't let me into the living room to talk to them? I couldn't shout this kind of thing from the kitchen door. Even if I managed to tell them somehow, there was no guarantee they would take me seriously. "Oh, Nelson, you're just imagining it." What if they *did* take me seriously, but were only concerned that they were going to lose their baby-sitter?

If I went to the doctor, he might confirm that I had a brain tumor and, frankly, I'd rather not have it confirmed. Or he might say that it was all in my head and send me to a psychiatrist. That was the last thing I needed. People already thought I was an oddball.

But I had to do something. My eyes were too dry, almost squeaking in their sockets when I turned them, and they let in too much light. I started wearing sunglasses. What would be next, a white cane? I couldn't eat. My stomach hurt whether it was full or empty and food was metallic-tasting. Only ice cream tasted good, but it made my fillings twinge. My hand shook when I held a pencil. What did the future hold? My hair falling out? My arms flapping around like Bobby Shook?

Every day was the same: the zoo, the park, the library, feeding the ducks, feeding the swans, the Arctic Circle, the clubhouse at the golf course, the bike shop, the cleaners, the five and dime, slides, swings, merry-go-rounds, teeter-totters. I was up to seven aspirin every two hours by July twenty-first. I had lost five pounds. I hadn't had an erection for a week and a half. If I didn't do something soon, I'd be one of those small, fascinating headlines in the paper: "BOY SHOOTS FAMILY, THEN SELF."

The wait was literally killing me, the wait for my fate to be sealed. Why not seal it myself and stick a stamp on it, too? Breaking a treasured heirloom or swatting my sister was not enough anymore. Something bigger was called for. I had to take charge, make a decision, do something to break the routine. Maybe in the process I would save myself. It was up to me; I was the only person to whom I was most important. What I decided to do made no sense—I knew this—but it was the best I could come up with, the only plan my aching head would allow. Desperate men do desperate things and desperate boys are even more desperate than that.

*   *   *

Mr. Crisp still hasn't said anything. Today I took time gathering up my books and papers, so that I would be the last one out of the classroom. I hoped he would stop me and say he wanted to speak to me. He didn't even look up from his attendance book.

It was almost two weeks ago, February 7, that I gave him my five composition books. I didn't rewrite them or copy them over, because that would have taken too much time and I might have lost my nerve. I just gave them to him as they were.

"I hope you can read my handwriting, Mr. Crisp."

"I'm sure I can. I don't have any trouble with your homework."

"Yeah, but this is messier because I've crossed things out and erased things."

"I'm sure I'll get the general idea. I'm glad you took me up on my offer to read your story, Nelson. I want to encourage you in your writing and help you as much as I can. As soon as I've finished it, we'll sit down and talk about it, okay?" That was ten days ago and he hasn't said a word.

"Oh, Mr. Crisp, there's just one other thing about it," I remembered as I was almost out of the classroom. I came back inside and lowered my voice to a Tim-like whisper. "You said if I gave it to you, it would just between the two of us. You wouldn't show it to anybody else."

"Absolutely. That's a promise."

What if he didn't keep his promise? What if he was so shocked by what he read that he gave it to the principal and the principal called my parents? If my mother and father knew about this, they would never forgive me.

That would be too bad because we've been getting along really well lately. A couple of nights ago we had a talk about where we were going on spring vacation. My father brought home information about vacation spots at the beach and in the desert. They seemed to want me to make the decision, even though they would be doing all the driving. I said I wanted to go fishing.

"Nelson, you hate to fish," my dad said, not critically.

"I used to, that's true. But I think I'd like it now."

"Why?"

"Well, I don't know. I remember how pretty it was with the

lake and the mountains and stuff. And just sitting there with my pole waiting for a fish to bite. It's nice and quiet. The boat rocks back and forth a little. And, you know, cooking on the camp fire and the stars and things. I guess I thought it was boring before. But it appeals to me now."

My dad and mom looked at each other and laughed. I wasn't trying to be funny.

"It *appeals* to you?" My mom couldn't get over this.

So we're going to Crater Lake the second week of March. But I don't think they would have been so nice and asked my opinion if they knew I had written down all the gory details of last summer and showed them to my teacher.

Mr. Crisp is probably mad at me for writing about him. I think I said something about how he doesn't have much hair and when he gets excited his head turns bright red. But that's the truth and it's a writer's responsibility to tell the truth, isn't it? I was unsparing when describing my own self, too.

I was very flattering about his book, *Hothouse Flower.* I sincerely felt that it was well written and entertaining. Perhaps I concentrated too much on the dirty parts, but I also appreciated his narrative ability and sense of character. Anyway, it's hard to write good dirty parts. That's a talent, too.

It's possible that he hasn't had a chance to read my story, but I think he has. He acts differently. He avoids looking at me and doesn't call on me in class. Yesterday he asked about the meaning of *The Lottery* and, of course, nobody had any idea what it meant and probably didn't even read it. My hand was up for almost ten minutes, but he never called on me once. Finally people were looking at me, so I put my arm down.

I should never have given it to him. It's nobody's business but mine, and some of it isn't even my business, like the parts about

Tim and Cat. If they found out there was a documented history of their relationship floating around, I don't know what they'd do. Pound me into the ground for starters.

If Mr. Crisp breaks his promise and shows my writing to anyone else, I'm going to take my copy of *Hothouse Flower* out from under my mattress, underline the parts about "coming" and "entering from behind," and show it to everyone in class, beginning with all the kids who got a C or lower on their report cards last semester. Maybe I can get the school newspaper to print selections. Or I could type them up myself on a stencil, mimeograph them off, and pass them around. Maybe I can even get him fired!

Calm down, Nelson. Have you ever heard the word "trust"? Mr. Crisp promised he wouldn't show your writing to anybody, so try believing him. He doesn't want to ruin your life or get your parents mad at you all over again. He has nothing against you. He didn't call on you in class the other day when you had your hand up because you always have your hand up. If this was Nazi Germany, you'd get a medal for being the best Nazi. You love to have your hand up.

When Mr. Crisp is ready to talk to you about your story, he will. In the meantime, scrape the price tag off that new black and white speckled notebook you bought, open the cover, write "Chapter Six" on the first line, and get to work.

chapter six

A night light was glowing in the corner of the room when I dropped through the window. The light made me feel I was expected. The half-screen skidded across the floor with a brief rattling sound and slid under a chest of drawers. I hit my head a little on the bottom of the window, but for my first time breaking into a house, I did well.

A single bed stood against the wall to my right. The bedspread had a design of spaceships and rockets. Smokey the Bear and Fred Flintstone sat on the pillow as if they were pals. The guard rail on the side of the bed was lowered almost to the floor.

Toys and games were stacked neatly on a shelf, the boxes not worn and broken like the game boxes at my house. They looked newly bought, the games never played. In a bookcase at the foot of the bed a hardbound set of world classics, arranged in alphabetical order by title starting with *Adventures of Robin Hood* and ending with *Walden,* looked like they had never been read. The night light, Donald Duck, plugged into an outlet near the bookcase.

Above the bookcase was a poster of the ABCs. The same poster hung in the children's section at the Laurelhurst Library where

Maude and I went for Story Hour on Friday mornings. I once tried to use it to teach Maude her letters, but she wasn't interested in learning to read. She was afraid she would turn out like me.

On the other side of the room, to my left, was a small desk and chair. Pens and pencils were held in a cup decorated with clown faces. There was also a box of 72 color crayons and a stack of coloring books. Pictures of hockey players were tacked to the wall above the desk and a hockey stick hung from two pegs.

Beside the desk, a world globe on a stand. Next to that, a Daffy Duck wastebasket. A child's record player was set on a low table with red, blue, and orange records slotted into a wire holder.

The dresser had four drawers. On the dresser top was a plastic place mat with an illustration of simple magic tricks: disappearing coins, handkerchief and card tricks. Bobby had gotten this by sending in a coupon clipped from the back of a box of Kix. I knew this because I sent in for one, too, when I was nine. I never got it.

Hanging from two hooks on the back of the door were a yellow rain slicker and a blue robe. A patch of Tramp the dog was sewn to the robe lapel.

Only the upper half of the walls were papered; the wallpaper showed farm scenes with horses, chickens, and two playful children. The paper was peeling above the door. That was the only untidy thing in the room, that and the half-screen I kicked out of the window frame when I came through.

I hurried across the room, retrieved the screen, and replaced it in the window. Before I did, I leaned out of the upper storey to signal to Tim and Cat that I was all right, but they were out of sight.

It had been eight days since I announced to Cat that I was going to break into the Shooks' house. We were at the roller rink.

A birthday party was in progress and fifty pairs of skates on the old warped wooden floor made a deafening sound. Skaters raced and pushed each other, laughed and screamed, and at one end some boys were organizing a whip, which the roller rink discouraged.

It was the perfect place to plan a crime. I reminded myself that if I ever wrote a spy novel to set a scene in a roller rink. I pictured Russian agents rolling around the rink wearing heavy overcoats and fur hats. The idea pleased me so much that as soon as I figured out who was spying on who, I could start.

Maude was struggling to get free and zoom off on her own. She whined and begged me to let go of her hand. She said "Nelson" about a hundred times. Finally, I released her and she sped away, disappearing quickly into the dense crowd. I yelled at her to stay in our end of the rink, secretly hoping the whip would come around and run her into the ground.

"What's that sound?" Cat asked as she skated backwards in front of me. Cat knew how to skate, I didn't. I kept close to the greasy wood railing.

"What sound?"

"That rattle." Every time I took a stride aspirin bottles rattled in my pockets so loudly they could even be heard above the din of the rink. When I went over the big warp in the floor I sounded like the maraca player in a mariachi band.

"It's Maude's candy. She wanted me to hold it."

"What kind? Give me some."

"No food on the rink," I said, pointing to the warning posted on the wall. Cat sighed; it drove her crazy that I always stuck to the rules. Then she did an arabesque.

"Anyway, the tree branch goes right up to the window with the screen," I said, continuing to describe my plan for the break-in. "That summer screen. I just swing through the window, knock the screen out with my feet, and I'm in the house." My heartbeat doubled. I had never thought my scheme through in much detail. As I spoke it aloud, the break-in seemed something only a hardened criminal with years of experience could pull off.

"That sounds good," was all Cat said.

"We've got to start watching the house again. We wait for them to leave like last time. Cat, careful! You're going to run over that . . ." But Cat had already seen the boy sprawled on the floor behind her. She executed a neat hop over him.

"You mean I watch the house while you baby-sit and Tim works. That'll be fun, me up in that fucking treehouse for ten hours a day all alone."

"I'll help as much as I can. Where's Maude?" I said, anxiously glancing around the rink. There she was, skating between two pretty pony-tailed girls. They each held one of her hands; every few strides they lifted her up and she squealed with delight.

"I thought you didn't even believe they did it," Cat said.

"I just said they're innocent until proven guilty. That doesn't mean they didn't do it. We have to have proof and the only way we're going to get proof is to get into that house."

"It would be great to nail them," Cat said, coasting to the side to tighten her skate lace. I glanced at my watch to see if we could quit soon and was dismayed to find we'd only been there fifteen minutes. We would have to stay at least an hour to justify the fifty cents admission and skate rental cost. I wondered if the skate shop sold Tums.

"What you do is, when you get inside, go right down to the front door and let me and Tim in," Cat said excitedly. Her lace tightened, she whizzed out on the floor again. I followed, ankles aching. "Then we can all go down to the basement together. We'll need tools to tear down that wall. And fingerprint powder. I bet Hugo can get us some. We'll dust for fingerprints."

"Cat, what good's that going to do? It's their house. Their fingerprints are going to be all over it."

"Okay, skating backwards is so easy," Cat said, ignoring the logical. "All you do is . . . Give me your hand."

"Cat, I can't."

"You weenie. Watch me." She arched her back, spread her arms gracefully, and glided away from me on one skate. Her old men's pants were gathered at the cuffs with antique bicycle clips and she wore a man's pale green short-sleeved golf shirt. When she arched her back, the shirt tightened across her breasts and my groin twitched, the first sign of life in several weeks.

Eight days later I was standing at the bottom of the Shooks' tree, emptying my pockets of aspirin bottles. Tim and Cat watched as I produced bottle after bottle like a magician with a string of scarfs. We had decided not to speak once we got into the Shooks' yard, so they couldn't ask about the aspirin. Mr. and Mrs. Shook had sped away in their De Soto an hour before. Tim was on guard and, as soon as they turned the corner, biked to my house, tapped on my window, and we rode over to Cat's.

Tim crouched down, I climbed onto his broad shoulders and he lifted me up to the first branch. It had been raining all day; the bark was soft and rubbed off on my hands as I grabbed hold. I easily pulled myself up on the branch. This was the kind of thing I could never do in physical education class—the sight of a chin-up bar gave me the willies—but that night it was easy.

Tim and Cat moved out from under the tree as I climbed. The tree shook a little as I went up and I was pattered with drops from above. I wore a dark maroon shirt with a pattern of Roman coins. This had been a gift from my grandmother, a surprise departure from handkerchiefs. The shirt was so ugly I had taken an oath never to wear it, but it was the darkest shirt I owned. I had on black jeans and my favorite shoes: high-topped basketball shoes with the soles worn smooth.

The branches were exactly the right distance apart and in seconds, it seemed, I was high above the ground. I felt exhilarated, charged by my own bravery. But as I reached for the fourth branch, my right foot slipped on the soggy bark. I grabbed at leaves and twigs to stop myself from falling. Everything was too slippery to catch hold of or too flimsy to save me. I tipped backwards off the branch, back diving out of the tree. I windmilled my arms, to no avail.

I heard Cat scream before I fell. This, I know, is impossible, but that's how it seemed. I heard her scream and the next thing I knew I was plummeting to the ground. I found myself surprisingly clearheaded during the fall, wondering if I would be killed or merely paralyzed. If paralyzed, I wondered if my parents would still make me take care of Maude or if I would be excused and receive disability pay. Perhaps Mr. Walsh would put in a wheelchair ramp at the Little Store just for me.

Then I hit the first branch, clutched the wet limb, and was safe. I don't know how I managed to do this, but I was pretty impressed. I sat up on the branch, took off my smooth-soled sneakers, which had made me slip, and tossed them down to Tim. He was looking up at me with a worried expression. Cat had her hand over her mouth.

My white crew socks gave better traction than the sneakers and I was up to the fourth branch again in no time. This was the branch that led upwards to the window. It was thinner than those below, so I lay on my stomach and pulled myself along it. I was concerned that the branch wouldn't support me, but it seemed strong and elastic. Although it bobbed under my weight, it didn't seem about to break. As I drew close to the window I could see that the small summer screen didn't fit perfectly into the frame. It was a little ajar.

I also realized that the branch didn't lead directly to the window as it had appeared from the ground. It ended several feet higher than the window and at least four feet away. When the branch became too narrow to move out on any further, I stopped to examine the problem. I straddled the branch. One of my balls slipped up into my groin.

There was only one thing to do: hang from the branch, swing my body toward the window, aim for the window, and let go. With luck and a little velocity, I would kick the screen into the room and fly through the two-foot opening. Hopefully the window wouldn't slam shut in the process, slicing me in two. There was, of course, another option: to forget the whole crazy plan altogether. But I had come this far and to back down would disappoint my friends. I had their attention and meant to take advantage of it, to amaze them with my daring.

I hung from the branch with both hands, my feet dangling in space. My hands were slippery and cold and I couldn't hang there for long. I had to do this quick.

I thrust myself back toward the tree trunk, kicking my legs as if on a swing. There was a gasp from below; Cat guessed what I was going to do. My first lunge toward the window was too timid and if I had let go I would have dashed myself against the loose gray shingles on the side of the house. I tightened my grip on the damp branch, threw my weight backwards, and thrust my butt into the air as I rocked again toward the tree. When I swung forward the second time I pointed my feet like an Olympic diver and straightened my back. I don't remember letting go—my hands released the branch by themselves. I flew toward the window. It occurred to me that I might have a future as a human cannonball.

My aim was perfect. I kicked out the half-screen and inserted myself through the slim opening as neatly as a mailman slips a letter through a mail slot. I landed on my butt on a furry oval rug. A moment later my ball dropped back down into its little sack. I was in.

After I replaced the screen in the window and centered the rug, which had slid out of position during my landing, I crept toward the door. Donald Duck seemed to follow me with his eyes. I turned the doorknob, opened the door carefully, and looked out. The upstairs hall was dark. A narrow, Oriental carpet ran along the floor.

"Bobby?"

I didn't expect an answer. It was a formality. Directly across from Bobby's room was the door to Mr. and Mrs. Shook's bedroom. It was open, a light was on, and I could see one post of a four-poster bed. I stepped across the hall and looked in the room. It was bigger than Bobby's bedroom and the window overlooked the street. I went inside.

A white bedspread and white, lace-edged pillows decorated the bed. A pair of women's slippers lay under the right side of the bed and on the nightstand rested a pair of glasses and a book. I glanced at the title: *My Antonia* by Willa Cather. I'd never read it. It looked too boring in the library.

On the opposite nightstand was an alarm clock and a folded magazine. Mr. Shook's worn leather slippers had been placed under his side of the bed. On the wall hung some faded sepia photographs in oval frames: a mustached man in a stiff collar and a woman with a stern expression on her face. Someone's parents. It seemed as though pictures like this hung on the wall or were propped up on top of the TV of every house I had ever been in. I wondered if I should persuade my mom and dad to get dressed up in old-fashioned costumes and have their pictures taken so I could hang them on my wall when I grew up. It seemed unlikely that they would cooperate.

I looked out the window. Tim and Cat were standing across the street, practically hidden under a thick maple. I waved to them. They were too far away for me to see their expressions. Cat was standing close to Tim's side. I couldn't tell if he had his arm around her or not.

Before I ran downstairs to open the front door and let them in, I checked the upper floor; there could be important clues. Bobby might even be a prisoner in one of the rooms. I tiptoed down the hall. The stairway led downstairs to my left. Beyond it was a small nook with a bay window and a window seat. A book of poetry lay on the cushion. At the far end of the hall stood a large china cupboard containing some mismatched china, several tarnished bowling trophies, and an antique Bible. I quietly turned the knob of the door beside the cupboard.

It was a sewing room. An old pedal-driven sewing machine was placed against the wall and a dress mannequin wearing half of a shirt stood in the corner. An unfinished quilt was stretched on a quilting frame and boxes of fabric and patterns were stacked at the foot of a daybed. Her room.

Across the hall was the bathroom. The huge tub had lion's paws for feet. Sets of towels hung neatly on towel racks—white towels on one rack, green towels on a second rack. People who lived in a house with such neat towels would surely commit a tidy murder. Finding clues might be harder than we anticipated.

In the ceiling between the sewing room and bathroom was a trap door leading to the attic, but I didn't have time to explore it.

I hurried down the staircase. The stairs creaked as I stepped on them and this seemed appropriate. The banisters were of dark, carved wood and at the bottom of each rail was a Greek maiden holding up a bowl of fruit. The fruit was artificial, dusty grapes and pears.

On the first floor, as Tim had described, an open doorway led into a living room. The room was dark, but I saw a couch, a television, and the back of a recliner. The dining room was on the right; Tim had also described this. I knew that the kitchen was through the dining room and in the kitchen was the door to the basement. I reached for the chain lock on the front door to let Tim and Cat into the house.

The sound of a garage door going up or down is a distinctive sound and can't be mistaken for anything else. There's a certain whooshing noise—air being let in and out—and the creak of wood and metal straining to find new positions.

My first thought was that Tim had successfully picked the garage door lock and he and Cat were already on their way inside. This wasn't entirely logical, as the plan was for me to admit them through the front door, but if I had been in a logical frame of mind I wouldn't have broken into the house in the first place.

Then I heard the sound of the Shooks' car, that wide pink and black sedan, pulling into the garage. I didn't panic. I stood still, fingers on the gold chain of the chain lock, wondering why the Shooks were home again so early. This was the second time they had returned suddenly to foil our break-in. When they go out, I thought irritably, they should stay out.

There was plenty of time to escape through the front door while they were getting out of the car and climbing the stairs to the kitchen. I had replaced the screen on Bobby's window, carefully shut his door, and hadn't touched anything else. The Shooks would never know their house had been broken into. I could try again another day.

But I wasn't thinking clearly. My brain was fuzzy from all the aspirin I had taken and my ribs hurt where I'd hit them on the branch. I had eaten a ham sandwich for dinner and a piece of ham was stuck to my stomach lining like a wet leaf on a hubcap. Or maybe it was simply that I didn't want the adventure to be over so soon. Whatever the reason, instead of escaping out the front door to safety, I ran up the stairs and hid in Bobby's room.

The moment I closed his door I realized what a stupid move I had made. Now I was trapped. There was no question of going out the window the same way I came in. I looked to see if the tree had moved any closer to the house in the last fifteen minutes. It hadn't. I heard the garage door come down.

I tried to think of another way out, but the Shooks' house didn't have a fire escape and it was the same distance to the ground from every window on the upper floor.

All too soon there were thumping sounds from below—the Shooks coming up the basement stairs. As a hiding place, Bobby's room was preferable to their bedroom or the sewing room in which Mrs. Shook might want to do some late-night stitching. The attic was the safest bet, but there wasn't time for that.

I stood still, paralyzed by my predicament, and listened. First, rapid clicking steps on the kitchen floor. Tim said that Mrs. Shook was a little fat and made noise when she walked. It was her. Then, her heavy tread on the staircase. Any second she would reach the landing and come down the hall. Most likely she would go to her bedroom or the sewing room, but to be safe I dropped to the floor and rolled under Bobby's bed, just barely squeezing under the guard rail. A moment later the door opened and Mrs. Shook walked into the room.

Bobby's spaceship bedspread didn't reach all the way to the floor, so I had a good view of Mrs. Shook's shoes. They were light brown with a small, narrow heel. Her feet appeared several sizes larger than the shoes and her flesh bulged over their sides like twice-baked potatoes.

She turned on the light and I slid back against the wall. I could hear Mr. Shook on the staircase now. His footsteps made the old house shudder. The bare wood floor vibrated under me.

"Bridget?" he called.

I never imagined Mrs. Shook being named Bridget. I'd known only one Bridget in my life: She sat in front of me in sixth-grade geography and played with her long, shimmering blond hair all through class. Every thirty seconds she would run her right index and middle fingers along the edge of her hair and flip it so the ends would fan out on the top of my desk. Then the glittering strands would gradually slip from my desk and dangle between us, swaying gently with the movement of her head until the next flip. This was very distracting.

I figured Mrs. Shook to be a Betty or a Marjorie. The sexy name Bridget didn't fit those swollen feet stuffed into the brown shoes that were coming closer and closer. She stopped at the edge of the bed. It occurred to me to suddenly grab her ankle, causing her to have a fatal heart attack and allowing me to escape. But Mr. Shook was already coming down the hall. Thump, thump, thump.

"Bridget . . ." he said again as he came into the room. He was wearing thick work boots, stiff with age and turned up at the toe. One shoelace was broken and had been tied in a knot to keep it together. His pants were olive drab slacks with worn cuffs.

"How long can we live like this?" Mrs. Shook said. She sat on the bed and it sagged with her weight. "I just wish it was over. I know you hate me for saying that." Her voice cracked and she started to cry.

Mr. Shook sighed in exasperation. "It *is* over, Bridget. He's gone." His voice was husky, with a little bit of an accent that I couldn't trace.

"Sometimes I think I'm going to go crazy."

"I don't want to hear another word about you feeling guilty.

We have to stop looking back. Life goes on," he answered philosophically.

"Sometimes I think I'm going to kill myself."

"Stop that," he said sharply.

There was a little silence and my brain spun, trying to fill in the blanks in their conversation. Mrs. Shook wished that "it was over." I guessed she meant she wanted the suspense to end, wanted the police to come to their door and arrest them. She couldn't live with her guilt and was thinking of ending it all. Mr. Shook had no misgivings. His attitude was, "life goes on." He was, of course, forgetting that life didn't go on for Bobby.

Mrs. Shook spoke again and I listened carefully, recording every word so I could report to Tim and Cat later.

"Why did it have to end this way?" she said in between sobs. "Why did God . . . ?"

"There isn't a God," Mr. Shook interrupted and this made Mrs. Shook cry harder. "Bobby's better off," he added.

"How can you say that?"

"It's the truth." The words were cold and callous and final.

I'd always doubted that they really did it. I wanted to believe that no parent could be so cruel and unforgiving. But the sadness in her voice, the harshness in his convinced me, finally, that it had happened after all. It was clearly Mr. Shook's idea and his hand that did the deed. I wondered if Mrs. Shook pleaded desperately for her son's life as her husband dragged him down into the basement. I pictured her covering her ears so as not to hear the boy's pathetic whimpers and the sickening sound of a hammer crushing his skull. I shivered and worried that the Shooks could hear my shiver.

"I keep thinking he's going to come back," she said. Her right heel tapped nervously on the floor as she cried. Mr. Shook walked over to the bed and sat beside her. The bed sagged more.

"He's not going to come back. The sooner we face that the sooner . . ." He didn't finish, didn't say what they could do then, but it was implied: the sooner we can go merrily on with our lives. Perhaps they would take a cruise to the South Seas. Cruises were unmanageable with a retarded son.

Mrs. Shook continued to sob—short, jerky ones, not unlike Maude's little sobs. Mr. Shook shifted impatiently on the bed. It creaked. All I could see were the two pairs of shoes, side by side. Mrs. Shook stopped tapping her heel. Mr. Shook moved his left boot and it touched Mrs. Shook's right foot. I heard a snap, the snap of a purse. A moment later she blew her nose.

"I just wish we could have him back, the way he was at first. Nobody ever had a sweeter boy," she said. The handkerchief dropped to the floor. Her hand appeared. She picked it up.

"Wishing isn't going to change anything. I wish we could have another son." Mr. Shook shifted again. The bed creaked again. There was the sound of a kiss. My God, I thought, what if they start doing it right on top of me? Bobby's bed didn't look that strong.

"I'm sorry. It's my fault."

"Bridget," he warned.

The tears again. Another of his weary sighs. "There's nothing we can do about it," he said in that same philosophical tone. "Nothing we can do about a lot of things." There was the sound of scratching. "We still have each other."

She didn't answer him. Perhaps this is what she dreaded: life with the man who butchered her helpless son. He would never let her go now, never trust her to keep their secret. If she tried to turn herself in, he would drag her down into the basement, too.

"I'm tired," she said and stood. Mr. Shook also got to his feet and they walked to the door.

"What are we going to do with his things?" She paused in the doorway and turned a little. She was probably looking at the ABC poster, the great works of literature, the world globe. Mr. Shook didn't reply. A moment later the light clicked off, the door shut, and I was alone.

I stayed under the bed and listened to the sounds of their feet padding up and down the hallway, going to and from the bathroom. A toilet flushed. The pipes groaned. As Mr. Shook was returning from the bathroom, he farted. "Chuck, do you want . . ." Mrs. Shook asked, but I couldn't hear the rest of the question. Hot chocolate? A bottle of champagne to toast their freedom? Later I heard Mrs. Shook's footsteps going down the stairs. Then she returned. She sang a little as she came along the hall.

I worked out a plan. When I was certain they were asleep, I would sneak out of Bobby's room, down the staircase, and out the front door. Tim and Cat would be waiting for me in the treehouse and I'd repeat Mr. and Mrs. Shook's conversation before I forgot a single word. Although we could immediately go to the police with the story, I would recommend that we try to come up with at least one piece of hard evidence, a bloody hammer or the like. This would take another break-in, but it would be worth it. Hearing with my own ears the Shooks discuss their crime—Mrs. Shook's guilt, Mr. Shook's carefree suggestion that life would continue—made me even more committed to exposing their cruelty. They could not be allowed to get away with it. Whatever reasons I had for breaking into the house, selfish motivations to some degree, vanished. There remained only the firm resolve that justice must be served.

Even now it seems incredible that I fell asleep during these thoughts. I wasn't tired; I was excited and scared. But I closed my eyes for a moment and when I opened them I realized that I had dozed off. I didn't know how long I was asleep. I left my watch at home so it wouldn't get broken and the one thing Bobby didn't have in his room was a clock.

The house was absolutely still. For once it wasn't creaking or groaning. No one was farting or sobbing. I listened for Mr. Shook's snores (I was sure he would snore), but heard nothing. I slid out from under the bed and tiptoed to the door.

I had been creeping around our house ever since my father hit me, so I was experienced at opening doors without making a sound. Bobby's door opened easily, noiselessly. The Shooks' bedroom door was closed and the crack between door and floor was dark. Down the hall the bathroom door was open, but the light was off.

Carefully I put a foot out, like a tightrope walker testing his high wire. My shoeless toe explored the floor, hunting for squeaks. I didn't rush. To rush was to make noise. The floor was squeakless. I stepped into the hall and closed Bobby's door. There was a tiny click.

I stayed close to the wall where the floor would best support my weight and be less likely to creak. Going down the stairs I kept near the banister, stepping on the thin strip of hardwood between the edge of the carpeting and the balusters. I didn't make a sound. I was almost there, almost out. I congratulated myself on my cunning.

Then I was at the front door. The doorknob was tarnished brass, a fancy detail like the elegant staircase that spoke of a grander time. My fingers trembled when I slid the chain lock along its runner. The chain jingled slightly, and I took it slow. To hurry was to make noise, to be caught. Then I turned the small keylike latch above the doorknob and felt the bolt easing back. The hard part was over. I was almost free.

He came out of nowhere. He must have been in the living room, sitting in darkness, hidden by the back of the imitation leather recliner. For a big man he moved quickly. He grabbed me before I even knew he was there, throwing his thick forearm around my neck, hitting my chin, and knocking my teeth together. He yanked my head toward him, then twisted my left arm behind my back. In an instant I was helpless.

"Who are you? What do you think you're doing?" he shouted in my ear. His breath smelled of coffee. No wonder he couldn't sleep.

"Let me go! Get out of here! Let me go!" I don't know why I said "Get out of here"; it was, after all, Mr. Shook's home. I must have meant something else.

"You're not going anywhere," he said viciously. "You're going to tell me . . ." I kicked backwards, aiming for his shin, but just kicked air. ". . . what you're doing here," he continued. "What you took!"

"Nothing! I didn't do anything!" I shouted. I pulled my feet up, intending to thrust them against the door and shove him over backwards, but he guessed what I was planning and dragged me away from the door.

I didn't have a chance. He was nearly three times my weight. I tried to squirm away, but his grasp was iron. I kicked my feet helplessly and each move sent pangs shooting through my twisted arm.

"Chuck, what is going on?" Mrs. Shook was coming down the stairs. I was faced to the door and couldn't see her.

"I found this little thief sneaking out the . . ."

"I didn't take anything! I don't want anything!" I shouted with what felt like my last breath. He was choking me with that thick forearm and any moment I felt I would pass out from lack of oxygen. A headache shifted from side to side as if it was loose in my head.

"Don't hurt the boy, Chuck," Mrs. Shook said, coming around

to look at me. I tried to turn to her to plead for my life—of the two of them, she seemed to have a vestige of humanity—but I couldn't even make this simple motion.

"What are you doing in our house?" she asked, more curious than angry.

"Nothing. Just let me go. He's hurting me!"

"Chuck, you're strangling the boy."

"Call the police," Mr. Shook said, ignoring Mrs. Shook's concern. He put a little more pressure on my left arm; another quarter of an inch and it would snap. I yelled with pain.

"Who is he?"

"Some rotten little thief. The police'll deal with him."

"Go on! Call them!" I screamed desperately. "I'll tell them everything!" This came out in broken, strangulated gasps.

"Tell what, you rotten little . . . ?"

"About Bobby! I'll tell everything I know! I know it all!"

The arm around my throat jerked downward in surprise and I gulped air. I hated being so close to him. His big chest was pressed against my back and thick hair on the back of his hand scratched against my cheek. The coffee smell was terrible.

"What about Bobby?" Mrs. Shook asked.

"You know what I mean. I know everything. So if I were you I wouldn't call the police." My voice shook as I uttered this melodramatic line. I'm sure I heard it on a television program the week before.

"Know what? Chuck, you're breaking the boy's arm," Mrs. Shook said. Mr. Shook reduced the tension a little and moved his right arm from around my neck to a position across my shoulders. Now I could breathe, but there was still no question of getting away.

"Know what?" Mrs. Shook repeated.

"And not just me, either. We all know," I added, making it

sound as if a whole squadron of junior detectives was on the case.
"Who's we? What do you know? What are you talking about?"
she asked. I could turn my head now to look at her. She was
wearing a rose-colored quilted robe. The slippers I had seen under
her bed were now on her feet.

"Bridget, call the police."

"I want to know what the boy means."

It was time to plea bargain, to make a deal. "I won't tell anyone,
I promise," I said, trying not to sound as desperate as I felt. I
couldn't show fear; I had to make them fear me. "Just let me go.
I won't say a word, none of us will. I swear on my life," I vowed.

"Tell anyone what?" she asked again. She seemed genuinely
puzzled. Was it possible that Mr. Shook had murdered Bobby and
never told her? Perhaps he told her Bobby was away at camp. No,
I had overheard her say, "Sometimes I think I'm going to kill
myself." She said she kept thinking he was going to come back
and there was that last melancholy question: "What are we going
to do with his things?" She knew; she was as guilty as he was.

"What you did with him," I said, looking right in her eyes. A
dark red blood vessel snaked across the white to her left pupil. "I
know what you did to him. You got rid of him. Didn't you?"

She tilted her head to the side and a tear fell out of her eye.
It missed her cheek entirely and dropped to the floor. Her bottom
lip trembled. She didn't need to be on the witness stand to
crack—she was cracking right here in the foyer.

Mr. Shook let go of my left arm. Numb, it dangled at my side
like an amputee's sleeve. He grabbed me by the back of my shirt.
It tightened over my chest and a button popped off.

"What business is it of yours? He's our son!" he shouted in my
ear, shaking me by the back of the neck like a cat. I suddenly
remembered their cat named Nelson, the one Mr. Shook ran over.

"What's your name?" He shook me again. I didn't answer.

"You're one of the kids from the neighborhood, aren't you? One of those kids who always made fun of him!"

"No, I never did!" I protested, and this was mostly true. "I felt sorry for him. It wasn't his fault he was retarded. He couldn't help it. He didn't have to die, just because you were sick of taking care of him. It isn't fair. He was your kid and you were responsible for him. You're not going to get away with it. Even if you kill me, too, you're still not going to get away with it!"

There was a dead silence. I could hear a clock ticking in the dining room. A car went by several blocks away. Otherwise, stillness. Mrs. Shook looked at me, her head still tilted to the side. A second tear was trapped in a wrinkle under her eye.

"Die? Bobby didn't die." She glanced up at Mr. Shook as if for confirmation. He said nothing. She brushed the tear away and it left a shiny smear. Her skin was pale and looked too thin to really be useful as skin.

"He's in the hospital."

"How come you don't visit him, then?" I shot back at her. "We've been watching your house all summer and you didn't go out for almost two whole weeks! If he's really in the hospital, how come you don't see him?" My voice broke a little. I pictured Bobby alone in the hospital without any visitors or flowers and too retarded to even read a book. "And what about the bricks?"

"Bricks?"

"The brick wall downstairs. That's where he is, isn't he? He's not in the hospital at all. You killed him and buried him behind that wall so you'd be rid of him forever. Didn't you?"

There it was, the words the whole summer had been leading up to: the accusation, the cards on the table. Neither Mr. nor Mrs. Shook said a word. She still looked at me with that tilted head. Mr. Shook still gripped me, still smelled of coffee. The silence returned. The clock ticked. The house shifted, making a sharp pop like a firecracker. Another car passed on the street, this one with a radio blaring. The song came and went and was gone.

Then Mr. Shook pulled me off my feet and dragged me through the dining room toward the kitchen. Again I fought to get free, but I was no match for him. Besides, I was dizzy with pain; my headache ricocheted off the walls of my skull like a ball in a squash court.

Mr. Shook yanked open the door to the basement and switched on the light.

"Chuck, don't hurt him!" Mrs. Shook said at his back, although her pleading for my life was less than I hoped for.

The unfinished staircase loomed before me like the entrance to a dungeon. I couldn't believe this was happening to me. He pushed me ahead of him and I grabbed the railing to keep from tumbling downstairs. "Get down there," he ordered. I took the steps as fast as I could. If I beat him to the basement maybe I would have time to grab some weapon to defend myself with.

"Chuck, don't do anything you'll regret," Mrs. Shook warned from the top of the staircase.

Suddenly I thought of it. The night Tim picked the lock we had seen Mr. Shook go into the house and emerge through the garage. There had to be a door in the basement linking the two. If I could get to it before him, I had a chance of escape. I bolted down the last few stairs.

The concrete brick wall was on my right. A washer and dryer stood against the wall directly in front of me and some washing hung on a line. I actually saw a pair of Chuck's shorts. Against the south end of the basement was a long workbench covered with tools; next to that, a power saw. I looked frantically for the door to the garage. There it was: in the west wall between a large water heater and some metal shelving. It looked ten miles away.

To my credit I got the door open before Mr. Shook caught me.

Again I was surprised at how fleet of foot he was, but perhaps he'd had a lot of practice catching Bobby, tying him up, and beating him.

He pulled me away from the door, kicked it shut, locked it, and took the key. Then he dragged me over to the workbench and picked up a hammer.

"Chuck, what are you going to do?" Mrs. Shook asked from the top of the staircase. She sounded less worried than intrigued; more anxious to get a front row seat to the slaughter than determined to throw herself between Chuck and me.

Chuck didn't answer. He was busy selecting a chisel. Several varieties were displayed on the workbench. He chose one with a sharp, wide blade, which looked heavy even in Mr. Shook's giant hand. In case two weapons were not enough, he also picked up a crowbar.

If there was a time for Tim and Cat to burst in with the police, it was certainly now.

"Don't do it, Chuck!" Mrs. Shook said anxiously. She took a step down the staircase, but just one. She was squinting, trying to see us in the dim light.

He paid no attention. He dragged me across the basement to the wall. I hit him with my free hand, but my fist struck solid muscle. I jerked this way and that, but his hand held me like a vice. The wall appeared to rush toward me. If blood had been seeping through the cracks I couldn't have been more terrified. A squirt of urine ran down my leg.

"Help! Tim! Cat!" I screamed. I had kept their names a secret, but in a moment that chisel would be implanted in my head and the time for courtesies was over. "Help! They're going to kill me! Stop them! Help!"

"Chuck, don't!" Mrs. Shook cried, but he probably didn't even hear her. It must have been exactly like this the night he executed

Bobby. Bobby had dribbled disgustingly once too often or wet his bed when he had been warned time and again not to, and Mr. Shook flew into a homicidal frenzy. Nobody, not even his wife, could stop him when he was like this. He wasn't satisfied until blood covered the unfinished basement floor.

We were at the wall. Four and a half feet high, it reached my shoulder. The large concrete blocks abutted the actual wall of the garage. Bobby lay behind them and now so would I. Mr. Shook let me go, confident that I had no means of escape: The door to the garage was locked and Mrs. Shook guarded the staircase to the kitchen. I looked around desperately for something to hit him with. A baseball bat leaned in a corner, but it was too far away. He shifted the chisel to his left hand and dropped the crowbar on the floor. I thought about grabbing it, but, as if reading my mind, he put his foot across it. He raised the hammer and turned to me.

"I'll never tell! I swear! I'll never say a word!" I screamed, but he tightened his grip on the hammer, his face contorting in an expression of maniacal hatred. Then he turned, put the chisel blade to one of the dried mortar joints of the wall, and slammed the hammer down on the head of the chisel. The sound split my skull as effectively as the blade split the mortar. It crumbled away and a brick loosened. He moved the chisel to the other end of the same concrete block, the hammer came down again and the mortar broke. He picked up the crowbar, jammed it between the water-stained cement garage wall and the wall he had built, and pushed. Two gray blocks pulled away and fell to the floor, one of them snapping in half. He picked up the hammer again, positioned the chisel, and bang! Mortar chips flew, a brick jumped. He grabbed the crowbar and pried at the blocks. Several more fell to the floor. He didn't stop until he had pulled down every single block in the wall.

He never looked at me once; in fact, he was so consumed with his task that he seemed to have forgotten me. I stood behind him, watching. He was bald in the front, but hair started at the crown of his head and was brushed straight back. Gray and white hairs were mixed. Silver stubble dusted his cheeks and chin like frost.

There was such fury and purpose in his work that I knew there was no point in trying to stop him, even when it was clear that Bobby was not buried behind the wall. There was only a dark, wet mound of earth, part of the neighbor's property, caving into Mr. Shook's garage. The garage wall had crumbled away, pushed inward by the advancing ground.

He even removed the bottom row of bricks, pulling them up one by one with his hands and tossing them into what was now a huge pile of broken concrete. When the bottom row was gone, he kicked at the gray crust of mortar on the cement floor to remove the last trace of the wall.

Only then did he stop. He still didn't look at me, but focused on the bulge of earth intruding into his garage. A rivulet of water trickling down the dark mound had formed a narrow puddle in the space behind the removed wall.

"You're just going to have to rebuild it, Chuck," Mrs. Shook said from her station at the top of the stairs. This was a reprimand, but a gentle one.

"I want the boy to see . . ." he said, but didn't finish the sentence and there was no reason to. I could see.

"This is worse than before," he said, crouching down and putting his hands on the convex mound of dirt as if feeling a pregnant woman's stomach. "I have to redo it, anyway," he added, suddenly fully absorbed in the problem of containing the creeping weight of earth. I could have taken advantage of his preoccupation and tried to escape, but now there was no need to. Anyway, I could not move quickly in my condition.

"What do you have to say for yourself now, young man?" Mrs. Shook asked in what I later learned was as stern a voice as she could muster.

"Could I use the bathroom, please?" I replied quietly. "Or I'm going to have an accident." My humiliation was now complete.

Mr. Shook stood outside the open door of the bathroom while I did my business. I could tell he hated me and hated the sound of my pissing, too. I wanted my stream to go on forever so that I wouldn't have to face them again, but it dried up all too quickly. A razor lay on the edge of the sink. I wasn't desperate enough to use it yet, but I filed it away as a last resort.

They told me to sit on the living room couch. The upholstery had a pattern of large pink camellias and was worn in a few places. Still, it was preferable to our lime green couch with the little gold threads in it.

Mrs. Shook talked. She started in the slightly stern tone she used before, but soon her voice softened and warmed. She seemed relieved to have a chance to speak about Bobby; perhaps she didn't have enough people to talk to. Mr. Shook stood in the doorway in case I tried to run. He only looked at me once. He wound his watch.

Bobby contracted meningitis when he was ten months old. At first the doctor thought it was the flu, but when the baby continued to be fussy and refused to eat, he did more tests and discovered a bacterial infection in Bobby's brain. Bobby was allergic to penicillin and some of the other antibiotics used to treat such cases, and a couple of very anxious weeks went by while the doctor searched for a cure for the infant. Eventually the symptoms disappeared all by themselves and Bobby appeared to return to normal. It wasn't until he was almost three that Mr. and Mrs. Shook noticed a slowness in his development, had him tested, and realized his brain had been permanently affected.

Still, he was a good son and didn't cause any more trouble, really, than a normal child does. (This was when Mr. Shook looked at me, his look implying that I could have taken a few lessons in behavior from Bobby.) Bobby could never really learn; he couldn't retain anything for long. He would stare at the ABCs, trying to distinguish one from the other, or hold plastic numerals and attempt to remember their names. Mrs. Shook never gave up trying to teach him these basic things and always managed to convince herself she saw a slight improvement.

In August of the previous year Bobby had a seizure. He never had a strong constitution and, when he was young, contracted every childhood illness at least once and sometimes twice. When he was older he was very susceptible to colds; he would get over one and immediately get another. But this seizure was something new and alarming. He flailed violently, convulsing and gasping for air. Mrs. Shook tried to stop him from hurting himself, but he was too big to control. She ran to the phone to call Mr. Shook at work. While she was gone Bobby chewed his tongue and banged his head on the floor.

Bobby had developed a brain tumor. The doctor did not recommend an operation. Since Bobby would never be other than he was maybe it was best to just let nature take its course. After all, what would happen to Bobby after Mr. and Mrs. Shook died? Mr. and Mrs. Shook consulted specialist after specialist, trying to find one who would give them hope. The doctors were sympathetic, but realistic. All of them discouraged an operation, which had no guarantee of success anyway and would be uncomfortable and frightening for the patient, and recommended that Bobby be put in a facility. He was only going to get worse and would become very hard to handle. But the Shooks refused to put Bobby away; they took him home and managed the best they could. Mr. Shook quit his job.

At the beginning of the summer Bobby had a stroke. His entire right side became paralyzed. Now the Shooks couldn't take care of him by themselves and, besides, he needed daily physical therapy. They put him in the nearest hospital that would accept him—Greenpark Hospital only ten minutes away. They visited him every day, seven hours a day. They spelled each other at the hospital, taking turns.

In the second week of June Bobby began to have fits. Whenever he saw his parents he became very agitated and upset. The doctors said he was trying to show how happy he was to see them; it frustrated him that he couldn't express himself and this made him violent. The doctors suggested knocking Bobby out with drugs, but Mr. and Mrs. Shook couldn't stand this, so they stayed away from the hospital for almost two weeks to see if their son's condition would improve. That was when they locked themselves in the house and didn't come out. They had never felt so depressed, so despairing of their son. Mr. Shook built the wall, but was so distracted he built it badly. Mrs. Shook closed all the curtains and sat in the dark. They started having their groceries delivered.

The night we tried to pick the lock Bobby had a small heart attack. He was okay again by the time the Shooks got to the hospital, but he soon became upset at seeing them and they had to leave.

A week and a half ago he went into a coma. Now there was almost no hope for him, but the way Mrs. Shook said it, she sounded like she still had hope. Tonight the nurse had called to say that Bobby's blood pressure had dropped severely and the Shooks again rushed to the hospital thinking it was the end. But the doctor treated Bobby with a drug and his blood pressure rose.

"How old is Bobby?"

"Thirty-one."

Mrs. Shook had a difficult time giving birth. She was confined in bed for six of the nine months of her pregnancy. She always blamed herself for not making her boy strong enough to withstand the meningitis.

"Now Bridget . . ." Mr. Shook said reproachfully. They must have had this conversation a hundred times.

She was unable to have another child. Although she was pregnant two more times, she lost both children. So Bobby was dear.

"Do you still think we killed him?"

"No."

When she finished speaking I asked for some aspirin. I followed Mrs. Shook upstairs to the bathroom, she gave me two white tablets and put her hand to my forehead. It was an automatic gesture, one she must have done so many times with Bobby.

"You're warm," she said and felt my cheek. She took a thermometer from a plastic case, shook it, and placed it in my mouth.

I sat on the edge of the tub while Mrs. Shook showed me some pictures of Bobby she had taken shortly after he went into the hospital. He was sitting up in bed, although a little lopsided. A helium balloon was tied to his tray. His hands were half-closed like claws. He was trying to look at the camera, but his eyes went in opposite directions. He appeared thin and frail.

She took the thermometer out of my mouth. It was high. She made me stand on the scale and clucked her tongue when the needle came to a nervous halt. She asked how long I had been feeling sick. I said a few weeks.

"Do you eat three good meals a day?"

"I don't eat much."

She took me downstairs to the kitchen and heated up a blackberry pie she had baked the day before. I sat with Mr. Shook at the kitchen table and we ate blackberry pie with vanilla ice cream.

Mr. Shook had coffee and I drank a glass of milk. At first Mrs. Shook wasn't going to have any pie because she was trying to lose weight, but she scooped up some of the filling anyway and ate it from the pie server.

It is now six months later, but I can still taste that pie. I felt like a baby having his first taste of solid food. The blackberry filling was tart, but so smoothly tart that it soaked into my tongue and I don't remember even having to swallow. The crust was sturdy and crisp when Mrs. Shook was placing a slice on my plate, but at the touch of my fork it separated into hundreds of transparently thin flakes. We ate without speaking. The pie deserved that kind of respect. Mr. Shook had a second piece, I had another half piece and Mrs. Shook ate some more filling.

"Why haven't you been to the doctor?" Mrs. Shook asked when I was scraping the last violet traces of blackberries from my plate. "Why haven't your parents taken you to the doctor for a checkup?"

Later I told Tim and Cat that I cried to make them feel sorry for me and let me go, but the truth was that I just started crying and couldn't stop.

"My dad works a lot and he doesn't have time and my mom, well, she's busy with something, too. I just can't tell them right now, 'cause . . . It's complicated. I take lots of aspirin and I thought it would go away, but it just gets worse. Maybe I have a brain tumor like Bobby. I can't sleep at night and I'm afraid I'm going to die."

This poignant speech looks almost logical on the page, but accompanied by gasps for breath, sniffles, and wipings of my nose and face, it was mostly inaudible and completely incoherent. Mr. and Mrs. Shook simply stared at me. Mrs. Shook's head was again tilted to the side as if the fresh angle would shed some light on my explanation. Mr. Shook's mouth hung open a little in surprise. There was a blackberry stain on his chin, which made him look even more surprised.

So they let me go. I guess they decided I was a seriously mixed-up kid and punishing me would simply be redundant. They didn't call the police or my parents as they had threatened. Mr. Shook said he expected me to come back soon and help him rebuild the wall, but otherwise they let me off scot-free and even lent me Bobby's new Keds, since I had tossed my shoes down to Tim when I climbed the tree.

"What's your name?" Mr. Shook asked.

"Nelson."

"I'll drive you home, Nelson."

"It's just a few blocks. I'd like the fresh air."

"Are you sure?"

Mrs. Shook made me promise to tell my parents about my headaches and have them take me to the doctor. When I came back on Saturday to help Mr. Shook with the wall, I was supposed to report to her what the doctor said. If he gave me a prescription, she wanted to see the bottle. She warned me not to try to fool her, because she knew a lot about doctors from the years with Bobby.

They waved good-bye to me at the front door. I went down Thirty-fourth Avenue toward my house, then doubled back around the block, and ran to the treehouse to tell Tim and Cat about my experiences. The treehouse was deserted. My shoes lay in the corner. Three cigarette butts were crushed on the floor, one with a smear of lipstick on it. I put them in the coffee-can ashtray. I wondered how long Tim and Cat had waited for me.

It was midnight. The sky was blue-black with white clouds. Between the clouds, stars.

I thought how differently tonight turned out from what I had expected. I expected to break into the Shooks' house and prove that they killed their retarded son. Instead, I cried in front of them and promised to come back on the weekend to learn all about retaining walls. I wondered if the rest of my life would be like tonight, one unexpected thing after another.

I expected to become a writer. What if, instead, I ended up a Marine sergeant or a telephone lineman? Would I be disappointed or happy and surprised, like you are when you open a birthday present that you're sure is clothes and it turns out to be the model aircraft carrier you've wanted for months.

I expected to have girlfriends in high school, to go to dances, get good grades, and have a shot at the commencement address. But nothing was certain. I pictured myself a high school dropout in a black leather jacket, roaring off to a rumble on my motorcycle. Suddenly, life seemed more complex than ever: exciting but worrisome, and almost better than a novel.

chapter seven

"Mom, I think I'm sick."

"There's a flu going around," she said without hesitation as she studied the instructions on a package of frozen peas. She was making dinner. A meat loaf was in the oven. My father was in Boise.

"I don't think it's the flu. I have this headache that won't go away."

"Take some aspirin." I couldn't think of a reply to this, so there was a pause.

It was the evening after the break-in and I was determined to keep my promise to the Shooks: to tell my parents about my symptoms and make them take me to the doctor. I had tried to tell my mother that morning, but she was still in her bedroom when Maude and I left the house. I tapped on her door to say good-bye and she called out, "Tell Maude to be good," in a froggy voice. I wondered if she was also sick, but when we got back from our travels she seemed fine.

"I mean, I've had a headache for three weeks. My stomach hurts, too. I can't eat. I think I should see the doctor."

"Let me feel your forehead." She turned toward me. She was

wearing a different perfume from her usual and it was like suddenly having a different mom. "You're not especially hot," she said after feeling my head with the hand that had held the frozen peas.

"There's this buzzing in my head that won't go away. And it hurts when I urinate." I thought about throwing in the erection problem, too, but there was boiling water on the stove and I didn't want to risk an accident.

"Nelson, at your age a boy goes through certain changes. Puberty. Your body is changing. You're becoming a man. You should feel lucky. The things girls go through . . ." The dot-dot-dot was in her voice.

"I don't think it's puberty, Mom. I think it's a brain tumor."

"Don't be ridiculous."

"I'll call Dr. Holt and make the appointment and pay for it out of my savings account, but I wanted to tell you first because I know he'll call."

She dropped the solid block of peas in the boiling water and sighed the sigh of a homesteader who has been up since dawn fixing grub for her menfolk.

"I don't expect you to pay your own doctor bills. What do you think we have insurance for? If you want to see the doctor, fine. I'll call him in the morning." She put on her glasses, studied the pea instructions again, and then turned the dial on the egg timer I had given her two Mother's Days ago. "But you don't have a brain tumor, Nelson. You're going through some physical changes, that's all."

"Now, this might be a little uncomfortable, Nelson," Dr. Holt said, pulling on a rubber glove. "But it won't hurt. Can you roll over on your side for me?"

I hoped Maude wouldn't choose this moment to burst into the examining room. She was playing in the waiting room. Dr. Holt's receptionist was supposed to be watching her, but Maude had already escaped twice. The first time she came in the room, Dr. Holt was listening to my heart with a stethoscope. Naturally, Maude wanted him to listen to her heart, too. I unbuttoned the back of her dress and pulled it down to her waist. When Dr. Holt put the stethoscope to Maude's chest, her tiny pink nipples puffed out in excitement.

The second interruption came when Dr. Holt was tapping my knee with his mallet. Maude wanted her knee tapped, as well. I didn't mind these interruptions; they broke the tension and postponed the moment when the doctor would tell me my case was hopeless. But I didn't want Maude bursting in while Dr. Holt had his finger up my butt. Maude would want him to do it to her.

Dr. Holt was not my idea of a family doctor. He looked more like a movie star. He was about the same age as my parents and had thick blond hair with matching blond hairs that lay in neat strips across his wrists and hands. They were so neat I wondered if he combed them. He had on a white jacket, but under it wore a blue and red checked shirt, no tie, and tight-fitting jeans as if he was going straight from my examination to a rodeo. His first name was Alan. I'd always wanted to be named Alan.

"Just relax. I bet you have a girlfriend, a good-looking guy like you," Dr. Holt said. I found this an ill-timed remark under the circumstances and, anyway, not a subject destined to relax me. I didn't answer. I studied a framed certificate from the University of Oregon Medical School on the wall. It said he was a real doctor. I wonder if they actually tested him or if he slipped through on his good looks.

I thought about Cat. She had appeared that day around noon when Maude and I were reading a menu taped to the window of a new Italian restaurant on Milwaukie Avenue. Maude was going to have pizza for the first time in her life. She wanted pizza not because she thought she would like it or even knew what it was, but because she liked the word.

"Your wallet's sticking halfway out of your ass pocket, Helen. You want somebody to rob you?" Cat said, a typical Cat-like greeting.

"Hi, Cat."

"Cat, we're going to have pizza!" Maude exclaimed. Cat knelt down and fastened the buckle on Maude's sandal. Cat was wearing white painter's pants with a man's T-shirt, and a band uniform jacket tied around her waist. On her feet were what appeared to be gold ballet slippers.

"You want to have lunch with us?" I asked her. She did and we trooped into the restaurant. It had been a Chinese restaurant only a month before. Now accordion music was gaily playing and lamps made from Chianti bottles sat on the tables. I insisted on a table near the back so Cat and I could talk privately.

Maude piped up as soon as the waitress approached the table. "We want pizza!" The waitress beamed at Maude. If I had whipped out adoption papers, she would have signed on the spot. I ordered a medium-sized tomato and cheese pizza for us to share, Cokes for Cat and myself, and milk for Maude.

While Maude drew on the paper place mat with crayons I carried for just such a situation, I told Cat the story of the break-in. She was mesmerized. For the first time in our friendship I believe Cat was truly impressed with me.

The pizza came. Whatever Maude had been expecting, this wasn't it. The pie frightened her, so I ordered an emergency grilled cheese sandwich. This was not on the menu, but the waitress seemed delighted to bend the rules. I wondered if Maude would go through life always getting what she wanted—Turkish food in a Mexican restaurant, a martini at a soda fountain—or if there would come a day when even she would have to stick to the menu.

"How long did you guys wait for me in the treehouse?" I asked Cat after I finished my tale of adventure. She was picking the cheese off the top of the pizza, leaving the tomato sauce and crust for me. "I kind of expected you guys to be there when I got out."

"We waited a couple hours or something," she said. "We would have come after you if you started screaming for help or we heard a buzz saw start up or something. We figured you were hiding in there till morning and then you'd escape. What could we do? So we watched for a while and then went home. That's what Tim'll tell you, too."

I puzzled over that last phrase, "That's what Tim'll tell you, too," while Dr. Holt examined me. Why did Cat feel she needed an alibi? The story made sense. I think they should have waited for me no matter how long it took, but the whole episode with the Shooks had turned out so well, I wasn't angry. "That's what Tim'll tell you, too" only made me suspicious that something secretive had happened in the treehouse. What could have happened? You can't take a bath in a treehouse. It would have to be something worse than a bath.

When the exam was over, Dr. Holt told me to get dressed and meet him in his office. I collected Maude from the waiting room in case it was bad news. I needed a hand to hold.

"It will be a day or two before we get the results of the blood and urine tests," he said fifteen minutes later when I was sitting nervously across the desk from him. "But I don't see a thing wrong with you, Nelson. You're a little underweight. I want you to eat three good meals a day and drink lots of milk shakes. That won't be too hard, will it? And I'll give you a prescription for those headaches, but my guess is they'll go away pretty soon all by themselves. You don't have a brain tumor." He chuckled as he tore a piece of paper from a pad and wrote on it. I wondered if he always laughed at his patients and if the American Medical Association condoned this.

Maude wanted a prescription, too, so he scribbled on his pad again and gave the piece of paper to her with a sucker. "I'll call your mother and tell her the good news," he said, putting a golden hand on my shoulder as we walked down the hall toward the reception area. "I bet you didn't know your mom and I went to high school together. We even dated for a while." This was a nightmarish announcement from a man who had just given me a rectal exam, so I thanked him quickly and hustled Maude out into the bright afternoon sunlight.

There was just enough time left in the day to swing by the drugstore and have my prescription filled. Then we went to Dairy Queen for milk shakes and hot dogs. I took my codeine with the milk shake, wondering if it was correct to mix the two medicines. On the walk home Maude asked if we could go to the doctor's tomorrow, too.

I watched for signs of gloating from my mother when we got home, but all she said was, "I'm glad you're all right." My father was back from Boise, but he said nothing. In fact, the only thing he'd said since he hit me was, "Don't forget to cut the grass."

Tim appeared at our back door while I was doing the dishes. I finished up and we went into my room. "Cat told me everything," he said, sitting on my bed and taking out a pack of cigarettes. I emptied a pencil cup for him to use as an ashtray. "I never believed they killed him anyway. It was all a crock."

"I know."

"They were real nice when I delivered the groceries."

"They are. They gave me pie and everything."

"The cookies were great."

"So was the pie."

"Cat's so full of shit half the time." I wondered how Tim felt about Cat the other half of the time. If she was full of shit twelve hours a day, that still left twelve more unaccounted for.

"Too bad about Bobby, poor slob."

"Yeah."

It was a typical conversation with Tim, both of us pretending to be bored to death. Pretty soon it would gain momentum.

"How long did you guys wait for me in the treehouse?" I asked as if I couldn't care less. I opened a drawer of my desk and pretended to be searching for something.

"Couple of hours, I guess. I didn't have my watch. We would have stayed longer, but I had to open the store the next morning and if I don't get eight hours of sleep, I'm a walking corpse."

"What'd you do all that time?" Again I tried for a casual tone.

"Nothing. Watched the house. Stared at each other's ugly faces. The usual. She rocked the treehouse, I told her to cut it out. She called me stupid, I called her a rusty cunt. Nothing new." He ran his hand through his thick, unkempt hair. "You ask Cat, she'll tell you the same. Mind if I take a leak?" He stood up and unzipped his pants.

"Long as you use the bathroom."

He nodded in acknowledgment of the joke, dropped his cigarette on the floor, stepped on the unlit end, and went out the door.

I picked up the cigarette butt, carefully ground it out on the inside edge of my map of the world wastebasket, and buried it under some balled-up pieces of paper and candy wrappers. Then I opened the window and used my Pee-Chee to wave the smoke out of the room.

"You ask Cat, she'll tell you the same," Tim had said. This was almost word for word what Cat herself said. Did they agree on this story? If so, they obviously did something they didn't want me to know. Perhaps they were afraid of hurting me. This was touching, but I wasn't a child. I was used to bad news by now. True, I did not handle the bath revelation with complete maturity, but I had learned from that experience and now accepted the fact that my two best friends were in love. What I imagined they had done in the treehouse was probably a hundred times worse than what actually happened. Unless, of course, it wasn't.

I had always thought of Tim as my brother, someone who trusted me as I trusted him. Now I realized this was something I imagined, like the Shooks killing their son and my brain tumor that turned out to be puberty. Tim was lying to me and keeping things from me, and that was something brothers never did. Or was this, too, a fantasy?

But Tim and I did have a friendship, hard as it was to pinpoint. We had interests in common—bike riding, swimming, television. We never shared our deepest thoughts and feelings with each other. Our conversations were often a series of grunts that could have been mistaken for a chat between two cavemen.

Affection isn't easily expressed among boys. Girls exchange each other's clothes, sleep over at each other's houses, fix each other's hair. A dirty joke and a unstifled fart is as intimate as two boys ever get. Tim and I never fought, never got out the gloves and went a few rounds. That is the other way two boys can show affection, to try to put each other in the hospital on a life-support system.

I never imagined Tim being my friend for life. I knew we would drift apart eventually, but not now, not this summer with my parents getting divorced, with Bobby Shook dying, with the relentless presence of Maude. When Tim came back from his leak he had two more cigarettes, we talked about last week's *Thriller* episode, played some records, and planned to do something the following Sunday. This was no different from what we usually did together and, in fact, was more than we usually did. However, when Tim left my house that night, I was convinced I would never see him again.

The next day Maude and I went to the science museum. I thought the exhibits and slide shows would be fascinating to someone with her innate curiosity, but I was wrong. Maude was particularly bored with the NASA space capsule that was on special display; even hearing that a monkey rode in it didn't perk her interest. She only liked the Transparent Man and Woman. She enjoyed seeing their organs and wondered where their Transparent Children were. Fortunately the zoo was close by.

She could now peer over the steel railings by herself. When we got home that night, I measured her and announced to my parents from the kitchen doorway that Maude had grown three-quarters of an inch since the beginning of the summer. My mother looked stricken, as if Maude had eloped with a teen idol, but my father was delighted and allowed Maude to run to him across the sacred living room carpet. He lifted her high and she squealed with delight.

Thursday, Maude and I watched the trial sailboat races on the Columbia River. The actual races would take place on the weekend, but I had promised my Saturday to Mr. Shook.

Maude and I ate sandwiches and potato chips and watched the boats from the side of a hill. Each boat was a little different, each sail had a different design. We picked out the boat we would take home if they allowed us, then named our boats. Maude called hers *Ginger*, which I thought was a sissy name for a sailboat. I named mine *Sea Wolf*, but Maude didn't get the literary reference.

I was tired and lay down on my back while Maude practiced

standing on her head. She had seen Cat do this and longed for the same skill. I took off my shirt and let the sun warm my anemic skin. I had forgotten to bring my codeine tablets, but didn't have a headache. I wasn't even tired, but I fell asleep.

I woke a little later and immediately looked around for Maude. I expected her to have rolled down the hill and be floating face down in the river, but, no, she was collecting dandelions and talking to herself. When she saw that I was awake, she ran over and dropped the dandelions all over my now pink chest. Then she jumped on me, thirty-five pounds of pure lead. It was a good day.

That night I almost went to see the Shooks. The blood and urine tests had come back and Dr. Holt told my mother that I was the picture of health. I thought the Shooks might like to know that I didn't have a brain tumor. I didn't want them to worry. Then I remembered that they would be much too worried about Bobby to even give me a thought, so I let it wait until Saturday.

Friday was, of course, Story Hour day—morning and afternoon sessions. While Maude listened to "Puss 'n' Boots" at the Laurelhurst Library, I looked up retaining walls in the fix-it section. I jotted down some notes so the next day I could be of use to Mr. Shook.

We had lunch at the Jolly Roger, something Maude had been begging for all summer. The restaurant sign featured a one-eyed pirate aboard a galleon, but I knew it was an adult restaurant that probably frowned on children dining there. I couldn't face another Arctic Circle hamburger, so we risked it.

Maude was expecting an authentic nautical atmosphere, perhaps something like the interior of her sailboat, *Ginger*, but she was enormously disappointed. The restaurant had portholes, but otherwise was a typical dimly lighted, wood-paneled restaurant. Predictably, the hostess reeled in surprise when I asked for a table for two. Maude piped up, "We want pizza!" This was now her standard demand upon entering any restaurant, no matter how absurd.

I warned Maude that the Jolly Roger was a seafood restaurant and she didn't like seafood. "Yes, I do," she insisted, a bald-faced lie. Of course there was not one thing on the menu she would let pass her lips. I conned the waitress into scaring up some fish sticks, which Maude would eat because she didn't believe they were real fish. She was probably not wrong.

The waitress took a shine to Maude and agreed to keep an eye on her while I went to the rest room. If there's a stall open, I usually take it. The men's room was empty, so I went into a cubicle and locked the door. I read the graffiti on the wall while I relieved myself. I wondered if any book in the world had been read by more people than the graffiti in that stall at the Jolly Roger. It was a disturbing thought.

When I finished and started over to the washbasins, I was faced with this sight: Dr. Holt standing in front of the mirror, combing his hair and humming. A moment later I was back in the stall, the door latched, my pants around my ankles.

It was not a crime for me to lunch at the Jolly Roger, so there was no reason I should be afraid of running into Dr. Holt in the men's room. But it would be awkward. It would lead to a series of questions: "How are those headaches, Nelson? Have you been taking your pills?" He might even want an on-the-spot examination of some orifice he overlooked. It was easier to stay in the stall until he went away, which he did a few moments later.

The hostess had seated Maude and me near the back (the last thing anyone wants to see when they enter a restaurant is a child), so I had a good view of all of the customers and knew that Dr. Holt was not in the dining room. But they also served food in the Captain's Bar. Curious, I crept to the swinging half doors with turquoise anchors on them, pushed one slightly open, and peered into the ridiculously dark lounge. A dinghy hung from the ceiling, another nautical touch. Dr. Holt was sitting in a booth, his back to me. His well-combed blond hair shone in the darkness. He was drinking a beer. On the table in front of him was a candle in a red globe covered by white plastic netting. Sitting opposite him, talking and laughing, sat a pretty woman with auburn hair. In fact, it was my mother.

I paid the check and hurried Maude out of the restaurant. The bus was just pulling up across the street and I waved to the driver to wait for us. In no time we were aboard and on our way to Story Hour at the Woodstock Library.

I took a household repair manual from the shelf, but found it impossible to concentrate on retaining walls. I couldn't stop thinking about my mom and Dr. Holt at the Jolly Roger. What were they doing there? Were they discussing my physical condition? Maybe the lab had made a mistake and Dr. Holt wanted to break the news to his old friend in person that her son was seriously ill and had only months or weeks to live. But my mother had been laughing and chatting with Dr. Holt. She was drinking something like a Manhattan, which is not a drink a mother would order after hearing that her only son was dying. A belt of Scotch, yes, but not a drink with a cherry in it. Then I recalled Dr. Holt smoothing down his shiny hair in the mirror and humming. I recognized the song, too: "Never on Sunday," a very sexy song.

Were they just talking over old times or were they having an affair? They had dated in high school and maybe even went all the way. If they hadn't gone all the way then, maybe they'd always regretted it. I had seen pictures of my mother when she was in high school. She looked young and pretty. I'd never seen a photo of the teenage Dr. Holt, but I could imagine him boyishly handsome in a letter sweater, a catalog of achievements under his class picture. Perhaps they were already at a motel, undressing each other as Maude innocently listened to *Madeline*.

I questioned the wisdom of sleeping with the family doctor, but at least it would be hygienic. I couldn't blame my mother for having an affair. My dad had been cheating on her for years. Still, I didn't think she should give up on him just yet.

Madeline was over much too fast and Maude and I were out on the street again. We ducked into Beckwith's Bicycle Shop where I checked the price on a red and black Schwinn I'd seen a boy riding the day before (too expensive), then walked to the drugstore to shop for birthday cards, although nobody's birthday was coming up. We had milk shakes at the counter and when Maude wasn't looking, I snuck a glance at the latest *Playboy*. Afterwards we swung by Cat's house, but she wasn't home. We dropped in at the Little Store, but Tim was out on a delivery. Hugo was behind the counter and asked if I wanted more sleeping pills. I said no. Maude pried money out of me for a coloring book.

That evening I looked at my mother closely to see if she had, as one writer put it, "the glow of a satisfied woman," but she looked pretty much the same. She made spaghetti and meatballs and ate with us, though she only picked at her food. My father was in Spokane. She asked about my headaches and I said they were better. Maude told her that I had looked at a picture of a naked lady at the drugstore and I tried to push Maude's face in her plate. My mom yelled at me to stop it, but ignored the naked lady subject. Perhaps that very afternoon she had been lolling on black sheets with a sleeping cocker spaniel at her feet like Terry, the July Playmate.

That night I picked out clothes for building the retaining wall. I didn't have anything as suitable as Cat's painter's pants, so I settled on some jeans that were torn a little at the crotch and mended with an iron-on patch, and a T-shirt with an orange stain on it (Maude, Kool-Aid). I set my alarm for seven A.M., but woke at six-thirty.

In the kitchen my mother was sipping coffee and disinterestedly turning the pages of the newspaper. On Saturday mornings she always had a desolate look on her face; it was the first of two consecutive days of Maude being underfoot. I half expected her to say that I had to start taking Maude on weekends, too, but she said nothing. I quickly mowed the lawn, edged it, raked the cut grass into the catcher, and emptied it in the garbage can. I turned on the sprinklers for fifteen minutes while I washed up. At exactly nine-thirty I pressed the little quarter moon on the Shooks' doorbell.

"Oh. Nelson."

Mrs. Shook stared blankly at me through the screen door and for a moment I wondered if I had the date wrong. No, this was Saturday—the same Saturday I had promised to Mr. Shook. Still, Mrs. Shook peered through the wire mesh as though she barely recognized me. I had a sudden fear that Bobby was worse, maybe even dead, and this was a bad day to come in my torn jeans. Then I realized why she looked at me so strangely: She didn't think I would return. They had made me promise to return, but were certain I would never show up. I'm sure they thought "a kid is a kid." It momentarily crossed my mind that I'd wasted a whole Saturday; I could have gone to the bookstores, to a movie, done my usual Saturday routine, and they wouldn't have reported on me. But it's important to keep your promises, I reminded myself, even if nobody expects it of you. A kid isn't always a kid.

"Mr. Shook said come back Saturday to help him with the wall."

"He's at the hospital." She unlatched the screen door and pushed it open. "But come in. He should be back soon." Now that her surprise was over, she seemed glad I had come. She even smiled a little, the first time I ever saw her smile.

"How is Bobby?" I asked in a hushed tone that seemed appropriate for the dark, gloomy house. The house wasn't much brighter in the day than it was at night. The curtains were closed and the dark wood floors, dark furniture, and Oriental rugs added to the funereal atmosphere.

"He's about the same," Mrs. Shook said as we moved into the kitchen. The kitchen was the only part of the house that didn't smell stale. It smelled of coffee and Ajax. The curtains were drawn back from the window over the sink and the window was open a little. The room was light and fresh and it was like stepping into a different house. "Have you had breakfast?" she asked, and, before I could respond, removed a big black skillet from the cupboard next to the stove.

"Some cereal."

"Breakfast's the most important meal of the day." She set the skillet on a burner, turned a knob, and lit the gas jet with a wooden match. A blue flame sparkled.

"I know. I just never have time, 'cause I take care of Maude all week. Maude's my little sister. And on weekends I have the lawn and other chores, too. I like to get them all done early so I can have the rest of the day to do what I want."

"And what do you like to do?"

I shrugged. "I don't know." She couldn't possibly be interested.

"You must know what you like to do, Nelson." She melted some butter in the skillet and took a carton of eggs from the refrigerator.

"Read. I write some stuff, too."

"What do you write?"

"Novels and stuff."

"What stuff?"

"Novels, I mean. Only I haven't finished one."

"Then we have something in common," she said mysteriously as she lifted the tin foil cover from a bowl of pancake batter and started stirring the lumps out. I had been in the kitchen less than a minute, but eggs and sausage were already frying in the skillet, bread was toasting in the toaster, pancake batter was being stirred, a pitcher of orange juice had been placed on the table in front of me, and I was polishing off the glass of milk she had poured. Mrs. Shook accomplished all this without much speed; in fact, she moved slowly and heavily. But her kitchen was like a little breakfast kingdom where the ingredients were right at hand and practically did the work themselves. I wouldn't have been surprised if she had sat down at the table with me while the eggs cracked themselves and the pancakes jumped and flipped in the iron skillet.

"In common?"

"I write poetry. Oh, little things in the paper. You know the poetry column on Sundays? In there, and in a couple magazines. Nothing very special. Robert Frost doesn't have to worry about me." She laughed a little at her literary pretensions.

"What are they about?"

"Oh, what is poetry ever about? Love. In all forms. Love of another human being, love of nature, love of God. Love of self. I haven't written too many of those, though." Another short, self-deprecating laugh. "They're all pretty old-fashioned. I try to make them rhyme, which is very old-fashioned, I guess. A couple of years ago, for my birthday, Chuck took my poems and had them made up into a little booklet. It wasn't sold in the bookstores, of course, but it was typeset and an artist designed the cover. It was a very sweet thing to do and I know Chuck thought it would make me happy, but . . ." She trailed off, sounding sad. I would have been excited to have a little booklet of my poems, but it seemed to depress Mrs. Shook. People are very strange about their writing.

"I'll show it to you sometime, if you'd like."

"I'd like that," I said, encouragingly. A sausage crackled and spattered. She prodded at it with a fork as if it had been bad.

"What do you write, Nelson? You know," she continued before I could answer, "you're the second boy I've met recently whose name is Nelson. I didn't think it was such a common name."

"I write a lot of stuff I don't finish," I said quickly, trying to steer the conversation away from the fact that I had sent a spy into her house with a bag of groceries.

"Who doesn't?" She scooted the disobedient sausages to one side of the frying pan, poured the pancake batter, then checked the toast. It was an old-fashioned toaster with little doors on the sides instead of slots in the top. The toast didn't pop up automatically when it was done, but still Mrs. Shook didn't burn it. When she opened the doors, the toast was evenly browned, crisp outside, but still soft inside.

"I have boxes of unfinished poetry. Oh, and once I started a novel. That's in a box somewhere, too. It's easy to start things, isn't it, but finishing them is something else."

I was almost dizzy from the smells in the kitchen, the fryings and toastings. The orange juice in the pitcher was the freshest and orangest possible, the milk in my glass the whitest and coldest I'd ever tasted. It seemed as if Mrs. Shook was inventing breakfast, a new and extraordinary meal that would change the world from this morning on. My stomach growled.

"Now I'm going to keep quiet and let you talk. Tell me about your writing. I want to know all about it," she coaxed, putting a stick of butter, a bottle of syrup, and a little can of cinnamon on the table and refilling my milk glass.

"Well, the first thing I wrote was about King Arthur and Guenevere," I began, but she immediately interrupted.

"I love stories about Arthur and the Round Table! I don't know how many novels I've read about them. And of course *Le Morte d'Arthur.* I read that in school. That's a wonderful subject."

"It was never published. I was ten. It pretty much stunk."

"I'm sure you're too hard on yourself, like I am. Would you let me read it sometime? Or any of your stories. I don't care if they're not finished. I love reading. That's my one luxury. If I had a dollar left to my name I'd spend it on a book. I buy hardbound books only. If I see one I want, I don't even think. I buy it. I love owning books. Love seeing them on my shelf. It almost makes me feel that I've written them myself. My father never let us read anything except the Bible and Mark Twain. Oh, he loved Mark Twain. I think he believed Mark Twain *wrote* the Bible."

Mrs. Shook set a jar of jam and a bottle of honey on the table, cracked some eggs into the fry pan, then chopped up some strawberries, chattering happily all the while. I got the feeling she and Mr. Shook didn't talk much, at least not about literature.

"He thought everything else would corrupt my mind, so I could never read the things I wanted to read. I wanted to read Dostoyevsky and, oh, I don't know, Hardy and Scott, everybody. Now I can read anything I want and I buy them all in hardcover. No paperbacks for me. Or library books. I always wonder where library books have been. Who had them last and where did they read them?" I thought of the copy of *Captains Courageous* I accidentally dropped in the toilet. I could see her point.

"Do you read a lot, Nelson? I bet you do," she said, answering her own question. "Well, if you ever see a book in this house that you want to borrow, just take it. Unless I'm reading it, but you can always tell what book I'm reading because I use the same bookmark every time. It's a bookmark Bobby picked out. It's a laminated plastic bookmark with a picture of an old motor car on it, a Duesenberg or something. Unless that bookmark is in the book you want, just take it. You don't even have to ask."

"Thanks, Mrs. Shook."

Breakfast was ready. The yolks of the fried eggs were centered perfectly in their circles of white, the three pancakes were all exactly the same size as if made in a mold, and the sausages spurted out just the right amount of grease when you cut into them. Mrs. Shook refilled my milk and orange juice glasses the moment the level dropped below the halfway point. Now that I was eating, she didn't speak. She sang a little, but not a recognizable tune like Dr. Holt's rendition of "Never on Sunday." Mrs. Shook sang aimless, tuneless bars of music. I don't even think she was aware she was singing.

The breakfast smells and the warmth in that kitchen made me feel like I was wrapped in a big warm blanket, just scratchy enough to be pleasant. Sunlight poured through the window, illuminating millions of dust particles that busily swirled and darted. The shine off the highly polished silver faucet over the sink was like the shine from a star. The kitchen was yellow, all yellow: yellow wallpaper, yellow sunlight, yellow butter on my golden yellow pancakes next to my bright yellow eggs. The table-cloth had yellow in it, as did the dishes. A red bread box across the room stood out like a gunshot wound.

Once my family went camping in southeastern Washington. Maude was only a year old, so she didn't come along. There was a lot of fishing, which I have already discussed my attitude toward. There was a nine-year-old girl at the next campsite with whom I spent some time. My mom insisted on taking pictures of us, as if Bonnie and I would want the photos to show our children in future years. In fact Bonnie was of no interest at all except for an ability to let out enormous, record-breaking belches. She could say whole sentences with her burps and also perform the ABCs. Once she tried the Pledge of Allegiance, but had to take a breath around "one nation under God."

But the most memorable thing about the trip was the camp fire. Each night my father made a big fire and my mother cooked over it. One night, fried hamburgers and baked beans. Trout, which my dad had caught, another night. Corned beef hash a third night. Afterwards we sat as close to the fire as possible; it crackled and the sparks shot up overhead like miniature fireworks. My dad put his arm around my mom. I toasted marshmallows.

In those moments it seemed as though nothing bad could possibly happen in the world: not to me, not to my mother or my father, not to Maude or the people at the next campsite, not even to belching Bonnie. Not to the United States of America or any other country in the world. How could anything bad happen when the stars were so visible, so close and so many above us, and the fire was popping like popcorn? The camp fire was hot on my face and the night cool on the back of my head. I was wearing my red and black plaid lumberman jacket and I turned the collar up so the raw threads scratched against the back of my neck in a pleasant way. My mother sang a song, something I didn't know, something from wartime. My dad tried to sing along, but he couldn't carry a tune and that made my mom giggle. The marshmallows caught on fire and tasted better burnt.

Now, in Mrs. Shook's kitchen, I felt the same quiet contentment: When something so perfect can exist in the world, such as this breakfast, this bright yellow day, how could anything be sad or dying or unloved in the world?

Of course, this optimistic frame of mind did not last long. Soon I had eaten so much I had a stomachache. My shriveled gut was straining to contain everything I plugged into it, so I put down my fork and took a last sip of milk. Mrs. Shook gave me a disappointed look. Bobby was probably a big eater.

"I went to the doctor," I said, taking the codeine bottle from my pocket and placing it on the table. "This is what he gave me. He didn't think it was anything serious. He said something about puberty." This last part I mumbled, embarrassed not to have gone through puberty long before this.

Mrs. Shook picked up the bottle and examined the label. Her lips moved a little as she read. A line of fine hairs grew above her upper lip, invisible except when she turned toward the light. She opened the lid and peered at the pills.

"Have you been taking one every four hours?"

"I started out that way, but I've been forgetting."

This was not acceptable. Mrs. Shook tipped the bottle into her hand and a solitary pill rolled into her palm. It was the gesture of a woman who had tipped a lot of pills out of a lot of bottles. She put the little red tablet by my place mat.

"I don't have a headache right now."

"The prescription says one tablet every four hours. Your doctor didn't write this for his health. He wrote it for yours. Take your pill." I took it.

"Do you like your doctor?"

Not particularly, but my mother likes him a lot, I wanted to say.

"He's okay. He looks like a doctor on TV."

"Holt . . . ," she said, squinting at the prescription label again, "I don't know him." He was probably the only doctor in the city Bobby didn't visit. "I don't like Bobby's new doctor. He's a specialist, which is fine, but there's something about him . . . I can't describe it. Yes, I can describe it," she said with sudden certainty. "He acts as if he's seen a million cases like Bobby and Bobby is nothing special. Well, maybe there *are* a million cases like Bobby and Bobby *isn't* anything special, but he shouldn't let on that he thinks that. Bobby is the most precious thing we have, we're scared to death, and he should be sympathetic." Her eyes were watering. I wondered what would happen if Bobby died. How soon afterwards would Mrs. Shook die of loneliness, of a broken heart, of having no one to tell to take his pills?

If anyone needed someone to cook for and launder for and fuss over, it was Bridget Shook. I suppose this was when I first thought of bringing Maude over to their house. Maude needed all those things and also required constant entertainment. She took up a lot of time and if Bobby Shook died, Mrs. Shook would have nothing but time. It was the perfect match. But this idea wasn't completely formed yet and got brushed aside when Mr. Shook came back from the hospital, there was a change of guard, and we went downstairs to build the wall.

The wall hadn't been touched since Mr. Shook tore it down. Bricks were scattered all over the floor and a big pool of water had gathered. My first job was separating the whole concrete blocks from the ones that broke when the wall came down. Mr. Shook said that even a chip in a block made it worthless. He had built the wall too fast and carelessly the first time; if he hadn't torn it down, it would have eventually fallen down by itself. We were going to rebuild it right.

While I separated the blocks into two piles, he carved at the mound of earth intruding into the basement, flattening it. The loose dirt turned to mud when it fell on the wet floor and guess what my next job was? By the time I had shoveled the mud and dirt into two wheelbarrows and mopped the floor clean, my torn jeans were filthy and there were brown smears on my T-shirt.

Then Mr. Shook gave me a hammer and chisel and told me to chip the dried mortar off the intact concrete blocks. The hammer and chisel produced a sharp Michelangelo-like sound and I enjoyed this part of the work. Mr. Shook laid a long fiberglass gutter under the flattened bank of earth, then used a skill saw to cut a small hole in the wall. The end of the drainpipe fit the hole perfectly. Now when water seeped down from the neighbor's property, it would collect in the shallow trough and run out to the street.

We didn't have enough bricks for a new wall, so Mr. Shook announced that we were going to the lumber yard. As Mrs. Shook had taken the colorful De Soto to the hospital, I pictured us carting back thirty mountainously heavy concrete blocks on the bus and wondered if we would have to pay an additional fare. But Mr. Shook had a truck he parked in a neighbor's garage a few blocks away.

It was a great truck, a real rattletrap from the twenties that chugged and banged and lurched its way along the street. Mr. Shook's attitude changed completely when he got behind the wheel. While we were working together in the basement he hardly said a word except to give me instructions. I couldn't think of a topic of conversation to broach, so I broached none. We worked side by side for three hours, barely speaking.

But once he was in the truck, he was a different man. He started right in talking and didn't stop until we got to the lumber yard. The truck was the first automobile he owned, he told me. He bought it second-hand and suspected that it was at least third- or fourth-hand, if not more. This was in North Dakota, where he came from. "This old truck has original dust from the Dust Bowl!" he said proudly, and uttered the first laugh I ever heard from him—more of a bark than a laugh. He took a pipe from his pocket and filled it while he steered with his little finger. We came to a stoplight and, as he was busy lighting his pipe, he told me to shift into first. The gearshift was so loose I thought it would come off in my hand.

"I drove out to Portland in this jalopy," he announced. I loved the word "jalopy," but it was so old-fashioned I figured I would never hear it used in my lifetime. "I was sixteen. 1918. Does that sound as far ago to you as it does to me?"

"Yes, sir." Woodrow Wilson's face swam up in front of me and then disappeared. So the truck wasn't from the twenties, as I had thought; it was even older.

"That was a godforsaken place, North Dakota. Too cold, too hot, too dry, too snowy—it was never just right. I remember driving away from Dunseith in this thing and yelping. Just yelping at the top of my lungs. I was so excited to get away from there I thought I'd piss my pants." He sounded almost that excited right now. I was afraid he would excitedly swerve into oncoming traffic; his pipe had gone out and he was again steering with his little finger. We came to another stoplight and he told me to shift.

"The first night I slept in the back of the truck. I didn't have money for a motel and there weren't any motels, anyway. They hadn't been invented yet. There wasn't much of anything between North Dakota and Portland. Butte, Montana," he said thoughtfully. "I remember Butte. I got into trouble in Butte."

He smiled to himself, remembering whatever trouble he had gotten into. I have a bad habit of thinking of older people as always being older, but Mr. Shook probably looked a lot different when he was sixteen and left North Dakota with a yelp. Maybe not handsome, but a big, brawny farm boy. A kid like that, all fired up at being on his own for the first time in his life, could get into a lot of mischief. "A girl," he hinted, but didn't go into details.

"Of course that was before I met Bridget. We met in twenty-nine, married in thirty. Bobby was born in thirty-one. He got meningitis the next year." Then we pulled into the lumber yard.

We stayed there an hour and a half, although the concrete blocks we needed were piled up outside the building not far from where we parked. Mr. Shook just liked looking around the store. He reminded me of Maude in the dime store, carefully examining each item, no matter how banal. Mr. Shook didn't buy anything in that hour and a half, except for the blocks, but he looked down every aisle to see if anything new had come in and had a long discussion with one of the assistant managers about metal garbage cans versus the new plastic ones. He was obviously a regular at Foster Lumber Mill; the store clerks all addressed him by name. He spent a long time in the small hardware aisle, trying to find a hook for Mrs. Shook's broom. He considered each one and asked my opinion on a couple of them, but none really suited him. I wasn't bored. Hardware stores always have something you never saw before and wish you'd invented. But I wondered if we were ever going to get the wall built.

Mr. Shook had a dejected look when the concrete blocks were finally loaded onto the back of the truck and he paid his $9.95. We rattled out of the parking lot and Mr. Shook asked me to steer while he got his pipe going again. The way he puffed greedily on it I could tell that Mrs. Shook didn't approve of it and didn't let him smoke in the house. I managed not to steer us into parked cars until the pipe was lit.

Then Mr. Shook realized it was past lunchtime and pulled into the A&W. We ordered through the speaker box and waited for the short-skirted waitress to bring our tray. In the car opposite us, a teenage boy and girl were feeding each other French fries dripping with ketchup and kissing between each one. I hoped this wasn't something I would find sexy the minute I cleared puberty.

"I used to own that place, you know," Mr. Shook said, and it was a moment before I realized he meant the lumber yard. "Started out as a clerk, then was assistant manager, then manager. About twelve years ago they were going to sell off the inventory, knock down the building, and turn the lot into a supermarket.

I scraped the money together and bought the place, lock, stock, and barrel."

I appreciated his use of the phrase, "lock, stock, and barrel" to describe a lumber yard and hardware store.

"I had it until a year ago when Bobby got really bad. It wasn't fair to Bridget to make her take care of him fourteen, fifteen hours a day. When I worked, I really worked. So I sold it off. A chain bought it. A lot of the same people work there, though. Nice people." His voice betrayed a note of regret: What if Bobby died? Shouldn't he have kept the store, let his employees run it, and have it to return to when the crushing sadness came? I wondered how often he went to Foster Lumber Mill. Once a day? Twice? Were his old employees glad to see him, or was he a ghost, haunting the small hardware aisle, never finding the precise hook he needed? I imagined a rush to the stockroom whenever he came through the doors, the clerks flipping coins to see who would go talk to him. I had the feeling that today was not the first time the topic "metal garbage cans versus plastic" had been debated.

Tracy, her name stitched on the collar of her uniform, delivered our tray. Her small breasts bounced like the balls in a sing-a-long TV show Maude liked. Mr. Shook struck up a friendly conversation with her. She went to Cleveland High; no, she was not a cheerleader; she was in drama and also a member of the swim team. Perspiration broke out on my forehead when I pictured Tracy in a swimming cap.

Silence fell while we ate. I remembered how Mrs. Shook, as chatty as the next-door neighbor in a comedy series while she was preparing breakfast, assumed a churchlike stillness while I ate. Eating was serious business to the Shooks.

I took my codeine tablet with my root beer float. Tracy returned to remove our tray and I made a note to brush up on my swimming and, with luck, get a place on the team so we could go to swim meets together. Tracy flashed a dazzling smile at Mr. Shook and carried our tray away. She didn't look at me once.

"We're taking a little detour," Mr. Shook said as he turned onto McLoughlin Boulevard and we passed the park with the ducks where I had spent so many Maude-filled days that summer. I didn't ask where we were detouring to. I knew.

The only hospital I'd ever been inside was Providence Hospital, where Maude was born. My dad took me there to visit my mother and see my new sister. Maude was, of course, a beautiful infant. Pictures of me at that age resemble the monkey embryo my biology teacher once brought into class. My mom couldn't stop saying, "She's a living doll." I was not jealous; she was a cute kid, but I could see trouble looming ahead. It didn't escape my attention that my parents had their two children just far enough apart so the older kid would be old enough to baby-sit the younger one any time they liked.

Unlike the huge, forbidding Providence Hospital, Greenpark Hospital was small and set in a wooded area. It looked more like a grade school than a hospital, but nevertheless smelled like a hospital inside.

Mrs. Shook looked up from her book. She was reading aloud from one of the classic volumes I had seen in Bobby's room. Bobby was lying in bed, covered by an oxygen tent. His breathing was unnatural, big gasps with long breaks between them. A needle was stuck in his left arm and attached to a tube that ran up to a bottle of clear liquid above his head. Another tube ran from under the covers to a plastic bag hanging on the end of the bed. It was a private room. A couple of stuffed animals reclined on the bedside table.

I couldn't remember when I had last seen Bobby, but it must have been some time ago. When Cat announced that he was missing and started the whole "buried in the basement" business, she made it seem as though Bobby had vanished very recently. But Mr. and Mrs. Shook stopped walking Bobby around the neighborhood the previous summer when he took a turn for the worse. Mr. Shook sold his lumber yard in early fall. No matter how long it had been since I'd seen him, Bobby certainly looked different. He was a big boy with big arms and legs, but now the flesh hung loosely on his body as if he were wearing the wrong size skin. His big head showed the shape of his skull. He was still tall, of course, but couldn't have weighed more than a hundred and ten pounds. And he was gray, a pale greenish gray.

"How has he been?"

"His hand moved. I held it and talked to him, but he didn't move his head or blink like before. His hand feels cold to me."

Mr. Shook took Bobby's limp hand and squeezed it. He put his face up to the oxygen tent and looked closely at Bobby. Mrs. Shook smiled at me. Her smile trembled. I wonder how many hours a day she spent crying.

"It's so nice of you to come, Nelson."

"I wanted to," I said, although this was not entirely true. Still, I was glad to see Bobby again after all this time.

I felt I should say something to him, but there was little to say. You would think a writer could come up with something original or comforting at a moment like this, but I was stumped. I took a step toward the bed and said in a loud voice, "Hi, Bobby. It's Nelson. I'm one of those kids who's always sitting out on their lawns when you go for a walk with your mom and dad." Then I added, in a voice not quite so booming, "I'm sorry I made fun of you sometimes."

Mr. Shook's big hand gave my shoulder a squeeze as if this apology to a thirty-one-year-old man in a coma was not wildly inappropriate, but the perfect thing to say in this time of need. I sneaked a glance at Mrs. Shook. She was smiling at me and her eyes glistened. The Shooks were hard to understand. I couldn't go wrong with them. Even breaking into their house turned out pretty well.

Having said my piece, I stepped back from the bed. I had a sudden feeling that I had done this before: the exact same one step forward, saying a little something, then one step back. The formality was familiar, but I couldn't place it. There was so little formality in my life. Then I remembered a funeral home, stepping up to the casket, pretending to kiss the corpse but not really touching it, saying, "Sleep tight, Grandpa," and stepping back to see the proud look on my parents' faces. It was strange to be doing almost exactly the same thing I had done when I was five. Was I destined to always be the same person or was some sort of change possible?

"How's the wall coming?" Mrs. Shook asked.

"We got a lot done," Mr. Shook lied.

"Did you eat?"

"We had a snack." I assumed that anything Mrs. Shook didn't personally cook was classified as a snack. "What about you?"

"I had something in the cafeteria."

"Let's go home."

"I hate to leave him." Mrs. Shook looked at Bobby. I read her thoughts: The moment I leave he will die. Her face was as translucent as a television screen, with an equally tremulous image. There was so little color there, she might as well have been in black and white.

"We'll come back this evening." Mr. Shook went around the bed and gently took her arm. She rose unsteadily to her feet; she had been sitting for hours. I wondered if someone had told Chuck and Bridget when they first met that thirty-three years later they would be in this hospital room, not knowing whether or not to leave their dying son, whether they still would have married or if they would have looked for other partners so that fate would lead them anywhere but to this moment.

She parted the oxygen tent and kissed Bobby's forehead. Mr. Shook did the same. He took Bobby's hand again, pressed it, and whispered, "Be brave, son." His voice was hoarse and he also seemed rocky on his feet. I thought of the man who just a few hours before had been steering with one finger and telling me how he yelped as he drove away from the Dust Bowl. I also thought of the man who barely said a word as we worked side by side for hours in the damp basement. He had been three different people already today and it wasn't even four o'clock.

We stopped at the front desk so that Mrs. Shook could ask the nurse to call her if there was any change in Bobby's condition. The nurse got a sympathetic look on her face as if she was sharing the Shooks' pain and said that of course she would.

I rode in the truck with Mr. Shook while Mrs. Shook took the sedan. As she got in the car, Mr. Shook asked if she was strong enough to drive. "Oh, I'm fine," she said, although it was obvious she wasn't. They spoke for a few more moments, softly, so I could not hear. Then Mrs. Shook drove slowly away in the big-finned car.

After we crossed the bridge over the railroad tracks on which Maude was fond of placing loose change, Mr. Shook pulled over to the curb and parked directly under a "No Stopping or Parking" sign. He got out of the truck and told me to slide over to the steering wheel. The truck was so old the seat didn't adjust and I had to sit on the very edge to reach the clutch and brake. Mr. Shook sat on the passenger side, lighted his pipe, and told me to drive down Twenty-seventh past the golf course and up Crystal Springs, just for practice.

"I learned to drive at thirteen. I don't see why you shouldn't. I don't hold with all these rules."

He didn't blink when I stripped the gears. "There's nothing you can do to this truck that hasn't been done to it before," he said philosophically. He didn't even mind when I hit the brake instead of the clutch, almost catapulting us both through the windshield. He laughed, another of his short barks. "You'll get the hang of it."

I drove up Crystal Springs, took a left, went as far as Tolman, then down Tolman to the garage on Thirty-first. The whole way Mr. Shook puffed on his pipe and coached me through it.

"Second. Don't forget the clutch. Okay. You can push it a little. Don't be afraid to step on the gas. You don't want it to die on you. Speed limit's thirty, you're nowhere near that. Good work. I didn't even have to tell you to shift. That was smooth. Couldn't have done better myself. Watch out for this little boy on the bike. Don't count on him knowing we're coming. Okay, here's the stop sign. Shift down. Grind, grind. That's okay. Don't worry about it. Look both ways. Nobody's coming. No police or anything, so let her rip. First! First! There you go. You're picking it up. The trees are nice along here, aren't they? My God, look at the color they painted that house! Second. That's the brake. You want the clutch. That's the one. No traffic, might as well give it a little juice. Hear that? You want to shift now. Third. Good. Clutch. Good work. Indianapolis here you come! I wonder how many race car drivers are named Nelson?"

*   *   *

I was so shocked by my grade that at first I didn't even see the note. My four-page essay on "How *The Red Badge of Courage* Relates to Today," if not one of my masterworks, certainly deserved better than a B minus. I believed that my comparisons of

the Civil War to the recent Cuban Missile Crisis (do we run? do
we stay and fight?) were particularly incisive. I even typed my
paper, to give Mr. Crisp a little rest from my penmanship.

"Nelson, see me after class," Mr. Crisp had written in the
margin, just above "Ambitious and creative, but not what I as-
signed. Stop showing off." I was hurt by this. I was only trying
to vary Mr. Crisp's reading material. Did he really want to read
twenty-seven analyses of the hero's character in *The Red Badge
of Courage*? I thought he'd appreciate a little variety. At least I
spent time on my paper and put thought into it. I stole a glance
at the boy across from me. He titled his essay, "What I Think
of the Guy in the Book." His first paragraph read: "He's a jerk!
He ran like a pussy. He should have blown those stupid Commies
away!"

Mr. Crisp looked summery in a tan suit, a white shirt, and a
bow tie. I wondered if he had a straw hat to go with the outfit.
As usual I waited until everyone else had left the room before
approaching him. He was packing up his briefcase. Inside was a
copy of *The Call of the Wild*, which I guessed would be our next
book. I would have to remember not to relate it to front-page
events.

"You wanted to see me, Mr. Crisp?" I asked formally. I was
determined not to be friendly. I had gone out of my way to write
an interesting paper and he gave me a B minus. He gave the "He's
a jerk" kid a C. Well, what could I expect from an English teacher
who wrote pornographic novels?

"Nelson, when I give an assignment, I expect you to do it. I
don't have certain rules for some students and other rules for
other students. Everyone is equal. I appreciate that you always
turn your papers in on time and don't have a lot of 'my dog ate
it' excuses. And I appreciate that you typed your paper. But if you
don't stick to the topic I have to give you a lower grade. You

should be getting straight As in this class. You're capable of it and I don't understand why you don't do what you're asked."

He said not a word about the content, not a single comment about my originality. He was happy I typed it! I vowed never to type another paper for him the rest of the year. If possible, I would write as sloppily as possible and then give my paper to Maude to color on. My face was flaming and there was a prickling behind my eyes. I'll be damned if I'm going to cry in front of him, I thought. I felt like spitting on him.

"Is that all, sir?" I said, trying for a military tone.

"I want to give you these back," he said, taking my five messy composition books from the top right-hand drawer of his desk. "Thank you for letting me read them. I'm sorry it took so long, but I've been busy." He handed me the books, closed the drawer and closed his briefcase. "I hope you don't mind, I made some comments in the margins. Mostly grammatical things: sentence structure, some spelling problems, use of profanity when it wasn't appropriate, use of cliches, that sort of thing. I realize it's a piece of creative writing, not a school assignment, so you can take my comments or leave them."

"Thank you, sir." I'd had enough of this. First he gave me a bad grade on my paper, then said I wrote in cliches, couldn't spell, and used a lot of filthy language. I should have known not to trust him. He probably read excerpts from my story aloud in the faculty room, making the other teachers roar with laughter. I turned away so he couldn't see my face. The hall outside was filled with hundreds of happy, uncriticized kids. I hated them all.

He erased the blackboard, raising himself up on his toes to reach the top part of the board. A quote from Walt Whitman disappeared.

"I made marks only in the first chapter," he went on. "That first chapter needs a lot of work. There's lots of repetition and quite a few detours from the main story. I know you're aware of this, because you mention it in the course of the narrative. By the way, I'm not sure a story about an Israeli freedom fighter is the subject for you. You want to be careful not to plagiarize."

He started to wipe his hands on the back of his pants, then stopped himself. His wife probably yelled at him about this. He took out a handkerchief and brushed the chalk dust from his hands.

"Anyway, you'll find that I didn't make any comments on the other four books because I was so wrapped up in the story. I kept wanting to know what happened next and I completely forgot to make notes."

He put the handkerchief back in his pocket and opened his briefcase again to check its contents. I stared at him, confused. It was *good* when a reader got wrapped up in a story, wasn't it? I thought a writer was *supposed* to keep the reader's interest. But Mr. Crisp seemed to be criticizing these things and blaming me for not giving him the chance to mark up the rest of my composition books.

"When I wrote that note to you on your paper I didn't realize I had a faculty meeting after school," he said, snapping the briefcase shut again in a businesslike manner, "so I've got to get going." A new picture of his wife and kids was propped up on the desk. I wondered if they had to starve while he was giving all his money to LuAnne so she wouldn't sleep with anyone else. They looked okay now.

"But, if you can stand a little more advice . . ." He looked around the room, saw that a window was open, and went to close it. "I think you should finish the story. You're starting to find your style. There are some very good sentences in there. Much better than anything you've turned in in class. The more you write, the better it gets and that's a very good sign. I know you have doubts about your writing. Don't worry about it. Finish the story and then go back. Remember, books aren't written. They're re-written."

He returned to the desk, glanced at his watch, then spotted someone out in the hall. He held up a finger and said, "Fifteen seconds!" to a pretty woman in a purple dress, who I recognized as the Spanish teacher. I once heard some boys in the lunchroom saying that she was the teacher they'd most like to bang until her head spun around. I wondered if she knew about this honor.

"Nelson," Mr. Crisp said quietly and I turned to look at him. "Reading your story made me very proud. Proud of you for writing it and proud that it's as good as it is. I stand up here day after day looking at all those blank faces and wonder what in the hell I'm doing it for. The other day I was so fed up I was ready to quit for good. Then I read your story and thought: Somebody's paying attention. Maybe it isn't such a waste after all.

"I can never tell what you're thinking—you're pretty secretive—but I imagine you were worried the past month or so that I've had this. I want you to know that I didn't show it to anybody or talk to anybody about it. I want you to finish it. It'll be good for you in a lot of ways to get that story told. And, anyway, I want to know what happens."

He smiled a little and patted my arm, then walked past me to the door. I was basically speechless.

"Nelson . . ." He stopped in the threshold. The Spanish teacher had struck up a conversation with another teacher in the hall. Mr. Crisp glanced quickly at her, then turned back to me and spoke in a low voice. "Is my hairline that obvious?" A hand automatically flew to his head to make sure his thinning locks were properly placed to cover his balding spot.

A writer's job is to tell the truth, but even a writer needs to fib once in a while. "No, Mr. Crisp," I said comfortingly. "I never even noticed until I started writing about you."

He seemed relieved. He gave me kind of a crooked smile, went into the hall, and joined the Spanish teacher. She was tall in her stiletto heels and could look down on him from a height. He didn't want to be bald to her.

I stayed in the room until the janitor came. I sat in a random seat reading over some of the comments Mr. Crisp had made in my first composition book. They were written in red ink in his pinched handwriting that was good for margins. There were the usual grammatical corrections, but also remarks such as, "Excellent use of humor," "Evocative description," and "Where is this going?" There weren't any marks in the section in which I wrote about him. I looked up the part where I wrote, "He doesn't have much hair, just a few blond strands that he combs over the top," to see if there were any tears dotting the page or if the page was ripped out.

I didn't want the janitor to think I was bad and had to stay after school, so I left when he started to empty the wastebaskets. I wandered down to the gym to see if basketball practice was on so I could say hi to Tim. We hadn't seen much of each other since school began, although we had gone to a movie a few weeks before and had a burger afterwards. He asked me if I would help him with his physics homework sometime. Aghast, I asked why he was taking physics and he announced that he was planning to become a doctor. He practically had his first patient right there. A chunk of hamburger lodged in my windpipe and I nearly choked to death before it popped out onto my plate.

Some boys were playing basketball, but none of them was Tim. I went outside. It was raining lightly. Leaves were starting to appear on the trees. Another three months and it would be sum-

mer again, a whole year since we started to watch the Shooks'
house.

I waited for the bus with some kids I knew only from seeing
them in the halls. The bus wasn't coming, so they decided to
forget it and get something to eat. To my surprise they invited
me along. I said okay, but then I realized that if I went with them
I would get home late and there wouldn't be time to write anything that evening. Mr. Crisp would never find out what happened if I didn't apply myself. I said thanks, but that I had
something to do and maybe I'd join them another time. They
didn't seem crushed and quickly disappeared up the street toward
the local burger joint.

As usual, the minute I refused the invitation I regretted it. It
was really starting to pour. The bus still wasn't coming. Pretty
soon those kids would have seats in a dry restaurant with warm
food on the table in front of them. I was tempted to run after
them and say I changed my mind, but I didn't, even when it
started raining harder and the wind blew some down my collar.
They might soon have good company and full stomachs, but I had
something they didn't and maybe never would have. I had a
reader.

chapter eight

The Whore was back in town. I invited Cat to my house for a Monopoly party on Friday night, August 3, but she couldn't come because she was having dinner with the Whore and the Prick. She didn't sound enthused about it. The Prick was the First National Bank loan officer the Whore ran off with.

"Why are you having a party?" Cat asked.

"I don't entertain enough."

It wasn't going to be much of a party, just Tim and another kid from our class, Dave Larson, who I bumped into at the Reed College pool the previous Wednesday when I took Maude in for her weekly lesson. Larson was already a champion swimmer, having won several ribbons for his feverish backstroke. I thought his friendship would come in handy if I decided to try out for the Cleveland High swim team in order to link up with Tracy. This was not completely out of the question. I was a good swimmer, though not exceptional. I knew I would have to excel at some swimming oddity to get a place on the team. If I sounded out Dave on the deficiencies of the squad, I could do a little training before school started.

"I've got a bottle of tequila," Dave Larson said when I invited him over. I tried to imagine what my parents would say if they discovered that a tequila-Monopoly party was being held in the backyard, but I counted on them being too wrapped up in their own troubles to notice.

Cat was disappointed that she couldn't come to my party. "We're having dinner at some fancy-schmancy place. I have to get all dressed up," she said in a disgusted tone, although she was pretty dressed up as it was. She was wearing a camouflage-patterned army shirt tied at the waist and a pair of khaki culottes. Hiking boots and plaid knee-high socks were on her feet; on her head she wore a military cap. A Rocky and Bullwinkle pin was stuck on her collar instead of a service decoration.

"How long is the Wh . . . your mom staying?" I caught myself just in time, remembering that Cat slugged anyone who called her mother the "Whore," although Cat rarely called her anything else.

"Till Sunday. Maybe I could come over after dinner. When are you starting?"

"Seven-thirty or something."

"Dave Larson is cute," she said, perhaps thinking of him in his swim trunks. She said nothing about Tim.

"I'd like to meet your mom sometime."

"Why?"

I shrugged. "Comparisons." I glanced over at Maude. She was rolling in the sawdust under the teeter-totters with a little playmate. Not far off was a girl I'd seen before. She sat cross-legged under a tree, drawing on a big tablet. Her long dark bangs completely covered her eyes. We were at Berkeley Park for the thousandth time that summer.

"I think my mom is having an affair," I said suddenly. "I know my dad is."

"With who?" Cat seemed mildly interested. She shook a cigarette out of a pack. A skull and crossbones tattoo decorated the back of her left hand.

"With our doctor." I told her about running into Dr. Holt in the men's room at the Jolly Roger, then seeing him with my mother in the Captain's Bar. "It's just a guess. Maybe they were discussing new developments in the medical field."

As usual, Cat didn't get the joke. "Is that all adults do, fuck around?"

"I guess."

I hoped that wasn't all I would do in the future. It wouldn't leave much time for writing.

"You know what?" Cat said, blowing out a stream of smoke. "Sex is bullshit. Somebody crushing you to death and breathing their bad breath in your face. Grunt, grunt, oink, oink. It makes me sick."

She scratched a bite on her leg. The bite looked like she scratched it a lot.

"You mean Tim?" I asked, venturing into dangerous territory.

Cat tossed her L&M, still lit, to the ground. A woman minding three children came over to the swings where we were sitting and scolded Cat, telling her that a child could step on the cigarette and what was Cat doing smoking anyway? She wasn't old enough and it was bad for her health. Cat only stared blankly, as if catatonic. The woman ground out the cigarette and returned to the children.

"When you get right down to it," Cat continued a moment later, "he's just another horny, mad sex fiend who thinks his dick is the Washington Monument, the Statue of Liberty, and the World's Fair Space Needle all in one."

I found this hard to dispute and a silence fell. I looked over at

Maude. She was standing on her head in the grass, her dress down around her shoulders and her panties completely exposed. Oh, well.

"Was it that night I broke into the Shooks?" I asked.

"He started kissing me and stuff. Nothing serious, but then he got all hot to trot." She took out another cigarette, shot a glance at the woman who had yelled at her, returned the cigarette to the pack, and exchanged it for a pack of gum. "I'm trying to keep an eye on the Shooks' house in case you're being slaughtered and he's got his fat tongue down my throat so far I think I'm going to puke. And his hands all over me," she added, folding a stick of spearmint gum in her mouth.

"Before I know it, he's laying on top of me, bouncing up and down and sweating like a hog. He weighs a fucking ton. I mean, we've got our clothes on and everything, but he's acting like it's the real thing. Grunt, grunt, oink, oink. He was killing me. I couldn't breathe, so I shoved him off. You can guess the rest. 'Cock tease!' 'Rapist!' I hit him, he hit me. The treehouse was rocking back and forth. I thought it was going to fall out of the tree and kill us both."

"What do you expect? You took that bath with him."

"We didn't do anything in there. I didn't think he'd think of it that way."

"You were naked."

"That was fun. This was . . ." She stopped, scared to say she had been scared. With Tim's big bulk on top of her, she wouldn't have been able to defend herself if he had wanted to go further. In a moment Cat's pleasure turned to panic, the person she loved becoming a person she feared. There was such a faint line dividing the two. As I watched Cat rocking back and forth in the swing, it seemed that the three of us had crossed that line so many times this summer, and there were still weeks to go.

"Finally we got sick of yelling at each other and just went home," she continued miserably. "I crawled into bed with all my clothes on and just . . ." She didn't say what she just did. Then she did say it: "Cried."

To my surprise she started to cry right then. A small involuntary sob sounded in her throat and two tears dribbled down her cheeks, one on each side.

"Fuck! The first time I try eyeliner!" She wiped at the tears, making black smears under her eyes. "Since then he hasn't called or come by or sent me a death threat or called me a rusty cunt or anything," she said in between sobs.

I took an initialed handkerchief out of my pocket and offered it to Cat. This seemed like such a sophisticated thing to do that I felt strangely mature. I wondered if I should put my arm comfortingly around Cat or if she would knock me into the next century.

"I love him, but I'm only thirteen," she sputtered. "I shouldn't of let him do anything, but I just want him to be happy. He's so fucking miserable all the time. That stupid family of his, he could die and they wouldn't even notice till he started rotting and smelling up the place. What's wrong with being happy once in a while? Is there a law against it or something?"

She blew long and hard into the handkerchief and then examined the result. Across the park the girl with dark bangs was staring at us. I stared back, hoping to shame her into looking away, but she didn't.

"When was the last time you were really happy?" Cat asked, but didn't wait for my answer. "Back when you were six months old and sucking on your mother's tit? That's about the last time I remember and I don't even *remember* that!" I tried to remember my last truly happy moment. The time we went camping and sat by the camp fire was a possibility, but that was years ago. Then

I saw the Shooks' bright kitchen and Mrs. Shook busily cooking and chattering. I remembered the buttery taste of the pancakes and eggs.

"I think he just got a little carried away," I said. "Remember, he's already fifteen. He's more grown up in that way." I always seemed to be defending sex-crazed men, i.e., my dad, Tim.

"Maybe it's because I keep saying my mom is a whore, so he thinks I'm one, too," she went on. "She isn't really. I just say that. I mean, if you were really pretty and were married to a man who all he does is drink beer and watch the fights, wouldn't you run away, too? I think she really loves the Prick. I think the whole reason we're having this bullshit dinner is they're going to tell me they're getting married and ask if I want to live with them."

"Would you?"

"I don't know. I don't want to live, period."

"You don't mean that."

She didn't respond. She blew her nose again.

"I hope you don't move."

"They live in Bend."

We contemplated the name of this town, so far away in eastern Oregon. It had such a lonesome sound.

I reached out a hand to Cat. We were swaying a little back and forth in the swings, so I didn't know where my hand would land. It landed on her shoulder, with my fingers just touching the back of her neck. She didn't react, but she didn't shrug it off, either. Her hair was very short at the nape of her neck, but didn't feel stubbly. It was soft and fine. Her neck seemed terribly thin, the nubs of her spine especially fragile. I wondered what she thought about my hand being there, whether it felt nice or was just a weight.

.   .   .

The Monopoly party lasted until twelve-thirty. My parents had gone out to dinner at the Jade Garden and come back around eleven. My father peered out the den window into the backyard where we were playing, but he didn't tell us to break it up. About midnight all the lights went out in the house.

Dave Larson collected the green properties, I had the yellow ones, and Tim got the orange and red ones, so it was pretty even. Tim bought Boardwalk and I bought Park Place and neither of us would sell. Tim's work experience seemed to have improved his mathematical skills and he didn't need help managing his money as he usually did. Finally, when it looked like nobody was going to become a pauper, which is the whole point of Monopoly, we quit.

Tim and Dave polished off the tequila. I'd learned my lesson from the strip poker night and stuck to soda pop. Dave encouraged Tim to join the swim team because you got out of class a lot to go to meets. Tim thought that was an advantage but mentioned something about having to be "wet all the time" that didn't appeal to him. I mentioned that I was thinking of trying out for the team, but Dave didn't take me seriously. As he left, stumbling into the darkness, he told us that the following night he had a date with a girl named Tracy, a fellow swimmer who worked at the A&W. He knew a guy who'd already had a hand down her pants and was hoping for similar luck.

Tim stayed to pack up the Monopoly set. As neatness was not his hallmark, I assumed he had something on his mind. We talked about how Dave Larson was a jerk and it was always the jerks who seemed to have it made. I asked how Mr. Walsh was. Mr. Walsh was okay, but he thought Mrs. Walsh, the invalid, was going downhill. More and more Mr. Walsh was putting Tim in charge of the store. Hugo had gotten fired for selling uppers to a fourteen-year-old boy and there was a chance he would go to jail. Also,

just in the past week, Tim's brother Sam had gotten a girl pregnant and was being forced to marry her. Tim's parents were upset
because the girl wasn't Catholic. Sam didn't want to marry the
girl and was threatening to run off to Los Angeles with his band.
The summer was turning out to be eventful after all.

"Have you seen Cat?" Tim asked, carefully putting the property deeds in order, starting with Mediterranean Avenue.

"I saw her today. No, yesterday," I said, recalling her crying jag
and my small attempt to comfort her.

"Yeah?"

"She thinks the Whore and the Prick want her to move to
Bend with them."

"Bend. Jesus."

A car roared by out on the street. The neighbor's dog barked.
A light went on in our upstairs bathroom. The summer was more
than half over. I would be fourteen soon, in high school, not on
the swim team, have new friends, maybe meet a girl. I felt my life
pivoting, swinging around as if on hinges.

"She say anything about me?" Tim asked, removing a white
one dollar bill from a stack of golden five hundreds.

"She said you hadn't seen her lately or called her or anything."
I didn't know how far to go.

"I've been busy. My job."

"She told me everything that happened in the treehouse," I
said, going for broke.

"A little dry humping. So what?" I had never heard this expression before. I supposed it was self-explanatory, but wasn't sure.

"She said she loved you."

He grunted, but didn't answer.

"You should call her. It isn't right to just dump her. She's got
feelings, even though she tries to hide them. She was scared,

that's all. She's only a kid. You don't have to go steady with her. Just be kind to her."

Tim reached up under his T-shirt and scratched his armpit. A toilet flushed inside my house, then the light went out in the bathroom.

"Yeah, well, I should get going," he said, not moving. He picked at a Band-Aid on his right index finger. It was a child's Band-Aid with stars and comets on it. "I just feel sometimes . . . ," he started to say, then didn't continue. He peeled off the Band-Aid. There was a purple slice across the underside of his finger. He held it up close to his eyes to examine it, then he replaced the Band-Aid.

"I feel sometimes like I'm going to explode. You ever feel like that, Nelson? Like you're going to explode?"

It was a difficult question to answer. Yes, sometimes; and no, maybe not in the same way Tim meant. I assumed that Tim felt he might explode in some kind of sexual way. I didn't feel exactly that, but I could certainly imagine myself someday dashing Maude's pretty head against a brick wall and walking away without a backward glance. If Tim's way of exploding was a little dry humping, there were worse things in the world.

Maybe there was more to it than that. I wished I knew exactly what Tim meant, but I doubt he knew. It was one of those unexplained feelings that perhaps you go through your whole life feeling but never fully understanding. It would be interesting to explode just once to know what it felt like, but I probably never would. Maude was, generally, pretty safe with me.

When Tim left that night he shook my hand. This was a strange gesture, a little on the formal side, but I suppose it was meant as a thank you or a sign of affection. He had a broad hand and a firm grip. The Band-Aid with little stars on it added a whimsical note to the handshake.

Tim doesn't appear in this book anymore, except very briefly toward the end. It's not that I never saw him again. We still sometimes went swimming or for a bike ride or to a movie. And, of course, I saw him at the Little Store where he soon worked six days a week and which was indispensable in my life. He paid back the money he owed me and tacked on a little interest, too. He called Cat and they continued to see each other until school began, but they broke up after that. I never asked, but I doubt if there was any more dry humping that summer.

I see Tim at school, although we don't have any classes together. He joined the basketball team which, I guess, he felt was a dryer sport than swimming. The team was so good they went to State, but didn't win the championship. Tim now has a steady girlfriend named Lisa who looks weirdly like him. They're almost twins, both with dark hair, thick eyebrows, and glasses that they slip on only when they think nobody is looking.

Tim didn't exit from my life, just from this book except for a couple of small parts at the end. But never again did I come so close to finding out what was inside my tall, gloomy friend as that night when he told me, "I feel sometimes like I'm going to explode." I don't know for sure, but I don't think he ever has exploded. You tend to hear about that kind of thing. It gets in the papers.

Tim was very important in my life from sixth grade until the time I'm writing about, the summer between grade school and high school. He was someone to whom I could feel superior on days when I needed to feel superior to someone and someone I could admire on days I needed someone to look up to. He was a flexible friend in that way, and that's what I needed. I don't know what he saw in me, but I hope it was something like what I saw in him.

As I have said before, I never thought we would be friends for

life. I don't know if I have any friends now who will be friends
for life; probably I haven't met my friends for life yet. But for
those three years that Tim was my closest friend, I couldn't have
had a better or a closer one. I'll always wonder how Tim is and
worry about him a little, maybe even when he's forty. This is not
a bad thing, I think, and is what being a true friend is all about,
even when the true friends have drifted apart.

The note read:

> *Dear Nelson,*
>   *We have gone to the hospital. Bobby isn't doing*
> *very well and we want to spend every moment with*
> *him, even if he doesn't know we're there.*
>   *Chuck says please don't worry about the wall.*
> *It will get done sometime.*
>   *Behind the door is a little present for you.*
> *Best wishes,*
Bridget Shook
> *P.S. I didn't choose the title.*

The note was attached to the screen door with a piece of tape.
Mrs. Shook's handwriting was rounded and feminine and she
wrote in straight lines even though the notepaper was not lined.
Behind the screen door was a small manila envelope. It contained
a thin paperback book with a drawing of a vase of flowers on the
cover. The title, which she didn't choose, was *A Bouquet of
Poems.*

I read it on the bus going downtown. There were twenty-four
poems, most of them not longer than a page and many were only
half a page. The poems rhymed, as Mrs. Shook had told me, and

mostly spoke of love and nature. One of them, "Boy in a Tree," was about Bobby. It told of a mother who tried to get her son to come down out of a tree, but he refused and wouldn't say why he stayed up there. It was getting dark and, although she pleaded with him to come inside, he still remained in the tree.

I liked Mrs. Shook's poems, especially this one. It was a relief to like the poetry, because I knew she would ask me what I thought and this was not a time for stinging criticism. She chose her words carefully and sometimes had beautiful ways of describing the rain or a sunrise. The book felt good in my hand and seemed just the right number of pages. I'd never known anyone who had written a book, even a book that was privately published. I felt proud to know a poet and would try to remember to tell her so.

It was Saturday morning and I had no responsibilities. The lawn was cut, my room was clean, and Maude's was picked up. Maude had been dropped off at a baby-sitter's house because my mother had errands to run. My father was spending the day at a stamp collector's convention.

I went to a movie, but it was a stupid comedy and I wasn't in the mood. I roamed the bookstores, but couldn't find anything to buy. I tried to think of a friend to call, but Cat was with the Whore, Tim was working, and I didn't think Dave Larson liked me so much he'd want to get together so soon after the tequila-Monopoly party. I didn't know quite what to do with myself.

The sob story I gave the bus driver almost brought him to tears. He was a big, cheerful Negro man who said, "Good day, ma'am" and "Step carefully" to every woman getting on and off the bus and asked each man the score of a baseball game that was in its final innings thousands of miles away. I felt guilty lying to him, but I needed him to make a special stop near Greenpark Hospital.

I told him my brother had been in a car accident and even

though I knew he would be all right, both of his eyes were bandaged. He wanted me to come read to him (a fat novel was conveniently tucked under my arm) so he wouldn't be scared. Even I had to blink back tears at this tender story. The Negro bus driver looked at me with a combination of sympathy and pride and told me that "family is everything in the world" and that I was to "take good care." He stopped at the side of the road just two blocks from the hospital. Cars were honking behind the bus, but he paid no attention. "I'll say a prayer for him, son," he called to me as I stepped down on the shoulder of the road. This was certainly kind, but a little beyond the call of duty. After all, I had ridden free on my student pass.

A little shop in the lobby of the hospital sold flowers. All of the bunches looked slightly faded, but I bought one anyway. I tapped on the doorjamb of Bobby's room. Mrs. Shook was sitting beside the bed, dozing. The book in her lap was about to slip to the floor. She heard my knock and looked up in gentle surprise.

"Nelson."

"I brought these."

I offered them awkwardly. They were wrapped in blue tissue paper, which crinkled loudly in the quiet room.

"You didn't have to do that." It didn't occur to me until then that Mrs. Shook had given me *A Bouquet of Poems* and here I was, five hours later, giving her a bouquet of flowers. She smelled them. "They're lovely."

I looked at Bobby. He looked about the same, but now he took very long intervals between breaths and there was a gurgling sound in his throat that did not sound promising.

"How is he?"

"Oh . . ."

Certainly he was dying. Even if he didn't have those long gasps between breaths, that gurgle in his throat, and such pale, almost

skinless skin, I would have known by Mrs. Shook's single "Oh."
She had aged in the two weeks since I broke into the house. Her
face was puffy and gray glinted at the roots of her hair. A wrinkled,
wet handkerchief poked out from her sleeve.

I put a hand on her shoulder. These days I was putting a lot
of hands on a lot of shoulders, but it gave me something to do.
Her shoulders were hunched forward and her back curved with
exhaustion, but I could feel her pulse beating steadily below my
fingers. She reached up and put her hand on mine. It was very
soft—a homemaker's hand, a mother who takes care of her retarded son's hand.

Mr. Shook came into the room during this tableau. He carried
two cardboard cups of coffee and had a newspaper tucked under
his left arm. He insisted on going right back out to get me a soft
drink. He appeared restless, so I let him go even though I wasn't
thirsty. After he was gone a nurse came in, turned Bobby on his
side, and wedged some pillows under his back and buttocks to
help his circulation. The nurse offered to put the flowers in water
and Mrs. Shook thanked her. They looked better in a vase, but
I suspected they wouldn't last more than a day.

"I liked your poems," I told Mrs. Shook when the nurse was
gone.

"You read them already?" She seemed surprised.

"I liked the one about the boy in the tree the best."

"That was published in *The Oregonian*. It was a while back,"
she added sadly, as if all writing triumphs were behind her and
now life offered only daily vigils at the bedside of her dying son.

"They were all good. I'd like to read some more," but she didn't
say whether there were any more to read. Then a minister came
in the room. I felt in the way and moved to a corner. He leaned
over Mrs. Shook and put his hand on her shoulder in the same
place I had put mine. He whispered to her and I concentrated

on something else so as not to overhear. Soon Mr. Shook came back into the room carrying my Pepsi. He glared at the minister who was making Mrs. Shook cry. The minister came over to Mr. Shook, took his hand, and held it for a long time. Mr. Shook wiggled impatiently as the minister murmured words of hope and everlasting life. "Yes, yes, of course, thank you very much," Mr. Shook said automatically. In the months Bobby had been in the hospital there must have been many visits from the minister like this.

Then we were alone again. I drank my Pepsi. Mrs. Shook sipped her coffee. Mr. Shook sat heavily in a chair and tossed his newspaper to the floor.

"Vultures."

Mrs. Shook sighed. "He's just trying to help."

"He can help by staying the hell away."

"I know you don't believe, Chuck, but I do, so please . . ."

"How does he know Bobby's going to be at rest?" Mr. Shook interrupted angrily. "Has he died and come back to life? He doesn't know any more than we do."

Mrs. Shook didn't respond. She warmed her hands on her coffee cup. It was time to go.

"Well, I just came by to give you those," I said, stepping up to the foot of the bed. Mrs. Shook thanked me for coming and for the flowers and I thanked her for the poems. I told Bobby to take care, although it was hard to see how he could accomplish this.

"I'll drive Nelson home," Mr. Shook said, heaving himself to his feet.

"I'm okay," I said, but Mr. Shook was already fishing deep into his pocket for his keys and I could tell he wanted to do it. He was a man more suited for building retaining walls than sitting hour after hour in a hospital room.

"Come see us again," Mrs. Shook said. She clutched at the hardbound classic in her lap as if it was a life preserver and she was far out at sea. The backs of her hands were spotted and the veins close to the surface. Her nails had been painted with pink polish, but were chipped.

I walked over to her and hugged her a little. It was awkward and not one of the world's great hugs, but she patted my back as if she appreciated it. She also made a "Mmmmmm" sound, a kind of purr, which made me think it had been a long time between hugs. She smelled of a kind of flower. I want to say violets, but I don't know my flowers.

"They don't do any damn good. All they do is upset her even more. It won't be long now. Why can't they just leave us alone?" We were driving fast along McLoughlin Boulevard. This was my first time in the De Soto. It had push-button gearshifts, which I longed to push, but Mr. Shook didn't offer them to me.

"If you were God, would you choose that man to represent you? I wouldn't hire that man as a nail salesman. Well, I don't think there's a God anyway. If there is, He should be fired and somebody more organized should take over. Look at the paper," he said, hitting it with his forefinger. It lay on the seat between us. I looked down and saw a story about trouble in Africa. "I used to believe in God. My mother was Lutheran, very religious. She used to sing hymns. But she's dead and buried. Maybe there was a God once, but He either got old and died, too, or just so damn sick to death with human beings He left us to fend for ourselves."

We came to a stoplight. I thought maybe Mr. Shook would want to go to the lumber mill to roam the aisles and talk to the clerks, but it looked like we were going right home. The light changed and he stepped on the accelerator. When he spoke again he no longer sounded angry, just tired and sad.

"Poor Bobby. I guess I won't have any trouble keeping busy, but God knows what Bridget will do with herself all day long. I can see her going right around the bend. Shut herself inside and never go out. Reading books. Books, books, books." I remembered Mrs. Shook clutching that world classic tight in her lap as if it would save her. "I might get a job. Doing what I don't know." He stopped talking for a moment. Maybe he was thinking about the lumber yard, how he wished he had it back. "We could travel. All these years we've never traveled. But . . ." He trailed off, making the idea of traveling sound a near impossibility.

"Poor Bobby," he repeated. "He had a lot of love." And then we pulled up in front of my house. I didn't need to tell him which house it was; he knew. The house looked deserted. Neither car was in the driveway. Maude must still be at the baby-sitter's, I thought, and reached for my key.

"That was a nice thing you did today, Nelson. Don't you worry about the wall. You did your duty. Don't think you have to come over every Saturday of your life to help me. You've got better things to do. Of course, I'd always be glad to see you and I know Bridget feels the same. You're always welcome, but you should be out having fun. You're young and you should take advantage of it. It doesn't last forever."

He wasn't looking at me as he said this; he stared straight ahead, out the windshield and up the street. If I lived to be eighty would I ever feel such a huge sadness as Mr. Shook felt as he sat in the car that day, with no place to go but back to the room in which his son was dying? Well, I probably would, whether it was my own son who died or my mother or my father or Maude or Cat or someone I hadn't met and didn't love yet.

"Guess I'd better be getting back to the hospital," he said, and I opened the car door. I wanted to say something, but was afraid that anything I said would only make it worse. Anyway, before I could think of a kind or comforting phrase, he spoke again. "If you ever need anything, you know where to come. I mean that sincerely. Whether it's money or anything."

"Thanks, Mr. Shook. I'll see you," I said, and meant it.

The next day at about six o'clock in the evening I suddenly had the feeling that Bobby was dead. This feeling was so unexpected and sure that it scared me. I tried to concentrate on a book, but kept reading the same paragraph over and over. I was so silent at dinner that my mom asked if I was still having those headaches. My dad looked at me as if he'd never seen me before. I excused myself as quickly as possible.

I waited until eight o'clock to call the hospital. The operator transferred me to Bobby's floor and I asked the nurse who answered if Robert Shook's condition was still stable. She replied, "Are you a relative?" and when I said I wasn't she refused to tell me anything.

"Can you just tell me if he's alive or not?" I asked. "I think maybe he died." After a moment, during which my hand trembled so badly the receiver rapped against my ear, she confirmed that Bobby Shook died at four-fifty that afternoon, August 5, 1962.

I never wanted to be Bobby Shook the way I sometimes wanted to be Tim or Dave Larson or a number of other boys to whom girls were attracted or who could do more than three pathetic pull-ups in gym class. But if I had to be someone with a short, miserable life, Bobby Shook had about as good a short, miserable life as you could get. He was loved. His parents thought the world of him. His mother tried to teach him his letters and numbers and cooked him three square meals a day. His father sold his business to take care of him. His parents only put him in the hospital when they couldn't properly take care of him at home, then sat by his bedside until the end. True, kids laughed at Bobby and imitated him, but everyone gets laughed at now and then and isn't imitation supposed to be the sincerest form of flattery? I'll never forget how happy he looked walking down the street, his parents on either side of him and his arms flying every which way.

I would rather have been Bobby than be either of his parents, who now had to live all alone in that falling down house with no one to take care of or worry over except each other. I guessed Mr. Shook to be about sixty and Mrs. Shook a little younger. If they only lived to their seventies, that still was a long time ahead. Mr. Shook said he would be able to keep himself busy, but I wondered about this. How many retaining walls can a man build? He could reroof the house, but that wouldn't take ten years. Nor would cleaning the gutters. He spoke of getting a job, but I doubted that Foster Lumber Mill would want him back. He would have too many ideas about how the place should be run and how much more efficient it was in his time. It was hard to imagine another line of work that a sixty-year-old man could go into when he had sold lumber and hardware all his life. I thought of the cheerful Negro bus driver and could easily imagine Mr. Shook driving a bus, telling people to watch their step and to move to the rear. He seemed happiest when he was on the move and perhaps a bus-driving career would be the solution. Otherwise, I couldn't think of a single job he might get.

Mrs. Shook, of course, could take up her poetry writing again, but would that really use up a whole life, day after day? She liked to read, but even I wouldn't want to read all day long, year after year. There was sewing and quilting, which she also liked to do, but ten or fifteen years' worth of quilting is a lot of quilts. Mr. Shook mentioned traveling, but I couldn't see the two of them on a windjammer cruise or camping in the Petrified Forest. I remembered the despairing tone he used when he talked of traveling. No, they would never travel.

How scared they must be, I thought, with all this time to fill and nothing to fill it with. As frightened as I was at having my whole life ahead of me and not a clue in which direction it would go or if I would ever be content, the Shooks must be a thousand times more frightened than I. I wanted to help them, but all I could think to do was to break the incessantly ticking clock in their dining room. Perhaps they wouldn't notice how slowly time passed if each second wasn't announced so loudly.

What I did, instead, was shop for sympathy cards. Maude and I went to four stationery stores and one drugstore before we decided on the right card. Maude didn't know what sympathy was and when she asked I explained it badly, but she liked the pretty pictures of flowers that decorated most of the cards. She didn't care for the ones with crosses and neither did I. I tried to find a card with a nice poem inside, but after reading twenty or thirty of them they all started to sound alike. Finally, I let Maude choose. The card she chose had a picture of sunbeams shining down on bright yellow daffodils.

At lunch I wrote a personal note on the card. I said that Bobby was a lucky boy for having such loving and devoted parents, that I thought he had been as happy as he could possibly have been, and I hoped that comforted them a little. Maude and I mailed the card at the post office, then I bought a paper and looked for Bobby's death notice. It was there, but there was no word of a funeral service. I wondered if the Shooks would cremate him at Maude's favorite crematorium, but I suspected not. They weren't the cremating type.

Later that day we ran into Cat and the Whore in the founda-
tions department of Lipman's. Maude spotted them from the
escalator and we snuck up on Cat as she was examining a pale
peach bra. She looked like she wanted to strangle me with it.

"Hi, Cat! We bought a simpatty card!" Maude exclaimed. She
was always happy to see Cat. Cat was her hero.

The Whore didn't look at all whorish. In fact, she was very
elegantly dressed, which was surprising for someone who lived in
Bend. I guess I had pictured her as one of those barroom ladies
in Western pictures who wearily take men to the rooms upstairs
and, when a fight breaks out, smash a vase over the head of one
of the bad guys. Instead, she wore a white linen suit and a matching hat, which sat like a small drum on her head. Her hair was
light brown like Cat's, but it was full and shiny and curled below
her ears. Her eyes were brown, also like Cat's, she had a fine nose
with sculpted nostrils and a wide, lipsticked mouth. Her neck was
long and would have been nice to touch.

"This is my mom this is my friend Nelson," Cat said without
punctuation. She quickly stuffed the bra into its box and put it
back on the shelf. The Whore took my hand. It was a thin, cool
hand, a nice hand if you were sick and needed a hand on your
forehead or cheek. "That's Maude," Cat added grumpily as the
bra box slipped off the shelf and she had to retrieve it from the
floor.

The Whore beamed at Maude and crouched down to her. She
did this with such grace that I suddenly remembered the Whore
had once been a runner-up for Miss Oregon in the Miss America
pageant. She had lost, but looked as though she could win today.
"Maude, would you like an ice cream sundae?" she asked as if the
answer might possibly be no.

We went to the coffee shop on the mezzanine. The Whore
held Maude's hand on the escalator and Maude chattered happily

to her, delighted to have another fan. Cat, as usual, insisted on riding the rubber railing, which was against the rules. She whispered that the Whore and the Prick were getting married at the end of summer and she was going to be the bridesmaid. As Cat had predicted, the Whore asked Cat to come live in Bend and Cat said she would think about it, but she guessed she would stay with her dad because she didn't want to go to school with a bunch of "yahoos and cowboys." The Whore bought her several expensive dresses and tried to take her to a beauty salon to get her hair and nails done, but Cat balked at that. Cat asked how the Monopoly party went and I said fine. She asked if we talked about her and I said no, though of course we did. She seemed a little disappointed. "Does Dave Larson know who I am?" she asked worriedly.

Cat adored her mother, that much was clear over our ice cream sundaes. She barely took her eyes off the Whore the entire forty-five minutes we sat in the clattery cafe. She didn't say a word and only picked at her butterscotch sundae. Maude carried on an endless stream of conversation that held the pretty lady in the white hat rapt and left Cat free to gaze at her mother. She was probably wondering if she should sacrifice going to school with yahoos, whatever they were, to live in the same house with the woman she loved more than anyone in the world. I'm sure she was thinking back to her small, depressing home across the street from a burnt-out house and down the block from some people who kept a busted car on their lawn. And inside her house, her father watching boxing, drinking beer, and not looking up when Cat came into the room.

Yet I never heard Cat utter one bad word about her father and she rarely referred to her mother without calling her a whore. It was strange, but somehow understandable. Looking at her perfectly sculpted mother it was also understandable why Cat cut her own hair and wore men's sports jackets. The satin underpants with lace trim were also understandable. It all had something to do with love. It's hard to hate someone you love, even someone who runs off and leaves you when you're young and have no other resources. You really have to work up a good hate, maintain it, and stoke it or it will fade away. It needs constant attention, like a pet. Who has the time or the energy? It's hard to hate the person who hits you across the face and only speaks to you about the lawn. It's easier to love him, wait a while, and hope things will change.

We left them outside the revolving door of the big department store. They were off to do more shopping. The Whore took my hand again and said she hoped she would see me soon; perhaps I would come to Bend. She kissed Maude, who gave her a big hug. Cat said she would call me and then they walked away. They were a strange sight, the Whore in her perfect suit, Cat in oversized work pants with loops for hammers and wrenches, and a white shirt with blue piping and the name "Rudy" sewn on the pocket.

We waited until Friday to visit the Shooks. I was a little nervous about what I would say, so I brought Maude along. I didn't know if it was appropriate to come so soon, though Mr. Shook said I was welcome any time. But I wanted to see if they got my card and to make sure they were all right.

Maude was appalled that we were going up to the creepy house. She pulled back and whined. I tried to entice her by talking about the yummy cookies made by the nice lady who lived there, but Mrs. Shook sounded so much like the witch in Hansel and Gretel that had been read at Story Hour the previous Friday that Maude tried even more desperately to escape. I had to hold her under my arm and carry her up the steps. She cried and pounded my legs with her fists. I told her to behave or I would drop her in the ivy and the snakes would slither all over her. She wailed even louder.

I deposited her on the porch, straightened her dress, which had hiked up in the struggle, and tried to distract her by asking her to ring the quarter moon doorbell. She put her little hands behind her, horrified that I would ask her to touch the strange button. I held her by the collar or she would have run.

There was no answer to my first and second rings and I began to think no one was home. It was only when I was reaching for the bell a third time that I heard Mrs. Shook's heavy footsteps inside. The bolt thumped and the door opened a few inches on the chain lock. Mrs. Shook peered out through the screen, squinting at the bright daylight. Maude shrank back as if a gargoyle had appeared.

"Hi, Mrs. Shook. I just came by to see if you got my card and if you were okay. I don't want to bother you."

She slammed the door in my face. I suddenly realized that I was the last person she wanted to see: a pestering kid who only reminded her of how unlucky she was to have had a retarded son. I recalled Mr. Shook's fear that his wife would go crazy with grief; perhaps it had already happened. I felt ashamed for disturbing her, but Maude had never been so relieved in her life. She began tugging me toward the edge of the porch, anxious to return to the safety of the sidewalk. Then I heard the rattle of the chain lock and the door opened again. I turned back, gripping Maude tightly. When the witch reappeared, Maude whimpered and hid behind my leg. Mrs. Shook unlatched the screen door and pushed it open.

"That's so thoughtful of you, Nelson. Your card was lovely. Thank you. Chuck went for a drive, but he'll be back soon. Come in."

She looked tired and her hair was mussed. Her print dress was wrinkled. I guessed that she had been asleep upstairs and that was why it took her so long to answer. I wished I hadn't awakened her.

"Oh, we have some stuff to do. We just came by for a second. We don't want to bother you," I repeated. There was a sharp pang above my right wrist. Maude had bit me.

Then Mrs. Shook noticed the squirming child behind me. She took a step onto the porch in order to see her better. Maude cringed and buried her face in my ribs, her small frame quivering with fright. A vein in her neck beat against the back of my fingers.

Mrs. Shook assumed the little girl was playing peek-a-boo and a smile flickered at the corners of her mouth. It was a mouth that hadn't smiled in weeks and had almost forgotten how. Her upper lip was creased with small lines I didn't remember seeing before. Stale lipstick was caked on her mouth.

The smile grew and spread and Mrs. Shook began to look less tired. The little lip lines disappeared and other lines formed at the corners of her eyes as her cheeks pushed up toward her temples. Her eyes grew bright; they were such a pretty gray. She seemed a little younger than she had been the moment before.

"Why, this must be Maude!"

chapter nine

The summer was mine.

Maude trembled with fear as we walked through the terrible dark house, but all apprehension suddenly disappeared when we entered the sunny kitchen and Mrs. Shook produced a heaping plate of homemade cookies and cold, fresh milk served in a Howdy Doody glass. The glass won her over; Maude had a crush on the bizarre marionette.

She liked the cookies, too. Each cookie was completely different. One was decorated with multicolored sprinkles, the next with silver stars, another with thin shavings of white and brown chocolate, a fourth was shortbread cut in the pattern of a leaf. While Maude greedily devoured the cookies, Mrs. Shook went up to Bobby's room and gathered together some of his toys. Before I knew it, my sister and Mrs. Shook were down on the floor playing Candyland.

When Mr. Shook came home, Maude ran to me for protection from the terrifying giant. She abruptly reversed her opinion when Mr. Shook suggested we all get in the car and go to the zoo. The rest of the afternoon Maude barely gave me a glance or a word.

She was at her favorite place with her newest best friends in the world.

Mr. and Mrs. Shook couldn't take their eyes off Maude. They were delighted by the bright child, with her comprehensive knowledge of the animal species. Maude had listened to the recorded information played through the speakers in front of each cage so many times that she was a fund of facts. She chattered endlessly in her bright falsetto about the digestive system of snakes and the mating habits of turtles. After four hours of this I would start looking for a brick to bash in the little expert's head, but Mr. and Mrs. Shook were enchanted.

Then the Shooks offered to take us to a restaurant with a circus theme, a place I had been careful never to reveal to Maude, as we would then have to go there every day for the rest of our lives. I said it would have to wait until another time, as our mother expected us home. Maude pouted and tried to summon up tears. The circus restaurant was already her favorite place to eat even though she'd never been there. Mr. Shook cheered her up by promising that the very next time we came over to the house we would go straight to the circus restaurant.

"When will we see you again?" Mrs. Shook asked as we stepped out on the sagging porch, Maude clutching an emergency ration of cookies to keep up her energy on the three-block walk home.

"Tomorrow!" Maude volunteered excitedly.

"Tomorrow is Saturday, my day off," I reminded Maude, and she was so dismayed that her chin quivered and her eyes dampened. Perhaps she was thinking of the dull baby-sitter my mother had dumped her on the previous Saturday who had only one measly slide and two swings that didn't go high enough in her backyard.

"Come anytime you like," Mrs. Shook said and touched the sad little girl's cheek. "You don't even have to call first. Just come right over. I'm always home."

This invitation proved timely. The following morning as I was rinsing out my cereal bowl my mom told me that I would have to take Maude for the day. The baby-sitter was on vacation, my mother had errands to do, and couldn't get them accomplished with Maude along. I wondered if her errands included the humming doctor. She offered to pay me double-time, but wanted no argument. My father was gone for the weekend, fishing with some friends from work.

Panic set in at the thought that perhaps the Shooks had made other plans for the day. I took Mrs. Shook at her word that we needn't call first. I dressed Maude quickly, gave her a sliced banana in milk and some apple juice, which she promptly spilled on her dress, and hustled her out the door. Even my mom looked startled at the eagerness with which we fled.

They were home. Mr. Shook was downstairs puttering with the retaining wall and Mrs. Shook was boxing up some of Bobby's clothes to give to charity. She kept everything, she once told me, from his earliest baby clothes to the slacks he wore on his last trip to the hospital. She would box them and rebox them, never quite satisfied and never calling the Salvation Army to come get them. She knew it was wrong and only prolonged the agony, but she couldn't help herself.

They had no plans for the day. The circus restaurant, which Maude had not forgotten about, didn't open until noon, so I helped Mr. Shook with the wall while Mrs. Shook got the stain out of Maude's dress and then baked more cookies. She let Maude decorate them any way she wanted with sprinkles, walnuts, M&Ms, chocolate chips, and an icing gun, which, in Maude's hands, turned into a weapon. "She's a very creative child," Mrs. Shook whispered as she wiped pink frosting off the refrigerator.

Maude fell in love with the circus restaurant. She didn't even care if she ate; she was happy to ride the merry-go-round, which twirled in the center of the room, and sit on stools shaped like elephants and tigers. Over lunch the Shooks made suggestions of places we could go that afternoon: Jantzen Beach amusement park; Washington Park, where the rose gardens were in bloom; Alpenrose Dairy, which had ponies for Maude to ride (another place I had made sure she didn't know existed); or we could just take a long drive in the country. Maude, of course, wanted to go back to the zoo. Seeing my crestfallen face, Mr. Shook suggested, "We can take her, if you want to do something else."

"We'll take good care of her," Mrs. Shook added and I knew they would.

So, the summer was mine. Whatever I wanted to do, I could do without my little sister tagging along. Mr. and Mrs. Shook took her for part of every day and sometimes for the whole day. Occasionally I went with them, to the amusement park and on drives to rivers and lakes around the city, but often I let them go by themselves. Maude rode the ponies two or three times a week, something I never would have had the patience for, and she got to go to the circus restaurant whenever she liked. Mrs. Shook cooked for her and played Candyland for hours on end. Mr. Shook repaired Bobby's old training bicycle and taught Maude how to ride.

Some days I helped Mr. Shook with chores around the house. He had let so many things go since Bobby became ill. Although Bobby couldn't help with complex repairs, he could hand his father a wrench or a handful of nails and Mr. Shook had become used to the two of them, father and son, working side by side. When Bobby became too sick to perform even these simple tasks, Mr. Shook lost interest in maintaining the house. It was an old house and needed constant care. With me for company the duties were not as lonely and Mr. Shook drew up a long list of things that needed attending to. I learned how to fix a leaky faucet and to patch and plaster a cracked wall. We were regular customers at the Foster Lumber Mill. Other days I went off on my own and had a summer.

It was the solution to everyone's problems: mine, Maude's, my parents', who didn't want us around, and especially the Shooks'. No sooner had they lost their retarded son than the doorbell rang and they had a new son who was well, could talk about literature, and help replace a termite-eaten post, and an adorable daughter who enchanted them with her charm and enthusiasm. I think, for the month of August 1962, Bridget and Chuck Shook almost forgot they were the unhappiest couple in the world.

I intended to spend the remainder of the summer writing a novel that would be published and become a best-seller without my parents knowing it. I pictured their looks of mortification when a friend would approach them at a future cocktail party and say, "I read your son's book. It was wonderful. You must be so proud." I spent so much time thinking about this delightful scene that I didn't get any writing done for several days.

If I wrote ten pages every day until school began I would have a three-hundred page book. I settled on the spy story, which began with the intriguing scene of the Russians on the roller rink. I was a little vague about what they were doing there and who was spying on who, but I solved this problem by having Vladimir and Kreshnik as confused as I was. They had no idea who they were supposed to be watching and their orders were to keep rolling around the rink until something happened.

I figured that somebody would get shot, though by now I was so fond of Vladimir and Kreshnik that it couldn't be either of them. It should be somebody completely innocent, I decided, the last person in the world who would get plugged at a roller rink.

Then it came to me. A four-year-old girl is skating ahead of them. She is pretty and sweet in her dress with a pattern of yellow daisies. Vladimir and Kreshnik smile at her. She reminds them of their small daughters so far away in Moscow. Bang! She drops. The gunman flees. Vladimir and Kreshnik skate frantically after him. End of Chapter One.

I was off to a good start. I had written fourteen pages, it was some of the best writing I'd ever done, and I couldn't wait to begin Chapter Two. Plot ideas and notions for characters came to me without even trying. The words flowed. I bought a two-hundred-sheet pack of paper and a new ring binder. By the time school started, every page would be filled. My writing career had finally begun.

But I never wrote another word of my potential spy classic. I did something else with my summer, something that surprised me as much as Vladimir and Kreshnik were surprised at the little skater's assassination. I fell in love.

Our romance started in a classic fashion: I yelled at her. I was sitting at a picnic table in Berkeley Park, polishing my first chapter. The girl I had seen several times before, with dark shoulder-length hair and bangs that hung into her eyes, was sitting on the ground not far away, drawing on a big pad. Every so often she would look up and glare at me from under those thick bangs. It's hard to write while you're being glared at and I made a number of stupid mistakes. After an hour of this my concentration was ruined and my Chapter One a sea of smudges and cross-outs. Finally losing patience, I jumped up from the table and stomped over to her.

"This is a public park!" I shouted. "I have as much right to be here as you do! I'm sick of you giving me looks all the time. If you don't like me being here, fine. There's plenty of other parks. Just leave me alone!"

She stood without a word, angrily threw her big tablet at me, and walked quickly away, her head down and her shoulders hunched. She didn't have a limp, but she was the kind of girl who looked like she would have a limp.

The tablet struck me in the chest, one of its hard cardboard edges digging into my breastbone. I caught it awkwardly and the cover fell open. There, on the first page, was a delicate pencil sketch of two little girls playing on the merry-go-round. The artist had captured the fast spin of the carousel and the girls' excited faces and flying hair. One of the girls was Maude.

"Hey!"

I shouted to the fleeing artist, but she didn't stop. She continued walking as quickly as possible toward the exit. I turned the pages of the tablet. It was filled with sketches of park life, scenes that had become familiar from my many visits there that summer: elderly people sitting on a bench and chatting, mothers rocking newborn babies, kids playing on the teeter-totters and slide, dogs rolling in the grass. Each drawing was as fine as the first one, and as filled with the joy of expression. There were several more sketches of Maude, and lots of me. Me reading a book, me playing with Maude, me sitting with Cat on the swings, me asleep in the grass, me writing.

"Hey! Wait a minute!"

I ran after her. She was already out of the park and I knew if I didn't catch her now I would never see her again. I didn't even take time to grab my spy novel. I left the fourteen worked-over pages on the picnic table and when I remembered to go back for them that night, they were gone.

"Wait a minute, just a minute!" I shouted between gasping, slightly asthmatic breaths as I ran up behind her. For a girl who looked like she should have a limp, she moved at quite a good clip. "I'm sorry I said that. I didn't mean it. Here's your pad back." I held the sketchbook out to her.

She didn't take it, didn't look at me, and didn't speak. She turned up Rural Street, walking in the same slouched but rapid style. With her head bowed, her thick bangs completely covered her eyes. It was amazing she didn't walk into a tree.

"I really like your pictures. You're a good artist. I didn't know that was what you were doing. I thought the way you kept looking at me you were mad at me or something. My imagination kind of runs away with me a little. I'm a writer. I saw those pictures you did of me. Those are nice. Maybe I could buy one and give it to my parents for a present sometime." I didn't say that my parents would probably rather have a portrait of Khrushchev. I really just wanted it for myself. "My name's Nelson. What's yours?"

She didn't offer her name and quickly crossed the street. I ran ahead a little, turned and walked backwards in front of her so she could see my apologetic look, but she didn't lift her head. Below the curtain of bangs I saw a pale, round face and naturally pink lips. She was wearing a plaid cotton blouse and a wraparound skirt held together with a large gold safety pin. Her legs were thin and shapeless. She wore loafers with a penny stuck in a little notch on the top of each shoe, a weird but appealing decoration.

"I've seen you in the park a lot. I'm usually there with my sister. Oh, I like those pictures you did of Maude, too. My sister's name is Maude. I went to Duniway. Where did you go? I'm going to Cleveland next year, are you? I bet they have good art classes there. I want to be a writer. Oh, I said that. That's what I was doing when you were drawing me, working on a book. A novel. Shit, I left it there! Well, I'll go back for it later. Who'd want it, right?"

She didn't say a word, didn't slacken her pace, didn't give me a look. We were passing the Catholic school now and weren't far from the Little Store. The streets were strangely empty. It was one of the hottest days of the summer, nearly ninety-five degrees, and everyone seemed to be either indoors or out of town. When I left Maude with the Shooks they were trying to decide between a visit to the Clackamas River or yet another ride on the ponies.

"Don't you want your sketches back? You should save them. They're great. How long have you been drawing? Did you have a teacher who taught you how or is it just natural? I really like the one of my sister on the merry-go-round. My parents would love to have it." I had never bought artwork before and wouldn't know what to offer if she agreed to sell one or two of her sketches. I was hoping lavish praise would get them out of her cheap.

Her straight, nearly jet black hair had just a tiny bit of red in it, which caught the sun. Her arms were as bony as her legs. She looked undernourished and frail, although I was the one breathing hard and struggling to keep up.

"Listen, I really feel bad for yelling like that. I've been kind of tense this whole summer. Puberty." A short, abrupt laugh popped out of me. "That's what they tell me. I think it's the onset of madness." "The onset of madness" was a peculiar phrase to come up with at that time. I was acting more and more strangely. I had never followed a girl before, never been so persistent when it was obvious the girl had no interest in me. I could not understand my behavior or control it. Perhaps it was the onset of madness after all.

"Would you like to stop and have a Coke with me or a milk shake or something? I'll buy. I hate losing my temper like that and I'd like to make it up to you. I mean, you shouldn't yell at somebody who does nice drawings of you and your sister. I'm usually more polite than that. There's a place right up on Woodstock. It's just a few blocks. I've got plenty of money if you want something to eat, too."

We reached a major intersection. A bus was coming with a few cars trailing behind it, so she had to wait to cross the street. She breathed an irritated little sigh. She stared at a broken pop bottle in the gutter. When she finally spoke, she didn't turn toward me, but kept her head lowered and her eyes veiled by the long bangs.

"Do you always talk so much?"

Her voice was soft and with the bus roaring by I almost didn't catch her first words to me. She fingered her drawing pencil, impatiently waiting for the string of cars to pass. Her fingers, like the rest of her, were slender, but had oversized knuckles and long fingernails coated with clear lacquer.

"No, I don't talk that much at all. I mean, compared to other people. I have this friend Cat, you wouldn't believe it. And my little sister, my God, sometimes my ear about falls off! No, I'm a writer, so I write a lot and talk just a little. This is real unusual for me to talk so much, but it's because I feel so bad about screaming at you like a maniac. What about the Coke or the milk shake? If you haven't had lunch, they have good burgers at the Arctic Circle and it isn't far. I won't talk the whole way there, I promise."

Looking back on it from a distance of almost a year I realize I was already in love, although this didn't become official for another week. What else could explain my extraordinary actions? I'd never impulsively asked a girl to have a hamburger with me. It took me almost a month to get up the nerve to ask Carolyn Messinger to the May Day dance. When I did she said, "No thanks, Norman," and I didn't even have the courage to correct her. All of a sudden I was aggressive and determined, unwilling to take no for an answer. Love was the only explanation for this irrational conduct.

"That's okay," she said in an almost inaudible voice.

"Great!" I answered enthusiastically, completely missing her meaning. "It's just a few blocks away."

"I mean, you don't have to buy me anything. Just give me my pad back and it's okay."

Her eyes never rose from the sidewalk. She remained hunched over, like a waif expecting a beating.

"Well, I'm kind of hungry, I don't know about you. I was going up there anyway. Why don't you come along?" I wasn't in the least bit hungry; in fact, I was so excited I thought I might vomit.

"I'm busy."

"Did you have lunch? You should eat something," I suggested, sounding more like Mrs. Shook than myself.

"Just give me my pad back." She reached for it, but I held it away from her and took a step backwards. If she wrestled me for it, I was sure I would win. She was probably the only person in the world I could pin.

"Over lunch."

She sighed that weary little sigh again. This, I guessed, was not the happiest child on the face of the earth. I wondered what twisted family she came from and if hearing about it would make me feel better about mine.

"I'm not hungry."

"Just have a Coke."

"I can't because of my teeth." Since she barely opened her mouth when she spoke, I couldn't see what her teeth were like.

"A milk shake. It's good for you. It's milk," I insisted.

She put a hand on the back of her neck and looked so sad at the thought of having a milk shake with me that I almost let her off the hook. But at that moment she gave in.

"If you promise to give me back my pad."

"Scout's honor," I promised, although I was never a Scout.

Her name was Shane, named after her mother's favorite movie. The fact that her mother named a baby girl after a Western hero indicated that she had parents as deviant as mine. In fact, she only had one parent. Shane was illegitimate. Her father never married her mother and deserted her before Shane was born. The child was named Shane because, at the end of the movie, Shane drifts away, never to be seen again.

I pulled this information out of her bit by bit, assaulting her with a battery of questions. Otherwise we would have sat at the soda fountain in grim silence. She never willingly offered a word. Every fragment had to be coaxed out of her and was spoken in a wistful tone as if her life story bored even her.

"Do you think you'll ever meet your dad?"

"No."

"Don't you want to?"

"No."

She spoke so softly and without opening her mouth that I was forced to lean toward her to catch these brief, mumbled responses. This quality, so annoying in others, made Shane as mysterious and elusive as her namesake. I had yet to see her eyes. Any glance at me was the quick look of a frightened animal and then her head ducked down again.

She had gone to the Catholic school, although she wasn't Catholic, because her mother wanted her to have a better than public school education. In September she would attend a high school on the other side of town that had a special art program. Her mother had to apply to the school board for permission and it was granted because of Shane's talent. She also took art classes at the museum downtown and after high school planned to go to a commercial art school in Chicago. She was hoping to get a scholarship, because it was expensive. Her mother worked for the phone company.

We didn't talk about the drawings. The pad lay meaningfully on the counter between us. I wanted to open it and look closer at the sketches of myself, but I was afraid she would think I was vain. I could understand why she would want to draw Maude; Maude was very drawable. But why so many studies of me? I tried not to be flattered by this, but couldn't help but be, a little.

I told her that my parents were possibly getting a divorce, but didn't go into the details of their love life. And I spoke about my writing, so she would know that I was a fellow artist. We shared some French fries.

I walked her home. She lived not far from Cat's house, but on a more attractive street. It was a small house with a low rusted iron fence surrounding the front yard.

"Thanks for the Coke," she said. She had ordered a Coke, despite her teeth. Perhaps she didn't want to overburden my finances by having a milk shake, or maybe she didn't want to be beholden to me for more than a dime.

"You want to do something tomorrow?"

"I have to work." She worked three days a week at Mode-O-Day, a dress shop.

"What about Friday?"

"I have class."

"Friday night?" I persisted.

She took a long time to answer. With her head permanently bowed she looked slightly Japanese. She was actually Irish.

"Go to a movie or something?" I suggested helpfully.

Her answer was so quiet I nearly missed it. "Okay," she said without looking at me and quickly opened the squeaky gate, latched it, and went up the steps to her house.

It wasn't until late that night that I realized I had my first date. The fact that I had yet to see Shane's entire face made the date seem even more romantic. It reminded me of tales of arranged marriages in which the bridegroom only views his bride at the wedding ceremony when he lifts the veil to kiss her for the first time.

But romance soon gave way to terror as a thousand questions crammed my mind: What should I wear? Should I choose the movie or ask her opinion? If she chose something I'd already seen, should I pretend not to have seen it or say I'd love to see it again? During the picture, should I try to hold her hand or put my arm around her?

Each question raised more questions: If I tried to hold her hand, should I hold it during a tense moment or a romantic one? What is the proper length of time to hold someone's hand in a movie, a portion of the film or the whole thing? Two hours of hand-holding might bring on cramps, which would endanger her artistic career. But if I let go after ten or fifteen minutes, should I wait a decent interval and reach for it again?

I thought about asking Tim some of these questions. After all, he walked hand in hand with Cat in the park, so he had experience in these matters. But I didn't want Tim to know I was such a rookie that the thought of reaching for a girl's hand could bring me to the edge of mental collapse. Anyway, he was past holding hands; he was already into dry humping. I couldn't see this happening with Shane, at least not on the first date.

As it turned out, the movie was so exciting that I completely forgot to hold Shane's hand or slip my arm around her at all. She insisted on paying for the ticket with her Mode-O-Day earnings, but allowed me to buy her popcorn—a small box that she managed to make last through the entire three-hour re-creation of the D-Day landing. It was a relief to see a movie with someone who didn't gobble everything in sight and then throw up just when they were storming Omaha Beach.

Afterwards we strolled down Broadway in search of a place to have a Coke, but every restaurant looked so adult that we gave up and came back to our side of town. Shane was impressed by my encyclopedic knowledge of the bus schedules; beyond that, she didn't seem particularly interested in me. She wore the same slightly bored expression whether she was talking about her il-legitimate heritage or trying to choose between red licorice and popcorn at the movie concession stand.

I was becoming obsessed with her forehead. It was constantly hidden by that sheet of bangs. What if she was concealing a disfiguring mark or a tattoo? As we walked to the bus stop, I hoped a breeze would come up and blow the bangs aside for a moment, but none did.

When I dropped Shane off at her house, my anxiety returned: Should I try to kiss her? Should I ask for permission first or surprise her? If I was Shane, would I want to be kissed by me?

We stood on the sidewalk in front of her house. The house was dark; her mother was working the night shift. I could tell Shane didn't want to be alone and I hoped she would ask me in.

"Maybe we can go to another movie sometime."

"Okay."

"There's lots to see."

Our conversations were composed of short sentences with long pauses between them. Shane mostly looked down at the ground, although she would occasionally dart a glance up at me as if checking to see if I was still there.

"Are you working this weekend?"

"Tomorrow."

"Not Sunday?"

"Uh-huh."

"Maybe we could do something then."

Shane wasn't someone I would have thought I'd be attracted

to. Tracy, the aquatic A&W waitress, was the kind of girl I always coveted: gorgeous, unreachable. I couldn't fathom why Shane appealed to me and why I wanted to spend more time with her. All I knew was that I wanted to hug her, wanted to feel those spindly limbs in my arms. I was bigger than she was, a little taller and stronger boned. It felt good to be larger than someone; to feel, if there was trouble, that I could protect her. Ever since I met Shane I had been trying to figure out what she reminded me of. That night it came to me: a polio child.

"Did you ever have polio?"

"No."

"Me either."

A trickle of sweat ran down the back of my neck and under my shirt. The night was cool, so it was Shane who was making me sweat. Again I thought about taking her hand. We had never touched, not even a casual brushing against each other in the theatre or on the street. But if I took her hand, I wouldn't know what to do with it, so I didn't.

"I better go in."

"Is your mom coming home soon?"

"I don't know."

She took a key attached to a large paper clip out of her bag. "Maybe you could pose for me sometime," she mumbled, then quickly added, "You don't have to." It was her longest sentence.

"Pose?"

"For a drawing."

"Oh. Sure." This was encouraging; it meant she wanted to see me again. I wondered if she meant posing in the nude. I wasn't sure I could do this without embarrassing myself.

"Well, thanks." She turned to go through the little gate, then stopped, turned back, and quickly glanced at me. I sensed that she wanted me to kiss her then, or at least try, but I waited a moment too long. By the time I jerked my head toward hers, she was already turning away to go up the path to her house.

I cursed myself on the walk home. The opportunity to touch Shane was lost, would perhaps never come again. Tears stung my eyes as I lay in bed that night. I wondered if I would ever grow up, ever be able to act without doubting myself, ever act simply from the heart.

It happened so naturally a week later that I was taken by surprise. The Shooks were planning a picnic lunch at Mt. Hood and I impulsively asked if I could bring a friend along. It surprised them, I think, that I had a girlfriend; I'd never mentioned Shane. Maude was jealous of my companion and huddled against the car door, a miserable scowl on her face. But when Shane made drawings and let Maude color them in, suddenly Shane was her dearest friend in the world. Maude admired Shane's long fingernails and stroked them tenderly—something I ached to do but had yet to find the nerve.

Snow still lay in little clumps on the mountainside and we discovered one large field of soggy snow in the shade of some tall Douglas firs. We made snow angels and then dried off in the warm sun while we ate sandwiches, homemade fruit cocktail, and chocolate cake. Shane drank coffee from Mr. Shook's thermos. He kept looking from Shane to me and from me back to Shane with a broad smile. Young love, I supposed he was thinking.

Later Shane and I took a walk. We stopped on the slope of the mountain under the ski lift. Tiny blue flowers grew randomly in the thick grass under our feet. One giant cloud strolled across the sky. A rat-a-tat-tat came from a nearby tree: a woodpecker. At that moment there was not one unbeautiful or less than perfect thing in sight and in the range of my hearing.

I needed someone to hold right then and it happened to be

Shane. I put my arm around her shoulders and she folded into me as if she had been waiting for this. Her body felt more substantial that I had anticipated. Yes, she was thin, but hers was a human body with weight and shape. Her small breasts were soft against my chest; I wouldn't have wanted them larger. Our heads rested side by side and her dark hair tickled the side of my face. My legs were trembling, but otherwise I was all right.

Her hands lay lightly on my back just below my shoulder blades. I hoped my back felt strong and protective. I turned my head toward hers and kissed her below her left cheekbone. I couldn't tell if her loud breathing meant she was excited or if it was simply that her nose was so close to my ear. I kissed her again between her mouth and cheek, where she might have a dimple if she ever smiled. She moved her hands, one to the angle of my shoulder blade and the other to the small of my back.

She lifted her head and touched her lips to mine. Our noses seemed to choose by themselves which sides they preferred. Her mouth was soft, but didn't make what I thought of as ordinary kissing movements. She didn't pucker her lips or produce any suction. She simply pressed her mouth against my mouth and parted her lips a little. I knew my eyes should be closed, but I opened one to see her expression. Her face was close and blurred.

A hand reached up and touched the back of my head. Her long fingernails combed through my hair, lightly scratching my scalp with their tips. It seemed a thing that would only happen to a star in a romantic movie, never to me.

Her tongue flickered into my mouth for an instant and then disappeared. I tried it next, but didn't know exactly what to do once I got my tongue in there. I rolled it around in her mouth for a moment, then pulled it out in case I was disgusting her.

Then we stopped kissing and just held each other a while. I worried about how we would end this, but after a time I felt her make a movement and I pulled away. My leg was falling asleep, anyway, from standing unevenly on the slope. I took her hand. It was surprisingly cold after our heated little episode, but I later found out she had permanently cold hands. A doctor told her it was poor circulation.

We walked a ways, saying nothing. From that little tongue flicker I guessed this wasn't her first kiss, but it was mine and I was a little numb from the experience. I worried if I'd done all right, if I should have made it last longer or something. But it seemed about the right length for the first one.

We rejoined the picnic. Mr. Shook grinned at us and looked knowingly at his wife. She swatted his hand and told him to behave himself and he laughed. Maude grabbed Shane's hand and pulled her off to show her something; I gathered it was a slug of monumental proportions.

"She's a nice girl," Mrs. Shook said, packing up the picnic basket. "I just wish she'd get that hair out of her eyes." Mr. Shook didn't say anything, but when we were walking back to the car, he put a hand on the top of my head and ruffled my hair a little.

"Who's that girl I keep seeing you with?"

"You mean Maude?"

"Ha-ha. Funny, Nelson," Cat said mirthlessly. We were on our way to Oaks Park for the afternoon, to ride the amusement rides and go skating again. The Shooks wanted to come along, but I had promised the day to Cat and I didn't think Cat and the Shooks would mix. Shane was working. It was the middle of August, a Thursday.

"I mean the girl you're going around with."

"Shane! She's neat!" Maude piped up.

"Shane? What kind of name is that?" Cat asked sourly, wrinkling her nose.

"It's Teutonic," I improvised, knowing it would shut her up.

"Huh." She shook a cigarette out of a crumpled package and lit up. We crossed the railroad tracks and headed down the slope to the park. Oaks Park was not a big amusement park, but the ride operators were lenient and allowed Maude to go on some of the scary rides if I rode with her. As far as Maude was concerned, the scarier the better.

"So are you going with her or what?"

"We're seeing each other," I hedged, knowing full well that hedging never worked with Cat.

"I know you're *seeing* each other. I didn't say you were blind, Helen. I said, are you going with her?"

"I guess. I like her. She's an artist."

"Oh, my, my!" The only picture I'd ever known Cat to draw was a crude sketch of a penis that she passed around history class and that got her sent to the principal's office.

I changed the subject to the Shooks. I said I'd become friends with them and wasn't that strange because I met them by breaking into their house? I told her about Bobby, about seeing him in the hospital and how he died. I described helping Mr. Shook build the retaining wall. I also told of our trip to Mt. Hood, but didn't say that Shane had come along and that we tongued each other under the ski lift. Before I could stop myself, I said that Maude, Shane, and I were having dinner at the Shooks that very evening, not thinking that Cat might like to be invited, too.

"You better be careful," Cat said under her breath.

"What do you mean?"

"Maude, run up and get three tickets for the Octopus," Cat

said, handing Maude some change in an unprecedented burst of generosity. "They could be child molesters," Cat continued when Maude had dashed up to the Octopus man.

"Come on."

"I don't believe that hoked-up story about meningitis. My aunt had meningitis when she was a kid and she was fine. I bet they poisoned Bobby with arsenic or something the doctors couldn't trace. There's lots of kid killers out there. I'm not worried about you. But Maude is a sitting duck."

I didn't try to hide my annoyance. It seemed as if Cat hadn't learned anything from the summer. I was already marked indelibly and would never look at things quite the same way, but Cat was still clinging to childish notions of murder and torture. For a moment I considered inviting her to the dinner, to prove once and for all that the Shooks were good people. But that would have been playing into Cat's hand, giving her just what she wanted, and for once I was not going to let her have her way. She had bullied me since we first became friends; it was my turn to have the upper hand.

Maude ran back with the Octopus tickets, shouting that she had persuaded the operator to let us ride until somebody else came along and wanted to get on. The park was almost empty.

"That's stupid," I said to Cat. "I know them. They're the nicest people I've ever met. I'd trust them with my life."

"That's just what they want. Your life. Or worse. You know, boys can get raped, too."

"Shut up. You're sick. Okay, Maude, let's go," I said, taking the tickets from her sweaty little hand. She was actually perspiring at the idea of being whipped around on the Octopus until she couldn't stand up straight.

I realized that Cat was jealous and lonely and simply wanted to be included. I sympathized—how many times had I desperately wanted to be a part of someone's plans and been ignored? It was a vulnerable time: Cat had lost her mother to another man and to a town far away, she had lost her father to the fights and she had probably lost Tim, as well. Now she was losing me, to the Shooks and to Shane, and she had no one else.

I felt sorry for Cat, but she had to be punished. Punished for going to Jantzen Beach with Tim on the Fourth of July, punished for spending time with him alone and leaving me with only a four-year-old for company, punished for the bath, punished for the dry humping. Well, now I would rub it in until it hurt that I had a girlfriend, was being taken on trips, and invited to dinner. Cat had to realize that I couldn't be taken for granted; that being my friend meant being my friend all the time, not just when it was convenient.

I loved Cat, otherwise there would have been no point in hurting her. I would rather have been Cat's boyfriend than Shane's, even though Shane was a more restful and feminine presence. But something in Cat touched me. Just the thought of those thin strips of bone in her chest was enough to make my throat feel tight. As long as I live I'll never forget how the back of her neck felt the day we sat in the swings and I tried to comfort her. No matter how many necks I touch, that will always be the best one.

The Octopus operator kept his word and whirled us around for a good ten minutes until two teenage boys wanted to get on. I felt nauseous, but Maude seemed stimulated by the experience and wanted to try the same thing with the Hammer, a torture device that threatened to dash its passengers' brains on the ground. I suggested the Haunted Mine and a little skating instead.

"When's the wedding?"

"Next weekend," Cat said with a groan. "I'm going there on the bus." I liked buses, but Cat hated the idea of sitting still for even five minutes, let alone enduring a three- or four-hour ride to Bend. "Mom wanted to tie ribbons in my hair, but it's too short, so I have to wear this crown of baby's breath. Have you ever smelt a baby's breath, especially after it's eaten Gerber's mushed peas and carrots?"

"How long are you staying?" I asked as we climbed into the cramped mine cart.

"School starts on Wednesday. I wouldn't want to miss that," she said sarcastically.

"What's the Pri . . . Your mom's boyfriend like?" I caught myself just in time.

"He tries too hard. Like talking about rock 'n' roll stars I don't give a shit about."

"Don't use that word around you know who." Our cart started up with a clank.

"My mom likes him. I guess that's what counts," she grudgingly admitted.

"How's Tim?" I asked as we rounded a curve and a vampire popped out at us.

"Why, did that remind you of him?"

"Stop talking!" Maude whispered.

"He's okay. He said he'd ride down on the bus with me and then turn around and come back, but that's stupid." Cat sounded slightly flattered by the offer and I'm sure she was tempted. "Anyway, they throw you off when you start calling each other 'cocksucker' and 'rusty cunt.' "

"Cat!" I reprimanded her again, but Maude was screaming at

the top of her lungs and probably didn't hear. If she starts swearing like a sailor around age six, I'm going to pretend I know nothing about it.

My parents had not met Shane. I didn't bring her to the house because I was supposed to warn my mother before I brought friends home and I didn't see her enough to warn her. She had begun taking landscape classes two nights a week. Another two nights she taught drawing and painting, but not at the art museum or I would have had Shane check up on her. I wasn't totally convinced my mother was really taking and teaching classes; I thought she might be spending her evenings with Dr. Holt.

My father was even less available. When he wasn't on a business trip, he spent his nights quarantined with my mother in the living room or den. When she was out, he played cribbage with his friends. They smoked, drank, and ordered in Chinese food. One night, shortly before the Shooks invited Shane and me to dinner, I ran into my dad in the kitchen where I was making myself a sandwich.

"Nelson . . ." He cracked open a metal tray and shiny slivers of ice scattered over the aqua drain board. He smelled of whiskey and chow mein. "Don't ever smoke," he said, a cigarette dangling from his mouth. He dumped the tray into a gold ice bucket and left the kitchen.

I wondered if my father would ever say anything to me that required more than three words. "Cut the grass." "Don't ever smoke." "Go to bed." I decided that if I someday had a son, I would try for longer sentences and perhaps a few positive ones.

I intended to tell my mother that Maude and I had been

invited to the Shooks' house for dinner, but she wasn't home the night of the invitation. A note was attached to the refrigerator with a ladybug magnet:

> *Nelson,*
> *Dinner is in the fridge. Just heat it up.*
> *Give Maude a bath. I'll be home early.*
> *Love, Mom*

Dinner was a large pot of ham and beans we'd had the night before.

I bathed Maude and dressed her in her best dress, one I never allowed her to wear on our daily wanderings. Cat's mention of the ribbon that wouldn't go in her hair made me think to tie one in Maude's hair. Maude was delighted with her appearance and couldn't stop looking at herself in the mirror.

I ironed a shirt and put on a pair of slacks. I ran next door and cut three roses from Mrs. Crow's garden hoping she wouldn't miss them and wrapped the flowers in newspaper. Maude and I met Shane on the corner and walked to the Shooks' house.

This is the memory I have of that evening: They treated us as adults. Not Maude, of course. She was treated as if she was the most special little girl in the world. But Shane and I were not children at the Shooks' table. We were equals. When we spoke, we were listened to. Our opinions were of importance.

Mr. Shook served us wine with dinner. Maude was annoyed that we got a pretty golden liquid in our glasses while she had to settle for everyday milk. Mr. Shook immediately took a fifth wineglass from the cupboard.

"Chuck!" Mrs. Shook was alarmed.

"She wants to taste it. A child's curiosity is a precious thing," he said, pouring a smidgen in Maude's glass. Fortunately, she found the wine revolting; a drunken Maude would have been a frightening prospect.

Shane looked pretty in a moss green blouse and a pleated skirt. Black tinted nylons gave her an exotic look. I know Mrs. Shook wanted to take Shane upstairs and whack off her bangs, but instead she asked Shane many questions about her aspirations in art. Mrs. Shook seemed a little recovered from Bobby's death. The lines in her face were not as sharply drawn and her hair had been recently styled and colored.

Mr. Shook got a little drunk, which made him more talkative at the table than usual. He still had that funny grin on his face whenever he looked at Shane and me, as if we reminded him of something pleasant from his past. He didn't envy our little love; he seemed proud of it and happy to be around us. After dinner he suggested he and I "leave the ladies" as if it was the nineteenth century and we were going into the study to smoke cigars and sip brandies.

We went out on the back porch and he lit his pipe. The sun was coming down a little earlier every night and by seven-thirty it was almost dark. An orange cloud hung in the west. Stars were switching on all over the sky.

"The moon always seems to be in a different place," he said, puzzled. We looked up at the pale three-quarter moon perched above a neighbor's chimney. "Have you ever noticed that? It's here, it's there. Sometimes it's low, sometimes it's high. It comes up early, it comes up late. Do you know anything about astronomy?"

"Not really."

"No, neither do I."

I felt I was letting him down. After all, I was the student and I should know these things. Then I remembered a simple fact.

"The moon revolves around the earth."

"Well, maybe that's why," he said skeptically, as if this couldn't possibly be the answer to the erratic patterns of the moon. I suppose he didn't really want an answer; he was content with having at least one or two mysteries left in his life. That moon, popping up in unfamiliar places and at unpredictable times, was something he wanted to be continually surprised by the rest of his days.

"I would give anything, anything on earth for Bobby to be here with us tonight."

He almost didn't get it out. I had never seen him cry or hold back tears, but now, three weeks after his son's death, he was breaking just a little. I looked away, letting him have his private moment of grief. I kept my eye on that stretched, orange cloud that was already darkening with the night.

"I'd give anything for you . . . ," he started to say, but that was as far as he went. Perhaps he felt it was wrong, with Bobby so freshly gone, to want me to be his son. I don't believe it would have been wrong to think that or to say it. Anyone would have felt the same. It was natural to want a normal boy, a son he could retire to the porch with, fix a faucet with, watch fall in love. I was flattered that it was me he had chosen and wished he would say more about it. But he didn't say any more that night and he never again spoke to me of these things. His sadness, like the trouble he got into in Butte and a thousand other parts of his life, he kept to himself. I doubt that he even let Mrs. Shook know these inner feelings. He needed to be strong so that his wife would have someone to lean on; if they both fell apart, there would be no hope for them.

"Well . . ." he said, tapping the ashes out of his pipe, "let's go rejoin the ladies."

We played Candyland until Maude fell over with a clunk. Mrs.

Shook thought Maude was having some kind of attack and wanted to call an ambulance. I reassured her that this was only typical. Since Maude was already asleep, Mrs. Shook suggested that she spend the night. I was afraid I'd get into trouble if Maude was missing in the morning, and said we'd better go home. Mr. Shook offered to drive us, but I wanted to be alone with Shane, so we walked. I slung Maude over my shoulder, knowing she wouldn't wake even if I dragged her behind me like a wagon.

As it turned out, Maude could have stayed with the Shooks because my mother didn't come home that night. My father was in Medford, scouting some new stores. I decided that if the Shooks ever again invited us to sleep over, I would accept. How nice it would be to wake up in the morning to the smells drifting out of that bright breakfast kingdom of a kitchen.

I posed for Shane a few days later. It was not a nude session as I had feared, although she did ask me to take off my shirt in order to sketch my shoulders. I held them up, hoping to fool her that they were square. "Just relax," she said, and in time I did.

That night we lay on the grass in a corner of the park and necked. I was on my left side, Shane on her right. Not far away some kids were playing on the rings, but we were in shadow and, anyway, I didn't care if they saw us. The grass was freshly mowed and small blades, like lint, clung to our clothes and hair. A high buzz hung in the air, but whether from a telephone wire or crickets I couldn't tell.

I worried that our mouths would get tired or our tongues knotted together, but neither of these things happened. It excited me to be close to Shane in this way. I knew she could feel my small, embarrassing excitement, but she didn't seem to mind. I slipped my hand under the back of her sweater and she didn't mind this, either. Her spine was as sharp as the teeth of a saw. I was surprised the bones didn't puncture her skin.

She rolled on her back and my hand naturally moved to her breasts. I didn't know how to take off her bra and didn't try, but she felt soft and young through the thin material. It was almost completely dark. The park lights switched on automatically at nightfall, but the timer was probably set for earlier in the summer when it didn't grow dark until eight-thirty or nine. Now the nights were closing in and summer would soon be over.

I wanted to do it so badly that I was afraid I wouldn't be able to stop myself. I wasn't used to having such strong desires. I had always been in control, always held back, never forced myself on anyone. But I was changing. I wanted to give in to these urges, which were new to me and would never be so new again. In fact, I didn't have a choice. That night I was powerless to do anything except what my heart wanted.

Shane lay on her back in the grass, eyes closed. One hand, her right, softly held my upper arm. Her sweater was raised to a level just below her breasts and her stomach rose and fell quickly, excitedly.

I leaned over her, supporting my body with my left arm until I was suspended above her. Shane kept her eyes closed. She knew what I was going to do and trusted me not to do it too fast or to hurt her. My body trembled with nervousness and longing.

With the flat of my palm, I pushed the dark bangs away to see her forehead, white and smooth and spread with freckles.

* * *

Minutes after we entered the crowded cafeteria, my date disappeared. It had taken all my nerve to ask Sherry Draper to the dance in the first place. Now I'd lost her. Six months had gone by since my relationship with Shane ended and I knew I was going to have to try again. Sherry had been my debate partner in speech class, so it was not wildly improbable of me to ask her out. But we only danced once and the entire time Sherry's head pivoted around to see who was with who at the last dance of the school year.

Then she excused herself to go to the bathroom and never returned. I wondered if she had fainted in the rest room or developed some kind of women's problem that delayed her. I considered asking one of the female teachers to go in search of Sherry, but intuition told me this would only lead to a grand humiliation. It was best to look busy and hope she would turn up.

I spotted Tim, dancing as if he was trying to stomp out a fire. He wore a letterman jacket with a big green C sewn onto it, a narrow black tie, tight black pants, and pointed shoes. At the last basketball game of the season he had scored the winning basket, elevating him to the status of a minor god. I watched him until he was swallowed up by the crowd.

I moved to the cafeteria line where soft drinks and cookies were on sale for a small price. I dug in my pocket for a quarter.

"Nelson, having a good time?"

Mr. Crisp stood behind the counter, one of the teacher chaperones for the evening. It was disconcerting to see him in the place where fat cooks served up steamed hamburgers and gluey macaroni and cheese during the week. He smiled broadly at me, showing his small, even teeth.

"Hi, Mr. Crisp. I'll have a Seven-Up."

He uncapped the bottle and handed it to me with a paper cup. He waved away the quarter I offered.

"What are you going to do with yourself this summer?" he

asked over the band's earthshaking twangings. "Lots of big plans?"

"I've got a job at Safeway!" I screamed over the music. "Box boy!" This wasn't strictly true, as I was still waiting for an answer from the manager who was a different manager from the one last year who asked how tall I was before he asked my name. This one also asked how tall I was. Still, I was pretty sure I would get it. It paid well and guaranteed thirty hours a week.

"Which one?"

"In Westmoreland!"

"I'll have to shop there sometime! Get some real heavy stuff and make you carry it to the car!" He laughed. He was very serious in class and in our little talks he had also been serious, so it was surprising to see him so lively. I couldn't imagine that listening to rock music and watching kids sweat and get horny on the dance floor would be much fun for him, but Mr. Crisp was more cheerful than I had ever seen him.

"I still want to know what happened."

"What?" I yelled back. The band had just gone into their ear-splitting rendition of "I Saw Her Standing There."

"Your story!" Mr. Crisp shouted back. "I still want to know how it turns out!"

"I'm working on it!" I said—also not true, but I meant to write the last two chapters as soon as finals were over.

"That's good." A teacher I recognized as the wrestling coach approached Mr. Crisp and whispered in his ear. I turned away and looked out at the dance floor. The cafeteria had no windows and without ventilation the temperature was soaring. Heat from the dancers' bodies rose and rippled like exhaust from a jet airliner. It was difficult to see anyone clearly, but Sherry was plainly visible dancing with Jeff Fee, a tall acne-scarred state champion hurdler.

He was grinding his loins into Sherry's in an obscene manner while Mr. Crisp, dance monitor, was giggling with the wrestling coach. This was high school and I had another three years to go.

"Nelson, grab a girl and dance!" Mr. Crisp shouted after the wrestling coach moved off. "There's a bunch of them over there just waiting for it!" He gestured across the room where four of the homeliest girls in the student body were gathered under a Canned Food Drive banner.

"I'm waiting for my date!" I shouted back. The band was now playing "Town Without Pity." This was a dance without pity. "My date went to the bathroom! She gets jealous if I ask another girl!" I explained, but Mr. Crisp's attention had shifted to the attractive Spanish teacher and he appeared to forget all about me.

However, as I began to walk away, I heard him shout again. I turned back. "Sorry, Mr. Crisp! I couldn't hear!"

"Don't start any knife fights! I'd have to break them up!" he said with another big smile.

I nodded, but didn't understand what he meant. We had known each other since the beginning of the school year. He should realize by now that I was the last person in the room likely to start a fight, unless I decided to punch Jeff Fee or slap Sherry around to teach her etiquette. Both these things were unlikely. Finally I realized Mr. Crisp didn't mean anything; it was just another joke. I supposed that he was happy to have only two weeks of school left and a whole student-less summer ahead. Even so, I wondered if that was the reason he was so jocular or if it was something else.

Not long after my conversation with Mr. Crisp I found myself near the Canned Food Drive sign and impulsively asked one of the wallflowers to dance. It was nine o'clock and I'd only danced once with a partner whose head swiveled around as though it was set on ball bearings. I was determined not to leave the cafeteria in defeat and if the only available girls were these drab creatures, so be it.

The wallflower's name was Paula. We danced three times and during the third number, a slow song, she placed her hand on my butt and whispered in my ear that she loved me.

chapter ten

Maude's screams could be heard from half a block away. I started running. When I was nearer the house, I heard my father's voice say, "Maude, shut up! Can't you shut her up? Where's Nelson?" A moment later I burst through the back door and ran up the three steps to the kitchen.

A broken serving dish lay on the floor. The dish once held beef Stroganoff. Now this, too, was on the floor along with a large serving spoon and one fork. My father was wearing a gray suit with faint blue lines. His left jacket pocket was brown with Stroganoff. Stroganoff also covered his left pants leg and shoe.

My mom wore a burgundy blouse, a black skirt, and high heels. A purse looped over her arm, gold earrings clipped on her ears, and her hair was newly done. She didn't look like someone who had just hurled a platter of beef Stroganoff at her husband.

"Mommy's going away! Nelson, do something!" Maude wailed in the same piercing tone I had heard four houses away.

"Nelson, get her out of here," my father said, gesturing to Maude.

"Nelson, fix Maude something to eat," my mom began even before my father finished speaking. "There's lasagna in the refrig-

erator. Or fried chicken, if she'd rather have that." Then she
turned and walked through the propped-open swinging door into
the dining room.

"Nelson, don't let Mommy go! Stop her!" Maude screamed as
she tugged on my arm. Her face was red and smeared with tears,
her hand was hot. I looked at my father.

"Never get married, Nelson," he said in a discouraging tone.
Then he looked down at the brown stain on his suit and said,
"Fuck!" I'd never heard my father use this word before and a
feeling of hopelessness overcame me. Now I knew their divorce
was certain: plates were flying, swear words were being used
around children, marriage was being discouraged.

"I want Mommy!" Maude howled. She pulled away from me
and ran toward the door. I winced as her bare foot aimed for a
wedge of platter, but she missed it and disappeared into the
dining room.

"I don't know what your mother told you about me . . . ," my
dad started to say, rubbing at the Stroganoff stain with a thin
paper napkin.

"Nothing," I answered quickly, although she had told me quite
a bit.

"But there's two sides to every story," he went on, forgetting
that I was a writer and instinctively knew this. "Don't believe
everything you hear. What a goddamn mess," he added, but
didn't clarify if he was talking about the suit, the floor, or his
marriage. He balled up the napkin and tossed it on the table
where it immediately rolled off the other side. He started for the
back door, then stopped dead in his tracks.

"Who's that?" he asked.

It was, of course, Shane, whom I'd brought home unexpectedly
to meet the folks. Standing on the first of the three steps leading
to the back door, she was blocking my father's way. As usual, her

head was bowed and hair draped her eyes. It struck me that she resembled a strange European dog, one that a rich woman in Switzerland might own. Then I remembered that I was in love with Shane and the resemblance passed.

This was a reciprocal visit; I had met Shane's mother a few days before. Doris McLeod was slight, like Shane, and small-boned. Otherwise, mother and daughter were very little alike. Shane's mother had honey-colored hair, which she brushed straight back from her forehead, blue eyes instead of Shane's gray-green ones, and an outgoing, if not bossy, manner. It made me wonder about the absent father, but there were no family pictures on display around the house. My own home was liberally decorated with photos of my mom and dad at their wedding ceremony and on vacation at Mazatlán, as well as pictures of Maude at various adorable ages. A portrait of me at age three festooned a wall some years back, but it had disappeared.

She insisted that I call her Doris. I did this, although it makes me uncomfortable to address parental figures by their first names. However, it solved the problem of whether I should refer to her as Miss or Mrs. McLeod.

Shane had rung Doris at the phone company where she was supervisor of the information department to say she was bringing me to supper. Doris had no objection and stopped for take-out food on the way home. I wore a shirt with palm trees on it, a festive outfit that alarmed Shane a little when she saw me. She sought out the most somber colors imaginable, browns and dark greens being her favorites. She wore no jewelry except for a tarnished ring that had been her father's, the only thing except Shane that he had left behind.

At dinner I talked too much about my writing, which tended to bore Shane practically into a coma, but Doris listened appreciatively and nodded on occasion. Doris then praised Shane's talent and expressed hope that she would have a successful career in commercial art, which she believed was a high-paying field. Doris made several remarks about how she was sorry she couldn't give Shane a better start in life, but that adversity was a great character builder. Shane toyed with a chicken wing, a dismal look on her face.

Doris criticized Shane for being too shy; nobody was going to open doors for her unless she knocked. Shane's head drooped even more until it hovered only inches above her plate. Doris probably delivered this lecture with annoying regularity—it had the flow a teacher gets from teaching the same subject year after year. All the same, she was sincere and believed in her daughter's talent. My parents had never asked to read a single thing I wrote.

Four days later I impulsively invited Shane home to meet my mom and dad. This was in violation of the rule that my friends weren't welcome unless I gave my mother twenty-four hours' notice, but I felt that mostly applied to friends like Tim who were likely to make noise, clean out the refrigerator, and smell up the bathroom. Shane was no threat in those areas. I was proud that I had a girlfriend and wanted my parents to know their son had a romantic future. Perhaps this would reassure them in their hour of marital strife.

Never before had I heard them raise their voices at each other, let alone known them to fling platters of Russian food across the room. Mostly they just talked quietly and endlessly. If my mom hadn't told me of their impending divorce, I never would have known about it. But I knew so little about them, anyway. I knew that my dad collected stamps and fished. My mom liked to paint and had a mother who gave me embroidered handkerchiefs year after year. I would be hard pressed to come up with a more in-depth description of either of them.

They married right before my dad went off to war. A box of love letters was stowed in the basement, letters he had written to her when he was in Italy, sometimes in trenches. This romantic beginning didn't fit with the sad, messy scene in the kitchen. It was as if reels of film had gotten scrambled in the projection booth and a wartime romance was mixed with a searing contemporary drama. I decided that if I ever got married I would try for a little consistency.

"This is my friend Shane," I said to my dad. Shane dipped her head and murmured something in such a soft voice that neither my father nor I could possibly hear it.

"Don't clean that mess up. Leave it," he said to me over his shoulder, then hurried down the stairs past Shane. She pressed herself against the wall like a leper not wanting to spread contagion. He went out the door and a moment later I heard the white Falcon start up and back out of the driveway.

Meanwhile, Maude's hysterical cries had moved to the upper floor. "Maude, please," I heard my mom say.

I looked at Shane, but she was still huddled against the wall, head down. I wanted her to see me shrug. I was embarrassed by the family chaos and wished her to know that I didn't take it too much to heart, although I did. Parents were parents; it was best to let them have their little scenes and try to keep a sense of humor about it. But Shane didn't look at me and I doubt if I could have conveyed such a complex idea with a simple shrug. I left the kitchen and headed in the direction of my sister's hysteria.

When I reached the staircase to the second floor, my mom was already coming down. She carried a small overnight case. Maude trailed behind her, clinging to her skirt. "Maude, please don't hang on me." My mother didn't seem upset; she was cool and businesslike and appeared anxious to be gone. I wondered if she was going to Dr. Holt's house. I had tried to picture my mother and Dr. Holt in bed together, but decided it wasn't good for my mental health and put it out of my mind.

"Nelson, take your sister," she said. Maude was howling incoherently, having reverted to an infantile, prelanguage state.

"Maude, let Mommy go," I said, knowing this would do no good. When Maude was tightly wound, nothing could calm her. I reached for her arm. Her fist shot out and hit me in the stomach.

"I left the number where I'm going to be on the refrigerator," my mom said as she moved briskly through the hall into the living room. "I won't be far."

"Don't go, Mom, we need you," I pleaded, although I wasn't exactly sure this was true. I fed Maude in the morning, took care of her all day, fixed dinner for her, occupied her until eight o'clock, made sure she brushed her teeth, and put her to bed. I did her wash and cleaned up the kitchen as well. This seemed to cover things pretty nicely. But I needed someone to pay me my weekly salary, so my plea was not a complete fabrication.

"If you need something, you can ask your father. He can do something for a change," she said and opened the front door. A yellow taxi cab was waiting at the curb. The sight of the cab made Maude shriek even louder and, I had to admit, the cab struck an ominous note. The fact that my mother wasn't taking the Ford Country Wagon made her departure seem final; perhaps we would never see her again. I tried to think of something that would persuade her to stay, but nothing came to mind. I wasn't even sure she and my father should stay together. They had given it nineteen years. That was a long time. They didn't resort to throwing gourmet dishes at each other until they had talked everything out. If they wanted to be divorced, who was I to prevent them? They were the adults, I was the child.

But there was Maude. What would happen after one parent

left by the back door and the other by the front door? I would then assume total responsibility. As she was too young for kindergarten, I would be the only freshman at Cleveland High accompanied by a four-year-old child. This might be good for picking up girls, since girls loved Maude, but the complications on a date were staggering.

"Mom, please don't go," I begged, but the request sounded hollow and she acted as though she hadn't heard.

"Maude, I'm leaving now," she said, crouching down and taking the distraught girl in her arms. Maude clenched her little hands on her mother's soft wine-colored blouse and pattered the material with her tears. "Nelson will bring you over to me in the morning. We'll see each other and we'll do something fun." I wondered if my mom would remember this promise or if, when I called the number on the refrigerator, she would find some excuse not to do something fun.

"I love you. Don't cry. You're going to be fine. Nelson and your father will take care of you," she assured Maude, not realizing my dad had already sped away. I opened my mouth to correct her, but would it do any good? The situation had acquired a velocity of its own, and would take more than reason or half-hearted pleas to stop it now.

"If I didn't have to go, I wouldn't," she continued, stroking Maude's sweat-drenched hair. "Please believe me. You're going to see me tomorrow. Oh, darling, please stop. I can't stand to see you cry. I love you so much." My mother's chin trembled for a moment and I wondered what was going on inside her head. Would I ever know? Would there come a time, when she was old and I was grown, that we would talk about this? Or would it simply be shuffled back in the deck of fifty-one other dramatic moments in our lives?

Maude was still bawling and finally my mom told me, "Take

her, the cab's waiting." I grabbed Maude and my mother quickly went out the door and down the steps to the sidewalk. The cab driver opened the car door and she slid in gracefully. Maude was choking on her own phlegm, but when I tried to get her to blow her nose on one of my grandmother's handkerchiefs, she cried louder and said she hated me. The cab drove off and as far as I could tell there was no wave or backward glance from our mother. Maude broke away from me and ran upstairs to her bedroom. The slamming of her door made the whole house shudder.

When I returned to the kitchen, Shane was gone. She must have slipped away as soon as she could, embarrassed by the domestic nightmare she had stumbled into. I thought about following her, but that meant leaving the suicidal Maude alone and it would be dark soon.

It was my house now. I sat in one of the two armchairs in the living room, trying to feel like a man of property. Now I could do anything I wanted with the place. I could redecorate. I could have a party. I could sell the house and move to New York to pursue my writing career.

It was a two-story house built in the 1930s. My parents bought it when I was a year old, so I had never known another home. The roof was so steeply peaked that the walls of the upstairs rooms were slanted. The house contained nine rooms in all and a large unfinished basement. My room on the first floor in the northeastern corner of the house was my favorite room, but I had other favorite places, too: the laundry chute in the downstairs hall that led to the basement and through which I once beaned my mom with a water balloon; the front porch, wide and flanked on both sides by bright rhododendron bushes; and the alley behind the garage where, as a young boy, I hid when I was in trouble and thought no one could find me.

Now it was all mine. I went into the den and took my place

in the big swiveling armchair at the desk. Some bills were stacked in a tray to my left. I glanced through them: telephone, electricity, gas, all of which would have to be paid if Maude and I continued to live in the house. There was also a bill from Alan L. Holt, M.D.

Complete physical for Nelson . . . $27.00

Lab expenses $11.20

Total $38.20

YOUR INSURANCE COMPANY HAS BEEN BILLED

That went in the wastebasket. I opened the center drawer and found a checkbook, "Lawrence D. Jaqua, Dolly C. Jaqua" in gold lettering on the leather cover. I opened it to see how much money I had. The account had not been balanced, but there were approximately four thousand dollars in available funds. This would see us through several months.

Further back in the center drawer was a jumble of papers and receipts, including a 1960 income tax return signed by both my parents, which would come in handy when I forged their signatures on the checks. I could cash them at the Little Store, where Mr. Walsh would not subject the signatures to FBI-like scrutiny. It sounded as though Tim was running the store now, anyway, and he wouldn't give me any trouble.

Under the box that held ballpoint pens, loose staples, and paper clips, was forty-three dollars in tens and smaller bills and these I took. I explored the other desk drawers to familiarize myself with everything necessary for running the household. The passbook for the savings account at U.S. Bank showed a balance of fifteen thousand dollars. This would be useful, but might be harder to get my hands on than the checking account monies. I found the combination to the safe and opened it. Inside were stock certificates, the deed to the house, and titles to the cars. The Ford Country Wagon could be sold off—that would keep Maude in Pixie Sticks for some time. A few pieces of my mother's jewelry were also stored in the safe and these could be pawned if Maude and I were starving.

I went into my parents' bedroom. I had never been alone in there before; it was forbidden territory. My parents were never champions of kids bursting into their bedroom in the morning, jumping on them, and shouting, "When's breakfast?" Once in a while my mom would talk to me while she was putting on her makeup before going out, but this was mostly when I was a lot younger.

It was my room now, if I wanted it. The bedroom was spacious even with one very slanted wall. It had its own bathroom and walk-in closet. Double windows looked out on Mrs. Crow's house next door.

I searched the drawers of the bedside tables. The drawer on my mother's side of the bed held a jar of face cream, a box of tissues, and a bottle of sleeping tablets. In my father's drawer were a Bible and a pistol. I took the pistol in my hand; it was lighter than I thought it would be. I stood in front of the mirror to see how I looked with a gun in my hand. I didn't look too dangerous. I wanted to check if it was loaded, but was afraid it would go off by mistake, so I put it back. I never knew we had a gun in the house and it somehow gave the house a whole new meaning.

My parents' closet was crowded with clothes, half my mother's and half my father's. I put my hand in the pockets of my dad's suit jackets, but all I found were a few stray breath mints, a couple of business cards, and a suppository. I didn't know he had hemorrhoids—I suppose it's the kind of thing you don't tell your kid. Above, on a shelf, were dozens of boxes containing my mother's shoes. On the floor were more shoes, some in a shoe rack and others loosely scattered. I felt inside a couple of my father's shoes; they were slightly damp and my hand smelled when I pulled it out, though not unpleasantly.

I was looking, I suppose, for a clue or piece of evidence that would tell me what my parents' trouble was, whether it was just the Other Woman or if it was more than that. If only I understood why they told me never to get married and left without even a wave, these things might be a little easier to take.

I was looking, too, for an answer to this: whether my parents would ever come back and if, in some small measure, we were loved. I did not begrudge them their personal problems. They were welcome to them. All I wanted was not to be left alone in a big house with a gun. Maude and I were not strong. Of the two of us, Maude was the more resilient. She forgot things easily and this gave her a certain bounce. Her moods shifted and changed, each shift leaving her renewed. I clung to every emotion like a leech, sucking it until it was dry.

Well, until our parents returned or our fate was certain, I would have to find adulthood fast. Maude was now my responsibility. I would not only have to get her dressed and fed each morning, I would have to try to persuade her that someone, even if it was me, loved her and had not forgotten her. It was now my duty to instill in her the belief that adversity makes a person strong, even though I believed adversity only makes a person expect more adversity. It makes you wary and suspicious, makes you keep a gun in the drawer next to the bed.

I needed to be kind to Maude and fair, and value her above everything else. Protect her and guide her, know when to be strict and when to be lenient. Most importantly, I had to love her with a parent's love: love without qualification, love without a price or an end.

I couldn't do it. When all was said and done, I was only thirteen. I could dress my sister, make dinner for her, and do her wash. I was capable of these tasks. But whether I could always decide what was right and good for her, I didn't know and didn't want to risk it. It had nothing to do with love. I loved Maude just fine. But I wasn't a parent and had no right pretending to be one. I wasn't mature enough, and was mature enough to know it.

In the end, of course, we went to the Shooks. I called ahead and said my mother was on a business trip with my dad, their flight home had been canceled, and they couldn't get back until tomorrow. We were scared to be in the house alone. Mr. Shook, who answered, said he would pick us up in five minutes.

We packed a few things. I took an extra pair of jeans and a couple of shirts. Maude refused to help, so I chose some dresses for her. We could always come back for more, although I had a feeling we wouldn't. It was either take everything or take nothing, so we took next to nothing.

I locked the house up tight. I put the checkbook inside the safe and locked that. I tucked the combination in my wallet, but took nothing else from the desk except the forty-three dollars. I cleaned the kitchen floor and made sure the stove was off. I left one light burning in the living room to discourage burglars.

Before we left I called Shane. Phone conversations with her were always troublesome, because she spoke so softly that the slightest static on the line or a truck going by on the street would drown her out. I made it quick. I said that Maude and I were staying at the Shooks until further notice and could I see her tomorrow? She said she was working during the day, but was free in the evening. I told her to meet me at the Shooks' house around six or six-thirty. Neither of us mentioned the scene between my parents, but it hung on the line like dirty laundry.

Mr. Shook arrived in less than five minutes. He waited patiently until I finished locking up, then held the door as we climbed into the De Soto. We all sat in the front seat, Maude in the middle clutching a stuffed Popeye. She was no longer crying, but her face had hardened into a "the world is against me" look. No convicted felon on the way to the penitentiary ever looked more wronged. I wondered if her childhood was over. If so, she was shortchanged—it might have lasted a few more years. I squeezed her knee, but she cringed as if being touched by the Blob.

Once inside the house, Mrs. Shook took over, enveloping Maude in a blanket of welcome. The house was warm and smelled of baked ham. Maude was suddenly the center of attention, Mrs. Shook tending to her every whim. If this did not make the little girl forget her newly orphaned status, it certainly distracted her. Mrs. Shook noticed immediately that Maude was wearing mismatched socks. She clucked her tongue disapprovingly and led Maude upstairs to find two identical socks in the many boxes of Bobby's abandoned clothes. She made it a game and Maude loved games.

"You better take a look at our wall," Mr. Shook told me and, as the women went upstairs, we went down. The wall was finished, solid and symmetrical. The mortar, part of which I applied, looked even. The bricks were perfectly aligned. I knew the small gutter behind the wall was carrying excess moisture out to the street. A small screen would keep out mice. This wall would be here long after the Shooks were gone, either gone from the neighborhood or from life.

"It's great."

"Well, it'll do," Mr. Shook replied as if the wall could have been more professionally built. "Now I've got to do something about that roof." He looked over to a corner of the basement where bundles of shingles were stacked as high as my shoulder. "How are you with heights?" he asked.

"Nelson, why don't we ever have ham?" were Maude's first words to me since we left our house. She had addressed Mrs. Shook exclusively, all the while desperately gripping Popeye, a doll she never showed the slightest affection for before. Now Popeye seemed the only thing that could console her in this troubled time. Even at the dinner table she clutched him with one arm until this proved too cumbersome, then she laid the gruff sailor in her lap.

"We have ham all the time," I reminded her. "You won't eat it."

"I love ham," she replied, darting a hurt glance at Mrs. Shook to emphasize how badly she had been mistreated. Mrs. Shook merely smiled. The table was laden with food, more than the four of us could eat in several dinners. Mrs. Shook never prepared anything complex—we were in no danger of flying beef Strogan-off at the Shooks' house—but even something as basic as baked ham possessed a quiet magic. The ham was the best ham in the world; the pineapple glaze the most pineappley glaze ever pre-pared. Even sweet potatoes, every child's nightmare vegetable, were crisp and colorful instead of gooey brown and orange.

As always, there was little talk at the table. We were there to eat. Mr. Shook chewed each bite ten times, a rule he must have learned as a child and now, half a century later, still obeyed. Mrs. Shook was watchful, eyeing everyone's plate for an empty space she could fill.

I felt safe here and young. Food was put before me and I ate. Milk was put before me and I drank. Life could be as simple as this. Far away was my empty house and the minefield of daily life. At this table were people to care for my sister and me, to feed us and hold off the dogs. I thought of the gun in my father's drawer and wondered if Mr. Shook also kept a gun. No, he had no need of a gun. He protected his loved ones with his heavy presence, with the bulk of his North Dakota body.

His voice on the phone: *"I'll be there in five minutes. Can you wait that long?"*

Yes, I could wait that long. No explanation was necessary, no persuasion. He would be there in five minutes and, in fact, was there sooner.

Her voice: *"Why Maude, you've got two different socks on! Cluck-cluck. We're going to have to do something about that!"*

The eagerness, the taking charge. And, not long after, the matching socks.

The Shooks never asked where my parents were stranded or when they would be back. They never suggested a long distance call to tell them everything was all right. I don't know if Mr. and Mrs. Shook believed my story or even questioned whether it should be believed or disbelieved. They were just happy to have someone to share dinner, someone to look at the wall with and think about repairing the roof with, a little girl to find socks for.

My thoughts that night did not come in complete sentences or in good English. At best they were glimpses of warmth and safety. The food filled and tired me. My brain slowed, shut down. For once I could not analyze what I experienced, could only experience it.

Dessert, apple crumble cake and ice cream. Coffee, my first real cup of coffee. Maude: *"Can I have seconds?"* Of course she could have seconds. The heaping plate. The napkin tucked under her small, crumbed chin.

Later, watching TV. There's nothing on TV. Talking about how nothing is on TV anymore. Playing a game with Maude.

Then Maude sleeping on the daybed in the sewing room, a duck-patterned quilt covering her. The light left on so she will not be frightened if she awakens in the night. The door open a crack.

Eight o'clock. Sitting up with the Shooks, trying to stay awake. His voice: *"We're going to take a look at that roof."* Her voice: something about a professional roofer. My eyes closing.

Later, or maybe not later, his voice: *"We can do it."*

A child, secure in the knowledge that his parents are close and watchful, drifts in and out of sleep. He catches the end of a conversation or the middle, and doesn't worry about following the whole. He is certain that nothing important will be discussed without him wholly present, life decisions not be made until he is back. And if one or two decisions are made, they will be good decisions and will take him into account.

Her voice, reading from a spiral notebook:

> *Two hundred dollars*
> *For one square of earth.*
> *I put my boy in,*
> *Now what is it worth?*

Her voice again: *"Oh, dear. I have to work on this."* An embarrassed laugh.

A car outside on the street slowing, stopping, a beep. I think it's my parents come to take me home. I start to get up. It drives on.

Later, his voice: *"I think he's asleep."*

My voice: *"No, I'm not."*

Rain starting, keeping time on the window above me. Under my head, a bright quilt.

Her voice: *"This is my favorite of hers. Oh, they're all my favorites. But this one . . ."* Then, reading from a broken-backed book of Edna St. Vincent Millay.

> *"Son," said my mother*
> *When I was knee-high,*
> *"You've need of clothes to cover you,*
> *And not a rag have I.*
>
> *"There's nothing in the house*
> *To make a boy breeches,*
> *Nor shears to cut a cloth with,*
> *Nor thread to take stitches."*

Her voice, later, holding back tears:

> *She wove a red cloak*
> *So regal to see,*
> *"She's made it for a king's son,"*
> *I said, "and not for me."*
> *But I knew it was for me.*

And still later, not looking at the book, the poem memorized:

> *A smile about her lips,*
> *And a light about her head,*
> *And her hands in the harp-strings*
> *Frozen dead.*
>
> *And piled up beside her*
> *And toppling to the skies,*

Were the clothes of a king's son,
Just my size.

Of course, it would be her favorite—the son so needy, the making of clothes to cover him. Her dream to be the harp weaver, weaving her life away to save her boy.

His voice: *"Now, now."*

Her voice: *"I know."*

His voice: *"Why do you read it if it makes you cry?"*

She doesn't know. She laughs. He holds her.

The rain stops. I turn over. The rattle of a newspaper. The soft click of knitting needles.

Finally, his voice: *"Nelson, we're going to put you in Bobby's room."*

I start to rise.

Her voice: *"Maybe he'd be more comfortable down here."*

His voice: *"Sure. Whatever you want, Nelson."*

My voice: *"No, that's fine."*

And so I slept in Bobby's bedroom, in his bed covered with his bedspread of spaceships and rockets. I think this was fate, but a tender kind of fate that I was unused to. When I walked sleepily into the room, Mrs. Shook was putting sheets on the mattress, white sheets bleached and ironed. "I put these out for you. I don't know . . . ," she said uncertainly, looking at a pair of pajamas way too big. "I thought I had some smaller ones."

"I don't need pajamas."

"You might be cold. It's going to be cool tonight, they said on the news. But anything you want. I know boys like to sleep in their underwear, I don't know why." She laughed.

I brushed my teeth with my finger, having forgotten my toothbrush. I tried on the pajama top, but it reached to my knees. I put my T-shirt back on and asked if I could look in on Maude.

She was sleeping peacefully. I tucked Popeye under the covers with her for company.

"We're glad you called us, Nelson," Mrs. Shook said, just before leaving me alone in Bobby's room. I was sitting on the edge of the bed, the bed under which I hid only a month before. I had taken off my shoes, but was waiting until she left to get undressed. "You can always call us for anything. Just think of this as your second home."

She stopped talking, but didn't go. She looked away from me and focused on the world globe, suddenly shy and out of words. I think she wanted to hold me for a moment, but felt it would not be right. I didn't know how to tell her that it wouldn't embarrass me. I should have gotten up from the bed, walked over to her, and hugged her. Nothing in the world would have meant more to her at that moment and it was such a little thing. I remember wanting to do it, wanting to give her that pleasure, knowing it would give me pleasure, too, and seal the bond. But I was thirteen and heroic gestures did not come naturally to me.

She hesitated at the door a moment longer, as if trying to think of something more to say, something that would unlock me from my self-consciousness and make me come to her. But again the words deserted Mrs. Shook and "Sleep well" was all she said. She turned to leave.

"Thanks."

She turned back and I could see in her face that it was this she wanted—not a hug or some grandiose gesture, just a simple thank you. Her face relaxed and her smile widened. Her eyes glittered; whether there were tears or not I don't know. She had been worried whether she had done enough, made my sister and me comfortable enough, fed us enough. This was the kind of thing Bridget Shook fretted about and my thanks was reassurance that we needed nothing more. For a moment the young Bridget Shook stood there, the Bridget she must have been before Bobby be-came sick and took so much out of her.

I felt bad that my thanks was so short. I could have added a "you" onto it, that wouldn't have killed me. But it would be hard to imagine an appreciation greater than she showed at that mo-ment. Maybe this was a word Bobby never mastered. Perhaps he never said "Thanks" and she had never heard it from a boy's mouth.

"Sleep in tomorrow," she said, then left the room and closed the door.

I undressed and turned out the light. Donald Duck glowed at me from the corner. I crossed my hands on my chest, but thought this might be the way Bobby had lain in his casket, so I put them under my head. I did not feel weird sleeping in Bobby's bed. It was a comfortable bed, a little softer than mine at home. The guard rail was down. I liked having all of Bobby's things, his phonograph, his great books of the world, his hockey stick around me. How many years he must have lain there, looking up at the chart of the ABCs and trying to figure them out. Well, was this really much different than me lying in my own bed, trying to work out a story or some bigger issue and not getting very far? How much of life was it possible to figure out, anyway, to really under-stand? I looked at the ABCs until the letters became meaningless shapes, some more pleasing than others, and none of them with any relation to me. I felt close to Bobby then, and sure that he had not really been unhappy. No child could be unhappy in that house, feel abandoned or be in need.

When I came woozily down the stairs the next morning at eight forty-five, having slept soundly and dream-free, Maude greeted me with a piercing, "We're going to the beach!" and we were. Mr. and Mrs. Shook had the whole day planned: a day at the beach. Everything was packed and they were just waiting for me to get up, get dressed, eat. Maude had tried several times to race upstairs and pounce on me, but Mrs. Shook held her back with a firm, "Nelson needs his sleep." Maude was excited. This would be her first trip to the beach, she swore, although we had gone the previous summer when she was three. But that was a lifetime ago.

Mr. Shook announced that we would buy whatever we needed—bathing suits, beach balls, sand pails—at Seaside. He was anxious to get in the car and get moving. I asked if we would be back by six; Shane was coming over. Yes, he assured me, we would be back. When he thought I wasn't looking, he grinned at his wife and winked. Breakfast was put in front of me, blueberry waffles and scrambled eggs. I ate quickly and by nine-thirty we were in the car and on our way to the coast.

It didn't occur to me until much later that my parents would not know where we were and might panic when they discovered us missing. They wouldn't assume that we were with the Shooks and safe, because my parents didn't know the Shooks existed. I had never mentioned their names. Maude, if she said anything, called them "those nice people." The Shooks were now an indispensable part of our lives, but a secret part. I had only told Cat about them and Cat did not believe they were sincere.

My mother had left a phone number on the refrigerator and had told me to call her in the morning, but in our hasty exodus from the house I forgot to take the slip of paper. Even if I had remembered, I still might not have taken it. The number might be Dr. Holt's, and the idea of asking him if I could speak to my mother did not please me.

When my dad left, he did not say where he was going or if he would return. I could have called him at his office to tell him where we were, but I knew that his secretary would say what she always said: "I'm sorry, Nelson, he's tied up." She said it kindly and I'm sure it was true.

So I made no calls. Mr. Shook was anxious to get on the road, and, because he and his wife had been so kind, I didn't want to delay them a minute more. It was not my intention to worry my parents or seek revenge for their desertion. I merely wanted to care for my sister as best I could. After all, that was my summer job.

Much later I asked my father and mother about the day their children vanished. At first they were reluctant, but I pressed them and then they seemed glad to talk about it. I was glad, too, that they trusted me to understand and not to judge them too harshly.

My father had come back home, late and drunk. He had had several drinks in a bar and tried to pick up a woman who was initially intrigued, but became bored by his incessant rambling about my mother and repeated showings of pictures of Maude and me. He drove home, miraculously avoiding arrest, to find the house locked and empty. He assumed Maude and I were with our mother, wherever she had gone. He hated himself for losing his entire family and wrecking his life. He drank half a bottle of Scotch, ate a can of cocktail peanuts, threw it all up, and fell into a drunken sleep still wearing his Stroganoff-decorated suit.

The phone woke him at ten o'clock the next morning. It was Friday, August 31.

"Larry?"

"Yeah. Wait a minute, the phone cord's tangled up . . ." My mom heard the receiver drop on the floor. A moment later his voice came back on the line. "Sorry. Dolly?"

"What are you doing home?"

"I'm getting kind of a late start."

"Are you sick?"

"I'm not sure yet."

"You sound terrible."

"I might stay home today."

"Are you all right?"

"I'm still in my clothes."

My mother filled in the blanks: late night, drunk, God knows what else. She changed the subject to avoid a fight.

"Would you put Nelson on?"

"I don't think he's here."

"Where is he?"

"Where are you?"

"Margaret's." Margaret was a friend who was always almost getting divorced from her husband, without ever actually going through with it. Her husband beat her and owned a company that made refrigeration equipment. This was the haven my mother had escaped to. "Did he already take Maude out?"

"I don't know. I haven't seen them."

"Would you please look?" My mom tried to keep the impatience out of her voice.

"Okay. Hang on."

My mom waited and rubbed her eyes. She had also stayed up too late, listening to Margaret talk on and on about her marital tribulations. While she waited for my dad to return to the phone, my mother tried to think of one couple that wasn't already divorced, in the process of getting a divorce, or contemplating divorce. After a couple of minutes, there was the sound of my father picking up the extension phone in the kitchen.

"They're not here."

"Nelson was supposed to call me."

"They weren't here when I came back last night."

"What?"

"The house was empty."

"What time was that?"

"Eleven, eleven-thirty."

"And they weren't home?" A note of alarm appeared in my mother's voice, the first of many that day.

"The whole place was locked up. Just one light on." This hadn't struck my dad as ominous at the time, but now, as he said it, the quiet house and empty bedrooms were so loaded with dark meaning that his legs felt weak. *I'm not a good father,* he thought. An image of two coffins, one small and Maude-sized, came into his head and wouldn't leave.

"Larry, why didn't you do something? Why didn't you call me? I left my number. What were you thinking of?"

"I thought they were with you."

My mother later told me that she felt an icy hand clutch her heart and even though that's the kind of cliche a writer can never use, it's something people really feel. She recalled Maude's shrill howls as she walked down the steps to the taxi. At the time my mother had thought, *I'll come back tomorrow. I love her so much. I can't stand to see her cry.* Now it might be too late.

My mother said she would come right home. My father stripped off the suit he had worn for over a day and took a shower, as cold as he could stand it. Still, he couldn't wash those coffins out of his mind.

Ignoring my dad's appearance—his gray unshaven face, his trembling hands—my mother called her mother as soon as she arrived home. No, Nelson and Maude hadn't visited for several weeks, my grandmother of the handkerchiefs told her. My mom then called other relatives while my father talked to the neighbors on either side of our house. No one had seen us, but Mrs. Crow asked to be alerted as soon as I turned up, as I had clipped some roses from her garden without permission and she wanted to give me a scolding. Other neighbors along the street were quizzed, but were no help.

"I'm going to call the police," my mother decided.

"Dolly, don't panic." My father felt panic rising in his chest even as he said this. "All they'll say is that someone has to be missing twenty-four hours before they're really missing."

"They're missing *now!*"

Opening the center drawer of his desk, my dad saw that the checkbook was gone. Almost fifty dollars in cash had also disappeared. *We've been robbed,* he thought. *The children have been kidnapped.* He was so blinded with terror that for a moment he had to sit with his head between his legs. Then he discovered the checkbook in the safe together with the titles to the cars and my mother's jewelry. Nothing else was missing. He remembered again the locked-up house, the one light burning.

"I think they ran away."

"It's Nelson," my mother said bitterly as she opened the phone book and looked for the number of the local police station. "He's been impossible this whole summer. I don't know what he's going through, but he better get over it fast. Why don't you do something about him, Larry? He's your son."

Annoyingly, the officer who answered the call repeated the very words my father had predicted: A person isn't officially missing until he or she has been missing twenty-four hours.

"She's only four! Are you going to do something or are you going to wait to find her body lying in a ditch? We pay our taxes and that's your salary!" my mother shouted. She hated sounding like a hysterical female, but she was fast becoming a hysterical female.

"Okay, we'll come on out to the house," Officer Constantine said, knowing full well that the absent children soon would be found at the park or a friend's house. There would be the usual awkward scene of the mother looking abashed and the father relieved, but furious at his wife. (I interviewed Officer Constantine for this part of the story).

Joseph Constantine had been a member of the Portland Police Department since he was twenty-two; he was now forty-two. Even as a boy he wanted to be a policeman. When his fourth-grade teacher asked her students to draw pictures of what they planned to be when they grew up, he drew himself as a policeman arresting a bearded criminal. He had arrested many people in his twenty years as a police officer, but never once had to shoot his gun except in target practice. He pulled it out a couple of times and waved it around, but never fired it. He was proud of this.

Missing children cases were part of the routine. Two or three times a week he received hysterical calls exactly like the one he received from the Jaquas. The parents always said the same thing: "We pay your salary." Kids ran away and kids came back; this was part of life and Officer Constantine was philosophical about it. He had three children of his own, all of whom ran away at one time or another. He sympathized with the frantic parents, but never got too excited until twenty-four hours passed. The kids usually showed up before then.

"I went to visit a friend, a sick friend," my mother lied to Officer Constantine when he asked her why she wasn't home the previous evening when the children disappeared. "And Larry had to work late. Nelson was baby-sitting. He's fourteen."

"Thirteen," my dad corrected her. The officer might not suspect the sick friend alibi, but my age was a matter of public record.

"Almost fourteen. He's very responsible, so we felt safe leaving Maude with him for a few hours," she went on, understating just a little the events of the summer. "Larry came home at eleven and they weren't here."

"Why didn't you report them missing at that time?" Officer Constantine shifted his weight and made a note on a little pad.

"I thought Dolly had taken them to her mother's," my dad answered. "It didn't occur to me that anything was wrong."

"Did you call home at any time between . . . ," Officer Constantine asked, checking his notes, "quarter of six when your wife left the children alone and eleven o'clock when you returned?"

"I was tied up in meetings," my father said, slipping into a lie as easily as my mother. "I thought Dolly would call."

"Where do they like to go? What are their favorite places?" were Officer Constantine's next routine questions.

"I don't know. The park . . ." my mom said vaguely, as if the park had not been mentioned a hundred times that summer. My dad said nothing; he had no idea.

"Did you check the parks?" No, they hadn't. Another little note went onto Officer Constantine's pad.

"Nelson likes movies, but movies don't run all night," my father offered unhelpfully.

"How about their friends? That's usually where children go when they run away. Did you check with their friends or their friends' parents?"

"Maude's only four. Her friends' parents wouldn't let her sleep overnight without calling me," my mother answered.

"Well, maybe they called and you weren't home," Officer Constantine said logically. My mother felt her temper rise: *He has no right to treat us like criminals. When is he going to stop asking questions and do something?*

"Who are Nelson's friends?" my father asked, hoping my mom

would be able to supply him with some names. "Who was that girl he was with yesterday?"

"What girl?"

"The girl he brought home last night."

"What girl?" My mother had not seen the diminutive Shane cowering against the wall during the Stroganoff War.

"The girl with the hair in her eyes," my dad explained, but this only drew another blank look from my mother.

"Nelson must have some other friends," Officer Constantine prompted.

There was a pause while my parents tried to think of some of my other friends. Since I was forbidden to bring them home without permission, and I was rarely granted permission, the names didn't leap to mind.

"There's that Tim," my father said, but couldn't think of Tim's last name or how to contact him.

"What about that girl . . . ?" my mother offered tentatively.

"That's the girl I'm talking about!" my Dad exclaimed. Now they were getting somewhere. "The girl with the hair in her eyes!"

"This girl doesn't have *any* hair. What's her name? Catherine, I think."

"A bald girl?" My dad was incredulous and wondered if this was something else my mother was making up, like the story about her sick friend.

"Catherine . . ." Officer Constantine jotted the name down. It was odd that two parents couldn't come up with the full name of any friend of their thirteen-year-old son. He began to wonder if the children were missing after all. Perhaps the Jaquas simply forgot what they looked like.

"Okay, we'll check this out. If you think of anything else that might be helpful, just call the station house. I'll put out an APB.

I suggest that one of you stays at home to answer the phone while the other drives around the neighborhood. Maybe you'll spot them. Get hold of some of their friends. Call Nelson's teachers. We'll find them. Try not to worry."

My mother felt Officer Constantine was being far too casual about this—there was a weary, "here we go again" in his instructions—but she had no better plan. She made some calls while my father drove slowly up and down the streets. He searched the parks and the library and went to my old school, which was closed. He found no trace of us because we were, by then, seventy-five miles away at the beach.

The waves were huge that day and crashed down upon themselves with a fury that made the ground tremble under our feet. The sun was bright, but not hot. There was a northern chill in the air, and a steady breeze that whipped my hair and made the whiffle ball fly. Four-storey clouds moved swiftly across the sky as if racing for a finish line.

Our first stop was Main Street. Mr. Shook took a wad of bills from his wallet and whatever we wanted, we got. I didn't want much and Maude wanted everything. After enduring my stinginess all summer—"One Pixie Stick, Maude." "A small Coke, you can't drink a big one."—she was finally being treated in the manner she believed she deserved.

He bought us both bathing suits and even wanted Mrs. Shook to put one on, but she just laughed. Maude got a shovel and pail, a beach ball, water wings, sunglasses, thongs, a sun hat, a kite, and saltwater taffy. I got a whiffle baseball set, not because I wanted it, but because Mr. Shook pressed it on me. I realized that he wanted it, wanted to play.

Mrs. Shook brought sandwiches, fried chicken, potato salad,

fruit salad, and Jell-O, enough for everyone on the beach. The beach was wide and long, and we had half an acre to ourselves. Maude ran along the edge of the water, scaring sea gulls. She collected seashells and played jump rope with a long, greasy piece of kelp, while Mrs. Shook and I talked about our favorite books. She wore shorts and a broad straw hat. Her legs were yellow and lined with long blue veins. Again she asked me to show her something I'd written, even if it wasn't finished, even if I wasn't proud of it. "If I was your age, I'd write and write and never stop," she said not sadly, looking out at the thunderous waves.

"What would you write about?" This was the question that plagued me nearly every waking minute.

"I don't know," she said, squinting against the bright sunlight. She looked down the expanse of beach, took a full breath, leaned her head back, and closed her eyes. "This."

I'm not sure I know what she meant by "This," but maybe I do. This day on the beach with the waves so high and the sand warm on top and more and more cool the further down you dig your toes. The smell of the beach, the fresh and rotting smells of the sea. The sound of Maude scaring the sea gulls and their furious screechings as they are forced up into the sky. The sky blue, the sand pail orange and yellow. Talking with a young boy about books, about writing, on a day made for just such a talk. The car parked not far away if we want to go somewhere, to another beach, to another place, back home. A day, in short, with no pain; a day containing everything good and beautiful in life and nothing that is small, unforgiving, unkind.

Later Mr. Shook wanted me to play whiffle ball with him and I did. I know now, and knew then, that this was the day at the beach they never had with Bobby. I was their son for those few hours, Maude their daughter. Maude and I also imagined that these were our parents, parents who wanted to buy everything new and brought far too much food for us to eat. Perhaps it was wrong to give in to this fantasy, but was it any different from the pretend games Maude played in which she was a princess or a rabbit for a time? Maude would admit, if you asked her, that she was not really a princess or a rabbit. She was merely playing, exploring the possibilities and escaping the harsh pull of reality for a time. Maude and I knew the Shooks were not our parents; the Shooks knew they had only one child and that they lost him; but none of us spoke of these things, or allowed them to touch the day.

Though, in this sense, the day was a dream, still it existed and we were there. The sandwiches were good, the waves as big as I'd ever seen them, the beach wide and clean. These things were real and grounded that day. Now, almost a year later, that trip is remembered while yesterday is already fading away. It was as true and lasting as anything in my life so far.

There was a sand castle, of course, and we all worked on it. It had turrets, a moat, and a tiny drawbridge. The sand was pliable and more cooperative than usual. Mr. Shook made a flag from a toothpick and a piece of red plastic wrap. He stuck it in the highest turret and we all agreed the castle was well made.

That was the way things went. Even when it clouded over and started to pour, the rain was warm and bathed us. In the car on the way home we smelled of salt, of wet towels, and wet hair. Mr. Shook wanted to stop to see a hillside where once, shortly after he moved from North Dakota, he cut timber. "We logged this whole hill," he said, looking at the trees that had grown up tall and thick since then. How long it had been. Mrs. Shook took his arm. Even Maude was silent, as if she knew that this was Mr. Shook's moment and she must give it to him as he had given her the beach ball, the kite.

Mrs. Shook wanted to stop to have coffee. I knew she just

wished to prolong the day, but no one objected. Maude had ice cream, I ordered hot chocolate. On the table was a small jukebox. I gave my sister nickels, she dropped them in the slot, and pressed random buttons, taking her chances. Country western music began to play through a faulty speaker.

Once again, there was little talk at the table, but I caught Mrs. Shook looking at me, simply looking. I knew the sadness had begun to creep back, coming closer as we came closer to the heavy gray house she lived in. I caught her eye and she glanced away, as if she had no right to wish, as Mr. Shook once almost wished aloud, that this could continue until she was old. I wanted to say something to assure her that I would not desert her, but was afraid I might phrase it poorly and make her feel even more alone. So, as usual, I said nothing.

It took my parents a long time to think of the Little Store. While my father was driving the streets, my mother made phone calls to anyone who might have seen us or to whom we could have run. She called my grade school principal and he gave her phone numbers of some of my teachers, but it was the beginning of the Labor Day weekend and most were out of town.

At about three in the afternoon my mother reached my eighth-grade history teacher. He suggested that Tim might know of my whereabouts, as the two of us were inseparable.

"What is Tim's last name?" my Mom wondered. "It's completely gone out of my head."

"Wooley, Tim Wooley."

The Wooleys were called. Tim was not home, Mrs. Wooley informed my parents, but he could be found at the Thirty-eighth Avenue Market where he worked. My mom and dad quickly drove there and questioned Tim. The last time he had seen me, he told them, was about a week before. Did he know where I might be, might have gone? Not really, he answered. Tim didn't know about the Shooks. He knew that I had broken into their house and gotten away with it, but he didn't know how close I had grown to them and that they had been taking care of Maude.

"Is there anyone else you can think of we could talk to?" my mother asked, her nerves frayed from five hours of anxiety.

"Well, Cat."

Cat was not at home. Her father was called at the outboard motor store, but he didn't know where she was. "She's wild. She could be anywhere," he said in a resigned tone. In fact, at that moment Cat was at the last place anyone would look for Cat: in a dress shop. She was being fitted for the wedding. The dress shop was, of course, Mode-O-Day, Shane's place of employment. Shane assisted at the fitting and the awkwardness of this encounter would require an entire chapter by itself.

The wedding would take place the day after tomorrow, Sunday, September 2. Cat had a ticket for the Saturday morning bus and was not looking forward to the long journey to Bend. She now regretted having turned down Tim's offer to ride with her. Even more than the trip and the ceremony, Cat was dreading the reception—forced joviality was never Cat's long suit.

After the fitting, Cat strolled through her favorite Goodwill store to see if anything new had come in. She bought a beaded Indian belt to go with the outfit she had put together to wear at the reception. As soon as the service was over, she planned to change from the frilly, girlish dress her mother had selected to a mustard-colored man's sports coat over a light green doctor's smock tucked into jodhpurs and, on her feet, her favorite shoes: gold ballet slippers.

Around five in the afternoon, as Maude and I were plugging coins into the jukebox at the Elsie Inn, Cat dropped by the Little

Store on the pretext of picking up something for dinner. She had decided to make supper for her father. He seemed pretty low on the eve of his ex-wife's wedding and maybe a home-cooked meal would cheer him up. Cooking was one of Cat's more surprising skills.

Cat loitered in the parking lot of the Little Store for ten minutes before gathering enough courage to go inside. There were lots of other stores where she could have bought the ingredients to make meat loaf; the Little Store was not the only store in town, but it was the only store in town in which Tim Wooley worked. She smoked two cigarettes, then cursed herself for not having any Dentyne to take away her cigarette breath.

Cat was not in a good mood. In two days, wearing a dress that made her look like a "geek," she would witness her mother's marriage to a man not her father. Later that week she would start high school and be bored to death for nine months straight. The only alternative was to stay in Bend and go to school with yahoos and cowboys who would not only make fun of the way she dressed and cut her hair, but probably take her out back and try to beat some sense into her. All of this would have been a little easier to bear if Tim didn't treat her like she had diphtheria. *This summer sucked the big weenie,* she thought, the only summation that seemed even close to accurate. "Oh, fuck it," she said, ground out her L&M in the gravel parking lot, and went into the store.

"Hi."

"Hi."

Tim was alone, stocking some toilet tissue on the paper products shelf. He wished Cat had come in when he was doing something a little more masculine.

"How's the ass-wipe moving these days?" she asked.

"Oh, we sell quite a bit of it," he answered.

Nice conversation, Cat thought. Kind of like *Romeo and Fucking Juliet.*

"What have you been up to?" Romeo inquired.

"Nothing much."

"Me either. Working."

"You gonna keep the job during school?" Cat pretended to be interested in her grocery list. If she looked at Tim's face she would start to cry.

"Mr. Walsh wants me to. I guess I will. Part-time, maybe," Tim answered.

"You want to give me a pound of hamburger?"

"Sure."

Tim went behind the meat counter and measured out a pound of ground beef. He was nervous and couldn't make it come out to exactly a pound, so he gave her a little extra, wrapped it quickly in white paper, and wrote the price in black crayon.

"I'm going to Bend tomorrow."

"Oh, right," Tim said. He suddenly remembered lying on top of Cat and how excited he felt, how good it was to have her face next to his, her hands in his hair. "You looking forward to that?"

"About as much as atomic war."

"Yep," Tim answered sympathetically. He took the package of meat to the front counter and rang up the amount on the cash register. He only charged her for a pound.

"I've got to get some other stuff, too."

"Oh. Okay."

Now he didn't know whether to void the 69 cents and ring it up again when Cat had selected all of her purchases or wait until she had decided what else she needed and hope another customer didn't come in in the meantime.

"School on Wednesday," Cat reminded him.

"That'll be interesting, I guess," Tim replied without conviction.

If he'd only say something nice to me, Cat thought. "It's good to see you. You look different today." Anything.

"Oh, jeeze, I almost forgot!" Tim suddenly exclaimed as loudly as Tim ever exclaimed anything. "Nelson's parents were in here looking for you."

"Nelson's parents? Why?"

He told her that Maude and I were missing and the Jaquas hoped she would know where we were. Cat immediately forgot the meat loaf, forgot that the summer sucked the big weenie, even forgot her desire for Tim to say something nice. "You bet I know where they are!" she said excitedly. "The Shooks'!"

"You're kidding."

"Call Nelson's parents and say I'm on my way over!" she shouted and ran out of the store. She ran all the way to my house and by the time she got there, Tim had phoned and my mother and father were standing on the porch, waiting for her.

"I bet anything he's at these spooky people's house, the Shooks. They're really weird. They had this son, this retarded kid. He just disappeared. I'm not saying they killed him, but one day he was gone and nobody ever saw him again. We were trying to find out what happened to him, if they murdered him or what, so we started spying on them. There was all sorts of creepy stuff going on over there. Finally, we broke into their house. I mean, Nelson did."

"Broke in . . . ?" my dad asked. They were the first words either parent had been able to get in.

"He climbed the tree by their house and jumped through the window. It was great, just like Superman or something. I thought he was going to kill himself, but he didn't. Except they caught him inside and ever since he's been this kind of slave to them!

He has to do everything they tell him, like go over there and do manual labor and stuff, or else they'll turn him over to the cops or even worse. Maybe do the same thing to him they did to Bobby."

My parents couldn't take their eyes off the girl dressed in baggy madras shorts, the new Indian beaded belt, a Fruit of the Loom undershirt with an "Adlai Stevenson for President" pin over her right breast, and snow boots. They had come to believe that something dreadful had happened to their children, and Cat's disjointed, incoherent tale only fueled their alarm. The mother's guilt for leaving, the father's guilt for coming home too late and too drunk, made them vulnerable to their worst fears. Cat sensed this and took advantage of it.

So she went a little bit further, stretched the truth, made those worst fears come true. At last she had an audience. It was all she really wanted—someone to listen to her and take her seriously. The worst thing was to be ignored; even being made fun of gave her a role in the universe. When you're young, the only really unacceptable life is an ordinary life, to be one of the vast crowd. Cat, like all of us, had to feel special to believe she existed. My parents, listening and believing as they did, made her special.

"Then they forced him to bring Maude over there. He didn't want to, 'cause he didn't know what they'd do to her, but they made him. So Maude became a prisoner, too. I bet anything that's where they are, trapped in that house and they can't get out. I'm not saying these people are perverts or anything, but why else do they want two kids that aren't theirs? It isn't Nelson's fault. They have him by the . . ." She stopped short of saying "balls." "They have the goods on him and I think they've kind of brainwashed him, too, because when he talks about them it's like, oh, they're so nice and all this stuff. I told him, 'Nelson, they're sick,' but he didn't listen. Nelson has more smarts than that, so that's why I think maybe they used Communist torture on him or something. Maybe I'm wrong and they're not child molesters, but they sure give me the creeps."

"Where do these people live?" my dad asked. His legs were rubbery. He couldn't make complete sense of the girl's story, but the words "perverts" and "child molesters" made him dizzy with panic. *I'll kill them*, he thought.

"On Thirty-fourth, I can't remember the address. I'll take you there!" Cat offered, jumping up and down a little in excitement.

My mother called Officer Constantine and told him her children had been kidnapped and were being held against their will, which she had suspected in the first place. Officer Constantine warned my parents not to go to the suspects' house by themselves, but to wait for him. If the girl's story was true, these people could be dangerous. He was on his way.

"If he's not here in ten minutes . . ." my father said, but he was. Officer Constantine arrived with his young, red-haired partner, Officer Pierce. Two additional officers followed in a second patrol car. Officer Constantine asked Cat to repeat her story, which she did eagerly. This time there were more details: the night she heard Bobby screaming and saw the shadow of Mr. Shook with a poker in his hand, the concrete blocks, the Shooks' suspicious conversation I overheard while hiding under Bobby's bed. Locked in a strongbox in her room, Cat said, was a detailed record of the Shooks' comings and goings, although the notes we kept when we first watched the house didn't fill five pages. Cat said she even had their fingerprints, but didn't say they were on the cookies Mrs. Shook had given Tim.

Officer Constantine listened attentively, occasionally shifting from foot to foot. He asked no questions and jotted nothing down in his little book. When Cat was finished my mother demanded that they waste no more time and immediately go rescue her children. Officer Constantine said, yes, of course, right away, and asked Cat to show them to the house. He doubted that Cat's story was anything more than a tall tale, but knew he had to investigate it anyway.

Cat rode in the backseat of the patrol car with my mother and father. She sat directly behind Officer Constantine, who was at the wheel. My mom was in the middle between Cat and my dad. My father sat on the right behind Officer Pierce. He carried his gun in his jacket pocket.

It was six o'clock and I was expecting Shane any minute. I planned to call home as soon as we returned from the beach to see if either my mother or father had reappeared, but we didn't get back to the Shooks' until a few minutes before six and there was just time to clean up before my date. Even if I had called, it's possible that I would have missed them. My parents left the house with Officer Constantine almost precisely at six o'clock. Things might have been averted if I had caught them before they left, but perhaps not. Cat worked my parents into such a frenzy of anxiety that it is possible they would not have believed me if I told them not a word of what she said was true.

There wasn't time to shower, but I scrubbed my armpits and changed my underpants. I had only one clean shirt left and I put this on, a short-sleeve, blue and white checked cotton shirt. I wore jeans and my high-topped black basketball shoes. My hair was thick with salt from the beach and wouldn't lie flat on my head. I did the best I could, gluing it down with a little hair ointment Mr. Shook kept in the medicine cabinet. A pimple had appeared in the crease between my chin and mouth and I was concerned that Shane would be repulsed by the blemish and not let me kiss her and feel her breasts until it cleared up.

Through the bathroom door I could hear Maude protesting that she didn't want to change out of her new bathing suit. She had worn it to the Elsie Inn and all the way home. She loved it and planned to wear it the remainder of her life. Mrs. Shook was trying to convince her of the impracticality of this plan. She patiently explained that Maude could wear the bathing suit tomorrow and the next day, but not tonight. It was getting too chilly to be wandering around the house without proper clothing.

"But it's so cute! I'm so cute!" Maude squealed. I didn't need to see her to know she was admiring herself in the full-length mirror in Mrs. Shook's bedroom, sticking out her stomach and looking over her shoulder at her almost nonexistent buttocks.

Mr. Shook saw the police cars first, or rather the reflection of their flashing lights as they played off the living room walls and the gray screen of the television. It was dusk and he had just settled into the recliner to watch the six o'clock news. He turned and looked through the window into the street. Two patrol cars were parked in front of the house. Mr. Shook assumed there was trouble next door. He didn't know his neighbors well—he and Bridget kept pretty much to themselves—but he liked to help out if there was trouble.

He decided to step out on the porch and take a look. He lugged his heavy body out of the recliner, reminding himself to eat lightly at dinner tonight, and took two or three steps toward the foyer. At that moment there was a knock on the front screen door. No, not a knock: a pounding that rattled the door frame and vibrated through the entire house.

I heard it from upstairs. I assumed it was Shane, although it struck me as unusual that a girl with such slender limbs would have a knock like a heavyweight.

*　*　*

318

At the beginning of the summer, when the idea of solving the murder of Bobby Shook was new and exciting, the three junior detectives sat in the treehouse eagerly anticipating the moment when patrol cars would pull up in front of the Shooks' house, police officers would climb the cracked concrete steps, mount the sloped porch, and pound on the front door to arrest Mr. and Mrs. Shook. That day had come.

When we talked about it afterwards, although I didn't care to talk about it much, Cat always said the same thing: "I made it happen." This was true. She began the investigation and she brought it to its conclusion. It didn't bother her that she had fabricated the entire story, lied to my parents and the police. The means justified the end.

Cat walked, or ran, through life without ever leaving a footprint. Nothing she did, it must have seemed to her, had an effect on anyone. She was just a dumb kid, a weirdo, an outcast. The entire summer had passed and what did she have to show for it? A small, unsatisfying love affair and the honor of being a bridesmaid when the Whore married the Prick. This was not enough.

And so she made it happen, made it a summer she would never forget, and for which no one would ever forget her. Cat finally left her mark. I'm sure she never thought about it in these terms; she wasn't a reflective sort of person. But I know she felt it inside and it changed her for good. When I see her these days, she is so changed. She is Cathy now, wearing dresses and no longer cutting her own hair. Her pierced ear has healed. She is a member of a group of girls, and when I look at the group I have trouble distinguishing her from the others. I have described her before, this new Cat.

I miss the old Cat, miss the toughness and the not giving a damn. I miss that fierce determination to be different, to scratch out a place in the world wholly her own. The new Cat would never play strip poker or light up an L&M in full view of the neighborhood. The new Cat doesn't call people Helen and thinks Helen Keller jokes are cruel. But for even a slight chance at happiness, the old Cat had to go. When Cat kept repeating proudly, "I made it happen," she meant that for the first time in her life she realized she was not a helpless victim of circumstance, nor a misfit. She was finally exactly like everyone else—a force to be reckoned with; and the door opened out of childhood into the rest of life, whatever that might entail.

I don't see much of Cat anymore except for a distant wave in the crowded hall and that part is sad. On the other hand, I will always have this: walking down the sidewalk, my nose in a book, and a voice behind me saying, "Freeze!"

* * *

When Mr. Shook unlocked the front door and opened it, he saw five people on the porch, none of whom he recognized. Two were police officers, there was a young couple in their mid-thirties, and finally an oddly dressed girl about Nelson's age. Mr. Shook worried that the old porch couldn't support so much weight. Shoring up the sagging floor boards was another project he had on his list.

"Mr. Charles Shook?"

"Yes, Officer. What can I do for you?" Mr. Shook replied politely. His body filled the doorway. He held the evening paper in his right hand.

"Have you seen these children?" Officer Constantine offered two pictures. One was a color portrait of Maude taken six months earlier in a photographer's studio. Maude beamed at the camera; unsurprisingly, she loved having her picture taken. The other was a black and white photo of myself, stiff and unhappy in a sweater and tie, my eighth-grade graduation still. Mr. Shook unlatched the screen door, pushed it open, and bent down to peer at the pictures. He needed bifocals, but that was another thing he hadn't gotten around to.

"Why, of course," he answered, and glanced up at my mom and dad. "Are you . . . ?"

My mother didn't let him finish. "What have you done to my children?" she said in a loud, belligerent tone. She took a step forward and my father also stepped forward, to stay in front of her. "Where are they?"

"They're right . . . ," Mr. Shook started to reply, but his thoughts were suddenly too confused to continue. This young couple must be the Jaquas, back from their trip to . . . Where did Nelson say they had been stranded? Chicago? Denver? Or did he say? They have come to pick up Nelson and Maude, of course, but why are the police along? Could the parents have been killed in a plane crash and these are relatives who will now take charge? But the woman said, *"my* children." It didn't make sense.

"If anything's happened to them, you're going to pay," my father warned. He wished he could say something more threatening so the man would know how serious he was, but he was only able to come up with these standard phrases. "You're not going to get away with it."

"Nothing's happened. They're . . . ," Mr. Shook started to say but once again his jumbled thoughts got in the way. He needed his wife to sort this out and turned back inside to call her. "Bridget?"

"Where are they?" This was my mother again. She found herself unable to say anything at a normal volume. She could only speak in a shrill and panicked voice. *"I want them!"*

As if on cue a piercing scream came from inside the house. Then, hurried footsteps: Maude's light, quick tread followed by a heavy, ominous clomp. "Come back here, you little scamp, or you'll be sorry!" a woman's voice called out. To two frightened, exhausted parents the footsteps and the threat validated everything Cat had said. Maude was fleeing for her life from the abominable Mrs. Shook. A delighted squeal became a terrified scream, a game became a nightmare.

"If the children are here, Mr. Shook, I want you to bring them to their parents now," Officer Constantine said authoritatively. "Then I want to ask you a few . . ."

"That's Maude! That's her!" my mother cried out. She grabbed the edge of the screen door and flung it back so hard it banged against the side of the house. The spring was broken, another neglected household repair. She brushed ahead of Officer Constantine and rushed toward Mr. Shook, who still blocked the doorway. My father also moved quickly forward.

Startled by the two parents hurtling at him, Mr. Shook took a step backwards into the house. He couldn't for the life of him make sense of what was happening.

At that moment Maude appeared. My mother saw her first, glimpsing her through the narrow space between the doorjamb and Mr. Shook's big bulk. "Maude!" she screamed, and hit Mr. Shook in the ribs with the side of her fist to knock him out of the way.

Maude heard her mother's voice and a second later, when Mr. Shook flinched from my mother's blow and moved a half step to the left, saw her. "Mommy!" she shrieked. She squeezed past Mr. Shook, pushing against his overalled legs, and threw herself into her mother's arms. My mom lifted her up and swiftly retreated to the safety of the porch. Maude, having thought she would never see her mother again, sobbed with relief. She buried her face in my mom's shoulder and clutched desperately at her neck. My mother rocked Maude from side to side and murmured in her ear.

"I've got you. Everything's going to be all right. Don't cry. Mommy's here." My mother had never felt anything as sweet as Maude's small hand on her neck, never touched anything as tender as her little girl's young skin.

Maude was, of course, completely naked.

Maude had finally been convinced to shed her bathing suit, but when Mrs. Shook approached her with a pair of panties and one of the dresses I brought from the house, Maude dodged her and raced down the hall. As I have mentioned, Maude found it great fun to run around naked. It was even more fun to make the nice fat lady clomp after her until she was puffing and had to sit down. Maude had played chase with Mrs. Shook many times before and, like most games, never tired of it. She was dashing down the stairs and screaming with delight when she heard my mother call her name. She forgot the game, rushed past Mr. Shook, and into the waiting arms.

"Goddammit, what have you been doing to my little girl?" my father shouted. Maude's wails seemed to him wails of relief that she had been rescued from her captors. Maude's nakedness spoke for itself.

Mr. Shook, still bewildered, again looked back into the house for his wife. He saw her descending the last few stairs, carefully holding the banister. She carried a small pair of panties and a dress, and was breathing hard.

"All right, Mr. Shook," Officer Constantine said, taking a step toward the suspect. Shook was turned away and Officer Constantine was afraid he might try to escape or lock himself in the house. "I want you to come out on the porch nice and easy. I don't want any trouble." He took hold of Mr. Shook's upper arm. The two men were the same height, but if one was the bigger man, it was Mr. Shook. He looked down at the hand on his arm, but did not try to pull away from it. He wished someone would explain.

"Chuck, what's going on?" Mrs. Shook gasped when she appeared in the already crowded doorway. She looked from her husband to the police officer, from the policeman to the young couple, and from the couple to Cat standing at the edge of the porch. Mrs. Shook was out of breath from chasing Maude and wore a half-smile on her face, as if embarrassed for being winded.

"Get your hands off me!" Mr. Shook said, ignoring his wife's question and yanking his arm from Officer Constantine's grasp. He stumbled back into the doorway and bumped into Mrs. Shook. All of a sudden, everyone spoke at once:

"Chuck, what on earth is it? Is something wrong?"

"Sir, I'm placing you under arrest. It will be in your best interests to cooperate."

"Maude, shhh. You're safe. Mommy and Daddy are here."

"Get off my porch! You have no right!"

"You goddamn monster! Move another step and I'll use this!"

My father doesn't remember pulling out the gun. One minute it was in his pocket and the next it was in his hand. Even so, it was the first thing he had done all day that he felt good about. He held the Smith & Wesson .22-caliber pistol straight out, with just a little bend in his arm so the recoil would not jam his elbow when he fired. Basic training had taught him how to handle a gun.

"For Christ's sake, Mr. Jaqua, put that away! I'm taking care of this!" Officer Constantine shouted, and a moment later Officer Pierce drew out his own gun. "Now! That's an order!" Officer Constantine barked, but my father did not obey. If anything, his finger tightened on the trigger.

Mr. Shook froze, but not in terror. He felt, instead, a detached curiosity. So this is how I'm going to die, he thought; well, it should be sudden. He didn't feel regret, except for leaving Bridget alone. He saw little in the future now that Bobby was gone, and perhaps it was just as well life ended now, quickly, in a second.

He remembered that he hadn't changed his will since Bobby's death. He supposed it didn't matter since everything would go to Bridget, but he hated this kind of loose string.

"Mr. Jaqua, I want you to drop the gun now," Officer Constantine coaxed in a steady, forceful voice. "We have the situation in hand. Officer Pierce has the suspect covered. Just lower the gun slowly."

My father kept the pistol trained on Mr. Shook. "Where's my boy?" he asked. "What have you done to him?" He hated that his arm was trembling, but he just couldn't steady it. Well, at this range it wouldn't matter.

"What have you done with him?" he asked again.

I was whistling. This was strange, because I never whistle and can't whistle very well. But whistling seemed an appropriate thing for a young man to do while getting ready for a date with his girl. After I brushed my teeth and put on a little cologne I found in the medicine chest, I looked in the mirror to decide whether or not I was handsome. Finally I decided this was something only an objective eye could determine, so I gave up and left the bathroom.

The moment I stepped into the upper hall I heard my dad say, "You goddamn monster! Move another step and I'll use this!" I was so surprised at hearing his voice that I didn't pay attention to the words. I was used to hearing my father speak only at certain times and in certain places: at home, on the phone when he called long distance, in the car. His voice was out of place in the Shooks' house.

I've always found it difficult to identify people, even people I know well, when I see them in unexpected locales. My mom in the Captain's Bar at the Jolly Roger is an example. I thought, Dr.

Holt is having a drink with a pretty lady. Then I realized the pretty lady looked familiar. Then I realized she gave birth to me. Once I ran into my grandmother of the handkerchiefs in the Arctic Circle. This was so startling I didn't identify her until she had spoken to me for an entire minute. I guessed she was a teacher I'd had in third or fourth grade.

So I didn't react right away to my Dad's voice. I thought, "That man sounds like my father," not, "My father is here." I walked to the top of the staircase and looked down. I could see Mrs. Shook standing at the front door and Mr. Shook straddling the threshold. There was at least one person on the porch, but I couldn't tell who it was. No one appeared to be moving or speaking. The house was dim and the light coming through the open door placed everyone in silhouette.

As I came down the stairs, I began to feel that something was wrong. Only a minute before my sister had been laughing and squealing. Now there was silence. Where was Maude, my Maude-sensor asked? The Shooks were still as statues at the front door. An unidentified someone was on the porch. That *was* my father's voice, I realized. What did he say, something about "using this"?

Then I heard his voice again: "Where's my boy? What have you done to him?" I thought, he can't mean me. I'm right here. He must mean some other boy. Does my father have another boy? My thoughts were slow, sluggish.

Then more voices tumbled over one another, some familiar, some not:

"Don't hurt him! Please!" I saw Mrs. Shook saying this, but not the person to whom she said it. She reached out a hand.

"Mr. Jaqua, put the gun down," a deep voice said.

"I've got him covered, Joe." This was a thinner, reedier voice.

"I'm not doing anything until I have my son." My dad's voice again.

"You're not going to get away with this!" another voice said, a voice I recognized immediately. It was the voice that told me so many times that summer to make sure Maude had something nutritious to eat, the voice that asked with which parent I would choose to live. So my mom was here, too, both my mom and my dad. I was surprised. I didn't know they knew the Shooks.

Then I heard Mr. Shook's gravelly voice and, right after, Mrs. Shook's voice, raised and desperate:

"There's some mistake."

"Don't hurt him! He's all I have!"

Someone shifted on the porch, thrusting something forward. Mrs. Shook cried out, a wordless cry.

"Use this," "put the gun down," "I've got him covered." The words, the phrases began to take on meaning. I still didn't know what was happening, but I knew it was trouble. I thought perhaps the Shooks were being robbed, although that didn't explain why my parents were present. It didn't matter. Someone was going to hurt Mr. Shook—*"He's all I have!"* she cried out—and I wanted to help. I took the last few stairs quickly and then was at the front door. It was curious that I thrust myself into the middle of what I assumed was an armed robbery. Up until then I'd avoided any physical danger; even tag football filled me with dread. I was changing, there was no doubt about it.

Neither Mr. nor Mrs. Shook had moved from the doorway, but through the gap between their bodies I saw a fat police officer reaching his left hand behind him. I couldn't see to whom he was reaching or what he was reaching for. I slid in front of Mrs. Shook to widen the angle. Next, I saw Maude's bare backside and an arm under it, supporting her. On the arm was my mother's gold charm bracelet.

No one knew I was present, not even Mrs. Shook who was intently focused on the gun. This I hadn't seen yet, but was just about to see. I noticed my father's body first, the way his left leg was planted in front of him and slightly bent at the knee, while his right leg was held straight with the foot turned inwards as if he was pigeon-toed. My mother stood directly behind him, so the effect was of my father protecting her. She was leaning backwards and clutching Maude tightly. Like my father she appeared slightly off balance.

My father's arm was stretched out almost straight and in his hand was the gun. I recognized it as the gun I had held the previous evening. His left arm dangled at his side. His face was tight and colorless.

No one noticed me.

"Okay, we're going to do this without any problem," the fat police officer said, although the tenseness in his voice indicated that he felt there might yet be a problem. He took a pair of handcuffs from a second officer standing behind him and a little to his left. This policeman was youthful, had angry red hair, and a matching stripe of red acne on his neck. I saw his empty holster. From my position I couldn't see the gun he held on my father, but I sensed it there.

"I don't want any trouble. We'll settle this all at the station house," the fat policeman said, extending the handcuffs toward Mr. Shook's right wrist. So it wasn't a robbery, I realized. Mr. Shook was being arrested. This made no sense and, at any rate, I would not stand for it.

"What do you think you're doing?" I shouted first, then, "Stop it!" and everyone looked at me.

My father gave me a quick glance, then his eyes returned to Mr. Shook. Army training had taught him not to be distracted while holding a man at gunpoint; that's how to get yourself killed. Mr. Shook looked at me with the same dumbfounded expression he wore during the whole of his arrest. Maude also turned at the sound of my voice. Her face was streaked with tears, but as usual she was able to stop her wails at will. My mother stared at me in surprise, as if she remembered me looking a little different.

Officer Constantine also looked at me. Later he said he was annoyed to see me materialize just then. He would have preferred to get Mr. Shook cuffed and convince my father to drop the gun before I entered the picture. He also didn't like my tone of voice. He wasn't used to being questioned while making an arrest or told to "stop it."

"Nelson! Come here! Hurry!" My mother broke the stunned silence that fell with my appearance. She fully expected my father to pull the trigger and didn't trust his aim although Mr. Shook was a large target and not three feet from the end of the pistol. But she knew nothing about guns. She worried that the bullet would ricochet off Mr. Shook and hit me.

"Son, do as your mother says. Just come out on the porch . . ." the fat officer holding the handcuffs started to say, but he got no further.

"I'm not your son!" I told him, then asked again, "What do you think you're doing?" My voice seemed unnaturally loud and high. I was embarrassed by my high voice and hoped it would soon change to a manly timbre.

The strange scene—my mother holding my naked sister, my father holding a gun, Officer Constantine extending the handcuffs, and Mr. Shook half in, half out of the house—was a puzzle until I looked past the small crowd and saw at the edge of the porch the thin, tomboyish figure of Cat. She was backed up against a peeling pillar, her arms crossed in front of her chest, hands clutching her elbows. She was breathless with excitement, the "I made it happen" spread across her face like jam on a small child. Had she been holding wires attached to the two police officers, my parents, and the Shooks, it couldn't have been more clear that this scene was her doing, the culmination of her efforts all summer. She wanted the Shooks to be arrested and they were being arrested. She wanted to be the one to lead the police to their door and she had led them there. I didn't need to be told of her lies; I could smell them on her. Our eyes met, but there was no apology in hers. Instead, she looked at me with the innocent interest of a moviegoer: Now Nelson's here. What's he going to do? This is getting good.

"Everything's all right now, young man," Officer Constantine said soothingly. "You're safe. Your parents are here. Just come out on the porch," he repeated as he slowly moved the handcuffs toward Mr. Shook's wrist.

I stepped in front of Mr. Shook and right into the line of fire. "Don't touch him! He hasn't done anything!" I shouted in that same high voice.

My small movement suddenly galvanized everyone into frantic action. Officer Constantine grabbed my arm and tried to pull me to him, Mrs. Shook grabbed my shoulder and tried to pull me back into the house, and my dad, keeping the gun trained on Mr. Shook, tried to shove me out of the way, toward the back of the porch.

"Get your hands off me!" I jerked away from all three of them and felt my shirttail come out. "They didn't do anything! They didn't kill Bobby! He died!" I announced, but the moment I said it I knew this was not why the police had come. Bobby is no longer the issue, I realized; I am. My parents think I'm in danger. Cat has told them something, something like the crazy suspicions she told me at the amusement park, and my parents believed her. The summer had sped ahead and left Bobby behind. I could do nothing about that, but I could stop Mr. Shook from coming to harm. At least, I could try. I stepped back in front of him and looked down the barrel of my father's loaded revolver.

"Larry, put the gun down!" my mother pleaded. "You'll shoot Nelson!" Maude watched the scene without comment. In fact, she was sucking her thumb.

"Please, Mr. Jaqua," Officer Constantine said in an impatient, I-want-this-over tone, "put it away. The boy is safe."

I could see the hesitation in my father's face; he liked how the gun felt, what it meant. The impotence he had felt all day disappeared when he produced the weapon. But he also realized that pointing a .22 in the direction of his son, no matter how badly he took care of the lawn, was not wise. He slowly lowered the pistol, but did not return it to his pocket, and still kept his finger on the trigger. Behind me Mr. Shook let out a heavy, coffee-laden breath.

"Stand aside, son," Officer Constantine ordered. He stepped toward me, still determined to clasp the handcuffs on Mr. Shook's thick wrists.

"I'm not your son!" I said again. I wanted him to understand this, that I wasn't anybody's son anymore.

"Nelson, come to me," my mother said, her voice softer now that the gun had been lowered. "It's all right."

"It's *not* all right! You're not touching them!"

"Nothing to worry about," the police officer tried to reassure me. "We're just taking them down to the station for some questioning."

"No, you're not!" I could feel Mr. Shook's oversized body behind me solid and sturdy, like the wall we built, and it gave me courage. "You're not taking them anywhere!"

"Nelson, this is something you know nothing about," my father said, his anger beginning to turn from Mr. Shook to me.

"I know everything about it! I'm the only one!" I insisted, and the streetlight at the end of the block clicked on like a visual exclamation point.

Officer Constantine reached for me, clasping a rough hand on my shoulder, but I pulled away before he could get a good grip. He reached again, this time grabbing me by the front of my blue and white shirt. I yanked back again and slammed my shoulder against the hinge of the screen door. Then my dad reached for me, trying to catch me by the back of the neck, but I ducked him, too. My reflexes had never been so quick. I could have dodged them all night.

"Go away! Leave us alone! We just want to be left alone!" I yelled, and my mother's face changed expression as quickly as a record spindle drops a new disk on the turntable. Motherly concern disappeared and a familiar "you're in big trouble, mister" expression took its place. But it was too late for such expressions; they had no more authority. "You're trespassing!" I continued. "This is the Shooks' house! It's private property! You don't belong here!"

"Don't talk to your mother and me that way!"

It was an ordinary phrase, the kind of thing every father says to his son at one time or another. He had said it to me before in our thirteen years together. However, it was the wrong thing for him to say at this moment with my friends being threatened and my parents reaching for me and telling me to come to them when for months they had ignored me. It was one more sentence from my father's mouth with a "don't" in it: Don't forget to mow the grass; don't ever smoke; don't get married; don't talk to your mother and me that way.

The sting of his slap, the click of the ice cubes in my mother's glass when she asked me how much I loved my father, the house so empty after they left—these were the things that carried the most weight that summer I was thirteen. They were things I could not forget, would carry with me forever, and made me feel very much alone. If I didn't tell my parents, they would never know that I was an unwilling participant in their life and could not live that way any longer. Their life would leave me feeling unloved and unprepared to live my own. If I didn't talk to them "that way," they would never know that through the Shooks I had learned that, although sadness was inevitable, life could also offer kindness; and, most importantly this: that I had found better parents and meant to have them.

"I'll talk any damn way I want!" The words burst out of me and took me as much by surprise as they did my father and mother. "You don't have any right to come here and arrest them! It's not fair! They've been through enough!"

"Nelson, just calm down . . ." my father started to say, but this only outraged me more.

"Calm down? *Calm down?* You've got a gun in your hand and you're telling *me* to calm down?"

"I want you to come here right now. We'll go home and . . ."

"I'm not going anywhere! The Shooks are my friends. They asked me here. They didn't ask you. Leave us alone. Leave *me* alone!" I said, even though this was what my parents had done all summer and against which I was rebelling. But it was hard to be coherent. How could I ever make them understand?

"What has gotten into you, Nelson?" my father asked, embarrassed that I was making a scene instead of throwing myself into his waiting arms as eagerly as Maude had flung herself into her mother's. "Why did you leave the house? Why did you run away?"

"Why did you?" I matched the sternness in his voice, the disapproval. "You were the one who walked out. So did you," I said to my mother, and the angles of her face hardened. "Where were we supposed to go? You put me in charge of Maude. What was I supposed to do? *What?*" I demanded, actually wanting an answer. If they had one, now was the time to reveal it.

"This involves a lot more than you know," my dad replied, underestimating me again.

"No, it doesn't," I said, suddenly no longer angry. "It's simple. You don't care about us and the Shooks do. That's all."

"Nelson, I won't have this."

"Okay, don't. Just leave. I'm used to it."

"Young man, you're looking to get hit."

"It wouldn't be the first time."

He took a quick step toward me, then checked himself. A small crowd had gathered on the sidewalk, drawn by the rotating lights of the two patrol cars, and my father hesitated to slap me with so many attentive witnesses looking on. The audience stood motionless as mannequins in the blue dusk, their faces upturned toward the porch.

"We'll talk about this later," he said in a voice that made it clear he didn't want to talk about it at all.

"You just drove off. You didn't even say where you were going," I went on. "You knew Mom was leaving. Why didn't you stay and take care of us if you're so damn concerned? You just walked out like we were nothing."

"I had business . . ."

"With who?" I asked. I had been waiting for this chance, saving up for it. "With that woman you've been seeing all this time, the last seven years? How am I supposed to trust you or believe anything you say after that?"

My dad opened his mouth to respond, but nothing came out. He stared at me for a moment, then turned to my mother for an explanation of how I came to know this. She avoided his look. He looked back at me, still at a loss for words. I took the opportunity of his silence to dig the knife in deeper. I was getting good at this.

"I don't understand why you have kids, and then don't bother to love them or spend any time with them. You just do whatever you want and forget all about us. I'm old enough so it doesn't matter, I guess, but what about Maude? She's only four and she doesn't have any parents. You guys might as well be dead."

"How dare you say that!" my mother objected. "We love Maude more than anything."

"We love you both," my dad added automatically.

"I don't believe you."

"I don't care if you believe me or not!" he shouted and glanced at Officer Constantine for understanding: *See what I have to put up with?* But the police officer only watched, neither interrupting nor passing judgment.

"How can you say that, Nelson?" my mother asked in a wounded tone, just loud enough for the onlookers to hear her sorrow and sympathize. "Of course we love you. We're your parents."

"That doesn't prove anything! All it means is you fucked twice. Anybody could do that!" I couldn't believe these words were coming out of my mouth. "If you love us, why don't you prove it? You don't do anything for Maude. I do everything. I get her dressed in the morning, I take her all day, I make her dinner, I play with her till bed, I put her to bed, and do her wash and the dishes. What do you do? You go to bars and drink with Dr. Holt."

My mother's face at this moment is hard to describe.

"I saw you there. Maude could of seen you, too, but I took her away."

"What have you been doing, following me?" she accused, the wounded tone turning to outrage.

"No! It was an accident," I said in defense, knowing she would never believe me. "Is that what you're doing all the time I've been baby-sitting? Is that why you don't want Maude underfoot?"

Now it was my mother's turn to be speechless. She gazed at me, lips tight, a muscle twitching in her cheek.

"What's this about the doctor?" my father asked her.

Instead of answering, my mother shifted the weight of Maude from her right arm to her left. "Larry, do something about him," she finally said in a flat, tense voice that betrayed an apprehension that nothing could be done now, that it was too late.

"And then yesterday you both just left and what do you say? You say," I reminded my father, " 'Don't ever get married.' Gee, thanks. After this summer, I don't have to be told that. And you say," I turned to my mom, " 'Take Maude, the cab's waiting.' That's all. Not even 'Good-bye.' And you say you love her more than anything."

"Nelson, stop this right now!" my dad demanded.

"I guess that means you don't love anything very much," I said directly to my mother and saw this hit its mark. The rest of it she could defend, but walking down the steps and getting into that cab while Maude sobbed and begged her to stay was something she knew was wrong. "If that's what you think love is . . . ," I started to say but didn't go further. After all, I was no expert on the subject.

"Show some respect for your mother," my father ordered.

"What about respect for me?"

"You're a boy. You don't understand . . ."

"You don't know anything about me," I answered, and he didn't dispute it.

"We'll settle this at home."

"I am home!"

The words surprised me. Everything else was familiar, the same old thoughts and worries that haunted me all summer. But this was a new idea. As I said it, I knew it was true and I repeated it so my parents would also know: "This is my home. This is where people want me. You don't."

"I give up," my father said, looking down at the old boards of the porch floor and shaking his head in despair. "I don't know what to do with you."

Then there fell a little silence in which no one spoke. We had reached an impasse; reached, really, the heart of it. At that moment I found it hard to believe that a whole world existed beyond that porch, lives being lived, routine being carried out. Here, it seemed, was the core of life, the quietly beating center.

"Their son died," I said softly, because my voice was starting to be raw and throaty, "and I've never seen anybody . . ." I began having trouble with words. "They took care of him better than anybody could have. They could have just put him in a home and forgot him, but they didn't. They did everything they could and when it was finished, I think maybe they wished they could do it all over again. Even the bad parts. I wonder if one of us was sick or helpless, if you'd take the time . . ." I looked at my mother and father. They looked back. Where did I learn to be so cruel?

"I used to think the Shooks killed their son because he was retarded and not like other boys. But it was exactly the opposite. His whole life they treated Bobby like he was the smartest kid in the world. Like he grew up and took over the lumber yard and married the girl next door and had kids of his own, but still came over here on the weekend to help with things around the house. That's the way they treated him, even though he couldn't even read or learn the ABCs."

"I'm sure that . . ." my mother started to say, but stopped, unsure of what she was sure of.

"They sat by his bed in the hospital. When they left they said where they were going, even if it was out for a sandwich. When they left at night, they said exactly when they would come back the next morning. And they came back exactly when they said they would. They never gave up on him," I told my father, who had just given up on me, "even when he had just a few minutes left. Maybe I'm selfish, but that's what I want. That's the kind of parents I wish I had."

My mother stared, her mouth slack and her eyes blinking rapidly. Then she started to cry. I looked away so I wouldn't have to see this and that's when I saw Shane. She stood beyond Cat on the cracked concrete steps between the two banks of ivy. She was looking up at me, eyes wide and for once not completely covered with the curtain of hair. I wondered how long she had been there, and guessed probably from the beginning.

"Maybe you think they did something to us. I don't know." I turned to Officer Constantine. The handcuffs still dangled from his hand, swaying slightly back and forth like a hypnotist's pocket watch. "But they didn't do anything except whatever we wanted to do. Like go to the zoo and to ride the ponies, lots of stuff. We had a picnic at Mt. Hood. We just got back from the beach," I explained, although the Seaside trip seemed several decades ago. "That's why Maude's like that. She was getting changed. Mrs. Shook always made sure she had clean clothes and her socks matched. She'd play games with her. She cooked and taught Maude how to make cookies. Me and Mr. Shook built a wall. What did we ever build together?" I asked my father, and he had no answer.

I would like to report that this "Friends, Romans, Countrymen" was delivered without tears, but I can't say that. Tears ran down the sides of my face and hung in tickling drops on the edge of my jaw. I hated crying in front of all these people: the police, my parents, Cat, most of all Shane. Only Mr. and Mrs. Shook, I felt, would not look down on me.

"I love you . . ." I choked on this, not because it wasn't true. "But I can't live with you anymore. I can't take care of Maude anymore." I looked at my mom to see if she had a stricken look. "I know you don't like to have her around all the time, but she's really not so bad. I don't know what I would have done without her this summer. But I start high school next week and I'll be too busy to have her all the time. Sorry, Maude," I apologized, but Maude seemed unaffected by my brotherly concern. She sucked her thumb and studied me as if I were a new species the zoo just acquired.

"I'm going to live here if the Shooks will let me. I'll sleep in Bobby's room. It has a good bed and there's a desk and everything I need. It's not like I'll never see you," I reassured my parents, although now this was probably the last assurance they wanted. "I'll just be a little ways away and I'll come visit and play with Maude and everything, but my life has to change and I'm the only one who can do that. I guess I know that now." This was not a happy discovery; it seemed a colossal responsibility. Welcome to the real world, Nelson. I suddenly wished Maude and I could change places: I would sit naked in the crook of my mom's arm while she told our parents they were not fit.

"If you make me go home," I said, addressing Officer Constantine again, "I'll just run away again until you get so sick of chasing after me you give up."

It was now almost completely dark and the red and white flashes from the patrol cars were especially sharp-edged. The stark beams made the scene on the porch even more bleak and hopeless. In the time it took for me to choose my next words, nobody broke in, no one offered a solution: There wasn't any and we all knew it.

"If it's okay, I'll come by in a day or so and get my stuff. I just want some books and clothes, that's all. I hope you don't hate me. I've tried to understand you all summer and maybe now you could try to understand me."

I wanted to say something more, something that would tell my parents that I did not blame them for everything they had done and everything I imagined they had done. That, in fact, I loved them more than ever because I had said it aloud and knew it was true. Even though it had been a long time since they told me they loved me, until that moment on the porch in the summer dark I could not remember when last I said it to them.

But these were complicated thoughts and, anyway, I had talked enough. I started to go inside.

As I turned, I saw Tim sitting astride his bicycle on the parking strip. He was looking at me, as was everyone, but Tim was the only person with a smile on his face. Tim rarely smiled and it was strange that he would choose this black moment to grin his dazzling grin. Then I remembered his question to me the night of the Monopoly party: "I feel sometimes like I'm going to explode. You ever feel like that, Nelson? Like you're going to explode?" Perhaps that was what had just happened. The hurt and anger I kept so carefully canned within me so no one would know of it and judge me harshly for it had finally exploded. Tim might not have been bright, but he knew some things instinctively, knew this, and it made him smile. I had spent years envying Tim and here he was, I think, envying me.

Turning my back on my parents, I walked past the Shooks into their house. I tensed, waiting for the bang and the bullet between my shoulder blades, but these didn't come. Nor did Mr. Shook move or try to stop me. I avoided Mrs. Shook's eyes, for I knew they were watery. I went quickly up the stairs, taking them two at a time so as to disappear off the face of the earth as soon as possible.

Then I was at the top of the staircase and then I was in Bobby's room, my room from now on.

chapter eleven

Shortly after I went inside my dad withdrew the charges against Mr. and Mrs. Shook. He slipped the gun back into his pocket and was certain that, during the ride home in the patrol car, Officer Constantine would lecture him about the dangers of keeping a firearm in the house.

"The child will catch cold," was the first thing that was said after I went indoors and it was said by Mrs. Shook. She stepped over the threshold and handed Maude's panties and dress to my mom, who put Maude down and quickly dressed her. "Thank you," my mother murmured almost inaudibly. She was glad to have something to do.

"I'm sorry," my dad then said to Mr. Shook without really looking him in the eye. "They disappeared and we got so worried. And this girl . . ." Suddenly remembering that Cat was the cause of the misunderstanding and the person on whom he should vent his anger and humiliation, my dad whirled around to confront her. But when he looked to the edge of the porch where Cat had been standing, she was gone.

"Well . . ." Mr. Shook said with his usual midwestern slowness, "We know what it's like to worry over a child."

Officer Constantine turned to his young partner. "Disperse those people," he ordered. The crowd remained on the sidewalk, still gazing upwards with anticipation at the Shooks' house. Officer Pierce told the group that the excitement was over and to get a move on. Disappointed that at least one of the guns hadn't gone off, but happy there had been even a small distraction in the normal course of their lives, the neighbors began drifting away. A paperboy continued throwing papers. Dogs barked and cars stopped at the curb drove on.

Officer Pierce switched off the flashing beacon on top of Officer Constantine's car. The beacon on the second patrol car also went dark and the car glided up the street. It seemed as if red and white lights had been flashing on Thirty-fourth Avenue for years, but a moment after they were gone it was as though they had never been there at all.

"What about Nelson?" my mother asked my father after she had dressed Maude and it seemed that they, too, were going home. "We can't just leave him here."

My dad glanced at Mr. Shook, expecting him to say something, but he was silent. He still stood in the doorway in the position he had taken when my father pulled the gun. Mrs. Shook had gone to gather up Maude's sandals and the few other possessions with which she had come.

"Maybe just for tonight," my dad said uncertainly. He wasn't sure what a father should do at a time like this. He found himself wanting to ask Mr. Shook's advice, but felt this might be awkward after nearly shooting the man. "We're all a little . . ." my father began to say, then couldn't think of what to say after that. He knew my mother expected him to take charge and he might redeem himself a little in her eyes if he said just the right thing.

"When he's a little more . . ." Again he stopped, stumped. The words simply weren't coming to him. "Tomorrow," he said, not sure what he meant, but leaving it at that.

"Come on, folks." Officer Constantine put a hand lightly on my dad's back. "I'll take you home."

Maude had been uncharacteristically silent during the Battle of the Front Porch, watching with the riveted attention she usually reserved for her favorite cartoons, but when she realized that I was not coming home with her, she began to howl. "Where's Nelson? I want Nelson!" she bawled.

"Nelson's going to stay here tonight," my mother said soothingly, but this only made Maude complain louder. "No! I want Nelson! I need Nelson! Let me go!" She broke away and ran to the front door. My mom was embarrassed by the little scene. It somehow made true all the accusations of her being a bad mother, and they weren't all true, she truly believed.

Before Maude could escape into the house Mrs. Shook reappeared carrying the remainder of Maude's clothes. The four-year-old grabbed Mrs. Shook's legs and pressed her face into the soft, worn fabric of her skirt. "He'll be all right, Maudy," Mrs. Shook said, leaning down and giving the girl one last sprinkle-covered cookie. "We'll take good care of him."

"I want to stay, too!" Maude pleaded, perhaps thinking of waking up to blueberry pancakes and cold milk in a Howdy Doody glass.

"No, you go home with your Mommy and Daddy. They love you and miss you," Mrs. Shook urged, but this had little effect. Finally my dad had to pick Maude up in his arms and carry her down the warped wooden steps of the porch and the old concrete stairs to the waiting patrol car. Officer Constantine held open the rear door. My father pushed Maude inside, climbed in after her, and my mother slid in behind him, clutching to her chest the few items of clothing Mrs. Shook had handed her. They were, of course, freshly laundered and ironed.

"Good-bye," Mrs. Shook called out and waved.

"Good-bye," Mr. Shook called out, too, and together they watched until the police car vanished up the street under the dark, broad-leafed trees.

Lying on Bobby's bed, I listened to the distant sound of voices on the porch, though words could not be distinguished and even individual voices blurred together. Only Maude's cries were unmistakable and provoked the old protective urges. I wanted to go to her, try to calm her, but I reminded myself that I had given over that responsibility, and someone else must now shoulder the burden. I covered my ears until the cries faded and were gone.

Bobby's room was dark and comfortable, his things already becoming familiar to me. I promised him silently that I would not make any changes. Everything would stay the same, except that a few of my clothes would hang in his closet, a few of my books would litter his desk. I also told him it was not my intention to replace him in his parents' affections. I just wanted to borrow his room to grow up in. I needed a place to live during my four years of high school, then I would move on to college or whatever fate awaited me.

I concentrated on this so as not to think about what I had said to my parents. Sometimes a phrase would trickle back into my consciousness and I would fight it and force it out. A month or a year from now I might be able to think of my words without shame, but I couldn't now and so I wouldn't think about them at all.

The sound of a step or a cupboard door closing occasionally drifted up from downstairs. The television was usually on at this hour, but I heard no television that night. I wondered what they were doing, the Shooks. Mrs. Shook was probably making dinner, Mr. Shook reading the newspaper. It was hard to imagine anyone going back to normal life after what had happened, but if anyone could do it, Chuck and Bridget Shook could. They were used to taking blows, then calmly picking up the evening paper, starting the evening meal. It was why I had come here: the calm, the routine. The assurance that ordinary life was still possible quieted me and before long I drifted to sleep.

I was awakened by a light tapping on the door. "Nelson," Mrs. Shook asked softly as if speaking to an invalid, "would you like some dinner?"

"No thanks." I said it before I was fully awake and knew how hungry I was. I hadn't eaten anything since the sandwiches at the beach, around one o'clock. My watch showed that it was a little after eight.

I rose, clicked on the light, and looked at myself in the mirror above the dresser. A pillow crease like a scar ran across the side of my face. The hair on the right side of my head was standing straight up, glued into that position by the hair oil I splashed on earlier in the Shooks' bathroom. I took a brush from the top of the dresser and tried to coax down the unruly bristles. This was the first time I used something of Bobby's except his bed, but I didn't get a chill or feel him watching over my shoulder. I didn't feel anything, only that the brush was there; it was a nice brush with a thick tortoise shell handle and it was heavy in my hand. In no time my hair was back in place.

Mr. and Mrs. Shook were seated at the dining room table when I came down the stairs. They looked up from their plates, but not in surprise. "I was hungry after all," I said. A third place was already waiting for me. I slid into the chair and Mrs. Shook was soon at my side, heaping food on my plate.

As usual nothing much was said during the meal, and I was grateful for this. Mrs. Shook asked, "More?" and "What can I pass you, Nelson?" Once Mr. Shook looked down at his lap and said, "I've got to lose some weight," then he took another helping of mashed potatoes.

Dessert was rhubarb pie. Mrs. Shook was anxious that I would not like it, but I liked it. It reminded me of the first pie I ate in that house: blackberry pie the night I broke in. I remembered the strangeness of the house when I crept through it and my fear of it. Now I lived here. I asked for another piece of pie.

I excused myself as quickly as I could. I wanted to tell Mr. Shook I was sorry my father almost shot him, that it was my fault, and I meant to make it up to him. I would reroof the house by myself, if necessary, and do any other household repairs that needed attending to. But I knew Mr. Shook did not require an apology and simply asking for seconds on the pie was apology enough for Mrs. Shook. I tried not to notice their looks of sympathy and, maybe, love as I went up the stairs to my room.

It was dark when I awoke. My watch read ten minutes before six. The house was still, the street outside also still. Nothing in particular woke me; I simply didn't need more sleep. I sat up. The room was a little cold. I needed to go to the bathroom.

I slipped on my socks and jeans and put on my checkered shirt, the one I had worn the night before. It was wrinkled from having fallen asleep in it before dinner. I carefully opened the door. Across the hall, Mr. and Mrs. Shooks' bedroom door was shut. I walked down the hall, stepping carefully in my stocking feet so as to make as little noise as possible. I reached the bathroom, entered it, and closed the door before turning on the light.

After relieving myself I ran water on my fingers and splashed some on my face. As I reached for a towel, I saw, on the small counter under the medicine cabinet, a new blue toothbrush. The previous day I mentioned to Mrs. Shook that I had brushed my teeth with my finger, but that it worked fine. She looked alarmed and scurried off to ask her husband if he happened to have an extra. Now a brand-new toothbrush lay on the counter in front of me, still in its plastic sterile container. Did she locate one she had bought for Bobby that was never used, or had she sent Mr. Shook, after my father nearly killed him, to the store to buy me a new toothbrush? Somehow I knew that this was the case and that he did it happily.

I was sorry they went to so much trouble, because I was leaving. I didn't know when I entered the bathroom that I was returning to my parents' home and cannot remember deciding this during the minute and a half I spent in the bathroom, but when I saw the new toothbrush I thought, "They bought that for me because they think I'm staying. I hope they aren't hurt when they find I'm gone." I hoped they would use the toothbrush when one of their own toothbrushes had worn down, but I knew, just as I knew that Mr. Shook had made a special trip to the store to buy it, that neither Mr. nor Mrs. Shook would ever use the new brush. It would be saved for me in case I came back, or another boy came to stay.

Now, when I live it through again after almost a year, I know that the decision to go was made for me the moment I awoke. I woke up cold in Bobby's room, and not a part of it. It was a child's room and that was one thing that could not be said about me any longer: I was not a child. I was responsible for my actions now. I was responsible for my own toothbrush from now on.

I switched off the bathroom light, opened the door, and returned silently down the hall. I made Bobby's bed, although I knew Mrs. Shook would unmake it after I was gone, to wash the sheets and air out the mattress. Chores like washing sheets and airing out mattresses kept her mind off her ache, just as Mr. Shook's endless trips to Foster Lumber Mill kept him moving, kept him alive.

The few remaining clothes I brought with me were either folded in the empty dresser drawers or hanging in the closet. I collected these; there wasn't much. Then I sat down at Bobby's desk, took a perfectly sharpened pencil from the pencil cup and a never-used pad of lined paper from the desk drawer, and wrote a letter:

> *Dear Mr. and Mrs. Shook,*
> *I'm sorry I left before you got up, but I was awake and it just seemed better that way. Thank you for letting me stay here the last two nights. I was really comfortable and slept well.*

This was the kind of thing Mrs. Shook worried about and a small reassurance might cheer her just a little.

> *I went back home. I don't think it's right to worry my parents and make them feel bad. I hope they can solve their problems and maybe if I'm there I can do something to help. Anyway, I want to make sure Maude is all right.*
> *Mr. Shook, I'll come over in a day or two to help with the roof like we planned. I'll bring something I wrote for you to read, Mrs. Shook, but I don't think it'll be very good.*

I wanted to tell them what their kindness meant to me and that because of them I had changed in some ways I already felt and

in others I would not know for a long time to come, but I didn't
trust myself to put these thoughts into words, at least not so soon
and so early in the morning. Finally, I just wrote:

> *Yesterday at the beach was one of the best days of
> my life. I'll never forget it.*

With love,
Nelson

The sky was lightening and the stars beginning to clear away
as I walked down Thirty-fourth Avenue and turned onto Bybee
Boulevard. The cool morning air raised goose bumps on my bare
arms.

I didn't think about what awaited me at home; I simply moved
in that direction and would let what would happen, happen. I
enjoyed the tapping of my smooth-soled shoes on the pavement,
the tingle along my arms. There weren't any cars, so I walked
down the middle of the street. Bybee Boulevard ran downhill and
I began to pick up speed, finally breaking into a trot. Moist air
blew through the open ends of my shirtsleeves and chilled my
sides and back. I tried to remember what day it was, but couldn't.
I didn't worry about it; it didn't matter.

The street on which I lived was deserted. Way down at the end
a pair of taillights blinked and disappeared. Someone was going
to work early. The houses seemed newly painted, although I knew
they weren't, and the flower beds freshly planted. The early light
made everything look created solely for my benefit. The bright
houses, the few dewy cars parked at the curb, the trees guarding
both sides of the street—these things had been put there specifi-
cally to please Nelson Jaqua and make him feel at home.

I began to think about my room, being in my room among my

books and clothes and things left over from my childhood. I looked forward to seeing them again, having the choice of them. Maybe I would even clean my room that day, sweep and rearrange things. But there was no rush. I would do it if I felt like it.

Our house was dark and vacant-looking. I stopped on the sidewalk and just looked at it. My parents brought me to this house shortly after I was born, so I had already spent twelve, nearly thirteen years here. I would live here another four years, if my parents allowed me, before I went away to college. Four years didn't seem long enough for me to thoroughly know the house, to know the people inside and be ready to leave. I was always wanting more time or less time. Time was either too short or too long and never just right.

The lawn felt springy under my feet as I crossed it to the driveway. The grass was in need of a trim, but was very green in the morning light and not embarrassingly brown and dried as I feared. The green looked nice in contrast to the pale cream-colored sides of our house. Big rhododendrons provided splotches of red.

Both cars were parked in the driveway, the Country Wagon and the small white Falcon. I would wash them today as a friendly gesture to my parents.

The back door wasn't locked and this made me feel welcome and expected. I closed it quietly and went up the three steps to the kitchen. All was exactly as I had left it a day and a half before. I could see my way without turning on a light; the first shafts of sun were already slipping between the houses across the street and spilling through our picture windows.

I walked through the propped-open kitchen door into the dining room. The room looked orderly and clean, as if spruced up just for me. I turned to go down the hall to the back of the house where my room waited. I was already thinking: What will I do first, what should I look at or touch? But a moment later these thoughts were gone. All hope and optimism was gone.

For, from my position in the dining room, I could see into the living room. There my parents lay on the couch, both on their right sides. My dad's back was to the back of the couch, my mom's back to my dad's front. My mother's arm dangled over the edge of the couch at an unnatural angle. Maude was curled at my parents' feet, her head on my dad's left lower leg. All three were motionless. On the long walnut coffee table rested the gun.

They were dead. Devastated by what I said to them, humiliated in front of the entire neighborhood, my father shot my mother and sister, then took his own life. I stood frozen, my heart thumping, a voice inside screaming: *Don't do this to me!* I never wished them dead, only for them to notice me, to know that I was still young and needy. Now that chance was lost and the only course left was to run back to the safety of the Shooks' house and hide once more under Bobby's bed.

As always, I imagined it was all about me. The world revolved because Nelson stood upon it, the neighborhood existed because Nelson walked down the street to see it, and people died because Nelson said the words to kill them. Why was it so hard to learn that I was just one small part, not inconsequential, but also not the be all and end all?

For I heard my mom's charm bracelet jingle, saw her arm move, and watched as she sleepily shifted position to find a more comfortable resting place. There was no blood on her body or the bodies of my father and sister. How could the gun have been placed so neatly in the center of the coffee table if my dad had shot himself? Anyway, the gun was a silver ashtray momentarily changed shape by a bright reflection of the sun.

I knelt down in front of them. They were breathing evenly, but not in synchronization. Maude's little breaths came more rapidly, my dad's were heavier with his mouth partly open, and my mom's long and even. Maude wore a nightgown with a pattern of Christmas trees; my parents were dressed as I had left them.

This was my family. I would never have another, at least not with this configuration: father, mother, sister. This was it; be satisfied. I watched them closely. Would I ever have another chance to study them, to be this close again to all three? A spattering of beard touched my dad's cheeks and chin. My mom's eyeliner was smeared, whether from tears or sleep I didn't know. Maude's skin was so smooth it seemed made that morning.

Then the beam of sunlight moved from the table, where it changed an ashtray to a gun, to my mom's face. She stirred at the brightness, raised her outstretched arm to shield herself from it, opened her eyes, and saw me.

"Nelson . . ."

I smiled a little; didn't trust myself to speak.

"Oh, honey, I'm sorry," she said. I changed position so the sun hit the back of my head and her face was shaded. "Things will be better. Your father and I will make it better. I just didn't know. Please forgive me . . ." One tear rolled out of her eye, traveled across the bridge of her nose, and fell to the edge of the lime green couch. This was the couch on which I had stretched so many times when I was sick, times when she leaned over me and put a hand or damp washcloth to my forehead.

"I thought you were gone for good," she said.

I shook my head. My chin was doing a dance. I longed for the day I would be too old to cry.

She reached out and touched the side of my face, her fingers resting softly across my ear. The bracelet tinkled as though calling attention to the moment. I dared to put a little pressure on her hand, leaning into it. She returned the press.

"I love you," she said croakily. "Don't ever think I don't love you with everything . . . ," but before she could finish I moved toward her, burrowing my face into her chest where I hadn't been since I was a child. She accepted me and softly rubbed my back between my shoulder blades. The sensation of safety was still there, almost fourteen years after the first time I was held against her in this way. It was not, after all, such a long while. I hoped I would always have somewhere like this to go, someone to lean into like her, but I supposed that was not possible and someday the memory of this moment would have to be enough.

My dad waked and raised himself up a little to see over my mom's shoulder. He blinked at the bright sun and looked down at my crouched and half-hidden figure. "Nelson?" he asked, and for once the name didn't seem like a reprimand or an omen of bad news.

I could not answer in words, but made a small sound of acknowledgment. I was too afraid to look at him.

"Is he back?" he asked.

My mother freed my head for me to respond, but I kept my face lowered, focusing instead on a bright patch of upholstery. My answer was muffled, I think, but clear enough.

"I'm back."

I expected something from him—a welcome, a scolding, an order to cut the grass—but nothing came and I felt cheated. Do not ignore me, I am yours. I heard him change position; the couch creaked; he took a breath. I remained bowed, steeling myself for anything that might come.

He put his hand on the top of my head. His palm was large, but curved to fit the shape of my skull, and his fingers spread out to encircle as much of me as possible. His wedding ring was hard against my scalp, but reassuring. He pressed gently with the least of his strength and I wanted him to press harder, press himself into me so that I could be strong in the future and never again fatherless. Then, as if he heard my wish, his fingers tightened and I felt his fingerprints printing themselves on my head, and deeper, for the rest of my life.

The small words, the simple change of positions woke Maude. She woke completely, as she always did, without a trace of sleep left in her little frame. She sat up, looked at my kneeling figure, and said in her high, insistent voice, "Nelson, where've you been? Where are we going today? Can we go to the zoo? You said we could! Please, pretty please? I promise I'll be good!"

She had forgotten everything.

*   *   *

Mr. Crisp lived on the west side of town in an area named Garden Home, a newish neighborhood of identical one-storey houses painted a variety of colors. Mr. Crisp's was turquoise with white trim. A tricycle stood on the lawn next to a tipped-over plastic birdbath.

No one answered the door when I rang, although this was not a surprise visit. I called a week before to ask when would be a good day to come. Mr. Crisp said he planned to be home on Sunday; anytime in the afternoon would be fine. School had let out three weeks earlier.

"Nelson!" Mr. Crisp appeared behind me on the front lawn as I was reaching for the doorbell a second time. He wore baggy plaid shorts and a white T-shirt. His knobby knees were smudged with dirt and his shirt soaked with water. "Sorry. Have you been here long? We're out in back and we can't hear the doorbell. I thought I'd better check. Come around this way."

He led me around the house toward the backyard. "My son just hosed me down," he said, pulling the drenched shirt away from his stomach. "He thinks that's really funny." Mr. Crisp didn't sound angry at his son. He sounded as though this kind of thing was inevitable when a family spends an afternoon gardening. We passed through a gate in the Cyclone fence that enclosed the small, treeless yard behind the house.

A woman was kneeling on the grass, digging in the flower bed. I recognized her from the picture on Mr. Crisp's desk. In the middle of the yard two kids played in an inflatable pool. The boy who sprayed his father was about Maude's age, the girl slightly younger.

"Honey, I'm going to . . ." Mr. Crisp said to his wife's back.

"Fine," she replied without looking up from her work. He must have told her a student was coming over.

"That's enough," he said to the boy who was still brandishing the hose. The boy laughed and faked turning the hose on his father again. "Come on in, Nelson. I'm just going to change."

I waited for him in the kitchen. Lunch dishes were piled in the sink and there was an open jar of peanut butter on the drain board, a knife sticking out of it. On the table a recipe book lay open to a chapter on barbecuing. Finger paintings decorated the refrigerator.

"Here we go," Mr. Crisp said as he returned wearing a short-sleeve shirt decorated with the flags of the world. He put my six composition books on the table between us. "I'm afraid we had a little accident. My daughter knocked over a glass of grape juice and it spilled on a couple of pages." He thumbed through one of the volumes until he found the soiled section. Two warped pages were stained a deep purple, but my ballpoint scribblings could still be made out. The immortal words were intact.

"Oh, that's okay," I reassured him.

"What are you going to do with this now?" Mr. Crisp took the book back, turned to a non-grape-juiced page, and skimmed the text.

"I don't know. Nothing, I guess. It was just an experiment."

"Can I make a suggestion?" He closed the book, stacked all six volumes, tapped them on their bottom edges to even them up, and placed them in front of me. "Put it away and don't even look at it for another twenty years. Twenty years from now you'll be what, thirty-four?" I nodded numbly at this astronomical figure. "That'll be a good time to take it out again." I wondered if thirty-four was his age, or if he picked the number at random.

"I wish I had a record of what I did and felt like when I was thirteen. I can just remember one or two things and the rest is a big blur."

He still hadn't said whether or not he liked what I'd written. I had a million questions to ask him: Did the second part let him down or was it as interesting as the first half? Did it bother him when I changed to the third person in Chapter Ten to write about my parents and the police officer? How did I come off as a person, sympathetically or kind of a brat?

"Mr. Crisp, I wanted to ask you if it was okay when I wrote, you know, in the part . . ." I reached for one of the books to illustrate my question.

"Nelson," he interrupted, holding up a hand to stop me. "This wasn't a school assignment. I'm not grading you on it. This is your own writing and you don't have to follow the same rules you do in class. The only guideline is: If it feels right, it is right. If it feels forced, it's wrong. If you're trying to imitate somebody else and not writing from here," he touched his chest above the Hungarian flag, "it's going to be false no matter if you spell everything correctly and use perfect grammar."

Suddenly, water pattered the kitchen window. Mr. Crisp rose

from the table and looked into the backyard. High-pitched screams and laughter were heard, then Mr. Crisp's wife's voice warned, "Now you heard what your father said!" There was a loud splash and more boyish laughter. I knew Mr. Crisp wanted to get back to his family.

"Mr. Crisp, you said you'd autograph this sometime as long as I didn't bring it to school."

I took my copy of *Hothouse Flower* from my shirt pocket and unwrapped it from the birthday wrapping paper in which I kept it safe. He turned back from the window and I handed the book to him. He looked at the racy cover, shook his head in amusement, and opened the paperback to the title page. "You'd think there'd be a pen around here," he said, glancing around the disorderly kitchen.

"I have one." I magically produced a fountain pen.

He took the pen, placed the book on the kitchen table, and leaned down to sign his name. But instead of signing, he raised his head and looked past me into the corner, his eyes focused but seeing nothing. I turned away, giving him the privacy a writer needs to write even a few words.

After a moment or two I heard the pen scratching on the cheap, coarse paper. When the scratching stopped, I turned back. He blew a little on the wet ink, closed the book, and handed it to me with the pen. "I'll walk you out," he said.

There was a friendly mess in the living room as we passed through: toys scattered around, a dress pattern spread on the rug, newspapers and magazines covering the couch.

"Whatever happened to that girl?" he asked. "The girl with the hair in her eyes?"

"She went to Lincoln High because of the art program there. It was kind of hard for us to get together after that. I guess we kind of broke up." I didn't tell him that Shane started going with another art student, a guy with ears like sugar-bowl handles and a chin with a dent in it. I saw them once on the bus, both carrying large art portfolios. When Shane noticed me she drooped her head so low she looked like a tiny hunchback. They got off at the next stop. "It wasn't meant to be," I said, as if we had been one of the great romances of the century.

"Well, we've all had some of those," Mr. Crisp remarked sympathetically.

We reached the front door. "Thanks for reading it, Mr. Crisp," I said sincerely. "And the good advice."

"Any time I can be of help." He leaned down to pick up an advertising flyer that had been placed behind the storm door.

"I'll see you next year." I pushed the storm door open and started to step out on the porch.

"Oh, I guess you haven't heard," he said. "I'm not teaching next year. I'm taking some time off."

Surprised, I turned to look at him. He was examining the flyer, which advertised summer specials, but he didn't really seem interested in them. "I have some things I want to do and Roberta is willing to work full-time while I indulge myself." He laughed a small embarrassed laugh. "I've taught seven years in a row," he added in defense of his unmanly behavior.

"The thing is," he went on, "I have a book I want to write. I can't do it when I'm teaching, because there's lesson plans and papers to correct and . . . Well, you know." I had never seen him look so uneasy. "There's never enough time, and with the kids . . ." He nervously rolled the flyer into a tight tube.

"Will it be another LuAnne book?"

That really made him laugh. Laughing relaxed him and his embarrassment disappeared. I suddenly recalled his high spirits when he was working the concession booth at the dance. He must have known then that he wouldn't be teaching next year and the relief made him giddy.

"No, no, I don't think so, Nelson." He laughed a bit more, then turned serious. "No, the fact is, reading your story made me think about something that happened to me when I was about your age. Well, a little bit older, sixteen or seventeen. I thought it might make a good book if I can write about it honestly, the way you wrote your story. I don't know if I can do it. It's been a long time since I've written anything except 'See me after class' and that sort of thing."

Now he seemed uncertain and apprehensive. It amazed me that he felt so insecure about his own ability even after he had published two novels and taught writing for seven years. So you never get over your self-doubt and fear of failure, I realized, even when you're thirty-four. This was not an uplifting thought.

"It wasn't anything like what you went through," he went on. "It didn't involve my family so much. It was more about a girl I got mixed up with and the effect that had on me and, well, a lot of people. You see, what happened was . . ."

He stopped and a change came over his face. It was the same distant look he had gotten in the kitchen. For a few silent moments he gazed out the glass of the storm door into the street without seeing anything. For a moment he forgot I was still there. Then he turned back, grinned, and tapped me on the shoulder with the rolled-up flyer as if he was knighting me.

"No, you'll just have to read it."

The visit was over. I went down the steps past the tricycle and fallen birdbath and heard him close the door before I even reached the sidewalk. Still, I walked to the end of the block and rounded the corner before I opened *Hothouse Flower* and turned to the title page.

In his pinched, concise handwriting that usually told me I

wasn't sticking to the topic or was capable of much better work than I was turning in, he had written:

For Nelson, my best student
the year 1962–3.

George Mitchell
(George Crisp)

I read and reread the inscription until every word was memorized. Then I carefully wrapped the book again in its colorful paper and put it back in my shirt pocket. I removed my composition books from between my knees, tucked them safely under my arm, and headed for home.